SPANISH EAGLE

SPANISH EAGLE:

The Restoration

Michael Wren-Hilton

The Book Guild Ltd
Sussex, England

The Book Guild Ltd
25 High Street,
Lewes, Sussex

First published 1997
© Michael Wren-Hilton

Set in Baskerville
Typesetting by Rowland Phototypesetting
Bury St Edmunds, Suffolk
Printed in Great Britain by
Antony Rowe Ltd, Chippenham, Wiltshire

A catalogue record for this book is
available from the British Library

ISBN 1 85776 247 9

This book is respectfully dedicated, without permission, to His Imperial Majesty Tsar Nicholas III of Russia and President Boris Stolypin who proclaimed him Tsar.

PROLOGUE

The Bolshevik Revolution of 1917 had swept away the Tsarist system and much of what it had stood for, for centuries, for better or for worse. The subsequent collapse of the Soviet Union, culminating in the storming of the Parliament Building in Moscow, witnessed by world television, had created a whole re-think of national and international politics. If there was re-thinking outside the old Soviet Empire it was almost as nothing to the excitement, concern, fear and patriotism within. The elections, held on genuinely democratic lines, had produced all manner of results, and the vast powers concentrated in the President caused the greatest hope and fear for the future. The Army had always been the keeper of the nation's soul, in liaison with the Tsar and the Orthodox Church, in earlier generations. Would that Army again come to Russia's aid and provide that sense of national pride which is the hallmark of all nations, large or small? Russia still had a large army, but what link was there with the Orthodox Church?

Above all there was no Tsar – only elected representatives, who might quite easily be thrown out by their new electorates at the next elections. These were the thoughts and questions that dominated the mind of General Stolypin, one of Russia's top Generals. The Tsar must be restored. The Army would serve the Tsar and all officers would take a personal oath of allegiance to him, or her, if a suitable male candidate for the office of Tsar could not be found. The old Romanov dynasty had been largely destroyed, but enquiries could be started in London, Paris and Madrid. The old KGB would be bound to have any amount of background and personal details. Within a week General Stolypin would be the best informed man in the world in relation to the Romanov dynasty and the contemporary scions of that family, but would any of them be up to the job that was required? The story of the restoration of the Tsar at the end of the twentieth century is almost beyond belief, but owed its origins and success to the flair, persistence and patriotism of General Stolypin and the man destined to be Tsar.

1

It was bitterly cold in Moscow.

Snowflakes fell in a strong, cold wind. The throng of people who were celebrating as best they could, with vodka at specially reduced prices, could have had no idea of the thinking and planning that was taking place at the highest level in one small room in a yet secret building within the Kremlin.

General Stolypin sat flanked by Colonel Viktor Maiski of Military Intelligence and Major Vladimir Renov, also of Military Intelligence. All three men knew what they were doing. They all spoke English, French and their native Russian fluently. Renov also spoke Spanish. They had developed in a hard school.

General Stolypin knew his family background, as did Colonel Maiski. Major Renov did not. Like so many others in Russia, he had no real family that he could call his own, but he had distinguished himself by hard work both at the School of Academic Science and at University, where he held a degree in Nuclear Physics. When he married two years ago he had purchased two faded sepia coloured framed photographs of a couple unknown and long dead, and these he had hung in the narrow passage that passed as a hall in his city flatlet. If he and his wife did have children, they could be told that these were the only photos left of their grandparents, who had died. Vladimir Renov had created his family backwards. Who could deny that they had been his parents? His wife Myra had danced with the Bolshoi Ballet, but was now expecting their first child.

Colonel Maiski was of Russo/Polish origins, and his family had enabled him to travel. His father had been in the Soviet diplomatic service. His abilities as a natural diplomat, coupled with considerable physical prowess as a trialist for the former Soviet Olympic riding team, made him very well qualified in Olympic diplomacy and generally. He could talk and ride with the best, and in the unlikely event of being 'cornered' he could look after himself with any two men at a time, since he was also possessed of a martial arts diploma. Viktor Maiski had never married, but he was always popular at parties, not least since, when pressed, he was an accomplished pianist.

The General, Boris Stolypin, was a regular soldier who had distinguished himself in various military fields. He might not have possessed the academic ability of his two junior officers, but what he lacked in terms of brilliance he compensated for by his experience and flair. The General was married to Olga, who had been a top mathematician employed, in former times, cracking would-be enemy military codes, but now a mother and grandmother. She had a cosy dacha 50 miles east of Moscow and the use of a second dacha in the Crimea where the family spent their summer holidays, on a shared basis, with Olga's sister. Olga's sister was married to an Admiral of the Black Sea Fleet.

'These papers are very interesting,' started Stolypin, 'but they are historical. Some of these memoranda are at least three months old.'

'Yes, General, but if you want them updating to, let us say, today's date, we will need to take a week, so as not to arouse any suspicion,' replied Maiski without expression. Maiski would have made a perfect poker player. He never betrayed any emotion except to himself when practising before a mirror. It wasn't surprising he had never married.

'Take your time, then, and let's have them all back, updated to today's date in ten days' time. I cannot and will not tolerate out-of-date material. Who do we have on the ground?'

'Where, General?' asked Maiski.

4

'In London, Paris, Madrid and Washington, of course.'

'You will have the names, General, at your office. The information is classified, but with your authority, in writing, I could obtain it.'

Colonel Maiski did know names, but he thought it prudent not to appear too knowledgeable in the presence of Major Renov, whom he was only slowly coming to know intimately, although they had served as fellow officers for some weeks on Stolypin's orders and instructions. No senior officer likes to lose the services of top subordinates, and Stolypin had been obliged to 'pull rank' to get these officers.

'I propose we divide our task. You, Maiski, will look after America, starting at Washington, and you, Renov, will look after Western Europe. That is London, Paris and Madrid. I will not be leaving Moscow unless I have to go to St Petersburg for anything special. You will of course, officially be helping our Olympic Commissariat in relation to the Atlanta Olympics, Maiski. You, Renov, will officially be visiting War Cemeteries and seeing what contribution we might make, in exchange for any help that they might give to us financially, in tracing missing officers and their dependants. There must have been any number of dependants of all those émigrés that our friends in the KGB have listed here. Hopefully we will be able to compile a short list for consideration. You both know what I'm looking for?'

Both men nodded. They stood up together as though they were on the parade ground and saluted. They folded their papers and moved to the door, opened by Stolypin pressing a red button on his desk. They turned at the door, faced General Stolypin for the last time that day, and saluted again. Stolypin returned their salute with a wave of his hand that owed nothing to the parade ground, but was sufficient indication that they could leave.

As they left Stolypin pressed the green button on his desk and the door to his office closed. Another opened and his two security guards entered.

The wives of top Russian military officers, particularly on the

Intelligence Sections, rarely met socially, but Olga Stolypin suggested to her husband before New Year that it would be nice if she could meet the wives of her husband's new aides, and she was disappointed to be told that Colonel Maiski was unmarried.

'He's a fine pianist, I believe, so we might as well have him. Major Renov's wife is expecting her first baby, so there is a basis of conversation. Don't ask Major Renov anything about his own family. He never had one, as you and I understand that term. He was brought up in a top school for orphans when his abilities were first recognized. I gather he gets a bit touchy, which may explain why he is so good at martial arts. No doubt his officer training will have helped him in that direction.'

Stolypin was well informed in relation to all his subordinate officers, their parents and children, indeed their extended families. It was all part of his job and his personal security to know these matters.

The evening was a great success. Olga was a good hostess. The dacha itself was well built and very secure. The whole compound of dachas was enclosed by a mined perimeter fence which was patrolled by armed guards with dogs. The meal was well prepared and was served with good Russian wine from the South – vodka flowed freely. Their guests would be staying overnight, and Viktor Maiski obliged, without too much pressure, at the piano. He thought Chopin and Tchaikovsky made a good compromise between his Polish/Russian background. More importantly, he played both well without sheet music. A few carefully selected neighbours attended the dinner and soiré, but after they had left Olga took the initiative in speaking to Myra.

There was the usual woman's talk about Myra's forthcoming happy event. Yes. The child would be born in Moscow. Everything had gone according to plan and she was sorry that Vladimir was being sent abroad, she didn't know where, but she understood it was important business in relation to the Olympic Games to be held in Atlanta. Olga was pleased to chat Myra along on this line of conversation, which came as second nature to her, as it does to all happily married women with families of their own, but she was equally happy that Myra seemed ignorant of her husband's purpose in sending him to Washington and the States beyond detailed work in relation to the Olympics. If she really did know, then she was a damned good actress as well as being a former dancer with the Bolshoi. Perhaps the two things went together.

Maiski the pianist, now relieved of his musical duties, continued to amuse as he mused over his future postings. 'Thank goodness all politicians think the same way on at least one wavelength,' he observed. 'I suspect it's the wives who make the arrangements. You never or rarely ever hear of summit meetings being held in large industrial centres. It's always Geneva, Paris, Rio or San Francisco. I'm looking forward to visiting Washington. I can't believe I'll be at Kennedy Airport, New York, in forty-eight hours.'

'I thought our friend Vladimir was going to Washington,' said Olga to her husband. 'Certainly that is what his wife thinks.'

'Yes. I guess she does, but there has been a last-minute change of plan. Viktor is going to the States. His knowledge of the last Olympics in Spain will be very useful. Vladimir will do the job he has to do very well in Spain, France and England. Funny thing, I can never bring myself to say Britain. I always say England unless I'm speaking professionally.'

'When do you ever not speak professionally?' sighed Olga.

The women's conversation drifted on to the changing fashions in Moscow and the future of the Bolshoi. The three men sat at the far end of the room. Stolypin drew a cigar from his small silver cigar case emblazoned with the hammer and sickle. He offered his case to his colleagues, but they both politely refused.

'I'm sorry you had to learn of the last-minute switch this evening, but I had thought that I had made it clear that you, Maiski, were going to America.'

'You did, Sir,' replied Maiski. 'I think Myra would rather

7

have Vladimir talking about the Olympics than talking about his visiting War Cemeteries.'

'You're right, Viktor,' interjected Vladimir. 'I rarely, if ever, talk about work at home, but I certainly didn't want Myra to be thinking of cemeteries when she's expecting our first child. These things can still be tricky.'

'Well, I'm glad that's settled,' said Stolypin as he drew on his cigar.

The Russian jet taxied down the main runway at Kennedy Airport. The Russian Military Attaché, in uniform, was there to meet Viktor. Viktor acknowledged the attaché's salute, although he himself was dressed in a two-piece grey suit with raincoat and trilby hat. No-one could have thought that he was an Army Colonel or have any military position. The two men spoke in Russian, of course, whilst in the Embassy car, but after visiting the Russian Consulate both men appeared dressed alike.

They travelled by train together speaking in English. The Russian Military Attaché had acquired quite a strong American accent. Anyone who had overheard their conversation would simply have thought that Viktor was British and Ivan American like themselves. At last they were in the Embassy in Washington.

'We don't know what contribution you are to make to our team here in Atlanta, Colonel. We were simply told to provide you with any information you required.'

'I think I can safely let you into a confidence, Ambassador.' Viktor paused to gain effect. 'I am not seeking to ride in our team, much as I would welcome the opportunity.' The Ambassador knew of Viktor's background and knew he would release no confidence without pressure, but what pressure could he exert?

'No, Ambassador. I have come for your help, and you must know I have come from the top. Moscow is becoming concerned that our new friendship with America may be making us lax in the field. I'm not making any accusations, you understand, but I would like you to see these reports I have brought with me. Presumably you have copies here in the Embassy or in some other safe place?'

Viktor opened his briefcase and laid out a quantity of sheets giving biographical details on any number of American citizens who were clearly of Russian extraction. Emigrés or the descendants of émigrés.

'Now you can see why I've been sent, Ambassador?' The Ambassador looked at the sheets. He looked again, but nothing immediately occurred to him. Viktor was not a man to miss the slightly bemused look in his Ambassador's eyes. 'You see the dates on those memoranda, Ambassador?'

'Yes I do. What of them?'

'They are nearly all three months out of date, Comrade Ambassador. That's what. My instructions are to have these brought up to date within one week and to require that they be updated on a weekly basis until further notice. If this information is not supplied and found to be correct by cross-checking, there are going to be questions asked as to fitness and loyalty. As I say, there is a feeling back home that a degree of laziness has set in, and I'm here to try and correct it. Living in the States is, I believe, what is termed soft. I wouldn't like to see any requirement for recall. I trust I make myself clear?'

'You do, Colonel, and you can rely on me to see to it that these memoranda are brought up to date immediately.'

'Good, Ambassador. I can see that we are going to get on well. Now let me see the programme you have for me. I understand that I'm to be a guest at a Reception at the White House tomorrow? I suppose you have a full guest list. I would like to meet anyone on that list with a Russian or Polish name. Could you let me have such a list?'

'Certainly, Colonel. Allowing for any unforeseen circumstances, say within an hour. Thank goodness for computers.'

'And now on a more personal note, Ambassador, could you find out where I might acquire some of the latest discs of top classical music for taking home. I think you will know my favourite composers from my personal file, but start with Chopin and Mozart. If there are any recitals being held at the

9

Embassy, I would appreciate an invitation.' Viktor allowed himself one of his rare practiced smiles, and the Russian Ambassador exchanged his look.

Viktor was tired, but he had been well trained. He went to the room placed at his disposal. He checked for any devices, set his wristwatch alarm and slipped off for 30 minutes sleep. His wrist alarm awakened him. He showered and changed into evening wear. He was ready for any reception that the Ambassador might have laid on for him or anybody else.

A knock at the door led to a document – a sealed envelope – being handed in. Viktor acknowledged, with a nod of the head and closed the door, relocking it. He opened the envelope neatly with his pocket knife, which he always kept in his breast wallet, and read. It was a full list of all those attending the White House Reception, with those of Polish or Russian-sounding names coloured in yellow, but perfectly readable. There were several names, and Viktor compared them to the lists he had brought.

There was one name missing from the list. It read 'Mrs Mary Orlanski'. Viktor noticed that she appeared to be without an escort. He immediately decided that Mrs Orlanski would have an escort downstairs. Viktor asked the military attaché, Ivan, who had brought him from New York, to make enquiries and in particular why her name was not on the list he had brought from Moscow. The reply he received was interesting.

'Colonel. There does seem to have been a mistake. Mrs Orlanski will have her husband Elmer with her. It seems that, accidentally, his name has been missed off the list. Enquiries were made, but the identity of the Orlanskis has not been traceable.'

'How do you mean, "not traceable"? Don't tell me that we have gone soft?'

'No, Colonel,' replied Ivan defensively. 'It seems that the Orlanskis came to the States in the early twenties. All that was gone into very thoroughly years ago, but they were Spanish, not Russian or Polish, as their name suggests. Any

10

number of people escaped from Russia, during and after the Revolution in 1917, and others who never had any connection with Russia or Poland assumed names to get here. You must know that any number of people who were very poor four or five generations back took to themselves the names of the estates or plantations on which they worked.'

'Mmmm. Yes, I see what you mean, Ivan. Thanks for your intelligence.'

Viktor went through the list with Ivan and settled on trying to meet five of the listed guests during the following night's reception, including the Orlanskis.

The wife of the Russian Ambassador invited Viktor to attend a small soirée she was giving on his first night, attended by invited guests from several Eastern European countries which had diplomatic offices in Washington. Viktor was grateful, and it gave him the opportunity of widening his growing knowledge of America. He concentrated his talk on the Olympics and even polished up on some of his French when introduced to the Romanian Military Attaché, whom he discovered had a genuine love of both music and athletics.

The reception at the White House was a dream – the sort of atmosphere that might have been described as a mixture of Buckingham Palace on a small scale and Hollywood. Seemingly everybody that was anybody in the world of Olympics, outside the ranks of athletes themselves, was present. The men were mostly in evening dress or dark suits.

Viktor wore his dress uniform which showed off his fine figure, and he was at once a centre of attraction amongst the less well-known. Within 15 minutes he had introduced himself to Elmer and Mary Orlanski.

Viktor noticed immediately that the Orlanskis were on soft drinks, notwithstanding trays of 'bubbly' on every hand.

'What a delight to meet you both. We have never met before, but I do hope we will meet again, Mr Orlanski.' This was Viktor's usual opening. It always went down well, particularly as he first shook hands with Elmer and then with Mary, kissing her hand with a slight bow. Mary felt

11

she was going to blush. 'I've heard so much about you, Mr Orlanski. I believe you are one of America's top bankers and that your bank are sponsoring the Games? If you have any money left over, no doubt you will be supporting Poland, but I'm only teasing. I have not introduced myself properly. My full name is Viktor Maiski – Colonel Maiski of the Russian Army – and I have been sent over here to try and assist our team. Riding is my sport. May I ask yours?'

'I'm afraid I'm not at Olympic level these days, but swimming and baseball were my games at Yale, and my wife's were judo and karate, but she too is not for competition. She has three young children to look after as well as me to put up with, but yes, we are sponsoring part of the Games, but I'm afraid we won't have any money over for the Polish or Russian teams at these Games – perhaps if there were Asian Games?'

The two men smiled at each other. Both were still weighing up the other, and both thought they were getting the measure of each other.

'Do forgive my appearing familiar, Mr Orlanski, but may I ask you an obvious question? What part of Poland did your family come from?' Viktor thought this a good ploy.

It was Mary who made reply. 'I suspect you must be related,' she started. 'Perhaps we are all related. I assume Polish people know the facts of life as well as we do here in America.'

Both Viktor and Elmer looked at Mary – Elmer had been through this before.

'We all of us have two parents, four grandparents and eight great-grandparents. Go back, say, sixty generations, and the family extended backwards must run into many thousands. There is almost certainly an Orlanski in your family, Colonel, and equally there will almost certainly be a Maiski in Elmer's family. If I'm wrong, go back another sixty generations.'

'That's a good one, Mrs Orlanski. I must remember that.'

'Seriously, Colonel,' started Elmer. 'I don't think we can help you beyond what my wife has suggested. I think a very wide circle of people know of my Spanish background of yesteryear, but there it runs out. Feel assured enquiries were made in depth years ago, but the trail runs out. I think it's best if you and I just agree to be distantly related, perhaps, and good friends for certain.'

'Mr Orlanski, I'm very glad to have met you, but if I may say so I think you're wasted as a banker. You would make the perfect diplomat. Now do please excuse me. I do have others to meet.'

As Viktor disappeared into the swirling crowd of well-dressed guests Elmer turned to Mary, saying, 'That was quite a man, darling. If ever we wanted a branch in Moscow I would like to have his address.'

'I'll tell you something else, darling,' replied Mary. 'That man is charm itself, and my guess is that he could easily take on any two of the security guards here. His eyes and body movements told me a lot. Mark my words. Riding may be his sport, but martial arts are his profession, in addition to any other qualities he may possess.'

The following morning Elmer wrote a short letter to Viktor which read:

'Dear Colonel Maiski,
    My wife and I were very pleased to meet you at the White House reception last night. I hope that we might meet again at or before the Olympic Games. In the meantime, may I say that if my Bank should ever open a branch in Moscow I would be very pleased to have you as a customer.
    Yours sincerely
    Elmer P. Orlanski'

Back home in Chicago, Orlanski was pleasantly surprised to receive a letter at his Head Office four days later which read:

'Dear Mr Orlanski,
    Thank you for your kind letter. I was pleased to meet you and your wife. I still smile at your wife's suggestion

that we might be distantly related. As to Banking, I shall be pleased to bear in mind what you write and have been pleased to pass a copy of your letter to our Commercial Attaché.

Yours sincerely
Viktor Maiski'

Viktor prepared his report on his Washington visit including his meeting with the Orlanskis, assisted by his secret tape recording of their conversation at the reception, but he did not rate them for the purposes of his engagement. He prepared to travel to Atlanta.

2

The plane that had taken Viktor Maiski to America had not flown direct from Moscow, but had touched down at Heathrow, London. A number of passengers alighted, including Vladimir Renov. No one noticed Vladimir except the MI6 operatives (Britain's top security unit) who checked all arrivals from abroad. No doubt the CIA in America and the Sûreté in France kept similar visual monitoring.

Vladimir was met by the Deputy Military Attaché attached to the Russian Embassy in London, accredited to the Court of St James. The Attaché had upon instructions invited a representative of the British Ministry of Defence in White-hall to meet him. Mr Dalrimple was a senior civil servant attached to the Ministry of Defence, with special responsibil-ity for the Commonwealth War Graves Commission. He had a good command of French and a smattering of German and Russian sufficient for social intercourse. His French was quite fluent.

The three men agreed, after formal introductions, to speak in English. The Attaché started:

'Major Renov has come over, as you know, on a rather sad errand. Basically he is here to try and trace Russian families, the descendants of officers who were killed during the First World War. We know that a great many served together with your officers and men in the years we fought as allies against the Kaiser. If there is any way in which we can assist you in return, Major Renov here is the best man qualified to help. I would only add that, despite what might appear his lowly staff rank, Major Renov has access to the

15

very top in Moscow, as I'm sure you, Mr Dalrimple, have here in London.'

This was calculated flattery. Dalrimple was flattered, yet he had the feeling that Major Renov possibly enjoyed seniority to himself. Renov, unlike Maiski, was of quite an open appearance, and he shook Mr Dalrimple warmly by the hand for a second time. Dalrimple thought this unnecessary, but perhaps that was the Russian custom.

'Major Renov will be staying at the Embassy, of course,' continued the Attaché. 'It is his first visit to London, and I will be escorting him around. We should be very pleased if you could accompany us wherever we go, or one of your deputies, since I feel that doors may be opened for you that might be difficult for us to prise open with simple polite words.'

'I'm sorry, Colonel Busov, I don't know that I understand you when you talk of prising open with polite words.'

'I apologize, Mr Dalrimple. I didn't express myself precisely. Now you are embarrassing me in front of Major Renov. What I meant to say was that, with your rank and position and your public-school background, you could almost certainly gain access to all your public schools and universities – particularly the two top ones – much more easily than two Russian officers, who until recently some of your headmasters and university Chancellors might have regarded as potential enemies of your great country. Nothing could be further from the truth, but I feel sure that you understand what I mean.'

Dalrimple and Renov both smiled as Colonel Busov finished. 'Look, Mr Dalrimple. Rather than chat here, why don't you come back to our Embassy now or let us come to your office in Whitehall, and we can show you what we have and where we feel that you could assist us. When Major Renov leaves us he is off to Paris and then Madrid – lucky man.'

Dalrimple thought it safer to take the Russians to his own office, and after arrangements had been made to have Major Renov's luggage, which seemed excessive for a single man, taken to the Embassy, the three men set off in Mr Dalrimple's Ministry car for Whitehall.

Vladimir Renov could not help wondering how simple it had seemed for him and his companion to enter Britain's Ministry of Defence Building within, as it seemed to him, minutes of his arrival at Heathrow. At the entrance to the Ministry Building Dalrimple formally introduced his guests.

'I take it you don't mind being searched for weapons or explosives?'

'Of course not, Mr Dalrimple. If we had any thought of doing anyone or anything any harm, we would hardly have come with you dressed as we are and unarmed. However, I would rather you carry Major Renov's attaché case since it contains classified information which may be above that permitted to be viewed by your security personnel. You can look at its contents, of course, that is what we want to show you once we are in your office.'

'Very well. Pass it to me.' Major Renov looked at Busov and then passed his attaché case, emblazoned with hammer and sickle, to Mr Dalrimple. Dalrimple opened the case, with Renov's assistance, and all he could see were sheets of neatly typed papers in English and Russian. Dalrimple nodded to the security officer, and the three men were waved through.

In minutes they were in Dalrimple's office, which seemed small to Renov, who had anticipated more stylish accommodation. There were further brief introductions to Dalrimple's small staff. Major Renov thought that his moment had come and he started a small speech which he had almost certainly practised before leaving Moscow.

'Colonel Busov and I would like to thank you all in anticipation for all the assistance you are going to afford us. I hope the word "afford" is the right one. You must forgive me if my English is not as good as it should be.' This was Vladimir Renov at his diplomatic humour. 'My mission here in England is to try and trace as many former officers of the Russian Imperial Army who may have died in your country, and to trace their descendants in case they are in requirement of financial assistance or indeed assistance of any kind. We know that many came to live in Western Europe between 1915 and 1925, and I know that my enquiries will be made much easier with your assistance. Naturally I would wish these enquiries to be completely confidential, and I understand that your Government has kindly arranged for a D Notice to be issued to your media, including the press. It goes without saying that my Government will be pleased to assist yours in reverse to what I am doing here. Upon the assumption that all goes well, no doubt your Minister of Defence will make a suitable statement in response to a planted question in your House of Commons, and likewise a suitable statement could be made in the Duma in Moscow at the same time. I do have a number of papers here listing names and addresses, and my hope is that with your assistance these can be brought fully up to date, and hopefully new names will appear. As a back-up to my enquiries here in London, I would wish to visit certain of your beautifully maintained War Cemeteries. I am certain that we can together help each other and our respective countries. If there are any questions you would like to ask of me, please feel free to do so through Mr Dalrimple. I would only add that a start has to be made somewhere. We are starting with what you may still style the officer class, but if we have success no doubt the scheme can be extended to what I think you still term NCO's and other ranks.'

General Stolypin would have approved his reception. The General had, after all, vetted and approved his draft speech before his leaving Moscow. In the privacy of Dalrimple's office Vladimir now warmed to his task.

'Do please feel free to call me Vladimir or Renov, without my title, Mr Dalrimple. We understand that it is all Christian names in the West these days, but if you are ex-public school please feel free to call me Renov, and I will address you as Dalrimple or John as you please. I think it might just sound more familiar and friendly. The choice is yours.'

Dalrimple was somewhat taken aback by Renov's approach, but he didn't wish to appear either stuffy or difficult and settled for surnames. 'Thank you very much, Major. If I may, I'll be old-fashioned and call you Renov. Feel free to call me Dalrimple.'

Renov extended his right hand as a mark of friendship. It was the third time, Dalrimple reflected, that he had shaken this man's hand this morning. 'Now, Dalrimple. Let me show you what I've got here.' Renov opened his attaché case and withdrew several sheets. He passed them to Dalrimple with a smile. 'Please take your time, Dalrimple. No doubt your Russian may be better than my English, but just in case, I've had them all translated into English. You can take my word for it that the English is as perfect a translation as is possible from Russian into English – allowing that certain phrases cannot be translated too literally.'

Dalrimple simply read the English version. He could hardly believe his eyes. Personal details of every description were there in black and white. He held no comparable details of deceased British officers of World War Two, still less World War One.

'I'm awfully sorry, Renov, but I couldn't possibly promise to undertake and improve on what you have here, and I gather you have a full case of papers. Relatives extending to first and second cousins and their schooling and marriages and offspring, and their schooling and universities. This is the sort of thing that might be supplied for a special programme on television. Colonel Busov will know the programme. We call it "This is Your Life", but that sort of enquiry takes weeks or months to prepare, and they are usually well-known people to start with. All these names! Somebody or some body of people have already done a vast amount of research. All I could hope to do is try and fill in a few blanks, but even that would take more resources than I have at my disposal. I would have to seek authority from a very high level. I'm sorry to say it, but it would be very difficult to keep all these enquiries, by a small army of civil servants, and all those with whom they had to make contact, completely confidential without any word getting to the media, either here in London or elsewhere.'

'I'm sorry to hear you say that, Dalrimple, but I had been warned that you might find it a tall order. Whilst you make your requests from on high, might I suggest that we commence our enquiries in relation to those Russian Officers who were related in any way to the old Imperial Family or who held rank above Colonel. That should limit the field of enquiry considerably. Perhaps we could start with your public schools, that I would describe as private schools, and then Oxford and Cambridge. Which did you attend?'

'I went to Oxford. Magdalen College,' replied Dalrimple. He had the distinct impression that his name would soon be recorded somewhere in Moscow. He just hoped that the Government knew what it was doing, allowing detailed personal details to be supplied.

'Good. Let's start with Oxford, then. Which schools would provide places for Russian students at Oxford in the 1920s?'

'I'm sorry, Renov. You've lost me already. It's the universities that offer places to selected students. The schools don't simply provide students, but I think I know what you are getting at. You want to know how many Russian students were attending Oxford University in the 1920s, and how many of those came out of Russia and might have had fathers who were Generals or Admirals, I take it, during the First World War?'

'Excellent, Dalrimple. That is just what I meant. You put it better than I could. That's just what I want. Then, when we know the students, we can go to their old schools and build up a complete picture. Most importantly, where are those students of the 1920s today, and if they have died, did they have children and where are they today? It shouldn't be too difficult. As you will see, I have marked with a red star those who fall into the first category, and we have over the years built up an extensive sum of knowledge. It's the blanks that you can help us to fill in.

'May I invite you to come back to the Embassy now, and can I offer you and your deputy a good Russian meal with vodka to celebrate our starting work together? I'm fairly sure that Colonel Busov could arrange that if you allowed him to use your telephone.'

Colonel Busov, who had anticipated Renov making such a suggestion, nodded his agreement. Dalrimple thought hard, but how could he refuse without giving offence to this Russian envoy?

Ten minutes later, four men, Renov, Busov, Dalrimple and a Major Carruthers, were on their way to the Russian Embassy for lunch. Major Renov made a point of leaving any number of his papers, but not all, with Mr Dalrimple. The papers he left were marked 'Confidential'. Those he retained were marked 'Classified' – his office in Moscow had copies of all his papers.

Over lunch, Renov toasted, 'To those in need of our joint enquiry.'

Back in his office in Whitehall, Dalrimple sat with Major Carruthers next to him, facing the two MI6 agents he had called to his room. 'I've invited you both to come and see us and allow you to debrief us as you think proper. We have both undergone an experience we have never had before.' Dalrimple went through all that had happened since he had first been introduced to Renov at Heathrow, and he produced all the paperwork that Renov had left with him.

Photocopies were taken and taken away by MI6. The Head of MI6 was, of course, given a full picture, but there seemed no harm done and Dalrimple was ordered to continue to co-operate, and if further assistance was required with enquiries, no doubt the Security services could provide it, provided it was all checked and properly allowable. But what a strange set of enquiries.

What could it possibly mean or be leading to? As for Major Renov's offer of reverse assistance, what could that amount to? There could not be many British Generals, if any, still less any members of the British Royal House who had taken refuge in Russia in the 1920s – or indeed at any time! Certainly the Department of Social Security was not aware of any persons on their registers claiming Russian Imperial or Aristocratic ancestry. It was perhaps an absurd enquiry, but the enquiry had to be made, and was to be made at some cost to the British taxpayer!

As for Renov, he made his own report, corroborated by Colonel Busov. This report would go in the diplomatic bag to Moscow. General Stolypin knew he had chosen his personal emissary well. His wife Olga made a point of buying at GUM – Moscow's well-known departmental store – a baby romper suit for Myra's expected baby, boy or girl. It didn't matter which. The first, or was it the tenth, move in the Restoration had begun. Stolypin was not the greatest chess player in Russia, but nobody of his rank made mistakes.

3

It was obvious to the Head of MI6, Britain's top security unit, that the Russian enquiry might have a political significance beyond the rendering of financial or other assistance to the descendants of émigré Russians following the Revolution in that country, and it was decided on the first day after the debriefing of Dalrimple to refer the matter directly to the Prime Minister.

This was a difficult and potentially delicate matter. The Foreign Office was asked for advice. On first principles no British Government could be in the business of supplying detailed knowledge of its citizens to a foreign power unless there were very good reasons, yet to appear to turn down help and decline to give assistance might so easily lead to a curtailment of assistance that might be required of the Russian authorities, and it wasn't as if the Russians knew nothing of these people who were the subject of Renov's present enquiries. They seemed to be extremely well-informed already – and certainly much better informed on the information they sought than our own authorities possessed. What was it all about? It couldn't simply be suggested that the Russians were up to no good. Knowledge of the old Imperial Family was already known in detail. Who were all these other people? The Russians were giving an offer of reverse information, but clearly there was nothing to be learnt in the same or similar categories. The Prime Minister knew exactly what was to be done.

The Russian Ambassador must be summoned and asked what he and his Government wanted and why. Enquiries of this nature should come from the highest level, perhaps at a summit level, certainly not at military attaché level, however senior or competent the officers concerned (and the rank of Major did not suggest the highest military level anyway). The Foreign Secretary was instructed accordingly to summon the Russian Ambassador to the Foreign Office to explain.

The Ambassador, together with the First and Second Secretaries from the Russian Embassy, arrived at the Foreign Office together with two security men. They were taken immediately to the Foreign Secretary's luxurious office overlooking St James' Park and Horse Guards Parade. After a formal exchange of greetings – in Russian, to make the Russians feel at home – the Foreign Secretary came straight to the point of the meeting:

'Your Excellency, I have summoned you and your colleagues to this meeting to seek your explanation of a seemingly impossible request by your Military Attaché, Colonel Busov, and his Deputy, Major Renov. It seems that your officers have sought highly confidential information regarding persons who are clearly British citizens, who may well have had Russian connections, family connections, going back one, two or even three generations. What is it all about? Our Prime Minister wishes to maintain and improve our relations with your country, but you must appreciate that we cannot simply provide information without reason and/ or the authority of the people concerned, assuming that is that they have the necessary qualification to give legal consent.'

'Your Honour,' started the Russian Ambassador politely, 'I hardly know how to start. Instead of inviting us here in person, surely you could simply have spoken to me on the telephone, and I could have made enquiries. As I understand the position, and I do not have full details, our respective Defence Ministries are seeking to assist each other in relation to War Cemeteries, the distribution of medals and the making of provision for dependants. Obviously I must make a report to Moscow on this meeting. Since we are only

24

asking for information at a low level, I hadn't thought it necessary to seek your personal assistance. I will, of course, speak to the officers you mention by name, but I can assure you that they are both excellent officers who would do nothing to damage your reputation or mine. What more can I say?'

This bland reply, which was carefully phrased, took the matter no further. The Ambassador was, of course, very experienced. The truth was that he knew nothing himself about the real purpose of the enquiries Major Renov was making, beyond what Renov had told him, which was no different from what Renov had told Dalrimple and the others.

The Foreign Secretary thanked the Ambassador for his attendance, offering to supply any information Major Renov might require, subject to Cabinet approval and subject to the individuals concerned being agreeable to information being given.

'Thank you for that, Your Honour. Since it is thirsty work driving all the way here from the Embassy through your crowded streets, may I ask for one of your delicious cups of tea? I think the late Lord Grey held your office before the First World War, so please let us have Earl Grey, if that isn't too great a play on words.'

The Ambassador had his own brand of humour which served to improve the immediate atmosphere. Tea was taken, and the Foreign Secretary reported directly to the Prime Minister later in the afternoon at the House of Commons.

The upshot of that report was that the Deputy Prime Minister – Dame Sylvia Sabita, formerly Mrs Sylvia Bartlett-Shearman QC, MP, who doubled as Minister of Information – was directed to take charge of the whole business, with instructions to report back to the Cabinet. Sylvia wasted no time. MI6 would provide the extra assistance that Dalrimple requested, and – so that she might have the most immediate personal report – Sylvia directed that one of her two Protection Officers, Chief Inspector Charlotte Johnson, would be one of the assistants seconded to Mr Dalrimple's office.

She would not wear uniform. What Sylvia wanted to know was what was the purpose of Major Renov's enquiries, if they were not exactly what he had said. Charlotte's opposite number to be seconded from MI6, Mr Smith, spoke fluent Russian.

The following morning, on the stroke of 9 a.m. Major Renov and Colonel Busov were at the entrance to the Ministry of Defence Building in Whitehall, where they were met by Dalrimple, Major Carruthers, Charlotte and Mr Smith of MI6. Dalrimple effected the introductions, and there was the customary shaking of hands. The only variation was that Major Renov made a point of kissing Charlotte's hand. Charlotte had half-anticipated this, and affected not to be taken aback.

Up in the lift and straight to Dalrimple's office.

There were six other Civil Servants already at work in the room. Renov took the initiative in speaking:

'I believe Colonel Busov and I are in your debt, Dalrimple. My Ambassador tells me that our names were mentioned in the presence of your Foreign Secretary and that he may have mentioned our names to your Prime Minister? I never thought that my name would be mentioned in such high circles within twenty-four hours of my coming to your country.' Turning to Major Carruthers, Renov continued, 'As one Major to another, I will have to try and return the compliment when you first visit Moscow, but obviously I cannot promise anything like so much.'

This was Renov trying to be amusing in his carefully prepared manner. Charlotte and Mr Smith never took their eyes off Renov. It was Dalrimple who made reply on behalf of Major Carruthers and himself.

'I gather that the meeting between your Ambassador and our Foreign Secretary went very well, and I have been able to obtain assistance from our Ministry of Information. Mr Smith and Miss Johnson are now attached to me until you have completed your enquiries, at least until you leave London.'

Renov smiled. Turning to Colonel Busov, he said in Russian, 'That sounds a very promising start, Sir.' Mr Smith heard exactly what was said and made a mental note. Renov continued in English, 'You are all so lucky in England having families and family trees. Sadly I have no family tree. I have no idea who my parents might have been. I was brought up in a school for orphans and then a junior military academy. I suppose I was lucky to be born Russian. I understand that I might have been killed at birth or earlier here in England. What is the word you use, "aborted", isn't it? I'm told you have aborted two million over the past twenty years – more than Hitler killed in England, I should guess. So you see why I'm very glad that I was born Russian.'

Renov was carefully weighing up his small audience and at the same time seeking to obtain any maternal instincts Charlotte might possess.

He was certainly making an impression. Dalrimple made as smooth a reply as was consistent with congratulating Renov on his having succeeded in life without family support and making as light as he could on the breakdown of family life in Britain. Renov proceeded to his next ploy:

'I do love your English language, Dalrimple. Not as good as Russian, of course, but so descriptive. Like all Russians, I particularly like Charles Dickens. What a writer! I think your tourist industry is to be congratulated on keeping the Dickens atmosphere, with men and women sleeping in cardboard boxes in shop doorways in the Strand, so near to your Parliament.'

Dalrimple and the others could hardly believe their ears. 'I do assure you, Renov, those people are to be pitied. They are certainly not there at the request or desire of our tourist industry. Quite the contrary. They are people who have sadly slipped through the net of our welfare system.'

'I'm sorry, Dalrimple. I didn't mean to upset you. I was trying to be complimentary. I will say no more and listen to what you have planned for me.' Turning to Colonel Busov, Renov said in Russian, 'I think you said, Sir, that our friends here plan to take us to Eton and Windsor?'

27

'Yes, that is the plan, Major,' replied Colonel Busov. It was only the second time that Busov had spoken that morning, so far as Charlotte could remember, beyond his formal 'Good morning' when they had first been introduced.

'I'm pleased to say,' started Dalrimple to carry the conversation along, 'that we plan to take you and Colonel Busov to Eton College, one of our top schools, then lunch in Windsor and Oxford University in the afternoon.'

'Thank you very much, Dalrimple. As a soldier, I should very much like to see how you defeated Napoleon at Waterloo. I seem to remember reading that "the Battle of Waterloo was won on the playing fields of Eton".' They all looked at each other and laughed politely. Secretly they all wondered how well-read Renov appeared to be. He might or might not have fully understood the word 'aborted', but his command of English seemed superb.

'Miss Johnson and Mr Smith will not be coming with us. They have their work to do here, but hopefully you will meet them again,' said Dalrimple.

'I'm sorry to hear that, Miss Johnson,' said Renov, speaking directly to Charlotte. 'I had been looking forward to your being with us. You could have told me all about your family. See. Look at my wife's photograph. My wife was a member of the Bolshoi Ballet, but now she is expecting our first-born – so I will have a family of my own.' Renov glowed as he said this, and he withdrew his wallet extracting two photographs, one of his wife Myra and the second of Myra and himself standing side by side – perhaps a wedding photograph.

Charlotte looked at the photographs and made some pleasant small talk before passing them to Mr Smith, who in turn passed them to Dalrimple and the Ministry men.

An hour later Charlotte was making report to Sylvia in the Home Office Building, having walked under Whitehall itself from the Defence Ministry. Mr Smith accompanied Charlotte and they made their report together, both to Sylvia and to a junior Home Office Minister and two representatives from the Prime Minister's office. Mr Smith had recorded the entire conversation on secret tape as standard practice. Although Sylvia and Charlotte always addressed each other by Christian names when on their own, in the presence of strangers they always adopted a formal style.

'Tell me, Chief Inspector, have you anything to add to what Mr Smith has told us in addition to what the tape tells us?'

'Yes and no, Minister. What Mr Smith has said is quite correct and the recording is perfect, but it is not always what is said, but the way in which it is said. I speak only a little Russian and I accept that Major Renov addressed Colonel Busov as "Sir", but I suspect that Major Renov was Colonel Busov's superior. I know nothing of Russian military ranks, but I'm under the distinct impression that Major Renov was senior to Colonel Busov, but I could be wrong. You know, Minister, it's a very difficult thing to put your finger on, but let me put it this way – if any Russian Police Officer was to come into this room now without a word being said, I fancy he would guess that you were the senior person in this room.'

Sylvia pursed her lips and then smiled. 'You are very perceptive, Inspector,' Sylvia turned to Mr Smith. 'Did you form the same opinion, Mr Smith?'

'I can't honestly say I did, Minister. Major Renov addressed Colonel Busov twice as "Sir", but of course, he could have been acting. If he *was* acting, he was a damned good actor. Some of the things he said sounded almost childish, but other things could have come straight out of a leading column in any one of our "heavy" national newspapers.'

'I'll just add this, Minister,' added Charlotte with an ever so slight chuckle in her voice. 'He may or may not be an enemy. I can't know. I will say this. If I was in a tight corner I would want to have the Major on my side rather than his Colonel, and I don't say that just because he kissed my hand!'

'Thank you, Inspector, I think you have been very helpful.' Sylvia paused and then added, 'I think you have both been very helpful.'

29

4

The snow still lay thick on the ground in Moscow when Maiski and Renov reported to General Stolypin on their visits to America and Western Europe.

Their plane had been diverted to Lubianka Military Airport outside Moscow, and the two officers were met at the steps of the plane by a large black staff car from the Kremlin pool. There were six outriders and three staff cars. Only Russian security could have known who was in which car as they sped through the deserted streets, inches deep in snow, that lined the river bank. The waters shimmered in the moonlight.

Major-General Renov and Colonel-General Maiski – their real ranks – felt and appreciated the warmth of General Stolypin's office after the cutting wind outside had chilled them in a matter of minutes.

'I think you both deserve a warm drink,' started Stolypin, pouring out three substantial vodkas. 'I have read your reports. You both seem to have done very well, but now I want to hear from you in person. In particular about those matters which you could not put in writing in case they fell into the wrong hands. I'm anxious to draw up a shortlist. Things have not been standing still here in Moscow, but I believe everything is under control. As a start I want you both to read each other's daily reports so that you can both give your objective views, and then I will give you mine. Once we have a shortlist of four we can invite them all to Moscow, separately, and assess them together. I'm thinking in terms of a natural reduction from four to two and two to one, unless any one of them appears outstanding. Do you agree, comrades?'

'Excellent, Comrade General,' replied Maiski without a smile.

'I agree,' Comrade General,' echoed Renov with a smile. 'Very democratic, I should say. I'm fairly sure Dalrimple would approve. I think that's how the top civil servants are selected in the United Kingdom. It's their Civil Service who run their country.'

'I think you may be right there, Renov, but we are in Russia. We must be quite certain that it is the Army which runs this country.'

'You are quite right, General, and that is why I'm so glad to be serving under you and not under some upstart politician.'

At this remark Stolypin laughed, as did Maiski. Neither of these officers could be described as a bundle of fun, but they both liked and trusted Renov. He had come from nowhere. He was completely loyal and, perhaps, had the best brain of the three. 'And now I have a surprise for you, Renov.' It was Stolypin at his best. 'Come along, both of you. I have arranged a little supper.' He pressed the red button. His office doors opened. The two guards outside the door saluted and Stolypin led the way down the illuminated · passage to a door marked 'Private'.

At the far end of the table stood Stolypin's wife Olga, and next to her stood Myra. Renov momentarily forgot himself as he ran forward and threw his arms about his wife. Maiski remembered his formality and kissed Olga's proffered hand. Maiski made a show of searching his pockets and then produced two American discs of classical music, giving one to Olga and the other to Myra. He was not an emotional man, but he was not ungenerous in his own way, and he always seemed to have the happy knack of knowing which type of music recipients of gifts liked best.

'I'm glad to be home in Moscow,' said Renov. The three men raised their glasses, followed by the ladies. 'To Russia,' proposed Stolypin. They all stood and downed their vodka.

Mr Dalrimple was always at his office at 8.30 a.m. or even

earlier. Britain might not be at war, but the Ministry of Defence was always busy, and it was said that there were more civil servants at the Ministry than there were soldiers, sailors and airmen in uniform. The correspondence addressed to the Ministry was like a mountain each morning, and a small army of civil servants were employed to open it. Understandably, the post had to be checked by security in case it contained explosives of various types, and particular attention was paid to all letters addressed to individuals.

On a particular Tuesday morning there was an envelope marked 'Strictly Private, Immediate and Personal'. The letter was addressed to Mr Dalrimple and had clearly come from the Russian Embassy in London. It was sent directly to Mr Dalrimple's office after being passed through a screen test. Dalrimple opened the envelope with care. He always did. One of his hobbies was stamp and envelope collecting. It hardly amounted to philately, but it gave him pleasure, and he had been permitted by his superiors to collect on the basis that his collection be retained by the Ministry until he retired.

The letter was typed, beyond being 'topped and tailed' in pen, and made fascinating reading. It had almost certainly been drafted with a wider audience in mind. It read:

'Dear Dalrimple,

I feel I must write to you to thank you and your colleagues Major Carruthers and Miss Johnson for all your kindness and assistance whilst I have been in London.

I will, of course, be reporting to my superiors. Please feel free to show this letter to yours. Do assure your colleague Major Carruthers that I know of no plans for us to alter the gauge of our national railways. There is no need for him to fear that our armoured trains will emerge at the Dover end of your new Channel Tunnel, and have no fear yourself that I have any plans to recruit you to our Foreign Intelligence service. No doubt there

32

are traitors in England and Russia who will always sell their country short for financial reward or professed idealism, but you and I do not come into those categories. If and when you should ever come to Moscow, with or without your colleagues, please let me know in advance in order that I may return your hospitality in my own modest way. My flat in Moscow is small, but my wife keeps what you term "a good table" at our small dacha. Hopefully when you come you will meet our first-born, due later this year.

Yours sincerely

Vladimir Renov (Major)'

Dalrimple re-read the letter again in case he had missed anything, but he hadn't. He went himself to a photocopying machine in his outside office and called MI6. 'I thought I must call you immediately,' he said as the two MI6 men entered – men whom he knew well and had known for some little time.

'We will have to let the Deputy Prime Minister know immediately, and it may well be that you will be ordered to send a reply dictated by the Foreign Office. You can be sure that this isn't just a pleasant letter of thanks which might have been expected,' said the tall thinner man – Mr Smith to the world.

Half an hour later Sylvia Sabita, the Deputy Prime Minister, was reading the original letter with two copies for her file. Charlotte was in attendance, as usual, in her role as Protection Officer, as were the two MI6 men and three senior Civil Servants. 'Read this, Inspector, and pass it back to me,' commanded Sylvia as she passed Charlotte one of the photocopies. Charlotte read and felt she was going to blush. She pursed lips before saying:

'A very nice letter, Minister, but it does seem somewhat creepy to feel that my name will forever be lying on some military desk in Moscow. Major Renov is sure to have taken copies, as we have. I imagine he is very thorough and he says, in terms, that he is reporting to his superiors, but he doesn't say who they are.' She passed the photocopy back to Sylvia.

'No he doesn't, gentlemen. Do we know who Major Renov is, beyond who he says he is, and what exactly is his position in Moscow or wherever?'

'No we don't, Minister. We have, of course, asked our Embassy in Moscow to make enquiries, but it is likely to take some time. The name Renov is, I suppose, as common as Smith, Jones, Robinson and Brown here in London, and there are many Majors in the Russian Army, which is much larger than ours, and his rank of Major might mean almost anything.'

Sylvia paused for a moment and then said, 'I will be showing this letter to the Prime Minister and the Foreign Secretary, but you must make immediate reply, Mr Dalrimple, and send it to Major Renov care of their Embassy. I'll draft it and will accept responsibility for it. How about this:

"Dear Renov,
    Many thanks for your kind and amusing letter. I will certainly bear in mind your offer of hospitality in Moscow. In the meantime, I'm sure all my colleagues trust that all goes well at your wife's confinement.
    Yours sincerely" '

Sylvia had dictated her draft reply for Dalrimple on her pocket dictation machine which she always kept available in her handbag for emergencies. The exchange of letters might have rested there, but there was a tail. The following morning a letter arrived at Harcourt, the country residence of the Deputy Prime Minister, a smaller version of Chequers. It was addressed to Inspector Johnson, c/o The Deputy Prime Minister – it was from Major Renov. It read:

'Private and Confidential
Dear Miss Johnson,
    I felt I must write to you personally to thank you for the kind interest you took in my wife and family when

34

we met at your Ministry yesterday. I am told that you live in the country, and I do not know your home address. I trust this letter reaches you. Please feel free to show it to Dame Sabita. I will be showing a copy of this letter to my wife!
Yours sincerely
Vladimir Renov (Major)'

Charlotte could hardly believe what she was reading. How on earth had Renov known that she was attached to Sylvia? She had said nothing about her normal duties, but clearly Major Renov knew. He must have been told who she was by his Embassy. After all, there were many photographs of the Deputy Prime Minister taken and published. She couldn't always be certain not to have appeared on them. She must report immediately to Sylvia. Sylvia obliged with a second draft which read:

'Dear Major Renov,
Many thanks for your kind note. I do hope that all goes well with your wife. It was very kind of you to write to me.
Yours sincerely
Charlotte Johnson'

Copies of these letters were also taken. Major Renov was certainly thorough, whoever he was.
A week later, at Prime Minister's Question Time, there was the usual question raised: 'Could the Prime Minister tell the House of his engagements of the day?' This was the traditional question set to lead to the real question. The Prime Minister replied almost as a matter of form, 'I would refer my Honourable friend to the reply I have already given three times this afternoon to the effect that I have been attending a meeting of the Cabinet this morning, and after leaving this Honourable House I have further meetings with Ministerial Colleagues.'
The Honourable Member rose immediately to ask his

supplementary: 'Could the Prime Minister say as to whether his future meetings today concern the information that has been leaked to the effect that confidential information has been supplied by the Ministry of Defence to Russian, and perhaps other foreign powers, concerning the private lives of British citizens of Russian descent, and will he assure the House that no such information, as that sought, will ever be given without the consent of the person or persons concerned?'

The Prime Minister, who spoke as though he had anticipated the question, rose. 'Madam Speaker, I am aware that enquiries are often made of the Government concerning private individuals resident in this country, but my Honourable friend can feel assured that the information sought by foreign countries is never given without the consent, freely given, by the individual concerned. If my Honourable friend has any information to the contrary, I would ask him to furnish it to my Right Honourable friends, the Minister of Defence or the Home Secretary, or indeed myself.'

Two weeks later, Sylvia, together with Carlos her husband, hosted a dinner at Harcourt attended by a group of friends, including two Ministers and their wives and Carlos's oldest friend from school days, Xavier de Sallas Lang of Madrid. They had attended Slapton College, the well-known Roman Catholic public school as boys, and Xavier had been Best Man at Carlos's wedding to Sylvia. It was Xavier who had identified the voice of Lord Michael Fuker at No. 10 Downing Street when the attempt had been made by a determined and well-armed group of politically motivated men to take over the country.

Xavier had been married, but was now a widower. His wife had died in Madrid of cancer. He still had his two boys at Slapton, where Sylvia and Carlos had their own two sons. They were, in fact, Sylvia's sons by her former marriage to Donald, her first husband, who had been tragically killed in a head-on collision on the M4 motorway. The dinner took its usual form. Everyone was formally dressed. The men wore black ties and the ladies a variety of dresses that collectively must have cost a small fortune. To many, any one of the dresses would have entered that description. It was when the table conversation switched to Westminster and politics that one of the ladies started:

'That was a very unusual question for the Prime Minister to be asked last week. Normally I never watch, but I saw it all on television. I thought his reply was very good.' The conversation drifted on.

It was Xavier who spoke to Sylvia after dinner, in the library, away from the other guests. 'Tell me, Sylvia, if you're allowed, what do you think the Russians are up to asking questions about their émigrés and their descendants?'

Sylvia felt instinctively that she had to be on her guard, even with Xavier, notwithstanding his friendship with her husband and the great service he had rendered to the country last year. 'How do you mean, Xavier? What do you know of any questioning by the Russians?'

'Come on, Sylvia, you do know what I mean, I'm sure – at least I hope you do. I met a charming Russian named Major Renov in Madrid last week. He was asking all manner of questions in fluent Spanish. I wondered how much he had picked up here in London.'

'He told you, did he, that he had been here in London?'

'Yes he did, and in Paris before coming to Madrid. He seemed very well informed. He had been to our Expo 92 in Seville and the Barcelona Games. If I hadn't known, I would have thought he was Spanish. He made one or two grammatical mistakes, as we all can in conversation, but he hadn't a trace of accent.'

'I never met him myself, Xavier, but Charlotte did, and she was very impressed.'

'Yes I know,' replied Xavier. 'He mentioned Charlotte, but not by name. He simply referred to a Miss Johnson, and I put two and two together, as I suspect he did. Have you heard from him since he left you?'

'No. Why should I?' replied Sylvia. 'As I say, I never met him myself.'

'Ah well, I did. He wrote me a most charming letter and he has invited me to attend a conference of architects and engineers in Moscow in March.'

'And will you be going?'

'Of course I will. It will be very interesting, I hope, and it will give me an opportunity of speaking Russian again.'

'I didn't even know that you spoke Russian, Xavier. Whenever did you find time to learn Russian? I thought it was a difficult language.'

'It is, Sylvia, if you have to start learning at our age, but I will let you into a secret that even Carlos might not know about his Best Man of yesteryear. My mother was half Russian, and I learnt my Russian at my mother's knee as you learnt English from your parents.'

'I'm lost for words, Xavier. You seem to have all manner of qualities. I must ask Carlos if he ever knew. Did they know at Slapton?'

'Yes, I think so. When my mother came over from Spain we always spoke in Russian or Spanish unless we were with the other boys, when we spoke in English, but my mother found English difficult. I do speak French and some German as well, as you know, but those languages I speak with a pronounced Spanish accent. I couldn't pretend to be German or French.'

At her office the following morning, Sylvia reported what she had learnt from Xavier the previous evening.

'It seems to me,' said Charlotte, 'that Xavier and Major Renov are very well matched. I really like Xavier. I would love to know him better, but he is still very close to his late wife and his programme seems to be almost busier than yours, if that's possible. He's known me for quite a long time now. Perhaps it's to his credit, but he's never given me so much as a smile with his eyes, as distinct from his lips, still less has he ever given me a "come-hither look". I sometimes think he just regards me as your shadow or a piece of furniture.'

'As a protection officer, that speaks very well of you, Charlotte. That's how he should behave, but I could tell you something although, perhaps, I shouldn't.'

'Go on, Sylvia. Do tell. What can you tell me?'

'Very well, but you mustn't say anything. I can tell you that he does notice you. He has for a long time, and I believe he likes you very much indeed. Why do you think he keeps inviting himself to Harcourt? It isn't just to talk to Carlos about Slapton, I'm quite sure of that.'

'Thanks, Sylvia. I won't be asking for a new posting, I promise you.'

The two women smiled at each other. A picture tells a thousand words. The two women might have continued their intimate conversation, but for the arrival of the civil servants with their red boxes, which brought it to a close. Soon Sylvia was ploughing through her morning paperwork and Charlotte withdrew to change out of her uniform. She returned a few minutes later in her grey suit, which made her much less conspicuous. She felt much more comfortable and at ease. Sylvia felt that she detected that Charlotte had shed a few tears, but had refreshed her make-up whilst she had been out of the office, but she kept her own counsel.

5

Enquiries at MI6 continued. Progress was slow. The where-abouts of Major Renov were seemingly impossible to trace from the time he had left Madrid. The Spanish and French security services were co-operating with the Americans. A Colonel Maiski had been asking questions in Washington and in Atlanta, but these enquiries all seemed to relate to the Atlanta Games, and he had returned to Moscow.

It was Charlotte who took the initiative one morning in raising the subject of Major Renov with Sylvia.

'May I ask, Sylvia, whether any more has been heard of Major Renov?'

'No. I'm afraid not. Perhaps it was all correct what he said, and we have been worrying unduly and spending a good deal of time and tax-payers' money in the process. I'm far more interested now in pressing on with our own Government's plans than worrying about Major Renov. I think your friend Xavier said he was pursuing certain enquiries of his own in Spain, and he also said he was going to attend a conference in Moscow. Perhaps he'll come up with something. He speaks Russian fluently as well as French, English and, of course, his native Spanish. You will have an opportunity, Charlotte, to brush up on your own French when we go to Paris next week to attend the Inter-Parliamentary Union Conference. It would be funny if Major Renov was to turn up in Paris.'

'I would like that, Sylvia, but I'd like it very much better if Xavier was to turn up. I really do like that man and his boys. I know they miss their Mum, but I don't like to say anything that makes me look as though I'm pushing myself, but I can't help thinking.'

'And hoping? I'll tell you what I'll do, Charlotte. I'll invite Xavier over to Harcourt with his boys this weekend, if they are not playing for the College. There will just be the four of us – Carlos and me and you and Xavier. It's up to you. Don't push yourself, but if he has any feeling for you at all he will at least have the opportunity of having you all to himself. Carlos and I will not play "gooseberry". You needn't have any fears for yourself. Xavier is a gentleman to his fingertips. Do say you'll come, and I'll try and get hold of Xavier and I'll cancel my scheduled visit to Lanchester.'

'You're very kind, Sylvia. I'll not let you down.' Almost involuntarily, she kissed Sylvia on the cheek and made her excuses, leaving Sylvia wondering just what she had let herself in for. She remembered now how she had successfully played cupid for Mary when she had persuaded Elmer Orlanski to come over to London from Chicago to look after American banking interests in the Severn Avon Project. Mary and Elmer were so happy, and Mary had given birth to triplets, who were now growing rapidly, judging by the latest batch of photos that Mary had sent. Although she had detected with feminine intuition that Xavier liked Charlotte, she had nothing really positive to go on as she had had, with Elmer sending flowers and his eyes positively starry in Mary's presence.

Sylvia pressed on with her reading. She was having lunch with Carlos at his latest restaurant in the West End. Carlos was on course to become one of England's leading restaurateurs. He would surely be selling out this year, if the price was right, and then he would be sitting on the Board of a National Group in addition to his interests and estates in Spain. She would break her 'Plan Cupid' to Carlos over lunch. She hoped he would approve and go along with her. The only obstacle Sylvia could envisage was the clear discrepancy in their ages. Xavier must be 48 and Charlotte 30. Still, if the old adage about dividing the man's age by two and adding seven had any merit, they would only be one year out. There was also the problem of background and religion, but there would be plenty of time for that if the chemistry was right.

She tried, with some success, to put these thoughts out of her mind as she ploughed through the minutes of the last two meetings of the European Inter-Parliamentary Commission. The Prime Minister had been to the last meeting in Oslo, and he and she went alternately to the meetings, which were held quarterly. It would be Britain's turn to host the event next time. The Prime Minister would be presiding, unless he could persuade the Speaker of the House of Commons to take the Chair.

At lunch, Sylvia told Carlos of her conversation with Charlotte and of her plan to try and play Cupid, and would he please be as helpful as possible if he approved. 'You do need to be very careful, darling. It's only twelve months since Sophia died, and he still feels fairly close to her. No Spanish woman would have a look-in at the moment, but Charlotte? He's never said anything to me. I think he does like Charlotte all right, but then he liked Mary and Susan. The Met certainly sent you three very attractive girls. With Mary married to Elmer and Susan married to her doctor, it only leaves Charlotte. I know you helped Mary and you didn't need to help Susan, but Xavier and Charlotte? I wonder. His mind is so difficult to follow. It always was at Slapton, but we'll give it a whirl, as you say.'

'Thank you, darling. I hoped you'd say that. Believe me, I will be careful. I still think it's a bit of a long shot, but Charlotte is absolutely bursting with affection for him, despite herself, and I know she's already shed a few tears and bitten her lip, even when she's been on duty. It's rather sad and funny at the same time when she excuses herself to freshen up with powder that doesn't really suit her.'

As they finished their meal it was Carlos who raised his glass and toasted across the table, 'To Xavier and Charlotte.'

There had been no difficulty in Father Rector being persuaded to grant exeats to the boys. Xavier arrived at Harcourt with his boys dressed in their college grey suits. The two boys, now 16 and 14, were quite the young gentlemen.

42

The elder boy, Miguel, had the same looks as Xavier. People had said that as long as Miguel lived Xavier would never die. Carlos was his mother over again – save that he was masculine.

The two boys greeted Carlos and Sylvia very correctly, shaking hands with each in turn. Miguel shook hands with Charlotte also, but Carlos put his arms round her and kissed her lightly on the cheek. Charlotte was as surprised as anybody, but Sylvia noticed and, more importantly, so did Xavier.

Dinner was deliberately taken early, at seven p.m., to give themselves a good long evening. Ostensibly the boys would not be kept up too late – in fact, the boys went to bed quite late after sitting up watching television.

After dinner the boys insisted on playing billiards against their father Xavier and Carlos. They had long since ceased calling him 'Uncle'. The boys would have preferred snooker, but Carlos stipulated billiards. The boys settled for billiards and won. 'It does make you wonder what you're paying school fees for,' said Carlos.

'At least you can see results, Carlos,' replied Xavier. 'Better than buying a brand-new car and losing thousands on depreciation every year. Who knows, they may make more money playing billiards and snooker than they will obtaining degrees.'

Xavier was in very good form as usual, fortified by a good meal followed by best Spanish brandy. Whilst the menfolk were out of the way, Sylvia took Charlotte into the library that served as Sylvia's official office when she worked from Harcourt.

'Charlotte, when the boys have finished their game I'm going to show Carlos and Xavier's boys some things upstairs, and we'll leave you and Xavier on your own – yes, I've spoken to Carlos, and you have his blessing.'

On their own now in the drawing room, Xavier started the conversation:

'Charlotte, do you get the feeling that our hosts have deserted us, or do you think they have deliberately left us on our own?' Charlotte felt she was going to blush, but Xavier continued, 'I say, it would be a bit of a lark if I took you for a spin in my new car outside, but we'd better not do that. Please tell me something about yourself. Have you any holidays planned?'

This was a pleasant start to any conversation. 'No, I haven't yet. It's rather early in the year, but I must start planning. I do get about quite a bit with Sylvia, but that's hardly holiday. I have to take my annual leave when she takes hers.'

'I see,' said Xavier, as if he was weighing matters in his mind. 'So if I ask Sylvia and Carlos to take a short holiday with me, as a "thank-you" for their kindness to me since Sophia died, I could ask you to join us without you losing any of your annual leave, as you call it?'

'That's a very nice thought, Xavier. When did you have that in mind?'

'I was thinking of the week after next. I assume you will be going with Sylvia to Paris as her protection officer next week, and then Carlos and I could take you both to my place in Chamonix for a spot of skiing – how would you like that?'

'I should like it very much, except that I can't ski,' replied Charlotte.

'That's no problem. You will enjoy learning, I hope, and I will be delighted to teach you – at least I will try to – my youngest, Carlos, has really fallen for you, hasn't he – kissing you at his age?' Charlotte was blushing. What a charming man this was. What couldn't he do? She wanted to throw her arms around him, but she remembered what she had promised both Sylvia and herself and affected simply to look coy. 'That's settled, then. All we need now is Sylvia and Carlos to agree. We shall need to have them with us, if only to act as chaperones when we are not on our skis!'

It was at this point that Sylvia and Carlos re-entered the room. 'Sorry to have left you both,' started Sylvia, looking searchingly at Charlotte, 'but there were one or two things I had to tell the boys about our television upstairs, and I needed Carlos with me – sorting out football boots and hockey sticks for my two boys.'

'You haven't missed much, Sylvia. Charlotte and I have just been arranging a short holiday in Chamonix, with you and Carlos acting as chaperones. You and Charlotte are off to Paris for another conference next week, to settle European affairs, and after that you and Carlos are coming over to Chamonix for a week's skiing. How does that sound? Do say you'll come. Charlotte and I can hardly go on our own!' There was an unmistakable twinkle in Xavier's eyes.

'My goodness, Xavier, you haven't wasted much time. You two have only been on your own five minutes. I don't know that I can just drop everything like that. The House is in session.'

'Never mind the House, Sylvia. You and Carlos have been very kind to me since Sophia died, and I want to give you both a little holiday, and I have invited Charlotte to join us, not as your protection officer, but as a novice skier who I'm going to help as best I can. I'm not the best skier in Spain, but at least I represented the University in the Sierras before I went into the Navy.'

Sylvia looked at Carlos and Charlotte in turn. What could she say? Events seemed to have moved much faster than she had thought possible. 'I'll have to see what I can do, but I won't be very popular at No. 10 or at my own office, and I'll have to apologize to my constituency chairman for missing a coffee morning that he had arranged.'

'Look, I'll tell you what I'll do, Sylvia. I'll send a cheque to your constituency chairman and I'll say it comes from the Chamonix Tories. How's that for you?'

'You really are very naughty, Xavier. It does sound awfully tempting.'

'Good. Then I'll take that for a yes,' said Xavier quickly. 'Now then, Carlos, there is work for you and me to do. We'll do it through the Embassy in the morning. Our Embassy will help me, even on a Sunday morning. No doubt you will tell your own Ministry, Sylvia, and I'll speak to Lyons to have suitable French security laid on. I find them very helpful at Interpol HQ, and they owe me from last year. Do you have anything to wear, Charlotte?'

Charlotte had been worrying about her lack of any skiing clothing, but she needn't have worried. Xavier had been planning well ahead. 'Just come in what you have, as though you were going out for a good walk in the snow in the winter, and leave the rest to me. We can fix you up when you're out there, and you haven't really the time to look round before you go to Paris. I guess you have a similar figure to Sylvia, so she might have some things, but we'll see to it that you look as smart as anyone.'

Xavier was in fine form, and the three of them wondered just what else Xavier had in mind.

'Accommodation will be a bit tricky at short notice,' went on Xavier, 'but I do have a few friends in Chamonix. One double and two singles – that shouldn't be too difficult. With luck, they might have inter-communicating doors, but don't worry, Charlotte, I'll make sure you have the key!'

Charlotte blushed. Oh, what a lovely sense of humour he had. She had never seen him like this before.

As she fell to sleep that night she was wishing that Xavier had been kissing her instead of his younger son from Slapton College. But perhaps the boy took after his father, even if his looks favoured his mother's side of the family!

The following week, Sylvia, in her role as Deputy Prime Minister, together with Charlotte in her role as Chief Inspector Charlotte Johnson, found themselves staying at the British Embassy in Paris. The Embassy is only a few hundred yards from the Elysée Palace – the official residence of the President of France on the Rue de Fauberg St Honore – and not that much further from the Hotel Bristol. Carlos and Xavier were frequent guests at the Bristol, one of the loveliest grand hotels in Europe. Sylvia and Carlos frequently travelled separately – as did a former British Cabinet Minister and his wife – as a precaution against them both being killed together in an air crash whilst their children were still at school.

It was a few days between their arrivals at De Gaulle airport, and it was during this period that Maiski and Renov worked together from the Russian Embassy in Paris on their final round of enquiries. It had occurred to both men that they were not going to be able to draw up a shortlist of four, as General Stolypin had commanded, and, with his consent, the list had been reduced to two. The method of selection would remain the same. The list was headed by the obvious scions of the Romanov dynasty – the living descendants of princes of the blood, both male and female, had been known for many years. The world media still pursued them from time to time in glossy magazines. The European Inter-Parliamentary Conference would bring any number of other possibles, including representatives of other Royal houses of yesteryear whose countries had become Republics since 1918, and yet more since 1945.

Maiski and Renov had their work cut out to cover all their potential candidates in personal interviews. These were conducted in Russian, French and German, according to need. The conference itself was held in the Palais Chaillot, from the steps of which there is the well-known and spectacular view of the Eiffel Tower known to generations in postcards and photographs of a personal nature.

The Conference was to some 'old hands' just another conference involving many well-meant platitudinous speeches delivered in different languages, with the delegates wearing headphones. The delegates obligingly clapped from time to time, particularly applauding those speaking in their own language. From the large public gallery, members of the public, separated from the delegates by large glass panels, took in as much as they could, and the world's media recorded all that occurred. Just how much would be beamed around Europe was a matter of debate. Most thought very little, and that even less interest would be taken. However, 'the show must go on', as the saying goes. As is nearly always the position, it was what was going on away from the podium and the television cameras that mattered.

Maiski and Renov were wearing their special glasses, not simply tinted, but made so that they could effectively see the nuances of delegates' eyes as they sat there in their

47

serried ranks. The Russians were well provided with every device, but so were the good-looking Spaniard Xavier and his friend Carlos. Xavier wore his special glasses which he adjusted carefully to the lighting in the large magnificent hall. Carlos chose not to wear his glasses, in order that the two of them sitting together did not too obviously look like 'observers'. Presently it was Sylvia who was called upon to speak. She went to the podium.

Charlotte's eyes never left her, although the French Sûreté was perfectly adequate protection. Not only were they thoroughly competent, but also armed, whereas she was not. Charlotte's role as protection officer was at a personal level, and her Black Belt in karate was quite sufficient for this purpose. She would never have been in Mary Orlanski's league. Mary could have killed any man within seconds, but that was not a necessary qualification.

Sylvia's speech was not remarkable in itself, but better than many. What brought her rapturous applause was that following a few well-chosen, if hackneyed, words in English she made the remainder of her speech in her polished French, as her compliment to Paris – 'where I spent my honeymoon'. The French Tourist representative was not slow to take this in. He already knew of the fact, but it was nice to hear it announced from the podium by a visiting Deputy Prime Minister – in French!

The two Russian officers never took their eyes off Sylvia whilst she was speaking beyond quick glances at the audience to check its reaction. Carlos looked at Sylvia, his eyes bulging with pride. Xavier did not. His professional eye was on the public gallery. There he was, Major Renov, and the man next to him, who was he? He, Xavier, felt certain that he had seen him before, but where?

Yes, that was the man he had met at Expo 92 in Seville, but who was he? He couldn't think, but certainly he was Russian. He had to be, sat next to Renov and wearing the same 'observer' glasses. 'I must let Sylvia and Charlotte know,' he thought to himself, 'that is, after I have informed Madrid via the Spanish Embassy in Paris.'

48

Xavier turned to Carlos as the applause for Sylvia's speech died down. 'You must be very proud, old man. What a lucky man you are, and what a lucky government to have a Deputy Prime Minister who can speak French so fluently. I'm sorry to have to leave you just now, but I forgot something I must put right at the Embassy. See you back at the Bristol.'

'See you, Xavier, and yes, I am very proud of Sylvia, and so are her boys.'

Xavier made his way to the Spanish Embassy as quickly as the taxi would take him. He spoke briefly to his Prime Minister and at some length to Spanish Security.

'Thank you very much, Señor, and feel assured that our Embassy will give you every assistance. We have sent two of our best men to Chamonix, just in case any problem should arise.' Xavier made his way back to the Bristol with a happy heart.

From his room at the Bristol Xavier called the British Embassy. He asked for Sylvia by name. He was put through to a senior secretary.

'Good evening,' started Xavier. 'You don't know me, but I'm a friend of your Deputy Prime Minister. I will be at your Embassy front gate in ten minutes. Please tell your DPM that it is important and that I'm a Spanish friend of her husband's. Do I make myself clear?'

'Yes you do, Sir, but can I have your name?'

'Yes. Just say Señor Lang.' Xavier replaced his telephone and prepared to leave after his 'five o'clock shave'. Minutes later Xavier was admitted at the gate, and three minutes later he was with Sylvia and Charlotte.

'Whatever is this cloak-and-dagger business, Xavier?'

'I didn't know who I was talking to, Sylvia, and I thought you would want to be the first to know – and immediately – that Major Renov is in Paris.'

'Major Renov? How do you know that? Have you seen him?'

'Yes I have, and he's seen you. He was at the Palais Chaillot this afternoon when you were addressing the Conference. I daresay he may have seen you too, Charlotte, but I can't know that for certain. He certainly saw you, Sylvia. He was wearing special glasses in the visitors' gallery.'

'I said that Xavier might find something out here in Paris with his speaking Russian,' said Charlotte, 'but I didn't think he would actually see him. Did you speak to him or try to, Xavier?'

'No I didn't, Charlotte. He was completely out of range, and I didn't know whether it was even wise to make conversation. There is still an air of mystery about that man, but I can't put my finger on it,' he continued. 'The best thing, Sylvia, if you and Charlotte would agree, is for Charlotte to write him a short letter saying how pleased she was to see him, but sorry she wasn't able to speak to him and wishing his wife well. That will give him something to think about.'

Sylvia thought. Her immediate thought was simply to tell MI6. 'Thanks for the thought, Xavier, but I don't think I could authorize Charlotte to write without London's approval, and how can you be quite sure? They will know that Charlotte would be unlikely to write on her own when she is here looking after me.'

'I don't know why we are in NATO sometimes, Sylvia,' sighed Xavier. 'You have my word for it. It was Renov all right. Don't forget, I had two or three quite long conversations with him in Madrid. I don't forget a face. Call London by all means, but a short note from Charlotte to Major Renov would be, how do you put it, an excellent idea.'

Sylvia decided to act on her own authority, and called the Ambassador. Within minutes a short letter was dictated, as from Charlotte, with copies for the Prime Minister in London, the Embassy itself and MI6. It read:

'Dear Major Renov,
    I was very pleased to see you this afternoon at the Conference. So sorry we could not have spoken, but hope we may meet again sometime in London or Moscow. Please give my best wishes to your wife.
    Yours sincerely
        Charlotte Johnson'

The letter was given an Embassy Seal and was hand-delivered to the Russian Embassy the following morning, after Sylvia and Charlotte had left Paris for Chamonix. At the Russian Embassy the letter was delivered immediately to Major General Renov after it had been infra-red checked by security. Renov opened the envelope with care, as he always did, and read the three sentences with amazement.

'How on earth could that have happened without my seeing her?' he asked himself a dozen times. 'I must be more circumspect in future,' he told himself. He simply could not bring himself to understand how she could have seen him with her own eyes without the lenses he had.

The two unmarked French police cars arrived safely in Chamonix over the Col d'Avorix, which had been cleared of snow. The Hotel Excel was not the largest hotel in the resort, but it was extremely comfortable, well-known to Xavier and equipped for all skiers from novices to Olympic hopefuls. The hotel was fully booked. Xavier was to say later that he had been fortunate to obtain the last double and two singles. He was indeed fortunate, but it was no accident. The hotel could always move clients in an emergency – whenever it suited Xavier's requirements.

Over dinner, following their arrival, Xavier made a point of saying, 'I'm sorry that I couldn't get the singles I wanted with communicating doors, but I felt that you, Charlotte, would want to be next door to Sylvia and Carlos. I believe there is a communicating door between those two rooms. So you can still feel you're on duty protecting Sylvia if Carlos should try to attack her!'

'What a great sense of humour.' She liked him better by the day. Charlotte was not to know that Xavier had reserved the accommodation exactly as it was, and he knew every inch of the hotel in terms of lay-out and security. The meal itself was French cuisine at its best. The choice lay between what is loosely described as 'International cuisine' and 'Haute Savoie' – local dishes of the highest quality. Carlos and Xavier went for the Haute Savoie; Sylvia and Charlotte

51

thought they would play safe and settled for the Poulet Kiev – a dish they both enjoyed. Since all four were tired and fully *au fait* with French, they sat after dinner watching the local television service which gave full details of the weather conditions in relation to skiing, with general advice to visitors to the region.

Charlotte had done as Xavier had suggested in relation to clothing, and Sylvia had been able to provide two skiing outfits from her extensive wardrobe, which was quite six times as large as Charlotte's. They all slept well – in their own beds – and ate a hearty 'English style' breakfast: none of your Continental nonsense of coffee and rolls!

Xavier had been up early to arrange for the skis, and the Professional had been his usual helpful self, with as much advice as he thought appropriate for Sylvia and Charlotte. Sylvia had skied with Carlos before in Spain, but was still something of a beginner. Charlotte was a complete novice, never having worn skis before in her life. Both Carlos and Xavier were very experienced. Xavier had skied both for his University, Seville, and for the Spanish Navy. Xavier relished the prospect of acting as coach to Charlotte, even if some eyebrows were raised when they saw Xavier making his way to the nursery slope. He came down the slope like the expert he was, but the same faces smiled when they saw him at the top again taking the hand of the terrified Charlotte.

After an hour's instruction Charlotte was just beginning to feel that the earth was truly standing still and that she was moving of her own volition. This after half a dozen falls which, no doubt, would produce bruises the following day. She felt so bruised in fact that she declined to ski in the afternoon, but contented herself with the swimming pool within the hotel, writing postcards to her mother, Mary and Susan, and watching Xavier and Carlos coming down the piste at a speed of knots. Sylvia stayed in her room working on her Ministerial red boxes, which seemed to follow her everywhere.

The following morning Charlotte didn't feel that she could play chicken again, and she put on a show of enthusiasm. Xavier seemed delighted, and within minutes of her draining the last of her coffee she was out with him again on the nursery slope. This morning it seemed much better. Xavier was a good instructor. By lunchtime she went down the slope on her own. In the afternoon the four of them went up the mountain behind the hotel in the funicular. They took an Alpine meal in the restaurant which overlooked the valley below, at a distance of many metres. Notwithstanding the date, it was quite warm in the crisp sunshine. Charlotte was wearing one of the two suits that Sylvia had lent her.

Whilst Charlotte was not what might be termed 'chocolate box', she looked at her radiant best and quite film-starish. Her height and carriage, combined with pleasant if not striking features, made any number of men look twice, perhaps, to the annoyance of some of the women! Xavier wasted no time in taking any number of snaps with his camera.

'I'll take a few and have copies made,' he said. They all took turns, and it wasn't long before the reel finished and the unmistakable sound of the reel winding back was heard. 'We'll get them developed at the pharmacy in the hotel in the morning.'

It must have been about 5 p.m. when Sylvia was ploughing through the day's red box, with Charlotte having a lie-down next door, when a knock came at Sylvia's door. Sylvia thought nothing of it, assuming it was the time for bed-sheets and covers to be turned back. She opened the door and was immediately knocked to the floor by one of three burly men, all masked, who entered. Sylvia screamed out in pain, and her scream brought Charlotte through the communicating door, dressed only in a negligée.

Charlotte ran forward. The burly man who had knocked down Sylvia went towards her, but with a kick that would have pleased Mary, her karate coach, she felled the man, who screamed as he clutched his groin. Charlotte went straight for the second man and closed on him. They both fell heavily on the floor over the coffee table. The third man grabbed Sylvia's red box and aimed it at Charlotte's head.

That had been his intention, but in the fall he hit his comrade instead and, concerned for his own future, he turned and ran from the room.

He had not gone one yard beyond the door when two swarthy characters of Spanish appearance grabbed him. One of these placed a half-Nelson hold on his left arm and the second man placed his right hand under his chin and thrust the man's head back with extreme violence against the wall of the hotel passage. The man crumpled like a stone. Sylvia had picked herself up by now. The second man was on top of Charlotte. Sylvia took careful aim with an unopened Champagne bottle and brought it down sharply on the head of Charlotte's assailant, who dropped like a log on to Charlotte's body. Charlotte had no difficulty now in pushing him off and away. The first man was still clutching himself and groaning in a most frightful fashion.

'Are you all right, Sylvia?' asked Charlotte, herself badly shaken.

'Yes. I think so. Are you all right? You saved my life coming in like that. Thank God you were next door,' cried Sylvia, who was white, shaky and breathless.

At that moment Carlos and Xavier arrived. The two swarthy Spaniards addressed Xavier in Spanish. Xavier, with a speed that terrified even Charlotte, seized the intruder who had attacked her by the throat and held him three inches above the ground against the wall of the room. This was with his left hand. In his right he held what appeared to be a pencil, but in the instant became the handle of a flick knife.

'Start talking. You've seconds only to live if you don't tell me all I want to know.' The man's face went a horrible red as Xavier's grip on his jugular tightened, whilst the blade of the knife cut slightly into his flesh below. Xavier released his left hand slowly, and the man appeared to recover his wits. Within two minutes Xavier knew all he wanted to know, and within a further five minutes the French Sûreté had the three men arrested for further interrogation.

The two Spaniards had melted away on Xavier's signal.

Before the arrival of the French police, Carlos had done his best to comfort Sylvia and Xavier had succeeded in comforting Charlotte. 'You have to laugh, Charlotte,' Xavier had said to her. 'I never planned to be in your room with you only wearing what you have on. You'll never know whether your bruises came from the skiing or saving Sylvia but thank God you're both all right. Please never be frightened of me. I was taught to box Queensberry Rules at Slapton, but I've had to learn to fight very differently since school days. From what I saw of that man you kicked, I think we must both be grateful to Mary, your friend and teacher. Come on. I'll leave you now. Have a shower and get dressed. Put some make-up on, if you feel you have to, but you look absolutely lovely to me just as you are.'

As he said this he held her to himself and kissed her on both cheeks. He left the room. Charlotte shook with emotion. 'What a man! I wish he was mine. If only he had kissed me on the lips!'

Fifteen minutes later both Sylvia and Charlotte were feeling better, but they were both still fairly shaky. It is one thing practising falling or even being thrown on the gym mat floor – it is quite another thing being attacked in an enclosed situation, falling over hard furniture on to a marble surface. At least Charlotte had known what she was about, and she was ten years younger than Sylvia. Both women had showered and repaired their faces as they thought appropriate – Charlotte had dabbed perfume behind her ears and on her wrists – when a knock came first on Sylvia's and then Charlotte's door from the passage.

Carlos opened the door, after he had checked the 'eye' in the door. One of the hotel staff was holding a bouquet of carnations which were out of season and clearly hot-house grown. Carlos took them from the girl, noticing that she carried a second bouquet which she was delivering to Charlotte's room. Carlos took them over to Sylvia, who was sitting at her dressing table applying the last touches to her lipstick.

Turning to Carlos she said, 'Thank you, darling. You needn't have bothered. It's Charlotte who deserves them. I

55

don't like to think what might have happened if she hadn't been next door.'

'Don't thank me, dear. Read the card. It's probably the management. I saw Xavier going downstairs.'

The card read: 'To an Honourable and Learned Lady from the Chamonix Tories'.

'You're wrong. They're from Xavier himself. Doesn't he have the very best sense of fun? I do hope he takes to Charlotte. I thought for a moment that he was going to kill the man who knocked her to the ground. At least I was able to help her with that Champagne bottle. Let's open it and ask Charlotte to come in and join us.'

Carlos went to the door that divided the rooms and dutifully knocked.

'Come in.' It was Charlotte's voice, but Charlotte looked as though in a dream. She had received red roses and she was holding the card that was delivered with them.

It read: 'To Charlotte, with love, X'. Charlotte was very full. She brushed past Carlos and went to Sylvia, holding the card in front of her as a child might run to its grandmother with a Christmas present. 'Look, Sylvia.' Charlotte showed her the card. There were tears in Charlotte's eyes, but they were tears of joy, not of pain. Any pains she might have otherwise have felt were a million miles away.

Sylvia put her arms around her and held her. There was no need for words. Both women knew how the other felt, but Sylvia felt that she had to say something. 'Just thank him, dear. Let him propose. You know he loves you.' Sylvia released her hold. Charlotte dabbed her eyes and went back to her room, sipping the Champagne that Carlos had poured. She sat before her dressing table. As she did so, she remembered a tune that must have been one of her mother's favourites in the long ago: 'I want to put some lipstick on a brand new tie. I'm a big girl now.'

6

In Moscow life was settling into a routine of sorts. There were those who appeared to be prosperous by world standards, including any number of visitors valued for their foreign currency. Side by side with this situation, there were thousands who appeared to be only a little above the starvation level, and perhaps any number who fell below it. There were communal soup kitchens and many scenes reminiscent of the most difficult days following Napoleon's retreat from Moscow in the early part of the nineteenth century. There were political commentators who continually made this very point. Take away the paraphernalia of the modern world and the scenario wasn't that far out, particularly with a heavy blanket of snow, with everyone wearing headgear for warmth rather than fashion.

The religious revival was apparent. The Cathedral of St Basil and many of the city churches had been cleaned and re-gilded, with large crowds attending services – crowds that might not have dared to attend only a few years ago.

Even Major-General Renov had thought it sensible to read extensively to know all that it was necessary for a man of education to know of Christendom and what had gone before. He still came out with some unusual requests for information: 'If it is right that only Christians can go to heaven after death, what happened to all those people who lived, say, ten thousand years ago – their souls, I mean – and what about all those people who lived, say, a hundred thousand years ago and one million years ago?'

57

Myra had long since given up trying to answer questions she couldn't answer. She referred him to the City Church Libraries that had not been destroyed and the priests in charge of them. Renov was not too keen. He knew of penetration by KGB and others. He would work things out for himself – when he had the time.

The most important thing now was his work and the forthcoming birth of Myra's child. General Boris Stolypin was making good progress. Beyond the detailed enquiries he was making with the aid of Colonel-General Maiski and Major-General Renov, he was preparing for the day when it would be necessary for the succession of the Presidency to be effected with the aid of the Army and other elements of the state apparatus, including the media.

The Winter Olympics had produced excellent programmes on television. Snow was neutral. It fell in Norway and across Scandinavia to St Petersburg and across the greater part of Russia. The Russian Army could be relied upon to produce all manner of competitors for the Winter Games, both men and women. Stolypin was determined that all competitors would receive as much publicity and promotion as was consistent with good order and military discipline.

Ivor Strydom was Chairman of the Parliamentary Committee charged with responsibility for media communication, and Stolypin made a point of inviting him to his dacha for consultations.

'I do feel, Comrade, that there is an unfortunate gap in our relations following the last Olympics in Norway. I would like to see the media playing a larger part in advancing the national interest in sport.'

This innocent introduction served to draw out the hopes of Ivor Strydom, who had felt repressed for years during Soviet rule that had obliged him to refer many matters for Committee consideration. This had resulted in the stifling of his own more liberal views on broadcasting. 'The great difficulty, General, is that as a nation we have become too stratified. I think you are the first man of your rank to invite me to your home for a discussion on the future of our national media and its requirements.'

'I find that very hard to believe, Ivor,' replied Stolypin. 'I should have thought you would have been inundated with invitations including security services anxious for their own future. Let me assure you I'm not in the business of seeking other peoples' jobs. I'm getting to the end of my service career, but I would like you to render one last service to the Army whilst I still hold rank.'

'What is it, General? I'll try and do what I can, if I'm allowed. What is it that you have in mind?'

'I was thinking of a twentieth-century history of the Russian Army,' replied Stolypin, 'starting in 1900 to the present time. It would be a fairly massive undertaking, but I think the Army would assist you, and over the years it would be a great, moving history of events. It would require considerable research and expense, but if you could put it to your Committee I would put it to some senior officers I know. Why don't we make a start with, say, the first fifteen years of the century?'

'1900 to 1915, you mean?'

'Yes, of course. We still have records of the Regiments and uniforms. They were very colourful at that time, so that should encourage the acting community, and what with the interment of the bones of the old Imperial family in St Petersburg and all the foreign visitors following that event, I should think you will have recent news coverage which you could slip into your first fifteen years,' added Stolypin, ensuring thereby that Ivor Strydom got the message that he, Stolypin, had given the matter more than casual thought.

The dinner that Olga provided was as good and substantial as any served in Moscow that night. In addition to the Stolypins there were the Renovs and Viktor Maiski, who added their support to Stolypin's views.

Ivor Strydom had the feeling that he was being set up, as indeed he was, but he knew the ranks these men held, and the prospect of such a huge field for acting and choreography was breathtaking. He made up his mind that he would seek to persuade his Parliamentary Committee to go along with the proposals. The period of 1900 to 1915 would not be too difficult, but it would be expensive, if only in relation to the uniforms that would be required. But again, there had been concern expressed in the textile and clothing industries regarding orders for manufacture, and the reduction in military expenditure regarded as a 'peace dividend', had not suited everybody in Russia any more than it had throughout the Western world. Any number of soldiers could be retained as extras, and the film would take all of a year and perhaps two to make. This would be the view of the Committee, to say nothing of the opportunity of mingling with military men of rank who they would not be likely to meet otherwise on pleasant social occasions.

Olga was like a second mother to Myra. Conversation covered all aspects of family life and photographs were passed around. Maiski was asked if he was related to the Maiski who had been the Soviet Ambassador to Britain at the beginning of World War Two and who had presented Russian wooden dolls to the young British Princesses, as they then were.

'No, I'm sorry, Olga. I can't claim that honour for my family, but I'll remember that question if ever I should find myself in that sort of situation. Fancy you remembering something like that.'

'It was all part of our training a long time ago. If we were ever called upon to make any gift to a foreigner, it always had to be wooden dolls to keep our woodworkers in work. I still have a few sets left, and one day, soon I hope, I will be making another gift of a doll set to Myra. Hopefully Myra's child will be able to pass the dolls on to her first granddaughter, but that will be well into the next century.'

Maiski's 'punishment' for not being the descendant of the former Soviet Ambassador in London was that he had to 'sing for his supper', or more exactly play the piano for an hour, which pleased him as much as it pleased his fellow guests. Baby talk was not Maiski's forte. It never had been and never would be.

*   *   *

Three weeks after the dinner at Stolypin's dacha the first 25,000 troops were assigned for film-making purposes. Ivor Strydom, on Stolypin's authority, was made an honorary Colonel in order that he could mix as required. No salary went with the appointment, but Ivor was suitably flattered, and he learnt quickly how to salute and receives salutes. He, Ivor, and other members of the Committee were taken on all manner of World War One reconstructed manoeuvres, always showing the Russians as being victorious against both the Germans and the Austrians.

According to the detailed military instructions sent from Stolypin's office, it was to be made clear that the Tsar and his officers were fundamentally decent men, if not very good commanders in the field, and more importantly it was to be shown that whenever a battle was lost it was due to the work of traitors to Russia, aided by the Germans, who were made up of anarchists of various types. Colonel-General Maiski was very well-informed, and he was quite determined that old scores going back to his grandfathers' day, not to say his great-grandfathers' days would be repaid with interest. There were certain objections to this rewriting of military history, but when those who objected came under KGB surveillance for advancing the cause of anarchy, the objections were quickly overcome, and it became apparent to many that the film would serve the nationalist interest of the Army. The troops were delighted to be dressing up in the colourful uniforms of their great-grandfathers' time, and quite soon literally hundreds of thousands of coloured postcards were in circulation, with colourful parades in both Moscow and St Petersburg and other cities throughout the Russian Federation.

Over the weeks following the Stolypin dinner more and more enquiries could be made quite openly concerning any number of people who had been connected with the old Imperial Army. Until 1915, the Army held its own, notwithstanding enormous losses in terms of men and materials, and it was the lack of materials that was the cause of so much human loss. There would be no such lack of materials in the film being made. Boris Stolypin and Ivor Strydom would see to that.

'We still only have four to choose from,' said Major-General Renov one day. He was right. The four would-be candidates for the office of Tsar were to be invited to Russia on various pretexts. The most obvious candidates, by reason of rank and descent, which some of them openly boasted, were invited by Intourist, the government agency involved with foreigners visiting Russia. Prince Popokovski's grandfather had settled in France immediately before Kerenski fell in 1918 and the Bolsheviks took over. His son had a gallant role in the Free French Forces in World War Two, but the present scion was a very different man. His photographs were often to be seen in glossy magazines, and he had given any number of interviews to journalists on the lines that 'if he was ever asked nothing would give him greater pleasure than the duty to serve his people in any position he might be offered'.

Upon investigation, this only meant some very high position indeed, giving him full freedom to come to the West and his various homes around the world, whenever it suited him. This was no part of Stolypin's thinking, but the man had to be asked, if only to give cover to the operation as a whole and make the numbers up to four.

A luxury liner making a Scandinavian cruise incorporating St Petersburg· was used in part by Intourist to bring the Prince and a small entourage of his to the former Imperial capital.

The Bolshoi Ballet was giving a short season, including *Romeo and Juliet* sung in French. What better bait than that? The Prince would have settled for any good musical rather than the ballet, and he did not relish being taken on what he regarded as a state package holiday. He quickly discovered that every minute of his tight schedule appeared to be spoken for.

Renov boarded the liner at Stockholm and made it his business to make contact with the Prince. Renov had very little contact with princes of any of the Royal houses, but he spoke French well without a pronounced accent, and he spoke as though he was travelling to Russia for the first time. He insisted that his fellow passengers should visit the Hermitage – one of the great art galleries of the world. It was during one of these excursions that Renov learned something that he felt he could only have dreamt, namely, that one of the Prince's entourage had been one of the men who had been convicted of attempting to steal from and assaulting 'Mrs Westlake', who in fact was the British Deputy Prime Minister travelling with her husband incognito at the Hotel Excel in Chamonix.

Renov was absolutely fascinated; the more so when he discovered the part that Charlotte had played travelling as Mrs Westlake's maid. All this he recorded and reported to Stolypin.

'I think that "maid" of yours must be quite a person. That's the one who writes to you, isn't it? I think Myra should meet her sometime.'

'Yes, I think she should, and I think you will enjoy meeting another person I have spoken about, who seems very friendly towards "the maid", and that is a Spaniard called Lang who has some Russian ancestry. He speaks Russian fluently in a rather old-fashioned way, but he's involved with Spanish Security, so I thought it necessary to be careful in Madrid. He went to Slapton College in England, which you and I would call "private", but which they call "public".'

Three American scions of former Russian émigrés were invited to Moscow, and naturally it fell to Colonel-General Maiski and his Olympic Committee friends to look after them. They were given the same 'treatment' as Prince Popokovski. They were housed in Moscow's new Hilton Hotel and taken to sporting centres and privately entertained at Maiski's country dacha on the same estate as Stolypin's. At the end of a further fortnight's deliberations the three men, Stolypin, Maiski and Renov, felt they were little further forward in their hunt for the man they wanted, but matters were going well in other directions.

The rouble continued to fall against the dollar, but there was hopefully continuing investment from abroad, but not on the scale required to bring any real advance in the national economy. The economic outlook appeared bleak.

It was whilst the three Generals were discussing matters with the film producer, Strydom, that Hollywood came under discussion with reference to the last earthquake in Los Angeles. The tremendous cost of reinstating the communications and prosperity of California as a whole was being met quite substantially by Federal Agencies, but the American banks were also involved. 'Maiski. You met a top American banker with a Polish-sounding name, didn't you, before you went down to Atlanta?'

'Yes I did. He was called Orlanski. Why, what of it?'

'I think it would be an idea if you were to contact him again. He did invite you to open an account with his bank, didn't he?

'More importantly, we could do with him opening a branch of his bank here in Moscow and St Petersburg. At the very least, that would enable us to get ourselves into the Finance Ministry and get it on our side, rather than us just going to them for money. You might be able to insist on one or two of our friends being appointed to the Ministry Board or Commissariat, or whatever they call it just now.'

'This will take some planning, General. Writing the letter to Orlanski is the easy bit. I don't know anybody who I could remotely call temperance, but no doubt they could be found, and if that's impossible we'll need a few conversions. Some of the ex-KGB would be only too willing to join a Temperance League if it meant security of employment with the added satisfaction of bringing American dollars into the country.'

'Good thinking, Maiski, but do get a letter off to your friend of one night, Orlanski. I can clear that for you whilst you make an approach to the Finance Ministry. We will, after all, have to have some evidence in writing that we have a contact.'

'Thank you, General. I'll draft one tonight, show you in

64

the morning and take it around to the Foreign Affairs Ministry for the diplomatic bag.'

It didn't take Maiski long to draft his letter. It read:

'Dear Mr Orlanski,

I do wonder whether you might remember me? It seems so long since we met briefly – too briefly – at the White House reception held for the Olympic Games. I remember the evening well, particularly your charming wife's amusing joke about the possibility of our being related sixty generations back. I am writing to you today to take up your kind offer to become a customer of your bank. You do not yet have a branch in Moscow, but since it is likely that I will be coming to the States from time to time, perhaps, I could have an account at your Head Office? I am not a man of means, as you are, but you may notice from this notepaper that I have had promotion since we last met in Washington so, hopefully, I will not require what I believe you call "facilities". Please give my kind regards to your wife. If there is any possibility of you both coming to Moscow, I should be pleased to meet you and offer you modest hospitality. If it is not your practice to have Russian clients who are not "temperance", I will, of course, understand.

Yours sincerely
Viktor Maiski (Col. General)'

'I wouldn't alter a comma, Maiski,' Stolypin had said the following morning. 'I must say, Maiski, your command of English is improving, and your style of letter writing. We shall have you becoming a Doctor of Letters if you carry on like this.'

The letter was duly typed up on a new American word processor that had been acquired by Stolypin for all correspondence addressed to Britain and America from his office.

Within four days it was being read by Elmer Orlanski at the Head Office of the Chicago Temperance Bank. Elmer called in his assistant Jim Rogerson – who had become his brother-in-law after marrying his sister Lucinda.

'Hey. Look at this, Jim. This is the guy I told you about. He was only a Colonel when we met him at the White House. How's that for promotion? I know little or nothing of Russian military ranks, but if they're anything like ours I should say he's in the fast lane.'

'Sure thing, Elmer. I seem to remember that Mary was very impressed with him. I seem to recall her saying something to the effect that she felt certain that he could handle himself. Perhaps he was a member or past member of the Soviet Olympic team.'

'Perhaps so. I will speak to Mary about him tonight, but for the moment it's a question of whether we give him an account. We can't let a Russian General slip through our fingers, but I suppose we'll have to have clearance from the CIA or some top trading department in Washington.'

'I don't know about that, Elmer, right now as I'm stood here, but I'll get right on to it and let you know for sure, and in writing, by tomorrow morning. No doubt you'll be drafting letters of acceptance or rejection within the next hour and despatch the appropriate one, depending on the result of my enquiries?'

'Quite so. Get with it and come back to me as soon as you can.' Elmer lifted his pocket dictaphone and commenced dictating:

'Dear General Maiski,
Many thanks for your kind letter of enquiry. Please accept my congratulations and those of my wife on your military promotion. It is always good to hear of one's friends getting on. I will be delighted to treat your letter as formal application to become a customer of the Bank, and whilst I seem to recall that you took the Champagne at the Reception rather than the orange juice, as sipped by my wife and myself, I may yet hope to persuade you to Temperance, if not total abstinence. As you read this letter you are now one of my valued customers. I have

opened your account with a nominal sum of one dollar, the price of a drink. I have no immediate plans to come to Moscow, but I thank you for your kind thought. Under separate cover I am sending you a formal letter together with application form and details of the bank's many facilities, which I am sure you will find interesting.
Yours sincerely
Elmer P. Orlanski'

Elmer's second letter, drafted in the alternative, gave him a tinge of annoyance as he dictated, but it read as well as his first. He proceeded to the next matter in hand.

At home, after dinner, Elmer told Mary all about Maiski's letter, a photocopy of which he brought with him. He also brought his draft reply. Elmer didn't discuss much business at home, but he knew that Mary liked all the personal news at the highest level – not mere dross – but so that she could hold her own in conversation and more importantly, perhaps, when not to know anything. Mary was quite certain that the bank should enrol General Maiski as a customer.

'Just think, darling, he might bring whole Regiments of customers.'

'Yes, and they might all require facilities in dollars – with the rouble falling. Where would our security be then?' answered Elmer.

'I don't know, darling. That's your department. Remember, you are the banker. I know very little about Russia. I know they have lots of land. I suppose you take a mortgage or Legal Charge on the Kremlin or something. Ask Jim, your brother-in-law. He's meant to know all about foreign banking, isn't he? I can tell you all about breath tests for motorists in London and the Hounslow Uxbridge test – but Russia!'

'Yes, honey. Jim is good at foreign banking, but I can't think he's ever put his mind to seeing how the Bank can have security on a Russian Officer's pay or property.'

'If you want General Maiski, why don't you ask him or his

present bankers in Moscow? It's not like you, darling, not to know how to start. If Jim cannot find out, invite Viktor Maiski over here, and I'll have a go. You know I won't offer him anything but good food and pleasant conversation.'

'Good offer, Mary, but international banking just doesn't happen like that, but I'm not saying we won't have him – ever.'

The conversation drifted on to and remained with the children, who really were growing up. Maria, Mary's cousin from Malta, was becoming more and more at home by the day. She had been excellent with the babies, but the time was coming when she would have to return home.

Mary had been a serving officer in the Metropolitan Police in London before she had met and married Elmer, who was now the President of the Chicago Temperance Bank. Mary had been one of the original Protection Officers allotted to Sylvia when she had first been appointed Minister of Information in Britain by John Senior, the Prime Minister. Mary was of Maltese extraction. Her parents ran the Malta Cafe in Shoreditch in the East End of London. She had had a comprehensive school education, with a modest number of 'O' levels, but beyond her natural ability to speak Maltese, which she had learnt at her mother's knee, she was tops in judo and karate. Officially she was Black Belt at 7th Dan, but by virtue of her ITS, literally translated as Inner Tensile Strength, she was far above competition level and had trained many at Olympic standard. She had fallen madly in love with Elmer and was still besotted with him. The birth of her triplets had seemed to make them even closer. She had been very close to Sylvia, who was a Roman Catholic like herself. She had maintained a fairly constant letter-writing communication both with Sylvia and her two ex-police officer colleagues, Charlotte and Susan.

Susan had married a Registrar Doctor from St Bartholomew's – Barts – in London. Charlotte was not yet married, but Mary had learnt from Sylvia that Charlotte was coming under Xavier's spell – at least that is how it seemed to Mary, who was very bright if not as highly educated, in an academic sense, as Charlotte. Mary had liked Xavier from her first meeting with him, when he had been Carlos's Best Man and she had been Sylvia's Chief Bridesmaid. She had also been Godmother to Lucinda's little boy, of whom Xavier had been Godfather, so she was doubly fascinated at the prospect of Charlotte falling for him. They would make an excellent match, but she could foresee problems, quite apart from their age gap. Perhaps that wasn't too much of a problem, but there were other problems, including religion and nationality. Mary would write tomorrow to Sylvia and tell her that Colonel Maiski had been promoted.

Mary wrote a long letter to Sylvia with all her news, including news of the babies and the Orlanski family generally. She always wrote straight from the heart in her neat girlish hand, with nothing left to the imagination or to be read between the lines. Sylvia always enjoyed receiving a letter from Mary. It was such a complete change from all the Ministerial reading in her red boxes. Since Sylvia was an only child, she had tended to regard her three Bridesmaids of yester-year as her three young sisters.

It was one paragraph that made Sylvia re-read Mary's letter twice. It read: 'Do you remember, Sylvia, about my meeting a Colonel Maiski of the Russian Army, who came over to Washington for a reception at the White House? He was a charming man. He came into our life again yesterday, with a request to become a customer of the Bank. He really is a very charming man who could look after himself anywhere – if you know what I mean – and he's been promoted Colonel-General. You can see what a long way he has moved in a short while – nearly as far as me coming to Chicago from London.'

Sylvia added two and two, and came up with five. Could this Colonel Maiski – now Colonel-General Maiski – have any connection with Major Renov? Enquiries at the British Embassy in Moscow revealed that there was a Major-General Renov, but there was a complete blank when it came to his posting. There was also a Colonel-General Maiski, but again no one knew or was prepared to say what position he occupied. Both men might possibly be attached to General Stolypin, but he was at the head of Russian Military Intelligence. There was no chance of gaining any information from that quarter. Several agents of different nations had tried, but many of these same agents were officially posted 'missing, believed killed'. Whether they had simply been liquidated or tortured first no-one could know, but there were, understandably, few who would volunteer to find out.

Sylvia and Carlos had been back a fortnight from their holiday in Chamonix, with Charlotte in attendance. Xavier had returned to Madrid, and Charlotte was missing him. Sylvia was down to her parliamentary duties with her usual vigour, notwithstanding her experience of being thrown on the floor, but that was now a memory, albeit painful. Charlotte really had enjoyed her break, which would not be classified as part of her annual leave, since officially she had been looking after Sylvia. Sylvia had given her a glowing testimonial in relation to her bravery on taking on her three assailants – all well-made masked men. Sylvia did not attempt to be economic with the truth, and the doctor's examination of Charlotte confirmed that she had been quite badly bruised. Whether all the bruises had come from her defence of Sylvia or her falls on the nursery slope might have been a matter for speculation, but they were all bruises consistent with her having fallen!

Charlotte was thanked by the top brass at New Scotland Yard, but told that she would require further posting. She would be promoted Superintendent in charge of university recruiting. Her first duty, to please her, would be at Warwick, and then Birmingham and Aston, which was around the corner. Sylvia was sorry to be losing Charlotte, but she had known it wasn't a lifetime appointment, and if Charlotte was going to the top, and if she didn't marry Xavier, it would be selfish to have tried to hold her back and down.

7

The Conference in Moscow, held at the Palace of the People, was one of the most important conferences to be held in Moscow that year – outside the world of politics. Those attending were all architects and engineers of standing from many nations, with a liberal supply of translators of every language spoken.

It is hard and difficult work translating as speeches are made, particularly when the translator is obliged to give emphasis, that is the same emphasis as the speaker. Like the European Parliament in Strasbourg, the 600 delegates wore headphones and the translators, in groups of three or four, took up the work between them, translating for 15 minutes at a time.

Xavier was a member of the Spanish delegation, and he had received his invitation directly from Vladimir Renov, who had visited both Expo 92 in Seville and the Barcelona Olympics later in the same year. Xavier had been involved in both these projects and in the extensive roadworks on the southern coast, from Malaga to Marbella and beyond.

The whole purpose of the Conference was to attempt to exploit the massive natural resources of the Russian state in terms of scientific and engineering infrastructure. The Russian hosts made no secret of the fact that they wished to see Russia equal America in terms of industrial production, and equally important, to keep well ahead of the potential rivalry of China, with its vast natural resources, to say nothing of its expanding population, estimated at 1,000,000,000.

It was on the second day of the Conference that Renov

71

made his approach to Xavier. 'It really is very good to see you in Moscow. I was so pleased that you were able to accept the invitation of the Institute. I think you know that my speciality is nuclear physics.' Dr Renov was now wearing his academic title.

'It is very good to be here, Doctor. I thought that the two papers given yesterday afternoon were excellent. I do find that one problem in all international conferences is that you develop what you might term "a hot-house atmosphere" in the hall itself, with little opportunity of seeing the country as it really is.'

'I agree, Señor, but I do have an idea of how that might be overcome in your case. I do have some friends in the Army who might just be able to give you access to virtually any part of the country you wished to visit immediately after the close of the Conference for a period of, say, one week. Let me speak to my friends, and you can let me know which parts you would wish to see. My invitation could not, sadly, extend to your entire delegation, but two or three could come, and we could then travel together in several cars or one small aircraft, according to where we, that is you, wish to travel.'

The conversation proceeded over drinks at the bar – one of 17 in the building. Renov now came to his real purpose. 'I really must congratulate you, Señor, on your Russian. I seem to remember you telling me in Madrid that your mother had been half-Russian and that your grandmother had been wholly Russian, and that you felt that your ancestors had been in the service of our old Imperial family?'

'You have a good memory, Doctor,' replied Xavier, wondering just what this man, who was Doctor or Major as occasion demanded, was really after. 'It is true that my ancestors were in the old Imperial Service, but so were nearly all Russians. At least ninety per cent I should say, but my family's connection was a little closer. I believe that distantly we were related to the Romanovs, but that was a long way back – perhaps on the wrong side of the blanket, if you know what I mean. That is why my family, on my grandmother's side, took the name Romanov but why do you ask?'

'I ask only as a matter of social enquiry and to satisfy my curiosity. You must forgive me. I have no ancestors. I envy you.'

Renov was absolutely delighted with this latest information. General Stolypin was informed within the hour. There was now a definite list of two candidates. Renov felt that he had struck oil. Could he possibly have stumbled on to a gold mine of a chance? There was a clear case for a meeting of Stolypin, Maiski and Renov with Xavier. Renov and his wife Myra were the obvious hosts, and three members of the Spanish delegation would be invited to make up numbers.

The dinner was held at Renov's dacha 60 miles east of Moscow. Myra was now in a very advanced stage of pregnancy, and in that situation Olga, Stolypin's wife, had come across to organize, with paid help, the catering supplied by a Moscow restaurant frequently patronized by Russian Army officers. As the meal was taken, conversation flowed as the wine flowed. The more wine, the more conversation, as is generally the case. Of the three Spanish delegates Xavier was the most fluent in Russian, and it was agreed by the others that he would speak for the Spanish guests in proposing toasts to 'The Institute', 'Myra and her forthcoming happy event', and several other toasts.

Doctor Renov, as he was addressed for the evening, proposed toasts to 'His Majesty the King of Spain', 'Our Guests' and other toasts. Each proposal required a mini-speech, and it was quickly midnight before they left the table. The Russians, all of them, were both impressed and amused at Xavier's manner of delivery and style. In a word, it seemed 'quaint'. No Frenchman today would dream of asking *'Comme portez vous?'* when greeting another, even if this was how British children had been taught to speak French 60 years ago. Xavier's Russian was what might be termed posh pre-Revolution.

Stolypin and Maiski congratulated Renov on his discovery and agreed between themselves that night that Xavier was certainly one of the top two if matters were to proceed. Stolypin decided that he had to investigate further himself. He took the initiative in inviting the Spanish delegation to view the 'Skydrome' from whence pictures of the universe outside the solar system could be viewed day and night. By means of advanced radar the satellites of distant stars could be seen, and the Russians were already working with the Americans and other European countries in exploring outer space. It was during this visit that Stolypin drew out Xavier's views on international co-operation and defence security in particular. Although Stolypin did speak and understand both English and French, he thought it best to speak his native Russian, not simply so that he could clearly understand everything said without effort, but so that he could hear Xavier continue in his polished Russian of yesteryear.

'Tell me, Señor. How do you feel about the security of your country, now that the Cold War is over? Isn't it a fine thing that we can now co-operate in peace to conquer the whole of the universe?'

A clever question – the real point of the question being covered by the platitudinous second question. 'General. You ask me two questions at once. Of course, it's magnificent that we are working together at last. If we can repeat in the outer universe what we are trying to do together in the Antarctic it must be a good thing all round, even if they don't have penguins on the moon or beyond! So far as security is concerned, you must know much more about that than me, but I suppose we must all be grateful that we can obliterate each other by pressing buttons, pulling levers or whatever has to be done, to blow up the civilized world.'

'That's a very interesting thought, Señor. You don't believe in disarmament, then?'

'Yes I do, provided it's safe, but I suspect it may never be so. At least for the next fifty to one hundred years,' continued Xavier. He didn't, indeed couldn't, know what Stolypin was after, but for good measure he added, 'I think all those nations which have the bomb must keep it in reserve against the possibility of attack. Wouldn't you agree?'

'Yes, Señor. I agree with you, and I'm glad to hear you say it. I was pleased to be able to toast your King last night at Vladimir's home. We don't have one for you to toast, but we do have a President.'

'Now you make me feel embarrassed, General. I completely forgot to toast your President. I seemed to be proposing so many toasts, and the wine was so good. Do give my apologies to Doctor Renov, please.'

Xavier had forgotten nothing, but he felt he must apologize. Stolypin had the strong feeling that Xavier was covering himself, but he smiled a diplomatic smile and simply said, 'I know what it's like when you're landed with all the toasts in a foreign country and language. It's easy to forget the odd toast.'

Renov and Maiski joined Xavier and Stolypin, and the conversation continued on various subjects. By the time lunch was served the four men were beginning to feel genuinely at ease with one another. In fact Xavier was now not only thinking in Russian, but as though he was a Russian. He seemed to have a grasp of affairs far beyond what might have been expected.

The Russian Military Officers, for that is what they really were, smiled to themselves when Xavier came out quite airily: 'One big advantage we have over you is that we can damn the Government and cheer our King at the same time. We have his statue and photograph everywhere – in hotel foyers and so on. These are rarely vandalized, but photographs of our politicians are always being damaged or torn by members of opposition parties.'

Renov finished this conversation topic by saying that he was finding it difficult studying Western political philosophy. 'It seems strange to me that Members of Parliament are elected on the basis of their promises, which they know or should know they cannot keep. It seems to me the more honest the politician the less likely he or she be elected, but perhaps it is different in your country.'

There could be no quick answer to this remark. Xavier answered as best as he thought diplomatic. 'I think you have to take a long term view, Doctor. The Chinese, I believe, say it is still too early to say whether the French Revolution of 1789 was really a good thing for France. I'm certainly not going to say whether Lenin or Franco were good or bad for Russia or Spain. Perhaps we should ask one of our British friends attending the conference as to whether Cromwell was good for them. I don't suppose he was, or they would have carried on with their Commonwealth. I think most of the British – well, the English anyway – were glad for the return of Charles II, but I'm not a historian.'

The three Russians were not far out in their thinking when they thought Señor Xavier Lang was a very good historian. After lunch Stolypin, who was in his element, took his colleagues on one side.

'I propose to pop Señor Lang a question, in jest, to test him. I'll say, "If it was in my gift to make you Tsar of Russia, what would you say?" Do you both agree? I would like you to be present when I pop the question.' The other two nodded. An opportunity arose whilst collecting their coats from the cloakroom. There was some pleasant small talk, and then Stolypin came out with it:

'You remember our conversation before lunch. Do tell me something in confidence, Señor. If I had the power to make you Tsar of Russia, what would you say? Please think carefully before you answer.'

For once Xavier was caught off guard. It was such a strange question coming from a Russian General in a gentlemen's cloakroom. Xavier searched his mind for the right words. This man must be asking in jest. He would make a romantic reply: 'I would be very flattered to be asked, General, but I could not accept. I could not hope to be a successful Tsar of Russia, as I would wish to be, without the support of the woman I love – and I'm not yet remarried.'

The three Russians laughed, but they thought. Back at their headquarters they discussed their situation and that of the country. What needed to be done? There were so many things. Perhaps the most obvious, but not obviously their professional concern, was the state of the economy and the currency. What was required was a massive introduction of foreign capital coupled with a rigid control of development, whilst a strong nationalistic flavour must be maintained. Internationalism was a good thing, but not of itself. There must be no question of anybody or any organization simply coming into the country, robbing it and the people.

'We must get money in, and we must control it ourselves or through those we can trust. By that I mean who we can control and instruct. I trust no-one outside we three,' said Renov.

'You are quite right, Renov. You have done very well tracking down Señor Lang. I think, Maiski, it's your turn again – this time with your friends the Orlanskis. You are now a customer of their bank. What we need now is a branch of their bank here in Moscow, well staffed by ex-KGB men.'

'Certainly, General, but it won't be too easy. We shall need the Ministry of Finance to help. Who do we know?'

'Boris Chekov. He would establish a contact for us, but he does not have the rank to make any decisions.'

'Good. I will speak to Chekov in the morning. I'll get somebody else to stand in for me at the Conference.'

'No need. I'll do that for you and give your apologies to the Spanish. It's perhaps no bad thing for you to be out of the way,' said Renov. The three men grinned at one another.

Viktor Maiski was looking forward to his second visit to the States. This time he would be travelling as an engineer from the Conference to discuss highways and bridges. He would wish to know details of corporate finance for the development in the States, and could it help in Russia.

He, Maiski, would stay in a hotel in Chicago provided by the Embassy in Washington – payment would be made by the Ministry of Finance in Moscow. Whilst in Chicago he would be able to offer modest hospitality to the Orlanskis or anybody else that he thought necessary, but it would need to be, and appear to be, modest. He could not afford to appear affluent when he was essentially in a role where he was seeking very substantial finance. He would never beg for money. There was no need for that, and he, Maiski, would not have suited the role of beggar in any situation.

The Conference drew to its inevitable close. Closing speeches were made and an invitation was extended by the French Ambassador for next year's Conference to be held in Paris. It seemed that conferees at professional level were just as good at selecting attractive centres as politicians. Major-General Renov made a point of wearing his dress military uniform at the Conference Ball the night before the Conference broke up, and was on his very best social behaviour.

Myra was now far too advanced in her pregnancy to be waltzing round any ballroom floor, easy as it would have been in her days with the Bolshoi and as it would be in the future. Myra's absence had simply given Vladimir more time to engage on his military/social duties, which he performed with skill and charm. As the song went – 'He oiled his way around the floor, oozing charm from every pore.' He visited all the national tables in turn, well, not all the nations, but all the European ones, but he spent rather longer at the Spanish table, where he made a point of speaking to Xavier, finishing his remarks with one that Xavier was to remember word for word: 'Myra particularly asked me to thank you for your kindness in giving us the Spanish birth outfit for our child. I do hope you find a second bride for yourself and that you might then be free to be my Tsar.' Vladimir Renov gave his broad smile and a knowing wink as he said this, and without giving Xavier time to reply he was off to the German table.

At O'Hare airport Chicago Maiski felt almost at home. Like so many Eastern Europeans he was quick at adapting himself to different surroundings, and his command of English, with a slight American accent, made him no different socially to any American host or hostess he might meet. He was met at the airport by the Russian Consul to the city and immediately driven to a small hotel used by the Consulate. He was natur-ally tired on arrival and decided to have an early night to recover from jet-lag. As he lay in bed he read over again any number of documents which he had brought with him, and fell to sleep having taken the elementary precaution of bolting the bedroom door and placing a chair against it like some old-fashioned filing cabinet.

Next morning he was as fit as if he had been in training, and his first call was to the Orlanskis' home. He had, of course, written to Elmer at his Head Office, but Elmer had insisted that he, Maiski, should feel free to call him as soon as he reached Chicago. Maiski considered this might prove too much of an intrusion. He decided on a good night's sleep before setting out on his important engagement. Sam, Elmer's butler at the Orlanski residence, a beautiful Colonial-style property with pillars to the front elevation and acres of mature gardens, answered the phone. Within minutes Elmer was speaking to Maiski.

'This is a pleasant start to the morning,' commenced Elmer. 'Have you just landed at the airport?'

'No I haven't, Mr Orlanski. I arrived last night, but it was late. I didn't think you would thank me for a late call. You might have been in bed. I waited until I thought you might have had breakfast, and I'm really ringing for an appointment to see you at the Bank.'

'Certainly, General. It's nice to be able to call you General now, and not Colonel. I don't have many Russian Generals as customers! How about you coming to the Bank at 11 o'clock? We can have coffee together, and I can show you around the office.'

'That sounds excellent. I don't know the way from my hotel, but I'm sure the taxi driver will know your bank,' replied Maiski.

At the Chicago Temperance Bank, the mirrored clock on the ground floor foyer announced to the world that it was 11 a.m. General Maiski was looking at the clock and then at his wristwatch to be certain they told the same tale. He approached the counter to announce his presence. He was accompanied by the Trade Consul from the Russian City Consulate, Ilya Novak. In a matter of moments the two men

79

were being escorted in the glass-sided electric lift to the tenth floor of the Bank's Head Office. Elmer Orlanski, flanked by two of his senior assistants, was standing at the door of his room, facing the lift as it arrived at the tenth floor.

'Good morning, General. It's very good to see you again.'

'Thank you, Mr Orlanski. May I introduce you to my colleague from the Consulate, Mr Novak?' They all shook hands in turn. Within minutes the five men were sitting at Elmer's large oval desk. The room itself was plain yet elegant. The clock on the wall indicated the time in Chicago itself, London, Tokyo and Valetta, Malta – to please Mary.

'I'm sorry I can't tell you the time in Moscow looking at my wall clock,' started Elmer. The other four men followed Elmer's gaze. 'If we were to open a branch in your capital, no doubt our engineers would make an addition, perhaps St Petersburg as well, if it's on a different time line.' This made a pleasant start to the conversation.

'That is just what we have come to see you about, Mr Orlanski. I know nothing of banking myself, but my colleague Mr Novak worked in our Ministry of Finance before coming to Chicago to help look after our trading position.' The three Americans looked at Ilya Novak, who had endeared himself to a section of the Chicago population by virtue of his ability as a tennis player. None of the Americans knew of his banking ability, but that would need to be tested in depth if there was to be any branch opening in Moscow or St Petersburg.

'Do tell us, General, or should I ask Mr Novak, what have you in mind? I don't imagine it would be too difficult opening a branch of our Bank in Moscow, but how many customers do you think you could find us? I wasn't aware of any large Temperance movement in Russia.'

'There is, in fact, quite a large and growing Temperance movement, as you put it, back home in Russia, based, I think, on the Baptist Church. I'm not a total abstainer myself, but I gather you do not insist on that. My thinking was in terms of your Bank investing in Russia for the mutual benefit of our two countries. As I say, this is all outside my work as an

Army officer. This is Mr Novak's department. I am really here simply to introduce Mr Novak to you. I'm in the States to examine your road and rail communications and the engineering involved, following our recent International Conference in Moscow.'

'Excellent, General,' replied Elmer. 'Then you have done your duty very well. Let me show you round the office so that you can see how we work. Mr Novak will know well enough – and then we can leave Mr Novak with my two colleagues, and he can explain exactly or more exactly what he has in mind.' Poor Novak was, in truth, simply the Ministry of Finance contact who Boris Chekov had ordered to meet and escort General Maiski. It would have been unfair to say he knew nothing of international finance, but he knew little more than he had needed to pass some very elementary banking examination before being seconded to the KGB. He looked vainly to General Maiski for support, but he, Maiski, was unaware of Novak's ignorance and he gladly rose to accompany Elmer around the superb bank premises, with every conceivable electronic gadget and machine whirring away and all the staff smartly attired in green.

This was the bank's dominant colour, to coincide with the 'green lobby' in the public domain. In former times the staff had dressed in grey, but Mary had thought that green was a good image colour, with full staff agreement.

'Whilst we are on our own, General, may I ask if you would be free to join my wife and I for dinner at our home tomorrow evening?'

'That's very kind of you, Mr Orlanski. I should like that.'

'Let us say then, 7.30 for dinner at 8. How does that sound? I'll send a car for you.'

'Many thanks, Mr Orlanski.'

'Please General, if we are going to be friendly, do let us drop our titles. My name is Elmer, and I believe your name is Viktor, so do let us be Elmer and Viktor in future. My wife's name, by the way, is Mary.' General Maiski shook hands warmly.

'Thank you, Elmer, I was beginning to wonder how much

longer we could keep up the formality. I do now believe I'm in America. Yes, please call me Viktor.'

Elmer and Viktor rejoined the others in Elmer's room. One of Elmer's assistants tactfully shook his head. Nothing was said, but Elmer correctly concluded that he had missed nothing whilst he had been out of the room and that Mr Novak's contribution had been minimal. Jim Rogerson, one of the two assistants, covered Novak's obvious embarrassment by saying that they had had a most interesting discussion on various aspects of banking from their early days as student bankers. For good measure, Jim added that he felt sure that there was a lot that they could learn from one another. The second assistant again slowly, but deliberately, shook his head, and Elmer got the message. The five men drank strong dark coffee together and then broke up. A lot and a little had been achieved.

At the Orlanski residence the domestic arrangements ran on well-tried and well-oiled wheels. It was definitely the home of Elmer and Mary Orlanski, but Elmer's mother Alice continued to live in the beautifully prepared 'granny flat' that was no flat in most people's estimate, but a second home that would have been the envy of any number of wealthy people. Mary and Alice were on the best and closest terms, and as occasion arose, Alice would join in the entertaining of Elmer's best customers, many of whom had been Elmer's father's customers – Elmer having succeeded his father as Chairman of the Chicago Temperance Bank.

Elmer's father Brett had during his lifetime better secured his home premises with Mary's advice, in co-operation with the Chicago City Police, but with Elmer's elevation to International Banker, the Federal authorities had virtually made the residence a fortress, but this was largely unseen by the general public.

Viktor Maiski first noticed the security apparatus when the car in which he was being driven stopped at the entrance to the drive and then again halfway up it. Not simply was the roadway gated, but armed security officers stepped out of the bushes as though from nowhere. Maiski was impressed. It reminded him of home. He couldn't help wondering whether the road might be mined. As the car drove up to the portico entrance Elmer was on the top of the short flight of steps with Mary.

Elmer walked down with Sam, who opened Maiski's car door and saluted. 'You sure have a great dacha, Elmer. It makes my place look like a shack.' Viktor Maiski was quick to adopt the American style of speech and remaining flattering at the same time.

'I look forward to seeing your "shack", as you put it,' countered Elmer. 'I'm fairly sure it would make good bank security, but come on in. First let me re-introduce you to Mary, my wife.' Viktor shook hands with Mary, not forgetting to kiss her hand as he had done at the White House Olympic Reception.

Once in the drawing room Mary introduced Viktor to her mother-in-law Alice and their two house guests, Sir John Bickerstaffe, now retired from his former high rank in the British Civil Service, and Lady Bickerstaffe, Sir John's wife. Lady Bickerstaffe, who before her marriage to Sir John had been Miss Florence Pairmaine, was Mary's great friend, notwithstanding the discrepancy in their ages.

Sir John and Florence were a generation older than Mary. Sir John had been Permanent Secretary at the Ministry of Information, and as such, Sylvia's right-hand man. Mary in turn had been WPC Farrimond, one of Sylvia's three protection officers supplied by Scotland Yard following upon attacks on Cabinet Ministers. The relationship between Mary and Florence was almost that of mother and daughter, but not quite. Mary's mother Maria would never be supplanted by anybody!

It wasn't long before Viktor knew all that he needed to know about the relationship between his fellow guests, and there was no strain in the conversation. There was no artificial stimulant. The Orlanskis were Temperance with a capital T when it came to entertaining within their own home in the presence of anyone who might remotely have been described as a stranger. It wasn't long before they were all sitting down to dinner. Mary had Viktor on her right-hand side and Florence sitting on her left. Mary knew that should there be any difficulty in keeping conversation away from politics, Florence was the one to keep cultural generalities to the fore with her enquiring mind, and was well-travelled and well-informed. She had never travelled in Russia before, however, and her curiosity was naturally aroused. Since Sir John's retirement, she had been on two world cruises with him.

'Do tell me something of your professional life, Mrs Orlanski, before you met Elmer. That is if you're allowed to. I understand that you served in the British Royal Protection Unit. That must have taken you all over the world. You should think of writing your memoirs. They would make very interesting reading!'

'You are very well-informed, Viktor – if I may call you Viktor – but you are not fully informed. No. I wasn't a member of the Royal Protection Unit, as you seem to imagine. Naturally I cannot really say anything about my early life, as I now call it, but you must know that to be of any use at all in security work you must be, how shall I put it? – part of the wallpaper. I still have what would be termed a London Cockney accent with slightly Maltese overtones, added to now by my increasingly American accent. Additionally, I cannot ride a horse, although I have had a few lessons since coming to America. You can't imagine me riding in Hyde Park with the Royals, can you? I would have been falling off and needing *their* protection.' Mary laughed at the very thought.

They all laughed. 'No, Viktor. My role was much less glamorous in terms of work and travel, but my job did one very good thing for me. It brought me into contact with Elmer, Florence and Sir John. It was Sir John that I met first, and I think you know the rest of the story.'

'Thank you very much, Mary. It's such a real thrill to meet honest security people, even if they are retired so young and so attractive. I'm sorry: Elmer wasn't meant to hear me say that, but I haven't come completely empty-handed. Would you allow me to make a small present to your three children, Elmer?'

Viktor was addressing all who sat around the table. As he spoke he produced from his pockets three small, perfectly made wooden dolls. Two were of Russian women in traditional dress, the third a traditional Cossack soldier. He passed them to Mary. Viktor continued without waiting for an answer, 'I'm sure they will enjoy them in the nursery. No doubt when they are bigger they will be able to discover the smaller dolls inside.'

'That's very kind of you, Viktor,' said Elmer. 'I will try and forgive your making advances to my wife over the table, but no more making eyes. Promise me.' They all laughed.

After dinner they all made their way back to the drawing room. The curtains were still drawn back and the lawns and gardens were floodlit. To Viktor it might have been a Hollywood setting, and he said as much. He did not fail to notice that the grand piano was inlaid mahogany. The word 'Bechstein' stood out boldly in gold. Despite himself Viktor could not resist the temptation of placing his right hand on the keyboard, striking a chord or two that sounded perfect.

'May I ask who is the pianist in the house? This is a lovely piano. I can't believe it isn't played.'

'I do play sometimes, Viktor,' replied Elmer, 'but only when I get time, which seems to be in such short supply these days.'

'That's a pity, Elmer. You really should try and make time. I do try and play myself sometimes, but like you, I lack practice. Being an army officer and an engineer doesn't give me the time I would like, as you might imagine.'

'Come on, Elmer.' It was Alice, Elmer's mother, who spoke. 'Give us a tune, as Daddy used to say. We all know you can play a tune if you want to. Please.'

Elmer could have wished, on this occasion, that his mother had not asked him to play. After all, he didn't know Viktor Maiski that well, and even from the way Viktor had played the two practice chords he sensed he would be hard put to it to please to the point of impressing, but there was no way of getting out of it. 'Oh, very well. You will have to excuse me, Viktor. I haven't played for some time.'

This was true in the sense that it was the first time today that Elmer had sat at his piano stool, but he had played yesterday, as he did every day he had the opportunity, which he often made. All the family and their guests took their seats, and Elmer commenced. It just had to be his favourite: Chopin's *Polonaise in A Major*. The family knew of Elmer's piano playing, but Viktor was thrilled. He too knew and loved Chopin, and in seconds realized that Elmer had been 'having him on'. Elmer was indeed a very good pianist. He might not be a concert pianist, but this particular piece he had played not less than one hundred times, and his playing would match many who did hold themselves out as professionals. At the conclusion Viktor called out 'Bravo', and all applauded. Jim Rogerson called out 'More', but Elmer rose and mockingly bowed. It was Mary who piped up:

'Come on, Viktor. It's your turn. Don't tease us like Elmer and pretend you can't play. I heard you play two lovely chords.'

'Mary, you should have been a diplomat, not a police officer,' rejoined Viktor. 'Very well. I will try to play something for you. If you don't know the melody, at least I should get away with it, with you, even if I can't deceive your husband.'

Everyone in the elegant room smiled as Viktor moved to the piano, mockingly following Elmer in bowing to the small audience. 'Pity I have not got my music,' he murmured aloud, 'but here goes.' His small audience listened and then gasped. Variations on a theme by Tchaikovsky, followed by Chopin's 'Tristesse' *Etude in E Major*, arguably the most evocative music ever composed, sounded like a dream. The appreciative audience exchanged meaningful glances. Elmer was full of admiration, as was Sir John Bickerstaffe, who had played to a high standard himself before his frightful injuries had robbed some of the use in his left hand. When at last Viktor stopped playing, they – the family audience – all rose and applauded loudly.

Mary's eyes fairly filled up. She never tried to conceal her emotions unless she felt it imperative. 'There you are, my friends. Not as good as Elmer, but I too have not played for some time. Well, not for a week!' He grinned broadly at Elmer, who returned a knowing smile. Both men felt they knew each other better. The time came for Viktor Maiski to leave, and Elmer insisted on taking him back to his hotel himself, with Sam acting as chauffeur.

In the rear of the car, Elmer quite suddenly said, 'I don't know how to say this, Viktor, but I can see you are a man of many parts. If ever you should retire and consider taking up banking as a second career – not just as a customer – please let me know. If we do open a branch in Moscow, I would like you to be one of our local Directors.'

'Thank you very much for that thought, Elmer. I haven't too long to serve in the Army, as you might guess. It's no good pretending to be a fighting fit soldier if you're not, and from what I've seen of your bank and know of your reputation, I think we could get on very well. Pity you don't speak Russian, but then if you did perhaps you wouldn't need me to be, what do you call it, "a local Director"?' The car, which Viktor did not fail to notice had bullet-proof glass, glided up to the front of the hotel like a destroyer coming alongside a naval quay. Sam, despite his huge size, was out in a second, opening Viktor's door.

'Very pleased you could come to my home for dinner and the music. Just think about it, Viktor. Have you any good schemes where I may be able to help you? If so, just let me know.'

'I will, Elmer,' replied Viktor. The two men shook hands, and Sam did not drive away until Viktor Maiski had disappeared into the hotel entrance. He did not forget to turn on the steps and wave. Back home, Elmer found all the family were still discussing Viktor Maiski.

'Darling. What a man,' started Mary. 'What else can he do?'

'I don't know, Mary, but he frightens me a bit, I must say. Just how many of our Generals in the Pentagon or elsewhere can speak Russian as well as he speaks our language – and play the piano like that? Last time he was with the Olympic Committee in Atlanta and the White House. If ever we do get round to opening a branch in Moscow, we must have him as a local Director, perhaps with you, Jim, nominally in charge, but I feel he would want that job and you don't speak Russian yet, beyond "Yes, No, Please and Thank you".'

'You're right, Elmer. We would have to have him as Moscow President with, perhaps, one other Russian of his choice and the remaining local Directors people we know, perhaps, one or two former Ambassadors, provided their Russian was up to his.'

Jim had enjoyed being a local Director in London, but his wife Lucinda – who was Elmer's sister – could hardly bring herself to think of living in Moscow, St Petersburg or anywhere else in Russia with two children. Her 'eldest' child was Jim's child by a previous union, and now she was pregnant and expecting Jim's child. Her very own 'eldest' was little Alphonse, born in Mijas, Spain, but his father, the late Sir John Penrose, had been nothing but a 'sugar daddy', and his subsequent murder had almost come as a relief, although she was in no way involved. It all seemed complicated, but it would shortly mean that Jim and Lucinda would have three children between them.

It was over breakfast the following morning that Sir John said, 'You know, I've been thinking. It came to me last night, but I couldn't be certain. Now I'm sure I have met our new friend Viktor Maiski before. It was a year or two back in Washington at a World Nuclear Disarmament Conference. I know I'm right, because I spoke to him then and he complimented me on my Russian. My Russian is not as good as his English, but you can take it from me that he must be very senior indeed. I would guess he's been a General for some time, I don't mean three weeks. I mean at least three years. He's certainly very senior indeed.'

'Thank you, John,' said Elmer. 'We'll have to be very careful how we go, and I must speak to "you know who" in

Washington.' Elmer prepared to leave. He kissed Mary good-bye as usual and set off for the bank.

The morning post was brought into the drawing-room by Sam in the old fashioned way, on a salver. It didn't take Mary long to sort it out. There was one letter addressed to Lady Florence Bickerstaffe. Technically, she was not entitled to this style of address, but Charlotte, who knew as much about etiquette as anybody needed to know, wanted to be sure that Florence would be the one to open the letter.

It read:

'Dearest Florence,

After Mum, I want you to be the first to know my news. Xavier and I are engaged. I feel a million dollars, as Mary and Elmer would say. He was absolutely divine. I can't give you any details yet about the time and place of the wedding, but you will be one of the first to know, and certainly the first person outside the family to be invited, with John of course. Please give my love to Mary and Elmer. Sylvia and Carlos know, and Sylvia sent round a lovely bouquet of carnations. Mum's house looks like a florists. Mum has said she will try and learn some Spanish. My Spanish is improving, but I will never speak Spanish as Xavier speaks English. I can't wait to sign myself Charlotte Lang!

P.S. Give a kiss to Mary's children for me.'

Florence smiled to herself. She passed the letter to her husband, and after he had read it with a smile, Florence passed it to Mary.

'Whoopee!' cried Mary. 'What a wonderful letter. I know why she wrote to you first, Florence. Sylvia told me all about the way you salvaged her position. What a lucky girl Charlotte is. I think she had begun to believe she was destined to be an old maid, but at thirty-something she is hardly an old maid, and with any luck there will be little Langs to come.'

'I'm sure there will be Mary, but I can see some problems.

89

I can't imagine that Xavier will want Charlotte to stay in London. He will want her in Madrid. One thing you can be sure about, her children will speak better Spanish than she does. Their English will be as good as their father's. Charlotte will see to that, and if they are favoured with sons I suppose they will finish up at Slapton, where Xavier and Carlos first met.'

'Charlotte isn't a Catholic, Florence.'

'No, Mary, she isn't. I think that could prove a little difficult. Elmer turned for you, but I don't think either of them would change easily. Xavier has his boys to consider, and he's very settled in his ways. He must be about forty-eight, and I think Charlotte is about thirty – and her late father was a vicar, I think. Anyway, that's their problem. I will remember to say a special prayer for them both tonight.'

'You're very good, Florence,' chimed in Alice, who had met Charlotte briefly at Sylvia's wedding to Carlos, and more recently when she had been in Chicago on escort protection duties. Alice didn't really know Xavier that well, but she liked him well enough and would always be grateful for the role he had played in relation to little Alphonse in rescuing him with Florence from Spain. She had always regarded Xavier as a man of mystery – as indeed he was – but she liked him. All women did.

'I think Scotland Yard is responsible for a great deal,' started Sir John, 'and a great deal of expense, but I must say that I have enjoyed it. I must be getting older,' he continued, 'I can't remember the name of the Superintendent, the lady Superintendent I mean, who nominated Mary, Charlotte and Susan to be Sylvia's protection officers. You were selected, Mary, I remember, as being the strongest and most capable, Charlotte was picked as being about the same size as Sylvia and able to "double" for her if required in terms of clothing, and she spoke languages, and Susan was picked for light night duties within Sylvia's home following her injuries in that frightful car smash. What a long time ago all that seems, and haven't you all done well! I feel very lucky to have been part of it all. I couldn't have dreamt of it happening four years ago. I suppose we'll have to start saving up for another wedding present.'

This was the longest speech that John had made since his own injuries caused by the explosion at his retirement party that Sylvia had thrown for him at Harcourt. Florence was delighted to hear John make his contribution to the romantic discussion. She was just a little concerned that John did not become too excited. She decided to take over.

'I suppose we must start with our congratulations. There is no point in our overdoing it. Charlotte says her mother's house is like a florists. The Spanish are fond of flowers, so I take it Xavier and Carlos will have sent profusions of flowers, but we must send some. How about one really nice bouquet by Interflora from us all? She will know that I have told you all, and she'll guess I have shown you her letter. You can't send flowers to a man, but I do have Xavier's address in Madrid. We could send him a card from us all.'

'What a good idea, Florence. You really do think of everything,' said Alice as she rose to pick up her own handbag, to extract her address book to look up the telephone number of Interflora.

'I've got Charlotte's mother's address here, Alice. Let me give it to you.'

The two women rummaged in their handbags. 'More coffee, John?' asked Mary. 'Your coffee must have gone cold with all this excitement and gossip,' she went on.

'I wonder, Mary, if I could make a suggestion?' Sir John was clearly feeling much more his old self. There really was a twinkle in his eye. 'Do you think Elmer would mind if we opened one of his special bottles of your non-alcoholic wines?'

'Good for you, John. Of course he won't mind. He'll only be sorry he isn't here to open it and drink with us, even at this time of the morning, but I can open it as easily as any man. Look, John. You get the glasses out of the sideboard there, and I'll bring a bottle or two bottles from the fridge in the kitchen. God, in all the excitement I had quite forgotten Elmer, but never tell him that. I'll give him a ring now and tell him we are raiding the fridge for his best Maltese wine.'

Mary couldn't get through to Elmer, which slightly annoyed her. Seemingly he had given instructions that he wasn't to be disturbed whilst he was on a coded call to the White House, but presently he returned her call.

'Darling. Do tell Sir John that he was right. I have spoken to "you know who". I am authorized to proceed with caution, and do drink some of that wine for me. Put another two bottles on ice for tonight and, yes, add my best wishes to the card. If you want the flowers to arrive as soon as possible, I suggest you call the Shire Bank in London – Sir John's bank now he's on the Board – and they'll get Interflora in London to deliver them immediately.'

'Thanks, Elmer darling. Trust you to think of that. The call to London may be expensive, but it will be cheaper than ordering by proxy.' Mary was glowing inside. Elmer knew he had in Mary a wife who always thought as a good treasurer should, even if he was the professional banker. He still could never forget that she had asked that the red and black dress she had bought specially for the Malta dinner could be 'taken in'. He had received quite a bit of ribbing at the golf club about this, but secretly any number of the members envied him.

Florence had positively refused to countenance her husband taking any position in the City following his terrible injuries, although he had been offered many, but last year she had agreed to John accepting a non-executive directorship of the Shire Bank – the British subsidiary of the Chicago Temperance Bank – on the strict understanding that he only worked at his own pace and from their home in Lanchester, with no more than monthly board meetings in London. This had given satisfaction all round and, of course, with Elmer being the chairman of the bank in Chicago, nobody, but nobody, questioned the wisdom of having one of Britain's top retired civil servants being a director of one of Britain's smaller, but most prestigious, banks. Florence, who could still operate a fax machine as well as she had ever done, faxed the message to the senior manager of the Shire Bank in Tib Lane, London.

Within the hour a large cellophane-wrapped bouquet was on its way to Palmers Road, near the Arnos Grove underground station. Charlotte's mother opened the door.

'This is getting embarrassing,' she called out to Charlotte, who was upstairs changing. 'Just look at these flowers. You will have to speak to Xavier. He has sent you three bouquets since you were engaged three days ago.' Charlotte came down and opened the small sealed envelope.

'Mum. It's not Xavier. It's Florence, John, Mary and Elmer and Alice. You might as well say "Uncle Tom Cobleigh and all" – it's from Chicago. I don't recognize the writing. Florence must have cabled from America. Aren't they beautiful? We must give them the place of honour.'

'Sorry, dear. I have no more vases. I only have three, and they're already full. Then I'll have to put two of Xavier's into one of the vases – the biggest – and put these into one of the others. Come to think of it, these will need the biggest vase. They must have cost a fortune.'

'Please let me ring them. It's nowhere near our time, but they won't mind. Mary is always on the go, and Florence will wake up if she knows I'm on.'

Within minutes Charlotte was speaking to Mary. Never was so much said by two women so quickly – unless it was by Charlotte and Florence!

8

It was ten p.m. on Saturday night in Moscow. The clock was striking on Red Square. The news in many languages was going out on television and radio. The Russian flag in its red, blue and white stripes was seen on the screen whilst the National Anthem played quietly in the background.

Quite suddenly, as it seemed, the screen changed and there appeared a man of 60 plus in the uniform of a General. He started to speak slowly.

'Comrades. It is my sad duty to inform you that earlier this evening our beloved President and Vice-President were taken ill. They have both been admitted to hospital for the best treatment available. In these sad circumstances, and at the request of the Supreme Army Council, I, Boris Stolypin, have assumed the high office of President of our beloved nation until democratic Presidential elections can take place next year. As I speak, units of the Armed Services, including the security services of the state, are taking up positions, if they have not already done so, to preserve the sovereignty and integrity of Russia. Even now, at this time of our national sadness, I wish to assure all our friends throughout the world that there is nothing to fear, but fear itself. All military and police leave is cancelled as from eleven o'clock to-morrow morning, to give all those concerned time to report back to barracks or to communicate their whereabouts and make arrangements for their return to duty. I count on all patriots to rally to our national flag at this hour, and I do not shrink from saying that anyone who seeks to defy any orders given by the Army, Navy and Police, acting upon my authority as

President, will be treated as an enemy of the people. Detailed instructions are being sent to all authorities of the State, and in the meantime I appeal to all of you who hear this broadcast, that will be repeated on the hour for the next twelve hours, to remain cool, vigilant and loyal. Our former beloved President, who presently lies in hospital in caring hands, asks me to send you his good wishes, and he has pledged to me his personal loyalty.'

At the conclusion of these words the red, white and blue flag again came on to the screen, with the National Anthem playing. Gradually the flag seemed to fade, with a picture emerging of military tanks, in tight formation, coming across Red Square. The picture again gradually faded, in a most professional manner, and the features of a well-known news-caster appeared. 'This is Radio Moscow. As viewers may just have seen, General Boris Stolypin has, at the request of Parliament, assumed the office of President of the Russian Federation, and Radio Moscow, for itself and its viewers, extends to His Excellency, the President, its loyal greetings. Now the following world news: from across the nation messages of support and pledges of loyalty are arriving at the Kremlin . . .'

The newscaster spoke for 20 minutes in this fashion. It was obvious to Intelligence Units of many nations that what they were hearing and viewing was not live, but had come from very well-prepared media sources. So far as the Russian people were concerned, it was simply a question of waiting for the next news bulletin. On the streets of Moscow, St Petersburg and other Russian cities, troops and police outnumbered the general public. Not unnaturally, there was consternation, to put it mildly, in all the world's capitals. What did it all mean? Russian politics had always been something of a mystery, but this was completely out of the blue and had obviously been most meticulously planned, and above all, who was this General – now Marshal – Boris Stolypin?

The world did not have long to wait. The Russian press was given complete freedom to print a good photograph of the new President with full narrative, reading: 'His Excellency, President Boris Stolypin, is one of the most highly regarded military men in the world. Feared by many in the Western world, he is the acknowledged leader of the officer corps of the Army. Able and articulate, he has wielded great power in the defence of the nation in his development of SS-20 missiles as Chief of Staff in Military Intelligence. Little is known of his private life beyond saying that he and his wife Olga are very happily married, with four children of their own and two grandchildren. It is understood that President Stolypin has appointed Colonel-General Viktor Maiski as First Vice President and Major-General Vladimir Renov as Second Vice President. All three officers are world-travelled. All three men are known linguists, with university degrees in nuclear and natural sciences.'

This article, together with any number of photographs, was copied by the world media. Mary and Elmer were completely stunned. So were Sylvia and Charlotte, not to mention Mr Dalrimple and Major Carruthers at the Ministry of Defence in Whitehall. Perhaps significantly, Xavier was not so stunned. He had met up with the three officers at the Moscow Conference, but even he could hardly take in what he was now viewing in Madrid. It all seemed like some dream or nightmare, but there was nothing for it but to await further news as it came out of that vast country. Naturally, through the usual diplomatic channels congratulations were sent to the new masters of the Kremlin. Almost nobody outside Russia could claim any personal relationship with the new President, still less any personal friendship. Elmer was hesitant at sending any message to Viktor Maiski, but Mary prevailed and a short message of congratulation was sent with a copy to the White House.

Xavier had no hesitancy. He sent a handwritten letter to Renov, which was taken to Moscow in the Spanish diplomatic bag. It read in Russian:

'My dear Renov,
    I feel I must write to you today with my personal

96

congratulations and best wishes for your future and that of your country. I could scarcely believe my eyes when I read that my genial host of last month was now Second Vice President. I do hope that we might meet again sometime, but at what level I cannot now imagine.

Yours in friendship,
Xavier Romanov Lang'

Within the hour of Renov reading this letter, it was being read by Stolypin and Maiski. It was Stolypin who spoke:

'Comrades. Xavier Romanov is our man. We must work it out carefully, but Russia will have a Tsar. We will be the "Gang of Four", and what's all this I read from London? Charlotte Johnson. Who is she, Renov? Would she make a good Tsarina?'

'Yes she would, Mr President. She would make an excellent Tsarina. Of course, she would have to marry him first, but by then he will, hopefully, be one of us. The wedding could be here in Moscow at St Basil's.'

'Good. I like that, but don't keep it to yourself, Renov. Who is this Charlotte? Is she British or Swedish?' asked Stolypin.

'She's a British resident with only one "s" in the middle of her name. I haven't got my file with me, but as well as I can remember she's the daughter of a deceased vicar, that is a Church of England priest, and she lives with her widowed mother in North London. She's an Inspector in the London Metropolitan Police and once served as bodyguard to the British Deputy Prime Minister. That's how she met Romanov.'

'How do you mean, Renov? Did Romanov try and attack the British statesman?'

'No, Mr President. He didn't. Romanov, as you call him, was at school in England as a boy with Carlos Sabita, who married the widowed Mrs Bartlett-Shearman, who later became Dame Sabita. It seems that Carlos Sabita had Romanov as his Best Man at his wedding, and his bride, Sylvia Sabita, the British statesman, had her three bodyguards, they call them protectors, as her Bridesmaids. I suppose it was then that Romanov first met Charlotte Johnson, but Romanov's wife was still living. After she died Romanov has got to know her well, and they went on holiday together, but occupied separate rooms, to Chamonix. I think you know the rest of the story.'

'You've done well, Renov, and you have a good memory, but what makes you think she would make a good Tsarina?'

'She has been a first-class bodyguard or protector for Sylvia Sabita. She is very good with Romanov's children – not too easy for a British woman, two grown-up Spanish boys – and she's obviously very fond of Romanov. She has a university degree and could learn Russian, given special training, in quite a short time. She does speak French and German fluently, as well as English, and she has no domestic ties except her mother.'

'Good. Very good indeed,' said Stolypin quietly as he thought. 'I take it she has no children of her own?'

'No. She hasn't. With her church and family background and her ability as a chosen bodyguard, I would guess she's still a virgin and will be until her wedding night. Romanov is quite the Spanish or English gentleman. He's got his two sons at Slapton, one of the top English public schools. We will need to get them into university over here as soon as possible, for security reasons, but that's something we can arrange. If there was going to be any problem we just might have to make an arrangement with Spain.'

Stolypin paused before proceeding. 'I think the first step is to invite Señor Lang to our Embassy in London, together with his fiancée. You could make a visit to the British Foreign Secretary to discuss Balkan security or anything else you dream up, and whilst you're there you could meet the pair of them and invite them to spend a short holiday in Moscow.'

'I hesitate to disagree with you, Mr President, but I think it best if we get Señor Lang over here on his own. We three can then confront him, on our own, without witnesses, and then it's up to him to propose our plan to his fiancée on his own, again without witnesses. Once he is one of us we shall all feel much safer, and there will be no chance of anything coming out in London, where secrets leak.'

'You're worth a lot of roubles, Renov. Yes, I think you're right. Let's play it your way. We leave it to you to make the arrangements with Señor Lang, and now it's your turn, Maiski. I gather you have received good wishes from the Orlanskis. Now what we want is an up-to-date version of the Marshall Plan. Say a loan of one thousand million dollars, repayable over a period of fifty years.'

'I've already started the wheels turning, Mr President,' replied Viktor Maiski. 'I've sent an urgent telegram to Elmer Orlanski.'

9

Some relationships are more difficult than others. Arguably one of the most difficult is the role of daughter-in-law elect. Much of the continuing popularity of Gilbert and Sullivan's *Mikado* hinges around that unfortunate, if preposterous, character. Another potentially difficult role is that of step-mother, particularly when the prospective stepchildren are foreign teenagers.

This was the situation that confronted Charlotte when she became engaged to Xavier. Charlotte did have two advantages. Firstly, she had known them both for four years – since she had served as WPC Johnson as protection officer to Sylvia. Secondly, long before Sophia – Xavier's wife – had died prematurely with cancer in Spain, she had deeply endeared herself to Xavier's youngest boy, Carlos.

The boys were now 17 and 14 years respectively. Miguel was quite the young man. He was very like his father – a tall boy, he was already six foot tall and broad in proportion. He carried himself well and would have been lined up to be School Captain or Head Boy had he not been Spanish. Father Rector had to be careful not to appoint too many prefects from overseas students, who seemed to be growing in numbers in direct proportion to the rising school fees and the reduction in size of the British Armed Forces. As it was, Miguel was Captain of the Second XV at Rugger and Captain of the Second Cricket XI. It was obvious that he would be Captain of both First teams next year. Miguel seemed to have all the attributes. He was a proficient skier, and at golf his handicap, on the College course, was six. What money and good training could do!

Charlotte had known him since he was 13, but she never really felt that she knew him as she knew little Carlos. She could read him like an open book. In many ways Miguel was like his father, Xavier, but he always seemed to have a cool reserve – very un-Latin – but his manners were always perfect and very adult, whether it was standing up if a lady entered the room or holding a chair for her, from behind, when she sat to a table. He was clearly destined to go to the very top of whatever he chose. There were times when Charlotte felt he was the same age as herself. Ridiculous. She was nearly twice his age, but she liked him – everybody did. He was very protective to his younger brother. Charlotte liked that side to his character. Miguel had always felt that he needed to be protective towards Carlos, with his mother being so ill for so many years. Carlos was now 14, but he had only been 10 when she first knew him. He was her dream of a boy – he was so boyish. He could be mischievous, as all healthy boys can, but he had a very warm heart and had warmed to her over the years. At 10 he had been young for his years, now at 14 he had a greater maturity than many three years his senior – perhaps it was the Spanish in him. Miguel would always shake hands. Carlos would put his arms around her and kiss her quite easily on the cheek by way of greeting.

The Lang brothers and the Sabita boys were good friends, which wasn't surprising in view of their parents' friendship and Spanish connections. Sylvia was a good mother, in every way, and frequently turned up to see her sons at the College. First she had gone with her first husband Donald, and now with Carlos, himself an 'old boy' of the School.

Xavier came to the College when he could, but poor Sophia had not been able to leave Madrid for six years and had not known her husband or her sons for at least four years. When Sylvia had visited Slapton College four years ago, Charlotte was invariably in attendance as protection officer, and she frequently found herself landed with looking after

101

Sylvia's younger son John and Xavier's younger son Carlos.

Charlotte was a 'sporty girl' in the best sense of that term. She had been Captain of her school netball team, she had been in the swimming Eight at Warwick University and she could run as quickly as most boys. Since joining the Police she had graduated to Black Belt in judo. She wasn't in Sylvia's team of three protection officers for nothing. Little Carlos had fallen in love with Charlotte the first time they had played together four years ago on Slapton Sands.

This was pure childish love – nothing sexual. He was fond of and good at sports himself, as good as any 10-year-old could be, and the strongest boy in his class. Carlos and John had running games with Charlotte. She always seemed to win. Charlotte always took the precaution, in the summer, of wearing her attractive swimsuit beneath her wrap-around cotton skirt, in case she was obliged to take the boys into the sea. She took her wrap-around dress off now to race against the boys, and Sylvia secretly admired her slim athletic figure. So would the older boys at the College she reflected, but Charlotte's figure meant nothing to the two young boys.

Eventually Carlos challenged Charlotte to wrestle with him. Sylvia and Charlotte were most amused, and Sylvia spread out the blanket she had brought with her for the picnic. Charlotte could, of course, have simply picked him up and thrown him wherever she chose, but to please him she went through the motions of 'wrestling' with him. He just couldn't understand how she, a girl, succeeded in putting him on the sand with her kneeling on top of him and holding his hands down with hers.

He lay on his back, looking up at her in bewildered admiration. 'Give in, Carlos. I win,' she said to him.

'Yes, Charlotte. I give in, but please let me try again.' Charlotte smiled at Sylvia, who nodded her agreement. Charlotte released her hold and jumped up. Carlos shook the sand from his hair and his clothes and faced Charlotte eagerly. He closed with her, as he thought, and all of two seconds later, at most, he was on his back again with Charlotte kneeling on top of him in the same position as before, with her knees on either side of his young body. The tops of her feet secured his legs to the sand and the backs of his hands were pressed against the sand with hers holding him down. There was a difference this time however. Charlotte felt that her left knee was pressing hard on a pebble beneath the sand. Thoughts flashed through her mind. She smiled at Sylvia, saying:

'Now, Master Carlos, you're a very brave boy, you deserve a reward. I'm going to put a real wrestler's hold on you. Please lie quite still. I won't hurt you. Promise.' In a second she changed her position. She placed all her weight on her right knee, raised her left knee from the pebble and placed it into the soft sand above and over Carlos' right shoulder and then, immediately, her right knee over his left shoulder, securing his arms in the process. In a classical wrestling posture, she held Carlos in a 'shoulder hold' from which there could be no escape. This was immaterial, since she was only playing with Carlos, who was thoroughly enjoying himself. He didn't move a muscle – he couldn't have done much if he'd tried. He was just so pleased that Charlotte had given him a second 'go' that he wasn't at all worried about her having imposed 'a real wrestler's hold'.

Although he was a child, he well knew that he had met his match. So far as he was concerned she was 'Superwoman' – she could do as she pleased. Charlotte released her hands from his. She did not need to hold them now, beyond guiding them. Her legs and weight fully secured little Carlos beneath her. She deliberately placed most of her weight on her knees initially, to save any undue pressure on him and then gently allowed her body weight to lie on his upper chest. He continued to look up at her with childish admiration. He was just happy to be where he was and wondered what would happen next. He didn't have to wait long to find out.

Charlotte smiled and winked at Sylvia. 'Now, Master Carlos. You've let me win a second time. Now I want you to do something for me.' She looked down at the little boy with his large bewildered Spanish eyes – which she loved –

103

and thought for a moment. 'I want you to choose the ice creams you've earned for letting me win, but I want you to do something else.'

Carlos looked up at Charlotte. He felt he was in heaven. He lay perfectly still on her instructions. She had his complete childish trust. He knew he had met his match. He was in no position to prevent her doing exactly as she pleased with him. He felt her legs on either side of his head and he knew her knees were immediately above his shoulders. She took his hands and placed them carefully, but firmly, beneath his head so that the palms of his hands effectively supported the back of his head as he looked up at her. The main weight of her body was resting now on his chest. He could not move and now she had both hands free, but she continued to hold his arms. 'Thank you, Carlos. There you are. You really are a very good boy. You've fully earned the ice cream I promised you. I'm now holding you down, and there's nothing you can do. Please listen to me, Carlos. I want you to make two promises to me. I promised you ice cream for letting me win. Now it's my turn to ask you to make two promises to me. Yes?'

'Yes, Charlotte. Whatever you want.'

'Good boy. Firstly, I want you to promise me that the first time you put me on the ground you'll take me out for dinner.'

'I promise,' Charlotte,' the little boy spluttered.

'Good, Carlos. I'll hold you to that, and now it's time for me to have a serious little chat with you. Although I'm speaking to you, Carlos, I'm speaking to you, John, as well, whilst you're sitting with your mother getting the picnic ready.'

John looked at his friend and Charlotte as did Sylvia.

'Please, Carlos. Just listen to me carefully. Just lie perfectly still as you are and continue to look up at me. I want to teach you and John a lesson this afternoon and a very important lesson in the presence of John's mother.' Charlotte said this to keep Sylvia on her side. 'If I was a nasty woman, or a nasty man for that matter, I could now hurt you, Carlos, and injure you by punching you, poking your eyes out or

104

worse. Now listen carefully and continue to look up to me.'

'I am listening, Charlotte,' replied the little boy.

'Good. Now please promise me that you will never, ever, let anybody else sit on you as I'm doing now. I'm not asking you a favour for my own sake, but for your sake and your own safety. I'm really asking for your Momma's sake. I know that if your dear Momma, if she was with us now, would want you to promise. Please promise, Carlos. I won't let you get up until you do.'

Carlos's emotions were now extended beyond anything he had ever known. He had over a period of many years built up what could only be described as a rose-tinted view of his mother, to whom he was deeply attached. For years she had not known him. He only had his early childhood recollections, but he always felt very close to her. Now Charlotte was appealing to him from her completely dominant position to make a promise as though demanded by his mother. His eyes filled with tears as he thought of his dying mother whilst in the complete physical control of Charlotte.

'I promise, Charlotte,' he murmured very quietly as his tears rolled down his cheeks. Charlotte looked down at him. She saw he was crying uncontrollably, but she couldn't hear him because of the sound of the waves breaking on the beach. Her every instinct was to jump up and let him go, but instead she maintained her commanding hold on him.

'I know, Carlos, that you're crying. I'm sorry. I'm crying for you myself inside, believe me, darling. It's only because I know that I'm doing what your Momma would want me to do that I'm behaving as I am. Please believe me, Carlos. I know that you'll thank me one day. What are you promising?'

Carlos could say nothing. He was trying to fight back his tears. The very mention of his beloved Momma brought new wells of tears to his eyes. His very vision of Charlotte, who was now bending close to him, was dimmed by his tears. In different circumstances he would have put his arms around her and kissed her for her kindness to him, but he couldn't move. Charlotte realized that she had, perhaps, gone too far.

The little boy was crying and quite helpless in her hold on him. Sylvia and John looked on: Sylvia with some concern. Had she let Charlotte go too far? Charlotte shot her a glance which conveyed an inner meaning.

'Come on, Carlos darling. Please let me help you. I know I'm being cruel to be kind, but you and your Momma will thank me. Please trust me completely, Carlos. Look up to me again. I will say the words of the promise I want you to make. All you have to do is repeat my words and mean what you say as you say them. Are you ready?'

Carlos smiled through his tears and nodded. 'Good boy. Now listen carefully and repeat them. I'll go slowly: I promise you, Charlotte.'

'I promise you, Charlotte,' he repeated. 'That I will never allow anybody else to sit on me for the rest of my life.'

'Good boy. You're the best and bravest boy I know. Now come on. Let's go and have those ices. I think you deserve two.'

Charlotte released her hold on his arms and jumped up, helping Carlos to his feet. 'Come on. Wipe your tears away, Carlos. Let me fasten this wrap dress again and we'll go together to get the ice creams. You have the first choice.'

Carlos couldn't stop himself. He threw his arms around her waist, burying his face into her. He had stopped crying. 'I do love you, Charlotte. Please hold me. You're the only person to have called me "darling" since my Momma last spoke to me, and she was speaking to me in Spanish. Even the Matron at Slapton only calls me Lang.'

Carlos continued to hold her. She placed her right hand on his tousled head of hair, shaking some of the sand away. Charlotte felt her own heart beating. She might have been doing the holding down, with Carlos in a classic shoulder hold beneath her, but he had completely drained her emotionally.

Charlotte took the two boys to the ice-cream van. Carlos

106

chose the chocolate and vanilla, Charlotte chose plain vanilla and John chose the strawberry for his mother, Sylvia, and himself. They made a very happy quartet as they licked their ices before eating the sandwiches that Sylvia had brought. One day Carlos would take Charlotte out for dinner, but he wouldn't have to wrestle with her first. As he grew older he liked her – perhaps 'loved' wouldn't have been a wrong word – more and more, but this was the love of a child for 'Superwoman'. She had made his day.

In the ministerial car that day four years ago Sylvia and Charlotte sank back on the rear seat. Both had enjoyed their visit to Slapton, but Sylvia detected that Charlotte was quiet and not her usual self. 'I think you were quite magnificent this afternoon,' started Sylvia. 'I did just wonder, at one stage, just what you were going to do and say, but I'll tell you one thing – that boy Carlos will dream of you for ever. You really have won both his mind and his heart. His mother would be grateful to you, if she could think at all.'

'You're very kind, Sylvia. I'll confess I did wonder how far I could go. I couldn't have done anything for the boys without you being there to support me. I don't know whether I ever told you, but I had a younger brother, Michael. He was killed in a road accident. He ran into the road chasing a ball. He was a lovely boy, full of mischief, just like your John and Carlos. I used to blame my sister Margaret for a long time for not making Michael see the dangers. She's older than me, quite a bit older, and she was in charge of him when they went out together to play. I just couldn't bear the thought of that little boy Carlos or your own boy being sexually abused by older boys or adults sitting on them and abusing them. You read such terrible things today, and we Police are often called out to absolutely sickening scenes. When he started crying, after I mentioned his mother's name, I saw my little brother Michael in Carlos's eyes. I was absolutely determined not to let him get up until I had extracted his promise in full. I just had to hang on in there. My heart was fairly pumping away. He was completely draining me. Luckily, I had an absolute hold on him, so I required

107

no physical effort, but I do believe today has been the best day's work I've ever done for you and your boy as well as Carlos. He's a real gem of a boy. I really do hope and believe, Sylvia, that nobody else will ever sit on him without a hell of a fight, and those judo lessons, which he will master, will prevent that ever happening.

'You know, Sylvia, I do think sometimes that I must have been born under a lucky star. I never dreamt of events turning out as they did today. I've absolutely no authority or standing, legal or moral, in relation to Xavier Lang's son, Carlos. I'm not a relative or his teacher or anything, and yet I put him on the ground, held him down and extracted promises from him. Just imagine what the press would have made of that little lot if anything had gone wrong! The very best I could have expected would have been immediate suspension, and I daren't think what might have happened, I couldn't have done it without your support.'

'Yes, Charlotte. We were both very lucky. These days teachers themselves have to be extremely careful. No teacher would have dared to do what you did, and yet now you have done more for that boy Carlos and my John than half the staff at Slapton could have done between them, but tell me, what made you do it?'

'It just came to me, Sylvia. I'd no idea that Carlos was going to challenge me to wrestle with him. It seems that your boy had dared him to do so, like little boys do. You remember he asked for a second chance, and you and I agreed?' Sylvia nodded, saying, 'Yes, I remember.'

'So I put him down again, and it was when I went down on top of him that the idea came to me. I remember reading last week in an old issue of the *Police Review* of a terrible case of child molestation, where a young schoolboy was sat on by his own father whilst other adults sexually abused the boy. Can you imagine such a thing? I was determined to do all I could to prevent the possibility of Carlos or your John ever being sexually assaulted. The idea came to me in a flash just as my left knee landed on a pebble. I know, of course, that I shouldn't have done it. I'll never make Inspector, but

I know in my heart that I did the right thing. Difficult things, consciences!'

'Yes, they can be, Charlotte, but half a pound of initiative is sometimes worth two tons of sociology training. I know you'll be an Inspector one day and, if I can help you, a Superintendent. Thank you for telling me about your brother Michael. I'm very sorry. I never knew. I feel so much in your debt. I know that Carlos – I mean my husband Carlos – will be very grateful for what you have done and gone through yourself this afternoon, and Xavier will be very grateful. You know, life can be very strange. That little boy Carlos still writes letters to his mother each week. All the little boys have to write letters to their parents each week after Mass on Sundays. Of course, his mother can't read them, but if and when she has a lucid interlude the letters are read to her by the nurses in Spain. Carlos always writes to his mother in Spanish, and he gives them to his father to send to save on his pocket money. He only writes short letters. Tomorrow morning he will be writing to his mother, and I'm sure he will be telling her about you. I'll bet you would like to know what he writes.'

'Yes I would, Sylvia, but I can't write Spanish and I would never seek to read anything Carlos wrote to his mother. Today I really did feel that Carlos did belong to me, but I dare not allow my feelings to get too close. I could be posted away from you anytime and then I would, perhaps, completely lose touch with him. I'll always think of him lying beneath me, with those lovely Spanish eyes of his flashing. He looked so bewildered at one stage and yet so completely trusting. I just had to do what I did for him.'

'Yes, Charlotte, and you did it very well. Whatever the future holds for that boy, I think he will always belong to you. Come on, let's forget the boys for a moment and get our diaries out and see what we have on together next week.'

Four years had passed since Charlotte had 'wrestled' with young Carlos. On the breakfast table Charlotte's mother had placed the morning's post. Two envelops were franked

'Slapton'. Charlotte recognized the handwriting on the two separate letters. She opened the first – clearly written by Miguel.

It read: 'Dear Charlotte, I feel I must write to you today, following father's telephone call late last night. Please accept my best wishes for your future happiness. I do trust that you will always find me a true friend and not just a stepson. Very sorry I could not be with you at the celebrations, but look forward to seeing you soon. Yours very sincerely, Miguel.'

Charlotte thought and proceeded to open Carlos's letter.

'Dear Charlotte, Congrats! I know my Momma, in heaven now, will be very pleased that you are to become my very own Mum. I know that you and Dad will be very happy. I am happy for you both. Lots of love, Carlos. P.S. Please try and come to Slapton on Saturday. We are playing The Mount. They won last year. With you watching, we will win.'

'What an adorable boy. I'm going to enjoy being his step-mother, starting on Saturday.' She was thinking and talking aloud. Her mother saw the look in her eyes, saying, 'I think you're already enjoying it, dear.'

Sylvia and Charlotte were on their own at Slapton College on Saturday. Sylvia's husband Carlos and Xavier were required to be at the Spanish Embassy in London – both were sorry not to be at Slapton. Sylvia knew that she could combine a visit to Slapton with a visit to Lanchester, her constituency. Charlotte, who was not on duty today, would not have missed the Under 15 match for anything. By happy chance, Sylvia's youngest was also a member of the team. They deliberately arrived a shade late so that the match could have started and they would not be held up unduly at the College itself. The grounds were like most good public schools. Normally the Under 15s would have played on one of the more remote pitches, but since this was an inter-school fixture and the top three teams were playing away, they had been given the privilege of playing on College Field immediately beneath the Lewthwaite Pavilion, named after the wealthy Old Boy who had donated it to the College in 1910. Sylvia paid her respects to Father Rector, and the two

110

women took their seats. Young Carlos had been disappointed not to see Charlotte before the match, but when the oval ball came into his hands, as he ran in the three-quarter line, he suddenly heard a voice he knew: 'Run, Carlos. Run.'

It was Charlotte, who was standing and shouting as loudly as anyone properly could. Carlos didn't really need to be told, but Charlotte's voice seemed to give 'wings to his heels' as he dummied and ran straight through The Mount's defence, throwing himself over the try line between the posts. A great cheer went up from all the college boys not playing in the games themselves, and an assortment of parents and friends of the College. Carlos jumped up and waved to the pavilion, where he knew Charlotte must be with Sylvia. Father Rector would insist on Sylvia – the Deputy Prime Minister – having a good seat in the Pavilion, and presumably Charlotte would be within two yards of her. That was his thinking, and he wasn't wrong.

Sylvia turned to Charlotte. 'Doesn't he play well? You must feel very thrilled. It must be all that training you gave to him on the sands four years ago, but Charlotte, don't embarrass him. Do try and remember this is Slapton. If you feel you must call out, and I'm not going to try and stop you, call out 'Lang', not 'Carlos'. You know that all the boys here are called by their surnames. It was very difficult when ours were called Bartlett-Shearman.'

'Thanks for reminding me, Sylvia. I quite forgot in the excitement.' On several further occasions Charlotte was on her feet. She simply could not resist encouraging Carlos, but she did not forget to call out 'Lang'. 'Thank God he has a short name!' At the conclusion of the game the respective teams lined up and cheered each other into the Pavilion, where a lavish spread of food was laid out. Slapton had taken their revenge for last year's defeat. Slapton 26, The Mount 12. Carlos came across with young Sabita, and offered his hand to Charlotte:

'I daren't kiss you in public, Charlotte. The lads would never let me forget – and I would cover you in mud. Do

please stay on. I want to go with you to the "White Hart".'
Charlotte knew what he meant, and secretly she was quite
glad not to have her nice new coat ruined with mud. Carlos
didn't forget to shake hands with Sylvia in his polite schoolboy manner, not forgetting to say, 'Very good of you to
come, Lady Sabita. John played very well today. He will be
in the Colts next year.'

Sylvia was pleased to hear this coming from Carlos, but
Charlotte was absolutely thrilled at the prospect of this
young boy becoming her stepson. What a boy. A player and
a diplomat! At the 'White Hart' Sylvia and Charlotte sat
down and awaited the arrival of the boys, who would arrive
changed into their smart clerical-grey suits.

'Let me pay today, Sylvia. It's the first time Carlos has
asked me, by letter, to come and support him.' Sylvia nodded
her agreement. The two boys tucked in as though they had
never eaten before that day. Nobody could reasonably have
thought that they had just consumed the splendid spread
at the Pavilion less than one hour before. At the conclusion
Carlos excused himself. He went to the Reception and
settled the account in cash. He received monthly 'pocket
money', and he could save when he wanted. Back at the
table, Charlotte called for the account. 'I'm sorry, Madam.
The young gentleman here has paid.'

Sylvia, Charlotte and John looked at Carlos, who was smiling his charming smile, and his Spanish eyes flashed. 'Don't
you remember, Charlotte? I made you a promise on the
sands one day, years ago, when I was a child. You were with
us, Lady Sabita. Charlotte wouldn't let me get up until I
promised to take her out for dinner one day. I know now I
would never try and put her on the floor. I marvel sometimes
at my own cheek, inviting her to wrestle with me. It was the
ice cream just now that reminded me. One day I will take
you out for dinner, Charlotte, I know you are going to make
Dad very happy.'

Charlotte was speechless. She took out her handkerchief
from her handbag and made some pretence at blowing her
nose. Sylvia silently signalled the boys to leave her alone

with Charlotte, and the boys quietly withdrew. 'That boy. He costs me a fortune in make-up. What have I done, Sylvia, to deserve Xavier and a boy like that? Just think – a childhood promise. I never could believe that I meant it or that he would remember making it. I was only teasing him. He will break many hearts. He's already broken mine this afternoon.'

'You're right, Charlotte. Now pull yourself together and listen to me. When you have children of your own you will learn quickly, but you have learnt a lot, I hope, this afternoon. Never make a promise to a child or extract one unless you mean it. You are very lucky, but you deserve it. May I make a suggestion?'

'Yes, of course, please do.'

'Mrs de Freitas has had to pull out of the College trip to Chamonix next weekend for the inter-school skiing sports. I'm going. My boy John is the Captain of the junior team. I know that he is hoping that Carlos will win one of the medals. Please let me put your name in Mrs de Freitas's place. I promise not to tell John or Carlos that you're coming. Do say that you will. We'll fly out on Friday with the others and stay at Xavier's hotel – the one he knows and where he's booked. You'll have to share my room, but you won't mind that. We'll see our boys skiing and hopefully winning something. After the race you'll appear on the scene. You'll insist on Master Carlos giving you a lesson on the nursery slope. However well he teaches, you're almost certainly going to have some slight fall or you'll fall accidentally on purpose, and then you can claim your gastronomic reward.'

'What on earth do you mean, Sylvia: my gastronomic reward?'

'Come on, Charlotte. It's not like you to be slow. Think of Carlos. Think of the promise you extracted from him, admittedly in teasing, when you were holding him down on the sand years ago. As I remember what Carlos said a few minutes ago, you made him promise to take you out for dinner the first time he put you on the ground. When you fall on the snow he will have "put you on the floor", in your own words, and I know that boy will be over the moon if you let him take you out to dinner. Just the two of you. He can't do it here, but in France! Just think how you would like to have had a top pop star all to yourself when you were his age!'

'Sylvia, I don't know what to say. You really are an angel in disguise. No wonder you are the Deputy Prime Minister. I could never have dreamt up what you've suggested, but thank you. Yes, I will come. I'll have to borrow one of your outfits again for the ski run, but I'll take two evening dresses, just in case of a real accident.'

At Chamonix the British camp was excited, but not optimistic. The Continental teams were strong, and there were visiting teams from the United States and Japan. Slapton's best hopes lay with John Sabita and Carlos de Sallas Lang (Carlos Lang for short). Their elder brothers would also have been entered in terms of ability, but the demand of public examinations had precluded their entry.

The boys were staying with other boys and girls in dormitories kindly provided by French schools, in Chamonix itself and surrounding towns and villages. Parents of those competing, of all schools and nations, were staying at hotels as they could find them and book them, together with observers and media representatives. The qualification runs on the Friday had reduced the total, by time limitation, to 50 for the Saturday finals.

Sadly, John Sabita just failed to qualify. The other Slapton boys were nowhere, except Carlos, who only managed to qualify with two seconds to spare. The competition was frightening. Twelve young competitors had been quite badly injured, but luckily there had been no fatalities.

Sylvia and Charlotte were booked in together, with other parents of the Slapton team, at the Hotel Excel where they had stayed before. Only John and Carlos had had any real chance of winning anything. They had skied from the age of three, and they appeared as professionals in comparison to their class-mates from the college. In real terms, any

114

number of the parents simply regarded the whole event as a very pleasant social outing with their young. The possibility of any British school students winning any medals or cups was regarded as minimal against the Swiss, the Austrians and the French.

The Slapton boys whose parents were present, joined them in their hotels. Those boys whose parents were not present joined together for jollifications of their own, with Father Turner in charge. Carlos had no idea that Charlotte was staying with Sylvia, and John had been sworn to secrecy. He, Carlos, decided, with Father Turner's approval, not to consume any alcohol, and he turned in early. He was given a private room in case there was any 'dormy party'. In the morning he was up early on the practice slopes. He wished his father and brother could have been with him.

The moment arrived: 'Carlos de Sallas Lang, College Slapton, Angleterre, quatorze ans.' The announcement over the loudspeakers was made first in French, then in English, German and Spanish. Charlotte felt her heart beating. High up, a tiny figure, as he appeared through her binoculars, was making a final fitting to his own tinted snow sunglasses. A flag waved, and he was coming down. Charlotte and Sylvia held each other's hands. It seemed like an eternity, but it wasn't. With a speed that could only be measured and appreciated by the roving television cameras that were strategically placed on the downhill course, Carlos came down the mountainside. He wound his way down, avoiding the limiting poles by inches, or so it appeared. He seemed to be in flight at times. Charlotte, notwithstanding her police training, could hardly bring herself to watch, but she did, as did Sylvia. Then he was at the line and the electric bell rang out.

'Thank God he's safe,' cried Charlotte.

'Look, Charlotte. Look at the computer board. He's leading. He's a whole two seconds down on yesterday. No-one will beat that. I believe he's going to win.' Sylvia threw her arms around Charlotte.

'He's done it, Charlotte. No-one is going to beat that,'

she repeated. 'Go to him. Seeing you now will make his day forever. Go quickly.' Charlotte needed no second bidding. Carlos was off the course proper. The next skier was coming down. Carlos was making his way to the area where all those who had already come down were meeting up with parents, coaches and friends. Charlotte ran as fast as she could in the snow. There he was. As loudly as she could she shouted, 'Carlos, Carlos.'

Carlos turned. He knew that voice. Within seconds they had their arms around each other. 'Charlotte, where on earth have you come from?'

'Carlos, darling, I've been here all the time. Please just hold me as tight as you can. You're safe, that's the main thing, and I do believe you're going to win. I couldn't bear watching you do that again in a play-off or jump-off or whatever they call it. You're so precious to me.' Charlotte's eyes were very full, and she was speaking to Carlos as a grown man and not a schoolboy of 14.

Eventually they released their hold on each other. Charlotte could not help but reflect that Carlos's hold on her felt as strong as any man's. Carlos recovered from Charlotte's embrace:

'I've never skied better, Charlotte. I'm so sorry that Dad and Miguel weren't here. I hope Momma saw me all the way. I skied for her today. She bought me my first skis when I was only three.' The young boy's face crumpled. Charlotte cradled his head down against her shoulder.

'Carlos, we're all proud of you. Your mother will know what you have achieved, and I'm only glad to be a part of your life. I always will be.' What more could she say or do? 'Come on, Carlos. We can't just stand here. Let's go and join the others.' As they walked hand in hand to the massed flagpoles the Slapton contingent started singing, 'For he's a jolly good fellow'.

Carlos was changing now after taking a long hot shower. So were the other competitors as they came down. It would be some time before the results of the morning Finals would be known. There was no undue hurry. He was feeling more happy than he imagined possible that Charlotte was there, but why hadn't she told him she was coming, and why hadn't John Sabita let on?

Charlotte and Sylvia were now having coffee in the 'View Palace' that overlooked the finishing arena.

'I know you will think I'm going soft, Sylvia, but I just can't bring myself into tricking Carlos and making him pay for dinner tonight out of his pocket money. He was only a child, little more than a baby, when I extracted that promise from him on Slapton Sands. I just can't do it. I should feel absolutely dreadful, and after all he's done today.'

Sylvia listened. She could hardly contain herself:

'Charlotte. Listen to me. You will feel a dead sight worse if you go back on the arrangement. Don't you realize that young boy virtually worships you? It's not a sexual love he has for you. It's the pure love of a boy who has lost his mother who was not, sadly, able to be any mother to him for years. It's pure selfishness for you to consider taking the easy way out by paying for his dinner. I'm not thinking of the money. If it was a question of money I would give the lad one hundred francs myself. It's the principle. Indeed, it's a lot more than principle. I know you're going to find it hard, but you will thank me one day, and hopefully tonight, for what I'm saying. Try and look at it from Carlos's point of view. One good dinner is much like another. You will have endless meals together over the years. You never have a second chance of making a good first impression. You did make a magnificent, if unorthodox, impression on that young boy on that sandy shore at Slapton, when you pretended to wrestle with him and held him down with your legs holding down his arms and shoulders, offering to buy him ice cream and extracting that promise from him. I was there too, remember. You just think of him as lying beneath you, like a baby, but he looked up at you and to you. You were "Superwoman" to him, and he fell in love with you that day. Please don't let him down. You really have something between you that thousands of women would give their right arms for. It's not sexual. It's pure and wonderful. No

117

stepmother wants to be a sex symbol to their stepson unless they are mad or evil. Please, Charlotte. Do fall deliberately, if you have to, on the nursery slope. Tell Carlos that he has put you on the ground and that the time has come for him to keep his promise in taking you out for dinner. That boy will be absolutely over the moon. Just think how proud he will feel entertaining his father's fiancée to dinner, ordering in French or Spanish. My God, you're a lucky girl. Please promise me that you'll think again. You must, for Carlos's sake. You won't have a second opportunity.'

Sylvia felt she had said enough, and she had.

'I don't know what I would do without you sometimes, Sylvia. I will steel myself. I will fall if it hurts me. I will never "let that boy down", as you put it.' Tears seemed to come to Charlotte too easily just now, but she held herself back from crying tears of happiness.

'Well, I'm glad that's settled, Charlotte. Look, here he comes with John.'

Carlos and John were coming over to the table, with Father Turner and a group of other boys.

'Carlos.' It was Sylvia who spoke. 'Charlotte wants to take up skiing. I've told her that you are tops in skiing and a better teacher. I think she would like you to give her one opening lesson on the practice nursery slope before the presentation ceremony this afternoon.'

'Yes. Please, Charlotte. Please let me teach you. I'd love to. I'll get you fixed up with skis just as soon as we've finished coffee together, and then we'll have to think of what you are going to wear.'

'That's no problem,' said Sylvia. 'Charlotte brought a set of my things over, in the hope that she might have a go. We had to keep it from you that she was coming just in case you started to look for her as you were coming down and missed a turning.' Sylvia thought she had covered that situation rather well. He would be bound to ask Charlotte why she had not told him that she was coming. Sylvia seemed to know Carlos yet better than Charlotte. She had two boys of her own! Charlotte had fully recovered her composure, and

118

joined in the conversation easily and with enthusiasm.

'When will the final results be known? We must ring your father and Slapton College,' she said.

'Don't you know, Miss Johnson?' It was Father Turner who spoke now. 'Carlos has won the Gold, and we're all going to celebrate! Slapton knows already.'

Charlotte jumped up. Neither she nor Sylvia had heard the result. They had been so busy talking, pouring their hearts out to each other. She virtually threw herself at Carlos. She kissed him on the lips. He might have been Xavier.

'My darling boy!' She broke down. This was too much for her to be told after the event. Carlos was embarrassed, but he didn't seem to care. He simply winked at Sylvia and Father Turner, and kissed her on the lips. In less than ten minutes they were all sipping Champagne, and Sylvia settled the account simply telling the head waiter to place the account to her room number. Normally he would have required immediate cash settlement, but the Deputy Prime Minister of Great Britain, that was different. On the nursery slope Carlos led Charlotte by the hand. She appeared like an old lady by her approach, even if she was only 30. Carlos showed her the basics as his father had done. Charlotte was off, and then she was down. She tried again and did a little better, but still she fell, and she was not pretending. On each occasion Carlos glided across to her as though possessed of wings and picked her up.

Eventually he said, 'Come on, Charlotte. You've had enough for one day. I do want you with me when I go to collect my medal at the ceremony. Come on. Let me help you up for the last time today.'

Charlotte looked at him adoringly. He had never seen her look at him like that. 'Carlos, when you were a little boy, you once made me a promise. You said you would take me out for dinner if you ever succeeded in putting me on the ground. Well, you have today. Please, Carlos, take me out for dinner in the hotel; just the two of us?'

Carlos could hardly believe his ears. It was the last thing he was expecting Charlotte to say or ask, but he was immediately thrilled to the marrow of his bones.

'Charlotte, you've made my day. I'd love to take you out for dinner. The other boys will be creased with envy. Come on, let's get back to the hotel, and I'll try and make some arrangements.'

They went together to the Professional's shop. Charlotte surrendered her skis. Carlos's skis were cleaned, polished and prepared for shipping. In fact, they would be going back by air in the same plane as the team.

At the Hotel Excel, Sylvia, in anticipation that Charlotte would steel herself as she had said she would, had arranged to join other parents and her own son John for dinner, leaving the table she and Charlotte had shared the previous evening for Charlotte and Carlos alone. These arrangements meant there was not the slightest difficulty for Carlos. Dinner would be taken early at 8 p.m., so that all the Slapton guests could get together later for celebrations.

At the presentation ceremony, Charlotte was as calm and collected, as she always was in her Police Inspector's role. She smiled and clapped as required, but she felt that twinge of all winners' supporters when the announcement came over the tannoy system: '*Première Classe. Medallion Etelon, Carlos Lang, College Slapton, Angleterre.*'

The announcement was given in four different languages: 'Will the audience please stand.' Charlotte leapt to her feet. She looked supremely happy, as did Sylvia and all the British contingent. Carlos bent down as the French Minister of Education placed the ribbon over his head, the Gold medal glinting in the bright afternoon sun. The Silver and Bronze awards followed, the winners of these medals being French and Austrian. The three boys, who looked like young men on the podium, shook hands. Then the familiar roll of the drums and the anthem 'God Save the Queen' was heard, not simply in the stadium, but along the walls of the mountain valley in which Chamonix lies.

As the last notes faded away there was loud applause from the 2,000 present. The television was going out 'live' all over

France and beyond. It would, no doubt, get a mention on the British television, but when it was known that Carlos had won, it was 'featured' with the Union flag being hoisted.

Back at the hotel, Charlotte changed for dinner. Sylvia had been quite right. This was a meal she would never forget. She would not pretend that Carlos was Xavier, nor would she attempt to pretend. She was just so thrilled to have Carlos as her prospective stepson. How proud his own mother would have been. She would like to have known his mother, but had Sophia lived she could never have married Xavier. These thoughts were flicking through her mind as she sat before the mirror on the dressing table.

Sylvia came in. They were sharing the same room. 'You did as you promised, Charlotte?' asked Sylvia, well knowing she had.

'Yes I did, Sylvia, and thank you. How do I look?'

'You look lovely. He will be the proudest schoolboy in Europe tonight. You couldn't have let him down. It's funny, isn't it. He will always see you in his mind's eye as you always first think of him. What a good job my Carlos and your Xavier went to that school. I wish I could be a fly on the wall of your alcove tonight in the dining room. You will both thoroughly enjoy it, and it's a meal you'll never forget. I don't really like to say it, but I'm almost glad Xavier and my Carlos are not here for your sake.'

'Thanks, Sylvia. You've been wonderful. For the first time since we have been engaged, I'm glad too to have Carlos by myself. I know I shall shed many tears over him, but he's worth every drop. I'm just sorry I don't seem able to get anything like so close to Miguel. He's very polite and kind, but he's remote in some way.'

Downstairs in the bar, Carlos kept looking at his watch. He was 14. He had never 'dated' a girl in his life, for all his seemingly urbane manner that many 18-year-olds would have envied. He had arranged, unknown to Charlotte, to have the two menus at their table typed in Spanish so that he could 'help', and he had ordered a corsage of flowers to match her dress, once he had found the colour she was going to wear from Sylvia. 'If I had been just ten years older I would have beaten Dad in proposing to Charlotte,' he mused to himself. He had missed his mother, as all sensitive boys do when their mothers die young. He had no sisters, and being away at an English boarding school from the age of seven, he might have been said to be sexually deprived. Although he never gave thought to Charlotte in a sensuous fashion, he had loved her from the start. She had been such a jolly good sport. As a tiny boy he could not conceive of any girl being his equal in a physical sense. The fact that Charlotte had been able to run faster than him, swim faster, and not least had been able to put him on the floor with seeming ease, and hold him down, had been beyond his belief. And she had been so kind and understanding. He had concluded that Charlotte must have been like his mother. Even when she had held him down all those years ago, she had not hurt him. Indeed, he had felt secure in her hold.

These were some of the thoughts that were going through his mind whilst she was dressing in her hotel room. One thing he knew now, at the great age of 14, was that he was dead lucky to have had the parents he had, and that his father had very good sense in asking Charlotte to marry him. He would always be loyal to his father and brother, but equally he would be loyal and affectionate to Charlotte. It seemed like an age to Carlos, but it wasn't really. It was just ten minutes past eight when Sylvia and Charlotte came down the staircase together. Carlos and John, who had been with him in the bar sipping sherry, greeted the ladies. Carlos had learnt well from following his father. He took Sylvia's hand in his and kissed it. He turned to Charlotte and kissed her lightly on the cheek:

'I'll try not to spoil your make-up this evening, Charlotte,' he said with his smile. Both boys were wearing their College clerical grey suits and their maroon 'colour' ties. They both had their 'colours' for skiing.

'You will both have sherry?' started Carlos. He was far more forward than John – the kind would say more mature.

Sylvia and Charlotte smiled at each other and nodded. They all sat down together away from the window, at the Manager's request, for security reasons. The French police and the hotel management were being very protective following the previous experience, and there would be absolutely no press coverage at the hotel this evening. The press had all the coverage they required of the events of the day. The time came to split up, and the head waiter led Charlotte, followed by Carlos, to the alcove at the side of the dining room. Carlos assisted Charlotte with her chair, as he had seen his father assist many ladies. The head waiter lit the three candles in the candelabra on the table, and Charlotte looked at the corsage.

'Is this for me, Carlos?' she asked as though there could be any doubt.

'It isn't for me, Charlotte. I thought you'd like it. It matches your dress perfectly, thanks to Sylvia telling me the colour of the dress you're wearing before dinner, and it suits your complexion.'

Charlotte felt she might have blushed. Could this possibly be the little boy she had first known only four years ago?

'Thank you, darling,' was all she could bring herself to say at the moment. It was enough for Carlos. He was already on cloud nine. He picked up the menus and passed one to Charlotte. At a glance she could see that they were printed in Spanish. She looked at Carlos. He was smiling and his eyes flashed. 'Charlotte, I had these printed specially. We are in France tonight, but my heart is still in Spain. I wanted you to feel that you were in Spanish hands tonight. I will translate anything you like on the menu, but if you really want a menu printed in English and French I will get you one.'

Charlotte thought. How could she best please this boy? 'No, Carlos. I'll put myself completely in your hands. What do you suggest?' Carlos purred to himself inside. What a lovely woman she was.

He translated easily and completely. Charlotte made her choice, and within minutes a Reserve Rioja was 'breathing' and a bottle of Cava was placed in an ice-bucket next to Carlos's chair. He poured two glasses and looked her straight in the eye. He lifted his glass and proposed: 'To you and Dad! I can't wait for you to get married.' Charlotte gulped.

'Thank you, darling,' she replied. Carlos had never been happier in his life. He positively glowed. The winning of the downhill for Slapton had been great, and he had been delighted to see Charlotte coming towards him immediately after he had come down, but the thought that he was acting as her host for dinner thrilled him.

'Charlotte, I laughed aloud in the bar just now, but John didn't know what I was laughing about. I hope you're not upset, but I'm so glad it was you who fell in the snow, and not me. I would have lost the race, but far more important, you would not have fallen on the ground and asked me to keep my promise. You have made me the happiest man in Chamonix.' Charlotte did well to keep her tears back. Could this possibly be being said to her, when only a few hours earlier she had thought, most definitely, that she was not going to allow herself to trick him into spending his 'pocket money' on her. Carlos continued, 'There is something I must tell you, Charlotte, now that we are on our own. I raced today, as you know, for my Momma. She was the loveliest person in the world. Look. Let me show you her photograph.' He took out his wallet and produced his late mother's photo – fading now, but obviously a very attractive-looking Spanish lady, who Charlotte had never met. The photo was obviously taken some years before her death. As she looked, Carlos went on, 'Now that Momma is in heaven, and no longer with us, I regard you as the loveliest person in the world.'

As a young boy of 14, he couldn't know the effect he was having on Charlotte, who was feeling completely overcome. This boy was speaking so innocently and yet tearing at her heart strings. What could she say?

'You're a very good boy, Carlos. Your Momma would be very proud of you, and so am I. I will never try and take your mother's place, I promise. I couldn't begin to try.' It was as much as she could say. Carlos did suddenly become aware that Charlotte was on the verge of tears, and altered course. He was learning fast, but he was still only a boy.

'Thank you, Charlotte, for saying that. Even when you do marry Dad, you won't expect me to call you Momma then? I would like to continue to call you Charlotte, unless you want me to give you a nickname like "Mater", but I would like to continue to call you Charlotte. You've always been Charlotte to me, and I hope you always will be. I regard you as my best friend.' Charlotte had not expected this. She would never forget this evening. Sylvia had said as much and she had agreed accordingly, but this boy was tearing her heart out in his boyish way and she had little resistance left.

Fortunately for her, the carrot and orange soup was just arriving. She felt she had been saved by the bell as she had been in the police gym when Mary had been putting her through her paces at karate and judo. That now seemed a distant memory. She felt she had coped better with Mary than with this young boy, but she loved him more by the minute. The arrival of the soup completely changed the conversation, and Carlos proved himself full of fun in any number of remarks he made. By the time the soup had been cleared and the chicken Kiev had arrived, Charlotte was her normal self. She pinned the corsage to her dress and raised the flowers to her face to scent them. The flowers themselves were not scented, but the florist had given them a spray of perfume that would wear off in the evening, but now gave that final touch.

'Charlotte. Dad told me how you saved Sylvia's life last time you were here in the hotel. He said you were "bloody wonderful". I wish I could have been with you. That man who brought you to the floor wouldn't be living today if I had been there. Perhaps it was a good job it was Dad and not me. Do tell me. When are you and Dad getting married? I can't wait to have you as my stepmum.'

'We haven't fixed a date yet, Carlos, but soon. I promise you'll be one of the first to know.'

'Charlotte. You made me make a promise to you when I was younger. I'm so very glad you did, and I can't tell you how happy I am that you called in my promise on that nursery slope. Now I want you to make me a promise, although I'm only a schoolboy. Really, I want you to make me two promises. Firstly, I want you to promise me that if you ever really feel upset or concerned about any matter you will come to me. I feel I take your friendship for granted. I want to be your best friend. Secondly, I want you to promise not to cry for me ever. I don't cry for you. I want to make you happy, not tearful.'

'Bless you, child, I promise.'

Charlotte took out her handkerchief and blew her nose. Carlos wasn't deceived, and he apologized in the only way he thought proper. He placed his hand on hers on the table. This only served to produce further tears in Charlotte's eyes, but Carlos, at his age, could not be expected to understand. Carlos poured out another glass for Charlotte and himself, and the arrival of the coffee Renoirs enabled Charlotte to recover. It was at this moment that the manager came to the table with an obvious telegram and a bottle of the best Cognac served in the hotel. He handed the telegram to Carlos and the Cognac to Charlotte. Carlos grinned his boyish grin. 'We can guess what this is, can't we?'

The telegram said all that was necessary: 'Congratulations. Dad and Miguel. Cognac en route.' He passed the telegram to Charlotte. Reluctantly, very reluctantly, Carlos folded his napkin. He pulled the table towards himself so that Charlotte could rise more easily. He followed her to the little group surrounding Sylvia and John.

The time came for Carlos and John to return to their temporary dormitory in company with other boys and Father Turner, who had been with other parents.

Sylvia and Charlotte were in their room now. Sylvia detected immediately – in fact, she had detected downstairs in the hotel lounge – that Charlotte had been crying. Even a repair job in the powder room could not completely disguise the redness in her eyes.

126

'Do tell me. How's the evening gone with young Master Carlos?'

'Sylvia, I can't begin to tell you,' started Charlotte. 'That boy. That boy nearly killed me. He's such a love. On at least three occasions I wanted to get up from the table, put my arms round him and squeeze him as tight as I could. I'm so grateful to you for making me call in his promise. He even showed me his mother's photograph and said he had raced his race for her and that now she was in heaven, he thought me the loveliest person in the world and his best friend. Perhaps most importantly, he made me make a promise to him which I'll do my damnedest to keep. He made me promise not to let myself cry about him. I promised, and to use your own words, "I won't let that boy down."'

'You're very lucky, Charlotte, and so is he. Don't tell Xavier about what you've done, and I shan't say a word to my Carlos. Let that little intrigue be something for ever special between you and that boy. I know he worships you, and he really does need you. I know it sounds silly, but beneath that frighteningly urbane manner of his, years ahead of his time, he suffers from loneliness and emotional insecurity. You can and do provide that for him in abundance, and you will continue to do so. Never forget, he only has the most childish, if cherished, memories of his mother, and he's not British like you and me. He's been at an all-male Church boarding school since he was seven. I do know that Xavier has done very well for both his boys, but Carlos needs you more than Miguel, who is almost a man today. He was years older than Carlos when their mother was first taken ill. I'll tell you something else – and this must be in complete confidence. You must never tell anybody that I told you, but it seems that Carlos has great guilt feelings sometimes. Some cow of a woman told him that he had caused his mother's illness and death by being born. It seems he weighed over ten pounds at birth!'

'God, no. What a bitch! Thanks for telling me, Sylvia. Naturally I'll never betray such a confidence, but I will make every effort to help him. I will thank him again tomorrow for tonight's dinner. I'm so glad you made me change my mind. You know, Sylvia, I have a confession to make. I have asked myself more than once how I would have felt if Xavier had been fifty-eight and Carlos twenty-six.'

Sylvia did not reply. She had pulled up her duvet. She was asleep. The following morning everybody packed up. Charlotte made a point of taking Carlos on one side.

'You made me the happiest woman in France last night, Carlos, darling. You made me promise to let you know if I had anything to worry about. Well, I want our dinner last night to be our little secret. I will never tell anybody about my falling in the snow and calling in your childish promise, and Sylvia has given me her word that she won't tell anybody. It's a secret that will die with us. Please agree.' She held him closely to herself. She didn't let a tear fall. She would keep her promise to him.

10

The Air France jet made its gradual descent to Heathrow. Xavier and Carlos were there to meet Charlotte, Sylvia and the boys. Slapton had laid on a coach to take the boys back to the College. No parents were going to object to that arrangement, and it did enable those fathers who had not been able to travel to Chamonix to have a victory lunch with their wives and sons. Sylvia had a very heavy week ahead of her both at the Ministry and the House of Commons, and Charlotte was on a university tour of the country, 'spreading the gospel', as she put it, recruiting for the Metropolitan Police. Secretly she was taking instructions with a view to converting to the Roman Catholic Church. She had understandably spent tormented nights about this decision. Her own mother was, to say the least, not best pleased. Charlotte's father had been a vicar, and following his death his widow had worked at a garage on the North Circular Road that ran around north London. It was Charlotte's mother's earnings and the small pension she received from her late husband's church that had helped Charlotte to go to university. It was enough that she was losing her daughter to a foreigner with two teenage children. He was so much older than Charlotte. He was 48, and she was only 30.

She had done so well in the Police and might have gone to the very top and married a person of her own age – at least another British subject. Charlotte had argued and pleaded in her own way with her mother.

'It's not that I'm "giving in", mother. If it was just Xavier and me, we could stay in our own churches. I don't think

Daddy would have been upset if he'd known all the facts. It's Xavier's two boys. They have been brought up as Catholics. They are Spanish. They go to a Roman Catholic school, and to expect them all to leave their Church and become Church of England would be asking the impossible. Just imagine us all living in Spain with no Church of England to attend, and the boys feeling that I had persuaded their father for selfish reasons. I hope that Xavier and I will have children. We couldn't all be going to different churches!'

These were the arguments that Charlotte had advanced, both with kindness and spirit. Charlotte could be quite formidable in any discussion when she wanted. She certainly was not the type to be told what she should do with her private life. She had been a good church attender herself and had gone to church with her mother for years. Her mother was still prominent in the local Mothers' Union, and Charlotte knew that her mother was concerned as to what the other mothers would say about Charlotte "turning", particularly with her father having been the vicar.

Xavier was charm itself when he was at Charlotte's home, which was as frequent as he found possible, but his Spanish charm had not served to warm Charlotte's mother's heart on the question of her daughter's proposed change of church. It was for this reason that Charlotte had thought it best to say nothing of her undergoing instruction. Xavier was aware of it, of course. He had suggested a church he knew in London where one of the Old Boys from Slapton was the Rector, but not a member of the Order which ran Slapton College.

Xavier had been summoned to visit Moscow. Naturally he told Charlotte, and she had relayed this information to Sylvia, who had now become a very close friend. Charlotte was very sorry that Xavier was going away. They were very much in love with one another, and there was no question of 'saving up to get married'.

Charlotte naturally wanted a church wedding. She would marry either at the church where she was receiving instruction, or Brompton Oratory, which Church Xavier attended when in London, or the boys' College.

When Charlotte returned home after her first week away touring the universities in the north of England – Manchester, Salford, Liverpool and Leeds – she found a number of letters waiting for her, including a large flat one with the postmark 'Slapton'. She recognized Carlos's writing. It wasn't her birthday until next month – he had got that out of her – what could it be? She went into the kitchen and opened the envelope carefully. She didn't have to look long.

Inside the large envelope there was a second one with a French postage stamp on it. That envelope had obviously been opened and re-sealed. She used the kitchen knife a second time and there it was – a photograph of Carlos and herself, taken by the hotel photographer at Chamonix. She remembered, now, that the photographer had taken the photo as they had sat together in the dining-room alcove. It was a good photograph – sometimes this sort of photograph fades quickly in the daylight. Charlotte was quite pleased her mother was out of the house. She had said nothing to her mother about Xavier's youngest having taken her out for dinner.

The letter, written on Slapton College notepaper, she would keep for ever:

'Dear Charlotte,

I do hope you like this photograph. I think you look super. I know it's not your birthday until next month, but I forgot to get you a card in London at the airport. I could get one from the village store in Slapton, but I have run out of this term's exeat cards so I can't leave the college grounds without permission. I could get Miguel to buy one for you, but that would not be from me properly. Anyway I'm a bit short of cash just now, but my allowance will be here at the weekend. I wanted you to have this photo as soon as possible. Please treat it as your birthday card and make Dad marry you as soon as possible.

Lots of love
    Carlos xxx'

131

Charlotte knew her mother would soon be back, and she placed the photograph and the letter in her slim black file case and proceeded to open her remaining mail, that was not that interesting.

She filed receipts and accounts and looked briefly at some junk mail, which she promptly deposited, without ceremony, into the kitchen bin. When her mother did come in with a pile of groceries, Charlotte talked of her trips round the 'Varsities' as she put it, whilst helping to put the groceries away. It wasn't until she had gone to bed later that Charlotte looked again at the photograph and the letter. She read the letter again three more times, without shedding a tear, and then after putting them away again for the last time, she fell asleep.

Sylvia had been right. She was as bonded to that boy as he was to her.

At the Spanish Embassy in London, where Xavier stayed regularly when on Spanish Government business, he was surprised to receive a message that the Ambassador wished to discuss a personal matter of importance with him concerning his own sons and his youngest son in particular. Xavier presented himself promptly at 11 a.m. He was never late, and translated every appointment as being five minutes ahead of the appointed hour. His wristwatch was always set five minutes fast.

'Do come in, Xavier. It's good of you to come. I don't know now whether I needed to have had you called, but I must confess that we were all very alarmed when we saw your young boy being accosted when he came off the snow. Congratulations by the way. You must be very thrilled.'

'How do you mean, Philip?' – the two men were good friends, so there was no need for any 'Your Excellency' between them – 'my son being accosted.'

'You obviously weren't watching, Xavier. As soon as your son came off the snow we saw a woman dashing towards him and throwing her arms around him. We knew it wasn't your dear late wife Sophia. It's a terrible thing today. It's no longer a question simply of providing security for athletes from foreigners, but from your own people. We have been lucky so far in Spain, but you must have read of assaults, and we didn't know who the lady was or even if it was a lady or a man dressed as a woman, with her running so fast. I can tell you now that we were mightily relieved when we got a call from Chamonix that the woman in question was your fiancée. I assume your fiancée is a good skier herself?'

'It's funny you should ask, but sadly no, she isn't yet, although I did give her one or two lessons myself when we were across there together a short time back.'

Xavier knew nothing of the incident of Charlotte having had a lesson from his son and their subsequent dinner date.

'There's another point, Xavier. Whilst we were very thrilled for you and your boy, our National Olympic Coach who was present and who was so concerned at your boy being accosted, as he thought, would like to think that in future meetings Carlos would ski for Spain – skiing for the Red and Yellow, not the Red, White and Blue!'

'I take your point, Philip. Tell Señor Dante that he's no need to worry. Carlos hopes to follow me to Seville University, and if he stays as good as he is he should stand a fair chance of skiing on behalf of Seville. I skied twice for the University after I left Slapton.'

'Never mind the University. Our national coach, Señor Dante, wants him to win a gold for Spain!'

'*Que sera sera*, Philip. We shall have to wait and see, but look we mustn't finish our conversation like this. I would like you to meet Charlotte. She's a lovely girl. I think I'm very lucky to have been at Slapton with Carlos Sabita. My Carlos is named after him, you know. Sophia's family were related to the Sabitas. Charlotte, I think you know, served as a protection officer in the Metropolitan Police. I came to know her when she looked after Carlos's wife. She was one of Sylvia's Bridesmaids, but why am I telling you this? You were at the wedding down at Lanchester. The best part of it, apart from she and me, is that she's proved a real hit with both our boys, particularly the youngest. It can be so difficult for boys of that age away from home without a mother figure.'

'You are indeed a lucky man, Xavier. Napoleon used to say that he preferred lucky generals.'

The two men shook hands after they had finished their coffees. Back at his private desk upstairs on the fourth floor of the Embassy, Xavier looked at his morning post – his personal post. His business post he had dealt with shortly after 8.30 a.m., following his morning swim in the Embassy pool.

There were two personal letters for him; one from Major-General Renov, now Second Vice President of Russia, that had been passed through security unopened, but checked by screening. The second letter had the envelope marked 'Slapton'. Perhaps understandably, he opened the Slapton letter first. 'Always put the family first' had been his motto in life. He had no cause to feel differently this morning.

He opened the envelope marked 'Strictly Private and Confidential'. This letter too had been cleared by the Security screening downstairs, but not opened. The letter read:

'Dear Xavier,

You won't mind my writing to you on a personal note I hope, but as an old Slaptonian yourself you will recall that we always have reserved the right to open boys' mail addressed to them here at the College – except, of course, from their parents – to protect them from possible contact with undesirable persons of every description. Since the sad death of your wife, your boys have received fewer letters than some of their peers, but recently your boys have received letters from a Miss Charlotte Johnson of London. We were greatly relieved to learn that Miss Johnson was your fiancée. Do please bring her over to the College for dinner. I know she has been with Dame Sabita, and she seems awfully good with your boys. I have shaken hands with Miss Johnson and made some small talk, but we would wish her to feel a member of the "Slapton Family". Don't let it be

134

too long before you bring her. I won't be Rector here for ever. Incidentally, your boys are both doing very well. Miguel is certain to get top "A" grades. I do hope you will think of letting him go to Oxford rather than Seville.

    Yours sincerely

     Father Rector'

Xavier smiled to himself. 'Father Rector doesn't miss a trick. I bet he wants to organize a wedding at the College as one of his last duties. It would suit him very well to have the deputy British Prime Minister and the Spanish Ambassador at Slapton.'

Xavier was never far out in his thinking. The second letter had come direct from the Russian Embassy and had clearly come to London, via the diplomatic bag, from Moscow. It read:

'Dear Xavier,

    We are very much looking forward to seeing you. My wife is very keen for you to see our little boy dressed in your kind birth gift. Now that he is strong enough to go outside we are arranging for him to be christened. Hopefully you will be able to be with us at the Orthodox Cathedral. If you would like to take the opportunity of being confirmed in the Orthodox Church of your ancestors, this would be a very happy occasion for us all, and General Maiski and I would be more than happy to act as your sponsors. Do please let me know the flight on which you are arriving, and I will meet you myself at the airport.

    Yours sincerely

     Vladimir Renov'

Xavier re-read the letter three times to be perfectly certain that he hadn't missed anything. He hadn't. He never did. 'Some would say damned cheek, others would be flattered,' he thought to himself.

He folded the letter and joined it with Father Rector's letter in his wallet. He would show them both to Charlotte.

'I wonder what she will make of them?' he asked himself. 'There is no problem about going down to Slapton, but being confirmed in the Russian Orthodox Church? Pity Charlotte was touring the universities in the north of England again. Perhaps she could alter it to Exeter and Southampton.'

Charlotte's mother had invited Xavier to join Charlotte and herself for supper at her home in New Southgate. Xavier did not drive that night, but took the Underground to Arnos Grove on the Piccadilly line.

On the stroke he was at the front door with flowers for Charlotte's mother and a bottle of best Reserve Rioja for Charlotte. He nearly always did this when he visited Palmers Road, and Charlotte's mother had almost come to expect it. Charlotte did expect it. She would have been very surprised if he had come empty-handed, particularly when he had been invited.

Conversation was very friendly, and Xavier was at pains not to discuss religion or anything that might touch on it – such as trouble in the Balkans or elsewhere. Charlotte had told him all about her mother's feelings. It was when Charlotte's mother went into the kitchen to make the coffee that Xavier took out Father Rector's letter and passed it to her, saying:

'Darling, I received this at my office this morning. Read it when you get the chance and let me have a few dates that suit you.' Charlotte took the letter from him. She noticed the Slapton postmark on the envelope and placed it in her handbag.

By the time Mrs Johnson had reappeared, Xavier and Charlotte were removing the best crockery and cutlery from the dining room table. Charlotte had turned the television on. It was one of her mother's favourite 'hospital' programmes, of which there seemed no end.

Xavier was going to have to be very long-suffering in viewing hospital films if he wanted to get at all close to his future mother-in-law! They sat down for their coffees and Charlotte made an excuse to leave the room. She shot upstairs, read Father Rector's letter with some amusement, checked her diary and wrote down four dates. She returned downstairs, made some small talk and then passed the dates to Xavier, saying:

'Darling, I think those are the dates you want when I'm going to be away.' Xavier took the hint from her smile that she would be happy to have dinner with Father Rector at Slapton.

'I wonder what she will make of the second letter?' he wondered. When the hospital programme was over Mrs Johnson announced, somewhat unexpectedly, that she was feeling a little tired and if they didn't mind she would have an early night. She had promised to arrange the flowers at the Parish Church tomorrow, and she had to get the flowers first from the florists before the shop opened to the public. Charlotte and Xavier were very understanding and offered to clear the dishes in the kitchen.

'I wouldn't hear of you doing them whilst I sat here,' he had said. On their own at last, Xavier gave Charlotte a big hug and kissed her on the lips. 'Darling, I thought that programme would go on for ever. Look, I have another letter to show you. Leave it to me to speak to Slapton. I'll let you know which date and we will motor down together – never mind his "small talk".'

They both laughed. Xavier produced Renov's letter. He said nothing and left it to Charlotte to comment or explode, as he anticipated.

'Christ. What a suggestion. I'll give him full marks for trying, but you tell him from me that I'm going through quite a difficult time as it is, with my poor Latin, and I've no intention of trying to learn Church Russian, even if you do have ancestors buried somewhere over there.'

Xavier was grateful that Charlotte had been so mild in her reaction. There was, of course, no need for any convert to his own church today to have any knowledge of Latin, but the priest who was instructing Charlotte had been impressed by the fact that she had been to university.

Xavier was off to Moscow. Charlotte went with him to Heathrow. She didn't like seeing him go even for a weekend. She could hardly wait for them to be married, but at least this weekend would enable her to try to get closer to Miguel, his elder son.

Miguel was so polite to her, but he was as cold as Carlos was warm. She had to be so careful. He was quite the young man, physically as well as mentally. There was no schoolboy about him, as there was with Carlos. He was 17 now, but had the bearing and manner of a man of 25.

Charlotte parked her car in front of the College. Miguel was there to meet her. He kissed her hand. He made no attempt to put his arms around her, and she thought it best not to try herself.

Miguel was Captain of the College Second Cricket Eleven, and they were playing at home against The Mount. This was always something of a 'needle' match. It often resulted in a draw. At the Pavilion, Miguel made a point of introducing Charlotte to Father Rector and getting her one of the best seats, with instructions to a younger lad to look, after her and 'make sure she doesn't have to queue for tea and cake'.

'He's just like Carlos, but older. They are both carbon copies of Xavier.' That was how she thought. Presently she was joined by Father Turner and two parents of new boys. There was pleasant talk between the four of them, and Charlotte explained that Miguel was not her son, 'but hopefully he will shortly be my stepson. His father is out of the country this weekend.'

These pleasant introductions over, they joined the clapping as the Slapton side went out into the field, followed shortly by the two opening batsmen from The Mount, who were obviously experienced players by schoolboy standards. They were wearing cricket caps that were clearly covering batsmen's helmets to protect themselves from fast bowling. Perhaps because she had played and been Captain of her netball team at school, Charlotte felt that cricket was a bit of a bore. The whole game seemed to proceed so slowly, the players changing places slowly, not simply to comply with the rules, in the sense of six balls per over, but changing of the field when batsmen made singles if one of them happened to be left-handed.

That was one thing she had in common with Miguel, but that, she thought was about all. She liked a game which was quick-moving, like football or hockey. She felt she could not participate, even as a spectator. She daren't call out her support for Miguel, or even Carlos for that matter. At best she could join in the clapping. It just wasn't her game, but it wasn't the game she had gone to see.

It was Miguel. How she wished the game would finish. It did eventually, after a break for tea. Charlotte would not embarrass Miguel in front of his fellow players – particularly as Captain – but she could not fail to observe that Miguel was addressed as 'Stumps' or 'Stumpy' by any number of the boys, and that he reacted to the name with pleasure rather than annoyance. She must try and find out why. It was another draw. The Mount had made 164 all out – Slapton had made 124 for four of their wickets. Miguel had 'carried his bat' with a score of 68 not out. He seemed very pleased with himself, but like all schoolboy captains, or any other captains for that matter, he wished his side had won. When stumps were drawn Miguel came up the steps of the pavilion to applause.

Ten minutes later he came over to Charlotte dressed in his blazer. He did look smart. There was certainly nothing stumpy about his appearance. At the White Hart Charlotte had booked a table for two. Normally that would have been out of the question on a Saturday, when the College had a home fixture, but the management knew Charlotte as the protection officer of the Deputy Prime Minister, so there was no problem. They assumed – incorrectly – that Sylvia was coming. Miguel was ever so polite, holding her chair for her as Xavier would have done and as Carlos had done at Chamonix. Charlotte decided to break the ice.

'Do tell me something, Miguel. I have been meaning to

ask you. Why do the boys call you "Stumps" or "Stumpy"? Surely a nickname. You're anything but stumpy.'

Miguel looked at her straight in the eyes. She felt he was going to pierce hers. She had never seen him look at her like this. He started slowly; 'I will tell you, Charlotte, if you promise not to be embarrassed.'

'I promise, Miguel. I am an adult and in the police, you know.' Charlotte wondered what was coming and a dozen thoughts flooded her mind, but nothing prepared her for what was to come. Miguel nodded:

'Very well, Charlotte, but it's a long story. I'll tell it as quickly as I can.' He paused a moment whilst he collected his thoughts. 'Charlotte, I don't know how it is with girls, but take it from me that in a boy's school there is always likely to be one of the older boys who likes to play with very little boys – do you know what I mean?'

'Yes I do, Miguel – go on.'

'Well, I'm big brother to Carlos, and both Momma and Dad always told me to look after him here. One day about two years ago Carlos told me that one of the big boys, he must have been seventeen then, had tried to play with him – you know what I mean – below the waist. Well, I took hold of the nearest cricket stump I could find and went after the bastard. He was a good deal bigger than I was then, but everybody knows that bullies are generally cowards so I went straight for him. Don't ask me what I did, but I gave him a jolly good poke with the pointed end of the stump in his groin where it hurts, and then I gave him a damned good thrashing. I would have continued to thrash him, but Father Turner and some of the Prefects pulled me off, and he was in the College Infirmary for three weeks until the end of term. He didn't come back. His parents took him away – not for what he had tried to do with Carlos and other boys, but for stealing from their lockers. The little boys don't have locks on their cupboards, to teach them honesty and all that. That's why they call me "Stumpy".'

'Miguel,' said Charlotte. 'I'm so glad you told me. You've done more good telling me what you have than you did

140

scoring all those runs this afternoon. Thank you very much, dear. Come on, have another cake. You'll never know or have the experience, Miguel, but it's not always easy being a prospective stepmother, but you really have made my day. I promise you I will never call you "Stumpy" myself, but I think it might be a good name say for a Manx cat if ever we have one. If there is anything I can ever do for you, Miguel, please never hesitate to ask me. I may seem old to you, but I'm only thirty. I'm nearer your age than your father's.'

'There is one thing you can promise me, Charlotte.'

'What's that, Miguel?'

'Promise me that you won't alter Momma's home in any way beyond replacement in Madrid until Carlos leaves Slapton for the last time. It would break his heart to find everything changed when he went home on holiday.'

Charlotte put her hand on his and said, 'I promise, Miguel. I certainly promise, and thank you.'

11

At Moscow Airport the VIPs were met by the usual fleet of large black limousines. As Xavier reached the foot of the mobile stairs that were placed against the aircraft, two uniformed officers greeted him with salutes. It was immediately obvious to Xavier that both officers spoke Spanish, and one of the officers Xavier recognized as a former military attaché from Madrid.

Xavier was escorted to the second in a short line of three ministerial cars. As he approached, Vladimir Renov clambered out of the rear door facing him. He greeted Xavier with the familiar 'bear hug' that Russians give. Renov was on top form.

There was more saluting, and soon Xavier found himself being driven to the Kremlin. Six motorcyclists were ahead and two more brought up the rear of the small convoy. Conversation in the car was personal, not political. If what was being said was being taped, it didn't matter so far as Xavier was concerned.

One hour after landing at the airport Xavier was in earnest conversation – in Russian – with President Stolypin, First Vice President Maiski and Renov in his capacity as Second Vice President. Russia's top three men and Xavier were locked in conference.

'We have been following your family's activities closely. Señor Lang,' started Stolypin. 'May we be the first in Russia to congratulate you on your engagement to Miss Johnson and your younger son's victory at Chamonix.'

'Thank you very much, Mr President. It's very good to

142

have your congratulations. If relations between our countries continue to improve, you will be in the European Union in no time. You never know, you just might be made an honorary Admiral in the British Royal Navy, and if you learn to speak Spanish we might find ourselves brother officers in the Spanish Navy.' Xavier could be equally flattering.

'I'm sorry, Señor, but we do have our spies. We think you're a very lucky man finding such a lovely lady as Miss Johnson after the sad loss of your wife.'

It was General Maiski who was speaking. 'Sadly, I have never married myself, and I'm getting a bit too old now, I think. Had I thought to seek a bride in England, I might have been ahead of you in the queue.'

Xavier realized that his family and the relationships within it had been carefully monitored since his last visit, but he could not disagree with what they were saying. He was very much in love with Charlotte, but he could not know whether these three men were serious or whether they were indulging themselves in comedy, the humour of which he could not follow. He had played chess himself, but not to top Russian standards!

Stolypin continued:

'You will recall, Señor Lang, that during your last visit to Moscow when I asked you if it had been within my power to appoint you Tsar of Russia you said something to the effect that you could not contemplate accepting such an appointment until you were remarried?'

'I do remember our discussion, Mr President. It was in the cloakroom of the Palace of the People. I think my exact words were "I could not think of being your Tsar without the support of the woman I love." I seem to feel that I was echoing the words of the late Duke of Windsor when he was giving up the British Throne.'

'You have an excellent memory, Señor. I stand corrected. Yes, I do seem to remember now that you used romantic language. I should think your fiancée would provide all the love you might require. We understand that Miss Johnson has already stolen the heart of your son Carlos. We'll be

143

honest with you, Señor Lang. Russia needs a Tsar. We may not be ready just yet. Your King was "groomed", if that is the right word, by General Franco. We feel that we could groom you, if you were willing, but there would have to be safeguards for ourselves.'

Stolypin was speaking slowly and deliberately as though he had practised his mini-speech, as he almost certainly had.

'We insist on complete secrecy on your part, and we guarantee complete silence here. It wouldn't just be your life on the line, but that of your future wife and children. Nobody, and I mean nobody, would have to know in advance of our plan to install you as Tsar. We appreciate this will impose great mental strain on you not even feeling free to speak to your future bride, still less anyone political in Spain or the West, but we are taking greater risks with our lives. What we would like best is for you to become Tsar Nicholas III in the year 2000. It took the Bolshevists and others many years to get rid of the old Tsarist Regime and establish the old Soviet Union, and it has taken us seventy years to get rid of them, so we are not exactly in a hurry. With you as Tsar and your future wife as Tsarina we could face the next century with confidence. We know you will want time to consider our proposal. Take your time. We have. But not a word to anybody but ourselves. If anything was to come out, we would know it had come from you. We would have to take appropriate action!'

Xavier looked carefully at the three men. 'Gentlemen. Thank you for being so open. You've certainly given me much to think about. I'll have to give your proposal the greatest consideration, and you have my assurance that no mention of anything that has passed between us will go outside this room. I assume that this discussion has been taped. I would appreciate a copy so that I can play it back. Make it a self-destruct version, if you will. I do know something about secrecy, as I think you know. Charlotte and I are planning to marry, but we haven't fixed a date yet. If she is not to know anything from me I shall need cover from you in the form of invitations to her as well as myself, so

144

that she can come to know and love Russia. If that doesn't work out, I fear I wouldn't be able to proceed, but if she really does take a liking to Russia, then . . .'

Back in Madrid, Xavier replayed the tape, which self-destructed. However, he first took the precaution of taking a copy on his stereo track recorder, which he would never part with unless he was to present it to President Stolypin at his Coronation at St Basil's Cathedral!

At Heathrow Airport, Charlotte was waiting for him. There was no fleet of cars with motorcyclists and no saluting. It was very much more agreeable putting his arms around Charlotte and pressing his lips on to hers. Today he held her to himself both tighter and for longer than she could remember. When he did release her, she simply could not prevent herself from saying:

'Xavier, darling. Your trip to Moscow has done you a power of good. You must go more often, but once we are married, you must take me with you. It must be something about the air in Moscow. Please hold me again.'

Xavier needed no further encouragement. He placed his arms around her, drew her towards himself and kissed her again on the lips with passion. 'Our next trip abroad is to Spain, darling, so that you can get the flat as you want it in Madrid.'

'That's very kind of you, Xavier, but I'm not going to change a cushion. I'll tell you all about that over dinner. Come on, we can't just stand here talking. The car's in the car park on one of those "pay and display" tickets.'

Charlotte drove Xavier to her mother's home in New Southgate. Mrs Johnson did like Xavier, but for his religion, and she had insisted on Charlotte bringing him straight to her home for supper and to stay the night – in the spare bedroom, of course.

They sat down. Charlotte thought her mother was not going to offer Xavier and herself a sherry, but at the last moment she did offer them a drink. Xavier reflected to himself that it was the type of sherry that might have been used to make sherry trifle, but as he sipped it he naturally

145

said it tasted very good and much nicer than the wine he had drunk in Moscow, but here he was telling a white lie.

'You were saying at the airport, Xavier, that our next trip abroad together must be to Madrid to get the flat changed. I think I said I wasn't going to change a cushion. I'll tell you why. When I was at Slapton to watch Miguel play cricket he took me to the "White Hart". He told me why the boys called him "Stumps" or "Stumpy". As you know, I've always tried hard to get to know Miguel. I really do feel that this weekend has been a turning point. I really think he likes me as much as I try to be fond of him. He made me promise not to alter your flat in Madrid until Carlos leaves Slapton. It seems that the flat in Madrid is much more than a flat to Carlos. He still feels very close to Sophia when he's in Madrid. I could never face Miguel if I was to go in and change things. It would completely destroy his confidence in me. You'll never have the experience, darling, but take it from me it hasn't always been easy trying to be the perfect stepmother. You want to think sometimes how you might have had difficulties if our ages had been reversed and that you had two prospective stepdaughters.'

'You've been marvellous, dear, and I do appreciate it. I know you have found Miguel much more difficult than Carlos, but that relates to that "Stumpy" business. I think he may have been a bit nervous, with you being in the police. What exactly did he say to you?'

Charlotte looked at him, flicking her eyes in her mother's direction before proceeding.

'He told me that he had given a bigger boy than himself a good thrashing for bullying Carlos.' She thought that explanation was sufficient for the dinner table in her mother's presence, and Xavier had the wit not to take matters further.

Later he was to be told exactly what Miguel had said, and he told Charlotte that Miguel had indeed given the older boy a very good thrashing.

'Thank God they found out he had been sealing from the little boys. If they hadn't, Miguel might well have found

146

himself charged with what you call GBH. Luckily Father Turner and some other boys arrived on the scene whilst he was going for him with that cricket stump. It could all have been very nasty. Miguel is so protective towards Carlos. He might just have killed that bastard bully. But he wasn't a bastard, that was the point. One day, unless the law is changed, he'll inherit a title and sit in the House of Lords. Everyone concerned was anxious to hush matters up. I think that Miguel will be relieved that he's got that off his chest, and you're quite right, we won't change anything in Madrid. You know both Miguel and Carlos are pure Spanish, allowing for any Russian they may have from me. Carlos nearly worships you, dear. I know from what he has said to me that he would cheerfully kill anyone who tried to lay a finger on you. If he'd been in that room when you were attacked in Chamonix with Sylvia, he would certainly have killed that man who brought you to the floor. I gather that it was you who persuaded Carlos to join the College Judo and Karate Club. I don't know what grades he's at, but Father Turner told me that boys in the club two years older than he are very reluctant to have a go on the mat with him. I don't know what it is, but he tells me that he skis for his Momma and he wrestles for you. He may win a Gold for Spain yet. You really are an inspiration to that boy. Sophia would be so grateful to you. I'm sorry you never met her.'

Charlotte smiled. 'He's so grown-up, Xavier. I just can't believe Carlos is the little boy I first came to know when I went on duty to Slapton with Sylvia. I always used to think he was young for his age. Now you would think he was eighteen at times. He's fifteen in a fortnight. In two years he will be a man in Spanish law, he tells me.'

'Yes, you're right and he comes into a great deal of money when he does attain the age of sixteen on Sophia's side. Fortunately, he has very good trustees – so there's no question of his blowing it. He's a very generous boy, but I think he's inherited a good deal of sense.'

'Xavier, I'm sorry not to be able to chat on about your boys and ourselves tonight, but I do have to be up at six

147

tomorrow morning. I have to go up to Durham and New-castle, as you know, so I will have to turn in. Oh, I do hope we can share the same bedroom soon. Mother would have a "canary" if she was to find us together. Please say "Good-night" to me properly before we go upstairs. Give me a Russian kiss, like you did at the airport.'

They both rose from their separate chairs. Xavier held her as tightly as he had at Heathrow and kissed her on the lips.

'If only she knew,' he thought to himself. 'If only I dare tell her,' he thought, 'but I daren't. She might be killed if it got out.' They both slept well in their separate bedrooms.

12

The journey down to Slapton enabled Charlotte and Xavier to carry on where they had left off discussion on their respective families last night. It was going to be a somewhat complicated – if exciting – relationship.

It wasn't just that Xavier was Spanish, but his interests were Spanish, both at family level, in commerce and in relation to Spanish security and politics at the highest level. Charlotte was going to have to give up her job as a Senior Recruiting Officer at Scotland Yard and make new roots for herself in Spain. Very few women, particularly young women just married, would relish the prospect of living in their husband's first wife's home, however opulent. Charlotte had given her word to Miguel, and she would not go back on it. She had met a number of Xavier's relatives when they had been in London, and she had known Xavier for close on four years in her role as Sylvia's Senior Protection Officer at Harcourt, following Mary's departure to Chicago.

All this said, she still wondered just what the future would hold for her in a country whose language she still spoke imperfectly. Very few of Xavier's family spoke any English at all, and she knew that some members of his family wished that Xavier had either remained unmarried following Sophia's death last year or that he should have married another Spanish lady – a widow, perhaps, who might have known and been a friend of Sophia years ago.

'I know it's not going to be altogether easy, darling, but I know all the family will love you once they get to know you, and I know you will find the boys are going to be very helpful. You will know that I will do everything I can, and you're not going to have to spend too much time in Madrid. You will be much happier near Seville. Incidentally, there are quite a number of English-speaking families in the wine trade there who are very good friends of mine.'

'I'm looking forward to being your "Lady of Spain" once we are married, Xavier. I just can't wait. Did I tell you that Carlos asked me last time I was at the College why I hadn't made you marry me already?'

'No you didn't. He really has taken a shine to you. Your real problems with him, I fear, will be when we are married and you have real authority over him and you have to start denying him. So far it's all been ice creams and supporting his sporting activities. Wait till you have to tell him he can't do this that and the other until he has done his vacation prep, or that he can't go out with any girl he meets in Spain. That will be the testing time.'

'Don't go on, dear. You'll have me thinking that you're jealous of him. Seriously, I will do my best for Carlos, and for Miguel too. I feel much nearer to Miguel since he told me all about that "Stumpy" business. I do try very hard not to show any favouritism. It's just that I seem to have known Carlos since he was a very little boy. He was only ten, remember, when I used to play games with him on the sands. Miguel always seemed so much older, and now – well, he's a young man. He's actually nearer to my age than you are, darling.'

'Yes. He only has one more year at Slapton, and then it's Oxford or Seville. I fancy he will want to go to Seville, and having you around the corner will be a great help to you both and me!'

The conversation drifted on. As they pulled up outside the College entrance they were joined by Father Rector himself, together with Father Turner, the boys' housemaster. Sylvia and her husband Carlos were coming to join them for dinner, with two couples they had not met before. Sylvia knew them well, which was helpful. One couple had been in Chamonix; the other couple had had to pull out at the last minute.

150

Dinner was served in a beautiful small dining room which was normally reserved for members of the Church Order that ran the College. The walls were lined by portraits, in oil, of deceased Rectors, two Cardinals and, surprisingly to Charlotte, a portrait of a former Tsar of Russia, who presumably must have had some connection with the Order in the past. Charlotte knew that the Russians had their own Orthodox Church, but perhaps centuries ago there had been some connection, but history was not her field and she wasn't going to make herself appear ignorant.

Before dinner, whilst they all chatted, the best quality dry sherry was served. It was said that the College had the best wine cellar in the county. Father Turner had been instructed by the Rector to sit next to Charlotte. Grace was said, and they all sat down in the knowledge that they were in for a pleasant evening with a quality fish meal, it being a Friday. There never had been an obligation to eat fish on Friday. It was simply a meatless day, but tradition dies hard, and it had been 'Fish on Friday' for longer than anybody could remember.

It was after the first course, orange and tomato soup, that Father Turner turned to Charlotte.

'Do tell us, Miss Johnson, when are you going to put us all out of our suspense. When are you and Xavier going to get married?'

'That's a very interesting question, Father. The answer depends, I think, largely on you.'

'On me. How's that?'

'Perhaps it's not you. Perhaps it's up to Father Rector. I would be married to Xavier now, given completely my own way and my resignation lodged at Scotland Yard. You know that I've been under instruction to join you. This is something we wanted to discuss with you. We have decided on a fairly small wedding, with Xavier's family being in Spain. What I would like, if it was possible, would be to be married tonight in Our Lady's Chapel here in the College, but I think Xavier is still wanting it in London at Brompton Oratory, where he has been going for years. If you and Father

151

Rector could persuade Xavier to marry me here – I don't mean tonight – I should be very happy, and I know that the boys would be delighted. I take it that a number of old boys do get married at Slapton.'

'They certainly do, Miss Johnson. Please leave this to me. I will speak to Ralph' – that was the Rector's name – 'immediately after dinner. Tell me, if I – I mean we – can persuade Xavier to be married to you here, what date do you have in mind?'

'I would like Friday, the fourth of October, Father. Normally I imagine most people would opt for a Saturday wedding, but a little bird tells me that Miguel is to be Captain of Rugger in the Michaelmas term, and I just couldn't be the cause of preventing him playing on the Saturday. I can't think of a poorer way of starting our marriage. I've really come to know Miguel, and I like to think I have his confidence. I'm certainly not going to do anything to shatter it.'

'You are a very wise woman, Miss Johnson. I can see why you have become an Inspector at Scotland Yard and why Sylvia Sabita is so fond of you. Yes, the fourth of October. Let's try and work together. I'll organize the College choir. Have you thought about the reception afterwards?'

'Yes I have, Father, but don't tell Xavier. He doesn't know what enquiries I have made, but the White Hart have offered to cater, and they have provisionally reserved me their best room. It all depends on you now. Isn't it exciting? This salmon looks delicious. The Sixth-form Prefects make excellent waiters, don't they? I suppose this is how Xavier's boys know how to order and look after guests?'

'We like to give an all-round education here at Slapton, Miss Johnson. May I call you Charlotte now? I always call Sylvia Sabita, Sylvia.'

'Yes, you may. I should like that. Xavier's boys both call me Charlotte. They never call me Miss Johnson, and I have told them to continue to call me Charlotte. I have made it quite clear to them both that I will never seek to take their mother's place, but I have to say that I regard little Carlos as near as being my own child as he can be, I still tend to call him little Carlos, but he's taller than me. He's certainly not the little boy I used to play with when I first came to Slapton as a young WPC.'

'You couldn't be more right there, Charlotte. That boy seems to defy nature sometimes. We used to think of him as being undersized when he first came to us, although we were told by someone that he was a big baby at birth. Now he is much the biggest boy in his class, and I fancy he may yet finish up taller and bigger than Miguel. Second and third children do often outgrow their elder brothers and sisters, I believe. There is one thing I would like your help with, Charlotte, if you don't mind my saying it.'

'What's that, Father? How can I help you?'

'It's this, Charlotte. I hardly know how to put it. That boy worships you. I don't mean in a religious sense, you understand, but you are a heroine figure to him. I don't know when it started, I suspect it started when you first knew him when he was a very little boy, and effectively he had no mother to whom he could relate, and no sisters either. He has built up an illusion of his mother, who he always sees through rose-coloured glasses. No doubt she was very fond of him and good with him when he was a baby, but you know she was desperately ill for years. It was during that time you came into his life, and now you have not simply taken her place in his affections, but he feels he has to prove himself worthy of you in almost a fanatical way, which I find difficult to understand. Perhaps it's the Spanish in him, but when I tell you that there isn't one boy in the College, including the Sixth Form, who would willingly wrestle with him on the gym mat, you will get some idea. If you could try and calm him down a little when you do marry Xavier, I think we should all feel a little safer. He simply says that he skis for his Momma and that he wrestles for you. I'm certain of one thing. He will certainly compete for Spain one day. Naturally, we'll continue to give him all the help we can at Slapton. We do have two very good men who come down from Southampton, but I'll tell you something – you mustn't tell him – I wouldn't dare take him on the gym mat

153

myself, and I did unarmed combat when I was in the Army before I joined the Church.'

'Thank you very much, Father. Trust me, I will speak to Carlos. I'm going to spend a holiday with the boys in Spain during the forthcoming holidays. They want me to meet all their family. I shall have to be on my best behaviour and try and improve on my Spanish. I sometimes wish that Napoleon had made them all speak French. I read French at Warwick. Come on, Father, we are letting this lovely salmon go cold.'

They smiled at each other. Both felt the evening was going very well and as they both wanted it. Xavier and his friend Carlos were at the far end of the table, thoroughly enjoying themselves. They were speaking in Spanish from time to time, and occasionally Father Rector joined in – he spoke Spanish fluently.

At the conclusion of the dinner Father Rector returned thanks and they all moved to his distinguished drawing room, where a bar had been set up offering a range of ports and cognacs. Old boys of the College who had come from Spain and Portugal seemed to send endless bottles. Father Turner went straight to his friend Ralph, the Rector, and it wasn't long before the Rector came over to join Xavier and Charlotte, who were chatting to Sylvia and Carlos by the empty fireplace, its marble glinting in the setting sun.

'Father Turner tells me, Xavier, that you want to be married here on Friday the fourth of October. What capital news.'

Xavier looked at Charlotte. 'What have you been saying, darling? We haven't discussed this together.'

'No we haven't darling,' replied Charlotte, 'but it's what I would like, if Father Rector could organize it. I wish he could arrange it tonight!'

Sylvia was almost as excited as Charlotte. 'Let me see my diary. What did you say? Friday the fourth of October? Yes. That's the week before the Conference at Bournemouth or wherever. That's no problem. I can go down to Lanchester the following day and do another surgery for them. What a wonderful evening we are having.'

'Hold on everyone,' started Xavier, feeling himself out-

154

flanked by these two women friends, obviously in league together. 'There will be arrangements to make, and we haven't even started.'

This was when Father Turner joined in. He had come over, hearing their conversation. 'Oh, I don't think there will be any problem, Xavier. Jefferson at the White Hart is an OS like you. All the best Slapton do's seem to be at the White Hart that aren't held here at the College. I'm sure he would be delighted.'

'How many guests were you thinking of having?'

'I hadn't got round to thinking about the number of guests yet. It won't be a large wedding. All my family, apart from the boys, are in Spain. I had been thinking of our getting married in London, but Charlotte seems to have jumped the gun.'

'Don't say that, darling. I think Father Rector's idea is absolutely wonderful. The boys will be very pleased. It was me that suggested a Friday wedding, so that Miguel could lead the team, which I believe he is going to Captain next term, the following day. He will play at his best with cava or Champagne in his bloodstream.'

Everybody laughed, and Xavier knew he was beaten and that Charlotte was going to be his wife on 4 October. The arrangements would be made with professional care. 'Thank you, darling. I hoped you'd agree. I'll work with Father Turner on the arrangements, but please, Xavier, grant me one more favour.'

'I will if I can. What is it you want?'

'Please let me tell Miguel and Carlos. You told them of our engagement. I want to see their faces and hopefully hold them both when I tell them.'

'All right, Charlotte. You win. You go and tell them, now if you wish, and bring them back here to have drinks with us. I'm sure Father Rector will agree.'

Xavier looked directly at the Rector, who nodded with a smile that was a scarcely concealed grin.

'Where will they be now, Father?' Charlotte was addressing Father Turner.

'I don't know, Charlotte, but let's go to the library and then to the seniors' billiard room to start with. We have tongues in our heads and we won't be long finding them, but they are not likely to be together.'

Charlotte and Father Turner were off. Within minutes they found Carlos, who had been scheduled to speak in the College Debating Club. As they entered the room quietly, one of the boys was speaking on that old chestnut, 'A woman's place is at home'.

Carlos saw them come in together. Within seconds he was with them. 'Come on outside, Lang. Miss Johnson wants to tell you something.'

Carlos could see that Charlotte was radiant. He took her hand and led her out of the room. Father Turner did the decent thing and lingered in the room where the debate was taking place, as though he was just looking in a supervisory manner.

'Carlos, darling, I have the best of news, and you are the first to know. Dad has agreed to marry me here at the College on Friday the fourth of October.'

She got no further. Carlos threw his arms around her and hugged her with the strength of a man. How he had grown!

'Thank God,' he said at last, and went on, 'Thank you, Charlotte, for telling me first. Let's go and tell Miguel. He'll be in the Sixth-form bar right now. I know he'll be very pleased, but no-one is more pleased than me, except you and Dad. I can't wait till the fourth of October, but why a Friday? Never mind, you can tell me later. Just let me hold you again. Tell me again. I can't believe it. I thought you were never going to get Dad to marry you.'

He threw his arms round her again, kissing her on both cheeks with a boyish passion that he had last displayed at Chamonix. Upstairs in the Sixth-form bar, ten senior boys were drinking. This arrangement had been permitted by the Rector in collaboration with the local constabulary, which was more than happy to know that these boys, some of whom were already over 18, could be under close supervision and yet feeling their way without the possible conflict of 'town and gown'.

The arrival of Father Turner, Charlotte and Carlos brought immediate silence to the room, and the boys who had not been standing, stood up.

'To what do we owe this pleasure?' started Miguel as he advanced to Charlotte, kissing her lightly on the cheek.

'Charlotte and Dad are getting married here at Slapton on the fourth of October!' Carlos couldn't contain himself.

'What here, in this bar, you mean?' This was Miguel at his funniest. 'Drinks all round, Barman!'

Miguel held Charlotte and kissed her again, on both cheeks this time. 'Come on, Father, you can perform the ceremony right now! Where's Dad?'

'He's with the Rector and all our other guests – where we should be. They will be sending out a search party for us shortly. It's just that Charlotte wanted you both to know before any official announcement was made, and also by fixing the wedding on the fourth, you, Miguel, will be able to lead the First Fifteen on the Saturday. They won't be on the touchline. They will be on their honeymoon.'

'Thanks, Charlotte. That's very decent of you. It'll be my first match as College Captain. I hope I can concentrate on the game and not be thinking of you and Dad flying off somewhere nice and warm.'

The 'barman', who was himself a sixth-former who played full back in the team, lined up ten half-pints of beer. 'And what can I pour for you, Mrs Lang – if I may call you that already?'

'You may, but you shouldn't really. Have you a white wine or something?'

'Yes, we have.' He poured out three glasses without asking further questions, passing one to Father Turner and one to Carlos.

'To Señor and the future Señora Lang,' toasted the barman. They all drank to that happily. Father Turner said something to the effect that he thought they all ought to get back to the Rector and his guests, where Miguel and

Carlos joined Charlotte and Father Turner for more drinks. It was a good job nobody was driving anywhere.

Whenever the Rector gave one of his dinners, guests were offered accommodation within the College, unless they had already made other arrangements, which often included the White Hart. Father Rector was to announce, after he had left the room to use the telephone in his office next door, that he had spoken to Jefferson, who would be very honoured to provide the wedding breakfast on 4 October, and by lucky chance he had the perfect room for up to 40 guests. The Rector naturally said nothing about Father Turner having told him of Charlotte's provisional booking, which he had now confirmed.

Before leaving Slapton the following morning, Charlotte made a point of taking Carlos on one side. 'Carlos, I'm so proud of you. I always want you to be my best friend. Now there is a favour I must ask of you, which I know you won't understand just now, but I'll tell you all about it when we are on holiday with Miguel in Spain, when we are on our own.'

'Whatever is it, Charlotte? You know you only have to ask me.'

'Yes I know, dear, but it's a lot I'm asking. Please, Carlos, just keep the judo trophy you've won. Don't wrestle any more this term. Please. Trust me, and I'll explain later.'

She put her arms around his young manly frame and held him tight. 'Certainly, Charlotte, if that's what you want. I don't understand. I won that trophy for you just like I won that Gold Medal for Momma, but give me your reasons in Spain.'

'Thank you, darling. I know you will wrestle again for Spain perhaps, but not again this term, please. You are my darling boy.' She held him close.

Before finally leaving she spoke again to Father Turner on her own, ostensibly to discuss preliminary arrangements for the wedding, but her real purpose was something quite different. 'You remember that little chat we had last night about Carlos and his judo?'

158

'Yes, of course, what about it?'

'I have spoken to him, Father, and he won't be wrestling any more this term. I haven't mentioned you by name, but I've asked him not to wrestle with anyone else this term, and he has given me his word. I will have a good talk with him during the holidays, the "vac" as you call it. I don't say he will never wrestle again, but if he does it will be for Spain and a Gold. I'll tell you something, Father. I used to be Sylvia Sabita's protection officer. I had to have a black belt in judo and karate, but I'll bet only a handful in Europe could take him on in five years' time. I'm so very sorry that I never knew his mother. She must have been a lovely woman. If there really is a heaven, Father, and you should know better than me, I hope I may meet her one day so that I can thank her for giving me Carlos and Miguel.'

Xavier drove Charlotte and himself away down the long drive around the lake, with its small island dominated by the statue. Father Turner reflected that Carlos and Miguel were indeed very lucky boys and that Xavier was a very lucky man. He would look forward to this wedding.

159

13

As they drove back to London, Charlotte and Xavier never stopped talking. Charlotte seemed unstoppable, but it was Xavier who started it.

'You were very persuasive indeed last night, darling. Forcing me into agreeing the wedding to be on the fourth of October, but I'm glad you did. I won't ask you now how you did it with Father Turner and Sylvia. You can tell me later. Did your mother know before me?'

'No, she didn't. She still doesn't. I'll let you tell her. It will be like asking her permission in the old traditional way. I think she will appreciate it.'

'I hope she does, Charlotte. It would be a bit awkward if she said No, wouldn't it?'

'She will. Come on, Xavier. It's not like you to be timid. Use your charm, as you have with me. She'll agree and enjoy every minute of it. She's really looking forward to her last holiday with her only unmarried daughter in Spain with your two boys. I wish you could be with us. Two single ladies with two young Spanish gents.'

They both laughed. 'It would make a good press headline,' mumbled Xavier, as he was obliged to swerve slightly to avoid a fool of a driver coming in the opposite direction on the wrong side of the road. 'I suppose you have the wedding list prepared already as well, darling?'

'No, I haven't. I'll want your help with that. As I've told you, I'm not going to alter a cushion in Sophia's flat in Madrid, but I have prepared a list of wedding guests, subject to your approval. You must understand, Xavier, I've been dreaming about this since you asked me to marry you, and what I'm doing really is saving Mother from worrying about all the details. Technically all the invited guests will be her guests, invited by her, but she will need my help, and yours, darling, when you have her permission!'

'All right. Let's assume she gives permission. Who have you got on your list?' Charlotte rummaged in her handbag, pressing the glove-box button to form a mini-desk.

'Here we are. On my side Mum, my sister and brother-in-law, my two Bridesmaids, Mary and Susan and their husbands, that is if Mary can come with Elmer, and Florence and John from Lanchester. I must have them and of course Sylvia and Carlos, but perhaps they are really on your side. Then for you, I have the boys Miguel and Carlos, Father Rector and Father Turner, the Spanish Ambassador and his wife, and that's as far as I've gone so far.'

'That's a very good start, dear. What's that, seventeen or eighteen, but there will need to be a few more. You will have to have Father Pearson who gave you instructions. I fancy he will want to come across and co-celebrate at the nuptial Mass. If we finish up at about thirty, that should be about right. I think one or two of my cousins will want to fly over. I don't know where they will all stay, but that's up to them.'

'Yes, it is, darling, but I do intend running up Mum's telephone account a bit letting her guests know the date so that they can be making their arrangements. I wouldn't be surprised if the White Hart isn't fully booked for that week-end, and a few of the other hotels in Slapton.'

'I'm sure, from what you are saying, that everything will be well taken care of. Just let me know what you want me to do, apart from marrying you and "being at the Church on time".'

Xavier hummed these last words from *My Fair Lady*.

'Yes, darling. You can leave most of it to Mum and me, but you will have to speak. I assume you will want Sylvia's Carlos to be your Best Man – he had you for his wedding – I have wondered who would propose "the Bride and

161

Groom''. I did think Sir John Bickerstaffe would be very good, if he felt strong enough.'

'Yes. He would be very good indeed. How is he now? I know you keep in touch with Florence.'

'They're both keeping very well. Florence is ageing. She has to do quite a lot for him, but she's very wiry. She has years in her yet and so has he, if he takes care, and I don't think Florence lets him out of her sights for too long. Who knows, one day I may have to keep you on a short rein.' Charlotte said this with a laugh in her voice, but secretly she could not entirely ignore the fact that Xavier was eighteen years older than herself, and she might be a widow herself one day like her own mother – and her mother had mentioned this, not once, but on many occasions.

Before they arrived back at Palmers Road, New Southgate, they had covered much of the ground in relation to the wedding arrangements, but no doubt they would be going over them again. Naturally Charlotte said nothing about her wedding dress. She had sufficient of the young bride in her to want her dress to be a complete surprise. Xavier knew it was to be a 'white wedding', of course, but whether white meant white, ivory or cream was entirely down to Charlotte and her mother. All that he needed to know was that the principals on the male side would be in morning suits – their own, hired or borrowed. He would ask Miguel and Carlos to make their own arrangements. Miguel at 17 would have been very put out if he had suggested anything else.

Home at last, Charlotte let herself and Xavier in with her own front door key. Her mother was out shopping, but she soon returned. Xavier decided to waste no time in 'seeking permission'. Charlotte discreetly went up to her bedroom, ostensibly to unpack her things.

'I'm glad to have you on your own, Mrs Johnson,' he started. 'You may or may not believe it, but only last night Charlotte and I decided to have our wedding at Slapton. We would both like you to organize it and know that we had your blessing.'

Charlotte's mother had half-expected this. She had not

been happy about it. Even now she was not really happy, but she put her small arms around Xavier and shed a few tears saying, 'Thank you, Xavier, for asking. Yes, I would like that. Bless you.'

Xavier for his part kissed her on both cheeks. 'Thank God she has taken it so well,' he thought to himself. 'Come along Mrs Johnson, put your handkerchief away. Charlotte seems to have worked a lot out already. She says she's done it to save you, but I want you to be the organizer. Charlotte tells me that you are very good at making all manner of arrangements with the Mother's Union, particularly with altar flowers and things. I'm sure you'll find Father Turner, the boys' housemaster, a very willing assistant.'

Xavier could flatter as well as the next man and better. He planted the idea of Mrs Johnson arranging matters, from the altar flowers, with all the consummate skill of Spain's leading honorary diplomat. Few in the Quai d'Orsay in Paris, and no-one in the British Foreign Office, could beat him in diplomacy. Spain needed the very ablest diplomats if they were to equal the European nations possessed of larger Gross National Production.

By the time Charlotte had returned downstairs she found her mother almost as excited as herself at the prospect of making her wedding day a success. Out of Mrs Johnson's gaze, Xavier smiled at Charlotte and nodded. 'There are a few telephone calls I must make, Mum. I'll find out how much they cost, and I'll let you have a cheque.'

'Don't be silly, girl. You make as many calls as you like. I know you'll want to ring Mary, Susan and Florence. If the bill is too big for me, I'll let Xavier have it.'

She smiled with genuine affection now at Xavier, who returned the compliment. Charlotte checked her watch and did a little arithmetic. What time would it be in Chicago? 'What the hell' she thought. She checked her diary in her handbag and dialled.

A voice she didn't recognize, clearly an American male accent, came on the phone: 'The Orlanski residence, Joseph speaking. May I help?'

163

Two minutes later Mary came on the other end. 'Say, what sort of time do you call this?' started Mary. 'Is there something I've missed on television? Has war broken out? What don't I know?'

'You don't know the time and date of my wedding, Mary. That's what. Xavier and I are getting married at Slapton College on Friday, the fourth of October, and you are to be the Chief Bridesmaid, Matron of Honour, or whatever you call it in America. Do say you'll come and bring Elmer with you.'

'Of course I'll come, and thank you. I've been waiting for this call for yonks. Do give Xavier our love and tell him it's not before time. You must let us have a list of presents . . .'

The conversation lasted 20 minutes. Fifteen minutes later Charlotte had made several more calls. The most important of these was to Florence Bickerstaffe.

'Florence, I just had to phone you to let you know that Xavier and I are getting married at Slapton on Friday, the fourth of October. Naturally we wanted you to be amongst the first to hear, but there is another reason. We would both very much like John to propose our health, if you felt he was up to it. I don't mean his ability to propose the toast. I mean, we wouldn't want to impose if you felt he would not feel strong enough.'

'Oh, Charlotte. He'll be delighted you've asked him. He's out of the cottage at the moment, but I'll get him to ring you when he comes in. Now do tell me all about it. We haven't been to a wedding since Susan's last year. To think, all Sylvia's WPCs happily married. You made a perfect trio for her. Have you told Mary yet?'

'Yes I have, Florence. I had to phone her first. She and Susan will be my bridesmaids – well, Matrons of Honour. That's the penalty of being the last one. Look. Xavier is with me as I'm speaking. Let me put you on . . .'

It was at the end of this conversation that Xavier made a suggestion which, understandably, gave great surprise. Would it be their first real argument?

'Charlotte, there are two people I haven't mentioned

before for the guest list, but I'd like to have them invited.'

'Certainly, darling. Who are they?'

'They're Russians. One you have met already, the other you haven't. It's Vladimir Renov and his wife Myra. They really are a very nice couple.'

'Vladimir Renov? You can't be serious, Xavier. Why on earth should we invite him?'

'Because he has proved a very good friend to me and to Spain. He's become very friendly with Elmer, and the Chicago Temperance Bank has opened a branch in Moscow with Renov on the Board!'

'Well,' she paused a moment, 'I suppose that does make a difference. So that's what you've been getting up to in Moscow? You really should have told me. I might very easily have put my foot in it with Mary and Elmer. Now don't you keep any further secrets from me. I'll have to get clearance from Sylvia on the political side, but subject to that, I will ask Mum to put them on the list, but you'll have to post the invitation. You seem able to do that best through your embassy. What did you say his wife was called, Myra?'

'Yes, Myra. You'll like her. She has just had a little boy. She was a lead ballerina in the Bolshoi some years ago. Of course, they may not be able to come, but I'm sure they would both appreciate the invitation.'

Charlotte called Harcourt. She was put straight through by Susan on the private confidential line. 'Sylvia. You will think this the most unusual call, but Xavier and I are already preparing the wedding invitation list, and Xavier wants Mum to invite Vladimir Renov and his wife Myra to Slapton. I have told him that I would have to get clearance from you in view of everything. It seems he has struck up a close relationship with Elmer through Viktor Maiski, and the Chicago Bank now has a branch in Moscow. Please let me know if they can be invited, and we can discuss details next time we see each other. Wasn't it a good do at Slapton?'

The conversation lasted 15 minutes, at the end of which the names of Vladimir and Myra Renov were added to the list. It was becoming impressive – the Deputy Prime Minister

165

of Great Britain, the Second Vice President of Russia, and His Excellency the Spanish Ambassador. A fax was sent from the Spanish Foreign Office in Madrid to the Russian Embassy in code:

'To Major-General Vladimir Renov,
    The Kremlin,
        Moscow.
Keep 4 October clear. Wedding at Slapton. Invitation to you and Myra to attend en route.
    Xavier Lang'

Xavier reported his forthcoming wedding to the King of Spain personally and Spanish Security. The Spanish Ambassador to the Court of St James, London, was alerted to attend. Xavier had already alerted him and his wife that they might expect to receive an invitation from Charlotte's mother. Xavier and Philip, the Ambassador, were personal friends.

Charlotte spent one or two restless nights. She was as much in love with Xavier as any prospective bride had ever been, and she really was looking forward to her wedding. Was it pre-marital nerves that affect any number of women, or was it something else? She decided that she simply could not confide in her mother and sister. They had both proved to be very understanding about her 'turning' for Xavier, but he was the cause of her anxieties.

At times he seemed secretive, and she knew he moved in the very highest levels of diplomacy, where there was always an element of danger, whatever precautions might be taken by national security services – and where were her most fundamental loyalties to lie once she was married to Xavier? Technically she would have joint British/Spanish nationality. Although she had signed the Official Secrets Act when she had first been attached to Sylvia by Scotland Yard, she would shortly be obliged to resign her commission with the Metropolitan Police.

She would be a nobody in Britain any longer, beyond being a private citizen abroad, whereas in Spain she would be the wife of one of that country's most important figures, albeit one who worked largely undercover under the highest patronage in the land. It was these thoughts, and nothing to do with the physical aspects of marriage, that were causing her to lose sleep. She must speak to Sylvia, and urgently. She would call Sylvia from Scotland Yard today. Was she just being stupid, or was there a real cause for concern? She must know or she would go mad.

After writing up her weekly report on her latest university visits, which wasn't that difficult since she made daily reports for this purpose, she ceased her dictation and dialled Sylvia's personal Ministerial office. She didn't need to consult her diary. Sylvia's office number would be ingrained on her mind for ever. Susan took the call and put Sylvia on.

Half an hour later Charlotte, wearing her smart uniform, was standing in Sylvia's office saluting. Susan, who at Sylvia's request was wearing her grey two-piece, withdrew, closing the beautiful mahogany door behind her.

'Sylvia, I just had to come and see you. I've not slept the last two nights. You know I'm madly in love with Xavier, but I've been thinking about my position. Supposing Britain and Spain were to be – I won't say at war, but on opposite sides in relation to, say, Gibraltar or any other serious matter? As I sit with you now, wearing this uniform and being close friends, there is nothing to discuss, but as from the fourth of October I would be on the other side, if you know what I mean. Suppose Xavier had been Argentine?'

'I had wondered, Charlotte, just how long it might be before we had this conversation. You do put me in a most difficult position in terms of giving you advice. I know you are as patriotic as anyone, but I honestly feel that in the final analysis you will have to act according to your conscience, and I think that if you wish your marriage to succeed completely you will have to put Spain first. I have given this matter some thought for you. Let me put it this way. No-one, but no-one, could have been a more loyal servant of the

British Crown and the British Empire than Queen Victoria – yet her eldest daughter was to become the mother of the last German Kaiser. You're not in the royal league, but my advice as a barrister, never mind my present rank as Deputy Prime Minister, is that you may safely become Spanish and owe your first duty to Spain, but like the poet wrote, you'll always be a "Daughter of the Sceptered Isle".'

'Thanks, Sylvia. I prayed last night that you might say something on those lines, but I didn't think you would be speaking to me in regal terms. I'll sleep much better tonight. By the way, Xavier thinks we will all be members of the United States of Europe one day, but certainly not before the fourth of October. I know that Mum is already looking at wedding patterns. Mary and Susan have given me their measurements. Susan, of course, can have her fittings here in London, but Mary will only have the night before to try hers on unless she comes across a few days before. Fortunately, Mary can use a needle and thread herself for any very minor adjustment. She wasn't Maltese for nothing. Did I tell you that your former right-hand man, Sir John, has agreed to propose "the Bride and Bridegroom"?'

'No you didn't, Charlotte, but you couldn't have a better man. You know it seems strange his not being here. His successor is very good, but I still miss Sir John. He never flapped. Of course, he was so experienced and nearly old enough to have been my father. Florence has made him a wonderful wife. He's looking so well. Now I must stop chattering. I have to go down to the House at 12.30 to sort out one or two of our boys. But do tell me, how are those two delightful boys of yours at Slapton? They seemed so grown up at the weekend. I don't know how much Carlos eats, but he seems so much bigger now than my John, and yet they are the same age, within a few weeks.'

'I know, Sylvia. Xavier always says that Carlos is cheaper to keep for a week than a fortnight. Sometimes I could feel he was seventeen and not fifteen. Already he is taller than me – and much bigger! Can I tell you something in complete confidence?'

168

'Yes, of course, you can. We are not on tape. Do tell.'

'The night before last, I had a real nightmare. I dreamt that Xavier and I had split up and the question of custody of Carlos was coming before the Court. You were representing me, and we won.'

'And you would too, if it came to it. Thanks for telling. I'm glad to think that even in your dreams you thought to retain me as advocate. It seems absolutely ages since I appeared in Court.'

14

The day that College at Slapton ended for the summer holidays was organized pandemonium. Hundreds of boys' trunks and parents' cars, not to mention the hundreds of boys and parents themselves.

The Langs and the Sabitas couldn't be away first. The two older boys of both families had their responsibilities within their Houses, and it wasn't until the middle of the afternoon that they got away. Sylvia had arranged that the four boys and their trunks could be taken to Harcourt and the following morning Charlotte and her mother would fly with Xavier's two boys from London to Madrid.

Xavier had arranged and paid for the tickets. He would join them in three days' time and then drive them to Seville. The flat in Madrid had been fully aired and prepared in anticipation of the invasion from London, and Charlotte's mother was excited and curious to see Xavier's Madrid home that was so soon to be her daughter's home. She thought that Charlotte had been very brave to accept Xavier's flat exactly as Sophia had planned it and known it.

The only possible advantage that she could see was that it would certainly be very fully furnished, to the highest standard, and being very Spanish, Charlotte would think that she had 'arrived' and wouldn't be too homesick looking at furnishings that would remind her of Southgate.

At the airport in Madrid, Miguel took command of the situation with his masterful Spanish. He was very much in charge, and Charlotte tactfully said nothing to diminish his protective manner. It was good to be away from work, looking after her mother and absorbing as she went along. She and her mother only had to carry their hand luggage. Miguel and Carlos wouldn't let them carry anything weighty.

The flat itself, in the centre of Madrid, was large and well appointed, but by most people's standards old-fashioned, with heavy oak furniture dominated by large pictures framed in gold that might more reasonably have been expected to be found in a good art gallery. Xavier had sensibly removed all photographs of Sophia, except those in the boy's bedrooms. Within five minutes of arrival, Miguel took down the photographs of his mother and placed them carefully in his top bedroom drawer, except for two which he liked best, which he kept out on the chest of drawers where he kept his shirts and ties. Carlos left all his mother's photos exactly as he had had them whilst she lived. Charlotte was not going to move anything in his room, but she was pleased to see a photograph of herself taken with Carlos on his bedside table.

'It will be the first picture he sees in the morning and the last one he sees at night,' she reflected to herself. This was exactly Carlos's reasoning when he sited the photograph which now stood in a rather old-fashioned solid silver frame. She would never enquire as to what had happened to the photograph it had replaced.

The four of them went out for dinner on the first night to a restaurant where Xavier was well known. He had arranged the dinner before leaving for London on his last visit. Charlotte's mother was surprised how late it was before they went out, but she entirely accepted that one dined late in Madrid. The meal was excellent and washed down with Reserve Rioja.

Mrs Johnson reflected to herself that she might just have been taken as the mother of one daughter and two sons, the boys seemed so grown-up. She would have needed to be an old mother for Carlos, perhaps, but they seemed far too old to be step-grandchildren. She was going to enjoy this holiday and really get to know these two young men.

171

She hadn't had a constant male escort since her husband had died, and Miguel was so attentive in such an old-fashioned way. She was very alive to the fact that Miguel could quite easily be taken for her daughter's husband, but sensibly she said nothing aloud and kept her thoughts to herself. As for Carlos, she thought he was something dreams were made of. She just couldn't believe he was only 15. How had we managed to defeat the Armada?

The following morning Miguel was up first, and he took morning tea to Charlotte and her mother, who were sharing Xavier's twin-bedded room, which Xavier had last shared with Sophia before she had been taken into hospital six years before. Perhaps it was foolish, but he had never changed the room. It was convenient now for Charlotte and her mother, but she would certainly install a double bed at the earliest opportunity. She wasn't going to start her married life with single beds!

Nor would she wish to sleep in Sophia's bed, however nice a lady and however good a wife and mother she had been. She sensibly didn't even ask which was Xavier's bed and which had been Sophia's.

Breakfast was continental. Charlotte knew that it wouldn't be the easiest of mornings, and she decided sensibly to wear little or no make-up which might get spoiled if she was to break down at Sophia's grave. She knew that Carlos was likely to break down, but she would help him as much as she could.

She had agreed to go with Carlos, on their own, to Sophia's grave that was like a shrine to him. Naturally, Xavier had had the monument erected and suitably engraved. There was a photograph of Sophia – obviously taken a long time before her death – framed in an oval-shaped glass case set into the marble. Charlotte purchased a small bunch of carnations at the entrance to the cemetery. She was slightly surprised that Carlos didn't, but when they came to the grave she fully understood why.

Carlos explained, 'Charlotte. I wanted Momma to have flowers every day. I bought them last year out of my holiday pocket money.' He held her left hand as a little boy might hold his big sister's before crossing a busy road.

Tears welled up in the boy's eyes as they looked together at the grave. Charlotte kept perfect control of herself. The plastic flowers were there in profusion. They would never die. They were regularly washed and cleaned as part of the cemetery cleaning service that Xavier had arranged on a long-term contract basis. They looked as fresh as the day they had been put in place. Charlotte never did like plastic flowers, but she could not fail to notice that 'those awful plastic creations' were everywhere. Her own carnations, which she simply lay as she had bought them, seemed almost out of place, but Carlos squeezed her hand and said quietly:

'Thank you, Charlotte, very much. I won't ask you to come again unless you want to. I have to come every time I come to Madrid.' He let her hand go before making the sign of the Cross. She followed his example. They stood together for a few moments side by side.

They turned together and walked slowly hand in hand without talking or turning back until they reached the cemetery gates, where Carlos kissed her lightly on the cheek and ordered a taxi. It had been a difficult hour for them both, perhaps particularly for Charlotte. Back at the flat they went to their bedrooms to wash and, in the case of Charlotte, to repair her make-up.

There was no reply at Carlos's door when she knocked. She entered and looked around. Carlos was not there, but there was something different about the room. What was it? Now she saw. She hadn't served in the police for years not to notice a change of scene. All Sophia's photos, save one, had gone. The photograph of Carlos and herself taken at Chamonix was still on his bedside table, but the only remaining picture of Sophia was the large one on the chest of drawers, which was clearly an enlargement of the one on the grave.

She could not help herself. She opened the top drawer of the chest of drawers, and there they were, perhaps 20 photograph framed pictures of Sophia. She closed the drawer. 'That boy. He'll kill me. He's growing up so fast,' she thought.

She returned to her bedroom and repaired the damage.

15

In Moscow Major-General Renov looked at his morning mail. He had, of course, received the fax from Spain, but now he had the formal invitation from Charlotte's mother which read:

'Mrs Alice Johnson requests the pleasure of the company of Major-General and Mrs Vladimir Renov at the marriage of her daughter Charlotte to Señor Xavier Nicholas de Sallas Lang at Slapton College, Hampshire on Friday, 4 October at 11.30 a.m. and afterwards at the White Hart Hotel, Slapton. RSVP.'

The card was very prettily printed on a violet shade of paper containing her address. 'Funny they have missed the year out,' mused Renov, 'but perhaps that's the English way.' Together with the invitation and the printed reply envelope addressed to Mrs Johnson there was Xavier's letter. Both the letter and the invitation had come through the diplomatic bag from London. There was no chance of the invitation going astray.

Renov read Xavier's letter and then, being the man he was, he re-read it to be certain that he hadn't missed anything.

'Dear Renov,

Please find enclosed Charlotte's mother's invitation to you and your wife. I do hope that you can both come over. I am sure you will enjoy it. Naturally there will be no politics, but I think you do know that Dame Sabita, the British Deputy Prime Minister, will be attending,

175

together with her husband Carlos, with whom I was at school at Slapton and who will be acting as my Best Man. I expect you will have the opportunity of talking to each other before or after the day itself whilst you are in London. Whilst I shall respect your wishes, I think you might like to attend as a private citizen rather than have the international press in constant attendance. I look forward to hearing from you if you wish me to make any accommodation arrangements, but I suspect these will be made through your Embassy in London.

Yours sincerely
Xavier Lang'

At the morning meeting with President Stolypin and General Maiski, Renov produced both the invitation and the letter.

'You will, of course, attend, Renov. You certainly have made a good impression, and you'll enjoy yourself into the bargain. I think we've made a very good choice in Xavier Lang. From what you tell us, almost as good a choice as he's made in Miss Charlotte Johnson.'

'Yes, Mr President. We don't know where they are just now, but we do know that Miss Johnson took her mother to Spain. She took Señor Lang's two sons with her, or rather they took her. They stayed in Madrid at his flat, and then I believe they went to Seville.'

'Good man. I'm glad you're keeping your eyes on them. We wouldn't want anything to happen to them, would we? Not after all we are investing in them, and with all the Temperance Bank of Chicago promises to invest with us. I believe we may all make out as good Socialist Capitalists.'

The three men smiled at each other.

'Your wife is going to enjoy her visit, I'm sure. I take it we can leave it to her to buy a suitable wedding gift?' asked Maiski.

'Yes, of course, leave that to me. I would suggest twelve vodka glasses. They are always acceptable, and it will get them into drinking vodka. We may need money from the

Temperance Bank, but there is no reason why Xavier Lang should be a total abstainer.'

They all laughed at Renov's humour. They made the most of this joke. They wouldn't be laughing much more that day. They had serious matters on their minds. At home in the evening, Vladimir Renov drafted his reply to Mrs Johnson. The formal reply provided no problem. That was simply sent in perfect script:

'Major-General and Madam Vladimir Renov have much pleasure in accepting, etc.' The letter that Renov was drafting was in more personal terms:

'Dear Mrs Johnson,

Please find enclosed the formal acceptance of your very kind invitation to your daughter's wedding at Slapton. May I say immediately, on behalf of my wife and myself, that we both hope that your daughter and your future son-in-law have many happy years ahead of them. My particular purpose in writing to you is to ask if you know whether your daughter and future son-in-law have what I believe you call a "wedding gift list"? I imagine they will receive many presents. Unless you know of any specific items they require, my wife and I had thought to give some top-quality Russian cut glass in the shape of vodka glasses, which I understand are not in general usage in England or Spain. I shall be pleased to hear from you at your early convenience and, in case it assists you, I enclose for your reply an envelope addressed to myself c/o our Embassy in London. Your reply sent to the Embassy will be in my hand within forty-eight hours. We look forward to meeting you on the fourth of October at Slapton.

Yours sincerely
Vladimir Renov'

This reply, which was approved by Stolypin and Maiski, was placed in the diplomatic bag for London and reached Charlotte's mother on Saturday morning, within 48 hours of

Renov signing it. Mrs Johnson was impressed by the envelope addressed to her from the Kremlin, which she would always keep with her souvenirs. Although the envelope was marked 'In Confidence', once she had read it twice she passed it to Charlotte, who was as delighted with its contents as her mother.

'How lovely – vodka glasses – Russian style. Xavier did say they were a nice couple. We'll find ourselves toasting their health before long and the health of their little son.'

The replies were starting to come in. Nobody had declined. Although it was not going to be a large wedding, in terms of numbers of guests, all the work involved was the same. Dresses, printing of stationery, arranging the transport and accommodation, flowers, catering, the list seemed endless. Mrs Johnson was enjoying it immensely, and Charlotte's sister joined in.

Xavier felt quite relieved to be out of it all. All conversation in New Southgate seemed to revolve around the wedding. Xavier's thoughts were on other matters, both short- and long-term. He too liked the thought of vodka glasses coming from Vladimir Renov. He knew they would be of top quality. He wondered how they would be cut and whether they would match any of his own cut glass, of which he had a fine collection both in Madrid and Seville.

Mrs Johnson wrote her letter of thanks to Renov. She didn't seek the approval of what she had written, but she did show her letter to Charlotte before posting it in the envelope thoughtfully provided by the Russian guest. The remainder of the holiday in Madrid and Seville had gone extremely well. Perhaps the best day had been the day they stayed overnight at Ronda. They had stayed at the Reina Victoria Hotel, which was Carlos's favourite hotel and where he said he would like to have his eighteenth birthday, if that was possible, when the time came. The hotel with its gardens enjoyed superlative views over the surrounding countryside, but best of all for Carlos, he felt close to his mother. It was whilst they had been staying at the hotel that his mother had ordered his first skis when he was three years old. He had completely forgotten the event in real terms, but he had been told many times that it was where the family had stayed, when they had been specially made for him.

Charlotte and her mother both fell in love with Seville – 'the loveliest capital city in Europe' – as Xavier called it. He should have known. He seemed to have visited them all. One matter did divide Xavier and Charlotte on this holiday. It was the subject of bullfighting.

Xavier regarded bullfights and bullrings with the same enthusiasm as many British regard county cricket matches on attractive cricket grounds. Many maintained that it was the tourist industry that kept bullfighting going. Charlotte was against all blood sports, and bullfighting in particular. Miguel had no strong views on the matter, but he wouldn't see his father going to the famous Ronda bullring – the oldest in Spain – on his own.

Carlos was loyal to his father too, but he decided without any prompting to support Charlotte. 'Dad, I've got an idea. You go with Miguel, and I'll take Charlotte and her mother to see the sights of Ronda. I know all there is to see in Ronda, from the Roman Baths to the Cathedral and the cliff walk. We'll see you back here in the hotel. We'll be down at the swimming pool.'

Both Xavier and Charlotte knew that Carlos was trying very hard in his boyish way to keep the pair of them happy.

'That's a very nice idea, Carlos.' It was Charlotte's mother who spoke up. She too knew in her own mind that the young boy's heart was being torn. The day itself was glorious and hot. Ronda is hot in the summer, but that day it was very hot. Carlos knew his Ronda well. He went there every year. He was almost like a junior guide. He started at the famous bridge that looks down on the gorge below. He took Charlotte and her mother for coffee and sandwiches to San Miguels at the side of and below the bridge, not forgetting to take his camera.

'I did think of ordering a bottle of white wine, but Dad always says that wine makes you thirsty. We'll have plenty of wine tonight with our dinner. When we've had these sandwiches I suggest we go first down to the Roman Baths. It's quite a steep walk down the hill past the Moorish Palace, but we can get some good snapshots there where Placido Domingo sang *Carmen.* I'm glad Dad and Miguel went to the bullring. I like having you all to myself, Charlotte, and you, Mrs Johnson, of course. You'll have plenty of time to have Dad all to yourself when I'm back at Slapton and you and Dad are in Seville with Miguel, but he'll be at the University.'

The boy was trying very hard. Charlotte knew this. She correctly suspected that her mother was quite pleased to have her with her on her own, and as for Carlos, she warmed to him by the minute. She would never introduce him to anybody except as her grandson. She would certainly leave him a small legacy so that he could buy something in her memory, not that he needed any of her money. She had discovered from Charlotte that at 16 he would inherit a small fortune. Both Charlotte and her mother found the Roman Baths somewhat disappointing, but the Cathedral was something different. Anyone hearing Carlos describe how the Cathedral had been added to the original mosque, with all the detail that might have been supplied by a professional guide, might have thought that he had committed the *Guide to Ronda* to memory. He pointed out how the tall wooden screens and altar were in fact wood, but so painted as to appear as marble. He seemed to know it all and yet he didn't seem big-headed, but was full of boyish fun as he tapped at the wooden screen to demonstrate that it wasn't marble. Stepping out of the Cathedral into the bright sunshine outside was like coming out of a matinee performance. The light is always bright in Ronda, but it seemed doubly so, and Charlotte and her mother were glad they had worn their broad-brimmed hats.

Carlos snapped away with his camera, making sure the background was right. This was something he had been taught in the College cine club which Father Turner ran.

'Always make sure you get foreground, middle ground and background if you take shots outside,' he had said.

180

Carlos now interpreted that as being Charlotte and her mother, preferably Charlotte on her own, directly in front of him, with the oranges on their trees as the middle ground and classical buildings – in this case the Cathedral – in the background.

In truth they were not great photographs for exhibition purposes, but attractive holiday snaps, and that was all he required. Mrs Johnson was fascinated at the trouble he seemed to take, and she insisted on taking snaps of Charlotte and Carlos standing or sitting together as they walked back to the hotel along the cliff walk. Once back at the hotel, Mrs Johnson announced that she was tired and would take the opportunity of having a rest. Carlos insisted that Charlotte come down to the swimming pool for a swim. She felt she could do with a short lie-down herself, but she couldn't very well refuse him, particularly when her mother said:

'You must go for a swim, dear. You don't have to stay in long. I suspect you can still swim faster than him. I know you said your feet were a bit sore, but you won't be putting any weight on them in the pool. You simply can't let him down. If we hadn't been here he would have been with his father and brother. You know as well as me that he only took us on that trip to please you.'

Mrs Johnson might have said more, but she had made her point and she felt she just might say something she might regret later. Carlos was down at the pool beyond the statue of the poet long before Charlotte.

'Why does it take so long for a girl to change and get ready?' he thought as he arranged for two deck-chairs, table and shade. The hotel pool was only small. He could dive in at one end and come up at the other without problem, but he would wait until Charlotte came down.

Years ago he would have grabbed at her and pushed her in without thinking, but now he was growing up. Charlotte was a very pleasant looking girl with a trim figure, but to Carlos she was a film star and heroine. Now she was here in her swimsuit beneath a striped bathing gown, carrying a towel, slim handbag and two glossy magazines. Several men sitting in their deck-chairs with their wives looked at Charlotte as she came down the steps, wondering who she was and with whom. They were individually and collectively surprised to see her place her belongings on the table which Carlos had produced, and yet more surprised when she stood at the side of the pool, testing the temperature with her big toe and then with a swift push or throw dropping Carlos into the deep end.

On surfacing, he immediately responded by hurling water at her. She smiled at him broadly, saying, 'You see, I can still throw you in when I want.'

On their own he would have swum to the side, climbed out and attempted to throw her in. She could still play games with him, but he was terrified of hurting her. He contented himself with continuing to splash at her from the safety of the pool, inviting her to come in. With a reasonable show of reluctance, she went in with a perfect dive that brought mini-gasps of admiration from her small audience who sat around the pool. Carlos could not contain himself. He swam over and ducked her head in the water. She responded, rising a little distance from him and then attacking him from below and pulling him below the surface. They both rose, shaking their heads and laughing. Charlotte now swam to the side, climbing out and making her way to the safety of the table and her towel. She only troubled to dry herself briefly and sat down on one of the deck-chairs.

'Come on, Charlotte. You're not coming out already. We've only just got ourselves wet.'

'I know, but you've tired me out with all that sightseeing. You've knocked Mum out completely. She's having a lie-down. You go in again if you want, but what I'd like you to do is go and get us both a drink from the hotel. I'll leave it to you to choose. A Coke would go down well. See. Take my purse – the drinks are on me.'

Carlos went to the hotel bar and returned. 'I've put the change back in your purse, Charlotte. I did think to give my room number, but you did say the drinks were on you.'

They both sipped at their Cokes and watched first an

elderly couple enter the pool and then a middle-aged couple. Carlos looked at Charlotte in a way that seemed to her both curious and protective, but he said nothing beyond commenting that Xavier and Miguel would be returning shortly from the bullring. Quite suddenly Carlos looked at her, asking:

'By the way – when do I start calling your mother "Gran" or something? I can't keep calling her "Mrs Johnson".'

'That's a very good question. Why don't you ask her yourself? I think she would like you to. I think she would like "Gran" better than "Grandmother". Ask her as soon as you like. She may say on our wedding day, but I suspect she would like you to start calling her "Gran" today. It would seem much more natural on our wedding day.'

'I will, Charlotte. I'll ask her before dinner tonight whilst we are having apéritifs.'

At this moment Mrs Johnson came down the steps. 'I don't know. I just couldn't sleep. I think it's this heat. The system is working, but it's so very hot.'

Carlos was standing up now and offering his chair: 'You'd better sit on this towel. I think the chair will be wet with my trunks.' He placed the folded towel where he had been sitting.

'Thank you very much, Carlos. That's very kind of you.'

'You've just come at the right time, Mrs Johnson. Charlotte and I were just talking about you. I was asking Charlotte what you would like me to call you after she and Dad get married. I suggested "Gran". What would you like?'

Mrs Johnson was quite overcome. She might have felt tired, but she didn't show it. She got up from her deck-chair, as quickly as anyone could, and flung her small arms around Carlos. If he hadn't been the strong boy he was, she might easily have pushed him into the pool and followed in herself. As it was she held him tight, tears flowing down her cheeks.

'You lovely boy. Please call me Gran. Don't wait till the wedding. Please call me Gran from now on. Bless you.'

Downstairs in the bar, Mrs Johnson was full of herself with Miguel. She liked her two 'grandchildren'. Carlos had told

Miguel of his discussion with Charlotte's mother at the pool-side, and he was also addressing her as 'Gran' as occasion demanded.

The three of them were sipping Sangria – a good one prepared by the hotel barman – not a proprietary brand. Mrs Johnson made no enquiry of Miguel concerning the bullfight, but told him all she knew about Ronda. Miguel listened dutifully, but he already knew Ronda as well as his younger brother. When Xavier and Charlotte came into the bar, Carlos started:

'What do you think, Dad? You and Charlotte simply have to get married now on the fourth of October. Miguel and I are already calling Charlotte's mother "Gran". So you can stop calling her "Mrs Johnson".'

Charlotte's mother beamed her pleasure. By the time they had ordered dinner the resident pianist was at his appointed place. His tinkling of the ivories formed a very pleasant background to the general chatter in the bar and the dining room.

The dinner itself was excellent. The two boys ate as though they hadn't eaten for a week. Xavier was to remind Charlotte and her mother that the pair of them were cheaper to keep for a week than a fortnight.

'I think I've heard you say that before, darling,' cooed Charlotte.

If Xavier's flat in Madrid could be said to be Victorian, his home in Seville was eighteenth-century. It was a superb mix of all that was best in Spanish domestic architecture, and furnished to the highest taste and, some would say, expense. The property was inhabited all the year round. The resident staff was only small. It consisted of Manuel and Maria, a husband-and-wife team who had been resident on the estate of Sophia's parents. They had been absolutely devoted to Sophia, and she in turn had been devoted to them. They were guaranteed continuing employment at the property under the terms of Sophia's will, and Charlotte was very happy to have them continue.

'I know you must have missed Señora Lang, my fiancée's

184

late wife, but I want you both to know that I want to treat you as friends and not as servants. I'm only sorry I never knew her myself. I do love her boys. I'm sure we are going to be very happy together.'

Charlotte now had sufficient Spanish to say this, and Xavier had already primed Manuel and Maria as to what a lovely person Charlotte was, as had Miguel. Carlos had told them exactly what they might expect, and they were not let down. Maria and Carlos were very close in their own way. Maria had been very sorry to see Carlos sent to school in England. He was always in her way in her kitchen, but she had missed him greatly. Manuel and Maria had been concerned for their future, but now that Charlotte was going to come and live with Xavier following their honeymoon, they were as happy as they had been since Sophia had been at home. Charlotte's mother simply could not believe that her daughter was coming to this property as her home. If only John had lived to see this, she thought.

On the Thursday before they were due to fly home, Xavier took Charlotte and Miguel to the University in Seville. This left Carlos and Charlotte's mother to themselves. Carlos was delighted.

'Come on, Gran. We'll go and have coffee on one of the boulevards. You don't speak any more Spanish than Manuel and Maria speak English, so I can act as guide again and you can pay for the coffee.'

He grinned his boyish grin, but he had other reasons of his own. When Xavier had left with Charlotte and Miguel, Carlos turned to Charlotte's mother eagerly.

'Gran, I'm very glad the three of them are out. I've asked Miguel to keep them at the University as long as possible. His interview is only meant to last twenty minutes, but he'll get Dad to show Charlotte all over the place. That should give us a good hour together shopping. I hate shopping myself, but having you with me will make all the difference. You can probably guess what I have in mind? I want to buy my wedding present for Dad and Charlotte here in Seville. We can leave it safely with Maria. She won't let me down.

She never has, even when she used to tell me off when I was in her way in the kitchen when I was tiny. You can help me make the selection. You will know Charlotte's tastes, and there is another thing. At Slapton I only have my pocket money. Here Uncle Paul at the bank will see to things. He is one of Momma's trustees. He will let me spend what I like within reason – that is his reason, but he's very kind – "Almost as kind as he's careful," Momma used to say, I believe, but Dad says he's more careful.'

Mrs Johnson was quite taken aback, but equally delighted at what she had just heard. She liked Carlos immensely, but this was a side to his character she could not have reasonably begun to understand. She was touched by his reference to 'pocket money' and his generous thoughts both to her daughter and herself, but his reference to his Uncle Paul as his Momma's trustee!

'What next?' She would be more than happy to buy the coffees.

'To save time we had better take a taxi, Gran, or better still, I'll ask Manuel to drop us in the centre, and we can then be at the shops as soon as possible to give us all the time we need.'

'A very good idea, Carlos.' Mrs Johnson had found Seville delightful, but tiring. It seemed so spread out like Paris, but so very much hotter.

'Tell me, dear, what do you have in mind to buy them?'

'I don't know yet, Gran. I thought you would have a lot of ideas. I think the thing I would like best, if I was getting married, would be a good dinner service. I always enjoy my food, and I know that Miguel ordered cut glass for them yesterday when he went into town on the pretext of buying some textbooks that he said he needed if he was going to Oxford, but I know he wants to go to the University here.'

'What a lovely idea. If he has ordered cut glass, as you say, a dinner service would be splendid. Let's start with the china shops.'

Manuel brought his small Fiat to the front of the house, and quite soon deposited Carlos and Charlotte's mother

186

in the centre near the Giralda, the famous cathedral and well-known Seville landmark. Five minutes later Carlos and his 'Gran' were looking at dinner services of every description, the majority with gilding in various patterns.

'The choice is very wide, dear, but if you want my honest opinion I would suggest one of the plainer ones that Charlotte or Maria can put in the dishwasher. The gold might come off in a dishwasher.'

'Good for you, Gran. I thought you would know best. I would almost certainly have gone for the one with the most gold on, even if it was the most expensive. You know, Gran, I'm going to miss Charlotte when she comes to live here with Dad.'

Mrs Johnson's eyes moistened. 'You don't know what you've said, Carlos. I shall miss her as much and more than you. Remember, she lives with me at my home. When Charlotte leaves home I will be all on my own, but I want you to feel that my home is yours whenever you are in London.'

'Thanks, Gran. I would like that. It'll be great having a real home in London. The other boys will be green with envy at Slapton when I tell them that I have a home in London as well as Madrid and Seville. They will think I'm rich. I'll try not to make a nuisance of myself. If ever it's not convenient just tell me – promise.'

'I promise, Carlos, but I don't think that will be very often. Now which one are you going to have?' She looked at two dinner services with floral patterns. Carlos settled on a pink-and-green service in pastel shades. The assistant addressed Charlotte's mother, who he naturally assumed to be the customer. Carlos immediately sensed that his Gran hadn't understood a word that the assistant had said beyond the word 'Señora', and he spoke for her accordingly:

'My grandmother doesn't speak Spanish very well. I will do the talking. I am buying this dinner service as a present, a wedding present. I wish to have this service properly wrapped in wedding paper and delivered to my home this afternoon, please.' He gave his home address, which

187

impressed the assistant, and the name of Maria as recipient.

'I can't give you a cheque myself, but if you will send the account to my uncle at the bank it will be in order. If you would like to phone him now, he will confirm.' Carlos produced his uncle's professional card.

'Certainly, Señor. Just wait a minute please.' The assistant, a man of 40 years of age, was obviously speaking to the Manager. A telephone call was made and the assistant returned.

'I'm sorry, Señor Lang. It was the name of the lady you gave me at your home that put me off. I do apologize. Certainly it will be packed and delivered for you this afternoon after siesta. Will 4 o'clock be convenient?'

Charlotte's mother, Alice Johnson, was so very happy. To have grandchildren like Miguel and Carlos had made her holiday. No woman in Seville had ever been happier to pay for two coffees. She insisted on Carlos having two Danish pastries – Seville style – and she had one herself to keep him company.

The interview at the University had gone well, and at noon Xavier, Charlotte and Miguel joined the shoppers. This was the excuse for further eating and drinks. Wine now, not coffee, and open Parma ham sandwiches. Xavier paid.

'I wish today would last for ever,' said Alice Johnson. 'With two grandsons already, you two can take your time in giving me any more.' She was directing her remarks in jest to Xavier and Charlotte. She was so happy. 'We've had a very busy morning looking at shops. They really are beautiful. I'd like to have had more time, but Carlos tells me that they will all be closed until 3 o'clock for Siesta.'

Returning home, Carlos related to Maria details of the shopping expedition. His secret was safe with her and at 4 p.m., on the stroke, she received the substantial parcel, which she told Manuel to take up to their private rooms which constituted a pleasant, yet old-fashioned, self-contained flat on the top floor of the house.

Alice took her Siesta. She could see why the Spanish liked Siestas. It was over 35 centigrade – well over 100 Fahrenheit.

Charlotte would have taken a Siesta herself, but first she must apologize to Carlos and have that talk she had promised him about his wrestling at Slapton.

'Carlos. Please come upstairs. I must speak to you on your own.'

'Certainly, Charlotte. What's the matter?'

'There's nothing the matter. Just come upstairs with me now. Please.' Carlos followed Charlotte to her bedroom, wondering whether she wanted to show him something. Perhaps something she had bought for Dad by way of wedding present? Once inside the bedroom Charlotte closed the door, and to Carlos's surprise turned the key.

'Now come and sit over here, Carlos – there are two things I feel I must tell you, on your own. That's why I turned the key. I don't want the others just walking in.' Carlos sat down, wondering what she was going to say. 'Now, Carlos, you will think I'm always making you promise me things. You are so grown up today. You're not a little boy any more. I don't really know where to start. I will start with Miguel. He told me all about the other boys calling him "Stumpy" and why. It seems he nearly killed that boy who tried to bully you when you were only very small at Slapton. Luckily, it seems, matters were hushed up, because they found that he had been stealing as well, but I'm telling you as a serving police officer, that if that matter ever became known, it could still make a lot of trouble for Miguel in both England and Spain. It might just spoil his chance of going to the University here in Seville, quite apart from making it impossible for him to go to Oxford, if he should want to go there. You must be wondering what all this has to do with you. It's this. I'm very proud of you, Carlos, and I'm very fond of Miguel. If you were to continue your wrestling at Slapton, you might quite easily, if accidentally, seriously injure one or more of the other boys. If you did, however accidentally, you could ruin Miguel's chances here in Seville or at Oxford, quite apart from any prosecution Miguel might have to face in England. People might say, "Wasn't it his brother who nearly killed Lord Wastwater" – or whatever he will be called – "one

189

day?" That's why I made you promise me that you wouldn't wrestle again at school without Father Turner's permission. I did promise both you and Father Turner that I would speak to you on this holiday. You don't have to prove anything to me physically. You wrestle and ski better than anyone I've heard of at your age. I know that you say that you ski for your Momma and that you wrestle for me, but I'm begging you not to wrestle any more whilst you're at Slapton. Promise me, Carlos. Please.'

'Thanks for telling me, Charlotte, but you needn't really have worried. I did promise not to wrestle again on the last day of term, but if it makes you happy, I will promise you now again not to wrestle with any of the other boys except in self-defence, but I will tell you again that if I was to find anyone laying a finger on you I wouldn't hesitate in killing them. It would be the best case of "self-defence" you ever saw in your police career! How's that for you?'

'Thank you, darling. I'll settle for that, but don't even talk about killing anyone. I can look after myself fairly well, as you know, and I'll have your Dad around to help, as I did in Chamonix. And now there is another thing. I really want to apologize for giving you such a good ducking in the swimming pool at Ronda and then getting straight out and not letting you try and duck me again. There was a reason. I was really off-colour that day and didn't really want to go swimming. I only went in at all to please you and your "Gran".'

'I know, Charlotte. Dad told me all about you. I'm sorry I didn't know there were days you didn't like to go swimming. Why don't you make me a promise now? Promise me that if I should ever want you to do something you don't feel up to, you'll just say to me "Remember Ronda" or "I'm Ronda" and then I'll know.'

Charlotte stood up from where she had been sitting and came across to him. She put her arms around him saying, 'Darling. You are the most understanding boy. Of course I promise.'

190

16

Friday, 4 October arrived. It was a day not to be forgotten.

Charlotte's mother Alice had booked herself in at the White Hart for the Thursday night for a double room with two single beds. She would spend Charlotte's last night, as her unmarried daughter, in a shared room. Effectively Charlotte would be married from the White Hart.

Xavier was coming down from London to Slapton with Sylvia and Carlos, his Best Man, in Sylvia's Ministry car, complete with Police escort. The boys, Miguel and Carlos, were, of course, already at the College. Father Turner had drilled both boys and the Sabita boys, who were acting as groomsmen, along with the altar boys and the College choir. Father Turner would be saying Nuptial Mass himself, assisted by Father Pearson of Wood Green, who had received Charlotte into the Church, but the actual marriage would be performed by the Rector himself, who was going to enjoy every minute of it.

Other guests made their own arrangements, including Vladimir Renov, the Second Vice President of Russia, and his wife Myra. They would also motor down from London from the Russian Embassy, together with two Russian security officers.

The Spanish Ambassador required no security, but he had with him both his wife and his Naval Attaché and his wife. Xavier knew the Spanish Naval Officer, and as Xavier had said to Charlotte's mother when they had completed the wedding list, they would help build up numbers on the Spanish side.

The Nuptial Mass had been timed for 11.30 a.m. to allow everybody good time to arrive. Those who were not motoring down from London all seemed to have booked into local hotels. There was nobody missing when the service started. Father Turner was not ex-army for nothing. He wanted a 'full house', and with the Rector's permission the Sixth Form were there en masse in their smart dark grey suits, white shirts and maroon ties. All these boys' voices had broken, and accordingly there was a good solid male voice choir effect to balance the young voices of the College choir, comprising many of the youngest boys in the school. A friend of Charlotte's who was a member of the London Symphony Choir sang the 'Ave Maria'.

Although enjoying himself, the Rector spoke little beyond what was required to marry Xavier and Charlotte. He knew there would be speeches after the wedding breakfast. He could not allow himself to say nothing with such a distinguished 'audience', and he was arguably one of the best speakers most of those present would be likely to hear in the course of the year. He had timed himself to speak for five minutes only, but in the event he spoke for six minutes. Any number of the boys had timed him on their stopwatches.

There was the usual appeal for confetti not to be thrown, but this request was honoured as much in the breach as the observance. It was to be several days before the last pieces of paper were to be finally removed from sight.

At the White Hart everything was in perfect order. Sylvia's security men, who had co-operated on this occasion with their opposite numbers from the Russian Embassy, had satisfied themselves that nothing was amiss. Both sides were secretly quite pleased that their 'charges' had not been staying overnight, as were the local Police. It was only to be a daytime affair in two locations. The dining room was bedecked with flowers, and as usual it seemed an eternity before the professional photographers would allow the breakfast to start.

Eventually, Father Rector said Grace and the lovely meal was under way. Charlotte herself looked like a fashion model in he bridal dress of cream silk trimmed with Brussels lace. Her pleasant looks were enhanced by a perfect facial make-up and her hair specially blown early that morning in Slapton village, an appointment for that purpose having been made back in July. She looked the perfect English bride. Her good carriage and figure set off her wedding gown to perfection.

Charlotte's two Bridesmaids, both Matrons of Honour, Mary and Susan – with whom she had served as WPCs in the London Met – were also beautifully attired in cerise, but neither could detract from Charlotte's looks that day. She positively glowed as all brides are meant to glow.

All the men present were in morning suits or uniforms. The three clergy were in their best cassocks as dressed for Speech Days and other important occasions. The meal itself – the main course was salmon, it being a Friday – was accompanied by the finest Spanish wines, and there was an unmistakable 'Spanish' atmosphere, although the Spaniards proper were a minority of the guests.

It was Sir John Bickerstaff who, as arranged, proposed the toast, 'the Bride and Bridegroom'. He made an excellent speech. It was obvious to all that not only was he a practiced speaker, but that he had prepared his speech with care, with considerable research in which he had been helped by his wife Florence. When glasses had been raised and wine consumed, the applause took some time to die down.

Now it was Xavier's turn. He rose to applause and, for fun, spoke his first few words in Spanish. This pleased those who spoke his native tongue, but after only two sentences he started again with the classic, 'Oh behalf of my wife and I'.

He thanked everybody who needed to be thanked. He mentioned Alice and presented her with flowers, and the Bridesmaids, to whom he gave boxed strings of pearls. In short, he made a very good bridegroom speech. Not a speech which would 'ring from shire to shire', but very well above any number of bridegroom's speeches. Perhaps he wasn't at his very best, but some of those close to him felt that his

193

mind might at times have strayed back to that glorious day in his early life 18 years ago, when Sophia had been his happy bride. He had, of course, spoken entirely in Spanish on that occasion.

Now it was the turn of Carlos Sabita, as Best Man, to return the toast to 'the Bridesmaids', that Xavier had just proposed. Carlos rose to the occasion magnificently, with amusing stories concerning the days when he and Xavier had been students at the College and when they had served as fellow naval officers in the Spanish Navy – 'Yes. We have a "Royal Navy" again now,' he joked. He said how true it was that the Bridesmaids were both delightful and experienced – how they had both been Bridesmaids to his wife at their own wedding. He too had prepared his speech with care, with the assistance of Sylvia, his wife. He deliberately refrained from reminding everybody that Sylvia was Deputy Prime Minister, but he did make a point of saying that this wedding must have done more good for Anglo/Spanish/Russian relations than any other wedding this year.

When he sat down there was more applause, and there matters formally ceased; but they didn't. Quite unexpectedly, 'Uncle Paul' from Seville stood up and started to speak.

'Bride and Bridegroom, Ladies and Gentlemen, You must all excuse my poor English' – he spoke well, but with a very marked Spanish accent that was completely missing from Xavier's and Carlos Sabita's spoken English – 'I know that this is England, but at home in Seville it is traditional for the youngest man present to make a speech. I do hope that young Señor Carlos is not going to let us down!' All eyes turned towards Carlos, who was sitting at the far end of the top table. Carlos rose to his feet to applause. 'How would the young man shape?' 'What a thing to do to put a young boy on the spot like that.' The audience needn't have worried.

'Reverend Fathers, Bride and Bridegroom: I had no idea, Uncle Paul, that you were going to invite me to speak, but Father Turner had warned me that somebody might ask me

194

to say a few words to maintain the family tradition. I'm glad he served as a padre in Gibraltar when Britain still maintained a garrison there and he came to know the traditions of neighbouring Seville. Now I have stood up, I don't really know what I am going to say. I will say three things: firstly, I know that if my Momma hadn't died last year she would like to have been here to join my brother Miguel and myself in wishing Dad and Charlotte every happiness in their future together. Secondly, whilst I have always, well nearly always, enjoyed having a big brother, I hope that you Dad and you Charlotte will make me an elder brother within the next few years. Lastly, I'm very glad to have a grandmother for the first time in my life who lives in London, where I can spend my exeats when you Dad and you Charlotte are out of the country abroad or at home in Spain. I've enjoyed today. I'm sure we all have. Thank you, Uncle Paul, for letting me say so in public.'

Carlos sat down. There were few dry eyes in the room. Perhaps surprisingly, it was Vladimir Renov and Elmer Orlaski who first rose, calling out 'Bravo, Bravo'. Everyone joined in standing and clapping. Xavier and Charlotte smiled their thanks. They were both full, but Charlotte was determined today not to ruin her make-up. Xavier simply maintained a 'stiff upper lip'.

Charlotte's mother couldn't and didn't. Nothing would stop her. She got up from her seat on the top table, went to where Carlos was sitting, and threw her arms around him. 'Bless you, child,' was all she could say. After Carlos's words and applause had died away, all stood while Xavier and Charlotte departed the dining room to the traditional rhythmic handclapping of all present. Conversation buzzed. The conversations were varied, but typical was that between the Sabitas and the de Freitas families.

John de Freitas was saying, 'My God, I wish I could have spoken like that when I was sixteen.'

His wife added immediately, 'I bet you wish you could speak like that boy did right now, dear, and I don't know that he's fully sixteen yet. I must say he looks and sounds like a young man of twenty or more. Xavier must be very proud of him. Did you see Charlotte's face as he was speaking? I thought she was going to break down. She only just managed to hold on.'

Vladimir Renov took it upon himself to congratulate Carlos on his prepared impromptu speech, and more importantly he made a detailed memo on his return to London, which was related via the diplomatic bag to Moscow. Vladimir was in overdrive. He introduced his wife Myra to Mary Orlanski – so that they could chat about their children, as he put it – whilst taking Elmer on one side to arrange an appointment to discuss the growing banking in Russia by the Chicago Temperance Bank. Everything seemed to be going well in that connection, but there is no situation that cannot be improved, and Vladimir was not the sort of man to miss an opportunity, nor was Elmer, and the two men talked earnestly for up to ten minutes, seemingly oblivious to all that was going on and being said around them.

Xavier and Charlotte toured the room, shaking hands and kissing as appropriate, thanking all they met for coming and their presents. Charlotte would be writing to them all with their thanks.

They made a particular point of thanking the Rector and Father Turner for all their help, and Charlotte's mother took the opportunity of extracting an exeat pass to have Carlos at her home the following weekend. At last Charlotte and Xavier were changed and ready to depart on their honeymoon.

They were off to Majorca, to a villa that was regularly let out to royalty and the jet set. Charlotte was dressed in a smart two-piece cream suit. Xavier was wearing his smart double-breasted navy blue blazer. The hired Rolls-Royce swept them away from the White Hart with yet more confetti thrown.

Outside Slapton the Rolls slowed down and pulled on to the forecourt of the South Coast Garage. They changed cars into Xavier's black Daimler and drove to Heathrow.

Mrs Alice Johnson had been looking forward to having Carlos at her home for the weekend almost as much as she had been looking forward to the wedding. Her elder daughter had been married seven years, and still had no children. Charlotte had stayed at home until she married, and she was now 30. Mrs Johnson had been an active member of the Mother's Union ever since her husband, her late husband, had been vicar, and she had played a leading role. For years she had been obliged to listen to all the other members of her own age group talking of their grand-children and admiring photographs of children that meant little or nothing to her. Now she had two ready made grand-children, and she was as anxious to show them off as anyone could be.

By happy chance, the Parish Summer Garden Party, in the vicarage grounds, was to be held on the Saturday follow-ing the wedding. Carlos knew that he was to be 'shown off' by his new Gran, but he would put up with that three times a year – once a term – if it gave the old lady pleasure and it gave him the weekend in London. He deliberately wore his best College grey suit, white shirt and colours tie in maroon and silver. The colours tie was not necessary for Mrs Johnson to remind those she met at the vicarage that Carlos had won the skiing gold medal. She had shown the video to them already, twice.

It was 11 a.m. before Carlos arrived at Arnos Grove under-ground station. Five minutes after leaving the station he was with Alice. She made a point of showing him 'his' room. It was Charlotte's former room and there were still a few things of hers about, but that didn't worry him. Alice made it clear that she was moving Charlotte's remaining things into the spare room, and Carlos was soon shifting things.

The room rapidly looked less feminine, and Alice insisted that he must feel free to bring anything into the room which he felt like bringing – 'and what I say to you applies to Miguel as well, dear.'

Two grown-up young grandsons coming to stay with her. After a very light lunch they were off to the vicarage, where she was in charge of the cake stall. This did not prevent her taking Carlos round all the other stalls. He appeared the perfect young gentleman, addressing the Vicar as Father, to the Vicar's slight surprise, and then, perhaps, he blotted his copybook by winning two coconuts with three wooden balls.

'You're very good at throwing balls, Carlos, but we don't really need two.'

'Yes we do, Gran. I want to take one back to Slapton and I want you to have the other one. I will make three holes in yours for you, and then you can hang it up in the garden at home for the birds.'

'What a good idea. We used to do that when my husband was living. Didn't it all go perfectly last Friday?'

'Yes it did, Gran. Well, nearly perfectly.'

'How do you mean, dear, nearly perfectly?'

Carlos laughed. 'To have gone perfectly, Gran, I should have married Charlotte. I have known and loved Charlotte longer than Dad. Nobody loves her more than you and me, but you're her Mum and I'm still at school.'

They both laughed, but it was a conversation that Alice was to remember.

17

Over two years passed.

Xavier and Charlotte settled in Spain. They made visits to London, Slapton, Moscow and Chicago. Their holidays in Moscow and St Petersburg were highlights, but there was something missing. With the enthusiasm of young lovers they had made love frequently, but there was no pregnancy.

As an educated woman, Charlotte had assumed that either she would become pregnant very shortly after marriage or, perhaps, she had been too keen or something. However, when two years had passed and there was still no sign, she determined not simply to speak to her family doctor, but have an internal examination in a top London clinic. The appointment was made, Charlotte attended and was advised that there was no reason at all why she should not conceive. Her mother, Alice, was very understanding, but she was mindful that her elder daughter Margaret had now been married seven years and still had no children.

It was against this background that the terrible news came. The front doorbell rang and Alice answered, to face two police officers in uniform. At a glance Alice recognized the local Inspector and Sergeant from the police station round the corner. They had been frequent callers when Charlotte had served in the Metropolitan Police.

'Come in, Inspector. What can we do for you?'

'I'm sorry to trouble you, Mrs Johnson. Is your daughter Charlotte at home?'

'Yes, she is. Come in, both of you, and I'll call her.'

Two minutes later Charlotte was downstairs. She immediately detected that the Inspector, whom she knew as George, was wearing a sad and serious expression.

'What is it, George? You look very serious this morning.'

'Please sit down, Charlotte,' he started, 'and you too, Mrs Johnson. I'm very sorry. I don't really know where to start, but I'll come right out with it. There has been a serious road accident in Spain.'

Charlotte felt her face draining. She had had to perform the duty that George was now performing on any number of occasions in the course of her police career. She looked at George without speaking, hanging on his words, hoping for the best and fearing the worst.

'It was late last night, Charlotte. Your husband was driving, and he had his elder son Miguel with him. There was a head-on crash and . . .' he paused and then went on '. . . I'm sorry. It seems they were both killed instantly, as was the driver of the other car.'

Charlotte crumpled, and Alice got up and put her arms around her and held her.

'Naturally, if there is anything we can do, Charlotte, you only have to ask. We have spoken to the Spanish Police. You can feel happy that your husband and stepson would have suffered no pain. It must have been instant death, but we're all very sorry for you, and if there is anything we can do, please let us know. Knowing how well-known you are to Dame Sabita and the Spanish Embassy, I'm sure they could have you on a plane to Madrid today, if that's what you wanted. There will, of course, be an enquiry and almost certainly a post mortem, but I don't really have to tell you that. I'm off-duty myself in one hour's time, but I won't go home. I'll stay at the station until you decide what to do. Don't attempt to drive anywhere yourself. Sergeant Gill will drive you to the Spanish Embassy or anywhere else you want to go. I understand that Dame Sabita may know already, in view of your husband's standing, but I wanted to break the news to you myself. I'm sorry. I have to leave you now, but if there is any help you want you know the station number.'

The officers left the house.

'Charlotte, love. I don't know what to say. Just hold on to me.'

Alice was at her most comforting. 'How could it happen? You'll have to tell Carlos. He'll be completely devastated. He'll need you. To have lost his mother as a child was one thing, but she, poor soul, had been dead in real terms for years, but now to lose his father and brother! The only thing is, dear, that you are not left with a tiny baby. I know you wanted one and you've tried everything, but at least you don't have the problem of bringing up a baby on your own in a foreign country. There's another thing. You'll be able to give Carlos all the help you can, and Xavier is bound to have left you a very wealthy woman. I know that money isn't everything, and you'd much rather have Xavier and his child or children than his money, but you do have to try and be positive.'

Alice felt she had to say these things to keep Charlotte both sane and going. The next few days were going to be difficult, but she would do all she could to help. Her mind was racing ahead. Hopefully Charlotte would in due course come back home to live with her and rejoin the Police. These thoughts fairly raced through her mind as she continued to hold Charlotte. Charlotte broke free.

'Mum, I must first speak to the Rector at Slapton. Carlos will have to be told. I shall find it very difficult telling him. It's so easy telling people you don't know, well not that easy, but when it's your own it's quite different. He only has me now and his Uncle Paul left and Paul's family. He'll never get over the shock. I think I must ask the Rector and Father Turner to tell him first. There are things I must do here right now in London. I'll go down to Slapton this afternoon. He'll know then, but I must go to him just as soon as I've been to the Embassy and spoken to Sylvia and one or two others. There will be so much to do. Why had it to happen to Xavier and Miguel?'

She could go on no longer and burst into tears. At Slapton, Father Rector was very understanding. It had often fallen to him to break sad news to boys at the College, but thankfully rarely had he to tell a boy of the simultaneous death of a boy's father and only brother. He first called Father Turner, Carlos's housemaster, and they agreed to call Carlos to meet them both at the same time in the Rector's office.

They sent for him in formal terms deliberately, so as not to break it to the boy in the presence of his peers. Carlos entered the Rector's office quite unaware of what he was wanted for or what to expect.

'Carlos. I usually call you Lang, but this isn't one of those occasions. I've asked Father Turner to be here with you when I tell you some very sad news that has just come to my ears. Sit down, Carlos.'

Carlos sat down, wondering what it could be. He thought that his new Gran might have been hurt in some accident.

'Carlos, I have to tell you that last night your dear father and brother were killed in a car accident in Spain near Madrid.'

He got no further. Carlos's face crumpled for the first time since his great victory on the skis in Chamonix over two years ago. He only had his handkerchief for comfort.

After some moments he spoke quietly. 'Where is Charlotte, Father? I need her now and she needs me.'

'You're quite right, Carlos, and I'm glad you're such a brave and sensible young man. Your father would be proud of you, and so would your mother and brother. We're all very proud of you. Take the rest of the day off. Go to the Chapel or your own room if you wish. Charlotte will be coming down this afternoon. She'll be very glad to be with you, I know. As you say, she'll need all the support you can give her. It's just two years since you made that excellent speech at the wedding.'

The Rector took out his own handkerchief and wiped a tear from his eye. Telephone calls were made.

Sylvia immediately offered any help she could. 'I'm very glad you have your mother with you, Charlotte,' she said. 'Don't go anywhere without her for the moment. You must be sensible and look after yourself. I couldn't bear hearing that you'd had an accident in your own car. Let your mother drive you to Slapton or take up that offer of the police or hire a taxi if need be, but please don't try and drive yourself. You've enough on your mind without worrying about all that traffic.'

Señor Paul de Sanches in Seville was the last of the immediate family to be informed, but he was to be a crucial factor. He knew his family obligations better than anyone outside the Lang family lawyers. He also controlled Sophia's trust fund that provided for the boys' education, Carlos's boarding fees at Slapton and much else besides. He was now going to require all his tact and firmness. He had always been very close to his sister Sophia. Spanish people generally are family-oriented at all levels of society, but 'Uncle Paul' was, if anything, excessively so and possessed of all the qualities that his obligations required.

As soon as he heard the sad news he telephoned immediately to Xavier's lawyers in both Madrid and Seville. After obtaining the information he sought, which was negative, he sought the advice of the bank's lawyers – the well-known firm of Abagodos in Seville. Their advice was unhesitating and correct. He had known general family law before he made his call, but they had confirmed it and would do so in writing. Señor Paul de Sanches was a valued client both in his own right and as a senior executive with the Seville Bank.

At Slapton, Charlotte and Carlos wrapped their arms around each other and both shed tears. Charlotte didn't care what sort of a picture her face appeared. She just wanted to comfort Carlos, who at 17 was now a well-made young man over six foot tall. Alice had travelled down to Slapton with her daughter, and the police had been very good in supplying a young WPC to act as chauffeur for the two of them, for which Alice offered to pay gladly.

'If it does cost money, dear, you deserve it, and as Sylvia said, you can well afford it now. You don't have any financial worries, thank God, like I had when your father died and I had to take that job in the garage to put you and Margaret through college.'

The three of them went to the White Hart for afternoon tea with Father Turner, who was kindness itself and helpful with suggestions too.

The Iberian Airways jet taxied down gently at Madrid Airport. 'Uncle Paul' was there to meet them. He was very helpful.

Within an hour of landing they were at the flat in the centre of Madrid. Alice, Charlotte, Carlos and Paul went to the same restaurant where Carlos and Miguel had taken Charlotte and Alice on Alice's first visit to Madrid. The meal itself went well, and Paul did his best to maintain conversation with his heavily accented English. Deep down, however, they were all very sad, and Paul thought it best to keep his own counsel as to what he knew.

It was back in the flat that Alice, quite without thinking, raised a matter that might have been better delayed.

'At least, Paul, we can all be grateful about one thing, sad as it all is. Charlotte is now a wealthy woman, so she won't have any financial worries as I had when my husband died and we had to move out of the vicarage – my two daughters and me.'

'I'm glad to hear you say that, Mrs Johnson. I confess I had been wondering about Charlotte's financial position, but I didn't think it right to raise the matter before the funeral. I'm pleased to hear you say that she is well-placed financially. I think your police are better paid than ours in Spain.'

'I'm not speaking of her police pay, Paul. That stopped when she resigned on retirement. I mean Xavier's money.'

At this point Charlotte joined them in the drawing room. 'I'm sorry, Mrs Johnson; may I call you Alice? I think it's a bit early to speak of Xavier's money, but I'm not aware that his money or this flat for that matter will pass to Charlotte. This flat certainly won't, because it belongs to Sophia's trust, but I think Charlotte will want to speak to Xavier's lawyers here in Madrid tomorrow morning. They will be able to explain the Spanish Inheritance Law better than me.'

Charlotte and her mother looked at each other, but said nothing. The following morning Paul left to return to Seville, but not before he had spoken to Carlos on his own.

'Carlos. Your Aunt Marie and I are terribly upset by the death of your father and brother. I think you are going to be able to help Charlotte more than even she and her mother imagine, but you must leave all money matters to me if you want to help them. You are only seventeen, but don't have any money worries yourself at Slapton or otherwise. You know you can always rely on me, even if I did let you in for it at the wedding! Your aunt and I were very proud of you that day. You spoke beautifully in your college English – much better than I could ever do. Always try and remember, Carlos, that you're Spanish. Your parents and brother were Spanish. Spain is best and always. If you really want to help Charlotte and Spain, please trust me. Your mother did.'

Señor de Sanches had prepared his little speech well, appealing as he had to Carlos's love of his late mother, Charlotte and Spain. 'Uncle Paul, I know I can always depend on you. I won't do anything in business without speaking to you first. You know that.'

'Good, Carlos. I did know, but I had to speak to you on your own, man to man.'

Charlotte went with her mother to the Madrid lawyers on her own. She had thought to take Carlos with her to act as interpreter, but her own Spanish was now quite good, and in any case she did not doubt that the Madrid lawyers would speak, if not perfect English, quite sufficient to make her understand both the extent of Xavier's estate – property and money – and its distribution under the terms of his will.

The offices were impressive, as were the two elderly legal gentlemen they met. They had no sooner settled down in maroon leather chairs than coffees were produced on a large silver tray.

'Mrs Lang. Before we say anything about your late husband's affairs, may we both say how dreadfully sorry we were to learn of his tragic death and, of course, the equally sad death of his elder son, Miguel. We will be attending the

205

main inquest in due course, but you must feel some relief that the accident must have caused instant death and no period of lengthy suffering in hospital.

'Now, as to your husband's "estate", as we call it. The starting point is your husband's will. Sadly, it seems that your husband didn't leave one. He did have a will, of course, but he destroyed it, intending no doubt to make another, and that means, effectively, that he died what we term "intestate". Our Parliament makes provision for the distribution of people's estates when they die without a will, and the provisions are very good for the family, but, and it's a big but, the provision goes downwards, not sideways.

'I don't know whether you understand what I am saying, but effectively it means that your late husband's property and money will pass to his second son, Carlos, not you. You will, of course, benefit, but the greater part of his estate will pass to his son.'

Alice, who had been through the trauma of widowhood with financial worries, couldn't contain herself.

'Are you telling us that my son-in-law has left my daughter penniless?'

'I don't think I understand you, Mrs Johnson. That is not what I said. I will repeat it all again if I did not make myself clear. It is simply the case that, having died without a will, all your son-in-law's property, including his monies in the bank, are what we call "frozen", and since Carlos is not quite eighteen, we will have to wait a very short time until he is, and then we can move. I have spoken to his uncle – his late mother's brother – who seems a very fine man. He has told me that we can keep everything on hold until Carlos is eighteen and that he will take care of all expenses, so you don't have any immediate worries. By the way, where is Carlos? I assume he has come out with you.'

'Yes, he has. He wanted to go to his mother's grave alone this morning. In fact, his uncle Paul went with him to make arrangements at the cemetery, subject to my approval.'

She felt she had to say this. Things seemed to be slipping away from her.

206

'Perhaps I should say something else, Señora Lang.' It was the older man who was speaking now. 'Whilst I know that what my partner has said is true, I would fully understand that you might like to have a second opinion. At the end of the day we have to look after Carlos's interests as our priority. Naturally we would not do anything deliberately against your interest, but I feel you might prefer to have another firm give you advice and act for you, particularly if you wanted to go to court to seek monies from your stepson by way of settlement or otherwise. I understand from Señor de Sanches that you and your stepson are very close. I'm sure that Señor de Sanches will prove very helpful. I would not like to see any upset within the Lang family. I'm sure you will understand what I am saying. You must forgive my poor English, but it is over fifty years since I first studied your language.'

After an exchange of pleasantries, Charlotte and her mother made their way back to the flat. Carlos was there, seemingly his usual cheerful self.

'I hope you had a good meeting with Dad's lawyers. Uncle Paul tells me that he will look after everything. He says that none of us need have any money worries, Charlotte, so you don't have to go back into the police or anything, unless you wish. I can take Dad's place and look after you when I'm eighteen, but until then Uncle Paul tells me he can look after things.'

Alice didn't know whether to laugh or cry. Charlotte simply put her hand on Carlos's shoulder and kissed him lightly on the cheek.

'Thank you, darling. You are my boy. I'm so glad you're here. I don't know what I would do without you. We'll have a lot of talking to do, but that can wait. How did your morning go?'

'We went to the cemetery, Charlotte. Uncle Paul spoke to the Cemetery Superintendent. He said there would be no problem and he will arrange the wording to be added after you have confirmed. Uncle Paul has suggested' – he looked out a piece of paper from his wallet – ' "Also her beloved husband Xavier and darling son Miguel. Treasured memories'', and that would leave spaces for photographs of Dad and Miguel.'

Although upset, with tears in his eyes, Carlos was speaking both clearly and in business-like terms. Charlotte thought for a moment and then said quietly:

'Yes darling, I think your Uncle Paul has chosen very nice words. He's a very good uncle to you.' Charlotte left the room, went to her bedroom and threw herself on the double bed she had installed in place of the two singles, and cried her eyes out. She did get up and put new make-up on, but she could do nothing to disguise her red eyes.

Both her mother and Carlos noticed, but Carlos was growing older by the day and he made no comment. He sensibly switched the conversation to where they were going for lunch. Alice's mind was full of thoughts. It was ridiculous, but Carlos seemed to have aged years in the last 24 hours. He seemed to have acquired that sense of command which she had first noticed in Xavier and Miguel. She found that she was filling up herself, but she wouldn't let it show. She had to hold on for Charlotte's sake.

At the funeral, everything seemed to pass as a dream. Charlotte, whilst fully conscious of all that was going on, felt that she was acting a part. The Requiem Mass was said in Latin, which she followed without too much difficulty, having studied Latin at school. It meant little or nothing to her mother, but at least with Carlos, Paul and his wife Marie present she sat, stood and knelt at the right time.

The church itself was full of people she did not know, but they all seemed kind, and an English-speaking priest from the British Embassy co-celebrated the Mass with the Spanish Parish Priest and took them to the cemetery. Charlotte kept her calm outward appearance as the coffins, both of them, were lowered into the vault containing Sophia's coffin. Carlos took her hand in his and squeezed. She knew it was his hand without looking at him. She daren't. She knew she might break down if their eyes met. She simply held his hand firmly and squeezed her acknowledgement.

After the funeral lunch Paul took Charlotte on one side.

'Charlotte, I do hope I can always call you Charlotte, I know you must have a lot on your mind. Please never think badly of him not having made a new will. He has left you treasure in that son of his, Carlos. I have already spoken to him. You will never need to be poor. You can leave it to me to look after the Lang fortune as I have looked after Sophia's monies. Don't ask me any questions now. Today isn't the day. Thank you very much for agreeing the wording on the tombstone. I know that Carlos appreciated your agreement. He was always very close to his mother, as she was to him. She knew she would never see him grow up. Be sure to keep him close to Marie and me. We do regard you as a member of our family. I hope you always will be.'

'Thank you, Paul. You and Marie have proved good friends.'

The inquest revealed the whole story. The facts were very simple. Xavier had been driving perfectly correctly. The other motorist had come round the bend facing him too fast. He, the other driver, had lost control and struck Xavier's car head-on. The first on the scene were two Russian businessmen on holiday – that was how they were described, but in fact they were security officers from the Russian Embassy in Madrid, who were shadowing Xavier on instructions from Moscow.

They had acted bravely. With their bare hands they had tried to drag Xavier and Miguel from the car, breaking the side windows to gain access for this purpose, but sadly they had both been killed immediately on impact. A detailed report had been sent to Moscow via the diplomatic bag, and the Embassy in Madrid had been told to send flowers to the widow. The card read: 'In deepest sympathy, Vladimir and Myra.'

The Spanish Police had taken statements. Post mortems had been held, and it transpired that the other motorist had been possessed of a considerable excess of alcohol in his bloodstream.

Señor de Sanches gave instructions for a claim to be

lodged on behalf of Carlos himself, not Xavier's estate, so that the benefit of the claim would pass directly to Carlos and would not be aggregated with the estate proper and thus escape inheritance tax as much as possible.

At home at last in Southgate, Alice felt she had to speak to Carlos on her own before he went back to Slapton for the remainder of the term.

'Carlos, you've been the greatest comfort to Charlotte and me. I do hope it hasn't all been too much for you.'

'No, Gran, it hasn't. I've still got you and Charlotte. I want Charlotte to be really proud of me. I can't bring myself to speak to her fully yet, as I would wish, but she is Mrs Lang to the world. I always want her to be Mrs Lang to the world. I don't think I could bear her becoming Mrs Smith, Jones, Robinson or Brown. I always want her to be Mrs Lang. Can you begin to understand what I am saying?'

'Yes. I do believe I understand, dear. I know she's very fond of you. I'm sure she always will be, but life is not going to be too easy for her. First, she will have to decide where she wants to live now that your father has died, and she will, I think, need to work to keep herself. She may not be able to get her job back. I think the Police would be glad to have her back, but she wouldn't be able to get her rank back.'

'Gran, that's up to her, but she doesn't have to work unless she wants to. I could keep her from Momma's trust fund. Uncle Paul says he will explain it all to me. I do know from what Charlotte has said to me already that she doesn't want to take money from me or my trust, but she is my stepmum. I know I'm only young, but I'm not stupid. I'll be a man in Spanish Law on my next birthday. Charlotte's thirty-two now and I'm nearly eighteen. You think I'm only half her age, but you must have done sums at school, Gran. When I'm twenty-one she won't be forty-two, will she? The difference between our ages will close up, just like it would have done between Charlotte and Dad.'

'Yes, you're right, dear. For the moment we just want you to continue to do your best at Slapton. I think Charlotte wants to work. She must keep herself going as you must. I think what she would like best is to work for her friend Sylvia as a personal assistant or researcher or whatever they call them in the House of Commons, but that may be tricky now that she's Spanish. She'll just have to wait and see.'

Charlotte phoned through to Sylvia at Harcourt. 'Sylvia, I must speak to you. Everything went very well in Spain. I'll tell you all about it when I see you. I'd like to see you as soon as possible, please. I'm taking Carlos back to Slapton tomorrow. I couldn't think of living in Spain on my own without Xavier.'

'I do understand, Charlotte. Come down to the Ministry Office tomorrow morning at 10 o'clock and we can have a chat over coffee before I go to Cabinet. Look after yourself and give my love to your mother. Mothers are very useful. Mine was when Donald was killed and before I met and fell in love with Carlos. See you.'

At the Ministry Office, Charlotte was on time. It seemed strange that Susan was still there in her role as Protection Officer, and now a Chief Inspector.

'Mrs Lang to see you, Minister,' announced Susan with a smile. 'Come on in, Charlotte,' called Sylvia. The two women embraced. 'Bring us some coffee, Susan, and one for yourself. I'm sure Charlotte would like you to be present. It'll save her repeating all she has to say when you two are on your own.'

Charlotte would have preferred to speak to Sylvia on her own, but she didn't feel she could object, and Susan had proved a very good friend over the years, quite apart from being one of her Bridesmaids when she'd married Xavier.

'It's a sad story I have to tell, Sylvia. I don't just mean Xavier being killed. That's the saddest part of all, of course, but you know all about that already. Quite simply Xavier didn't leave a will, and all his money, or the bulk of it, passes to Carlos. I could make a claim in the Spanish Courts, of course, but that would effectively be a claim against Carlos, and I simply couldn't contemplate bringing an action against him. Incidentally, he's been absolutely wonderful. He told Mum last night that I need never work again, that

211

he will provide for me out of his Momma's trust fund and he wants to see as much of me as he can. If he was my own son, I couldn't be closer. I don't want to live on his charity, as you'll appreciate. I want to work, and frankly I need to, in more ways than one. I need the money, and I'm too active, far too active, simply to sit at home. I was rather hoping you might be able to find me a job before I start enquiring downstairs in the Home Office or anywhere else.'

'Charlotte,' started Sylvia, 'you mustn't think of enquiring downstairs or anywhere else. I've a ready-made job for you right here and at the House. All Members of Parliament, as you well known, are entitled to assistants, researchers and secretaries, and you are the perfect candidate to be my Personal Assistant. I've been on the look-out for a replacement for John Hickson, who left a fortnight ago to go into the City. You'll be my top Personal Assistant from the first of December. I will have to get clearance from the Permanent Secretary, with you now having Spanish nationality. Your first allegiance will again be to the Red White and Blue, but you've already signed the Official Secrets Act Declaration.'

'Thanks very much indeed, Sylvia. I really don't know what to say, except you know I accept your offer very gladly indeed, and you know I will do my very best for you. I know very little about British politics just now beyond what I read in the papers. Luckily I've kept reasonably abreast reading the papers flown out to Madrid, but I think I know more about Spanish politics. I suppose that in twelve months I will be in reverse and be fully up to date here and dead ignorant about what's going on in Madrid.'

'Good girl. It'll seem quite like old times. We must be careful about one thing. We don't want Susan losing her job. The Treasury are getting keener by the day watching expenditure. We don't want them saying that I don't need a Protection Officer now that you are working with me. Some of them are trying to get rid of Chief Inspector rank!'

'Thanks, Sylvia. I'm glad you said that,' put in Susan. 'If they do try and push me out, I'll resign my commission and you can appoint me a PA. I'll be quite happy to work along-side Charlotte again, in uniform or dressed as I am.'

The three women laughed.

'Look, I've got to go to the Cabinet meeting now. Why don't you two have a second coffee, and you can fill Charlotte in on any and all the changes that have taken place since she held your job.'

'Certainly, Minister,' said Susan, with more than a twinkle in her eye. Sylvia departed with one of her red boxes that seemed to follow her everywhere, with her smart black leather handbag hanging from her shoulder.

'You don't need me to come with you to Downing Street, Sylvia?'

'No, you stay chatting to Charlotte. I think I can manage. I'll take the Home Secretary with me.'

18

The tragic death of Xavier Lang was not simply a personal tragedy. It was a matter of the greatest concern to the three top Russians. President Stolypin summoned Viktor Maiski and Vladimir Renov to his secret headquarters within the Kremlin.

The meeting was held immediately the news of Xavier's death had been confirmed from Madrid. By happy chance, all three men were in Moscow when the news came. Vladimir gave an order for flowers to be sent to the widow as soon as it was known that she was at the flat in Madrid, and one of the security officers at the Madrid embassy had been posted at the flat to report Charlotte's arrival.

'This is an extremely awkward development, comrades. We've spent a great deal of time and roubles on Xavier Lang,' started Stolypin. 'There are two matters that concern me immediately. First, was Lang as good as his word? Did he tell anybody, including any members of his family, of our plans for him? His wife, his sons or his government? Secondly, where do we go from here? Do we look elsewhere, or do we forget the whole thing?'

'President. We're not going to see all our time and effort and roubles wasted.' It was Renov who was speaking. 'If we stick with Lang's family, he does have a surviving son; the one who won that skiing competition at Chamonix last year, or it was two years ago? He's very bright. I know that myself, since I made a point of speaking to him after he spoke so well at his father's wedding. I could make further enquiries in London. I imagine that Lang's widow will return to her

214

mother's home. There won't be much for her in Spain. She would have made an excellent Tsarina, but I'm afraid that's now out of the question. If the young man Carlos was ever to become Tsar, then Lang's widow would be the Tsar's mother, but that would not make her Tsarina.'

'No it wouldn't, unless we altered the law to permit it, but that's a long way off,' put in Maiski. 'Let's stick to first things first and establish as a fact that he hasn't confided in anybody. My men haven't heard a whisper of anything. I would guess he kept his word, but we can't rely on guesswork.'

'Certainly we can't.' It was Stolypin who took charge of the discussion. 'Renov. I want you to go to London and find out all you can. I agree it's not likely she will stay in Spain, either in Madrid or Seville. Her mother lives in London and Lang's son is at school in England. Maiski, you let Renov know immediately you know that the widow is back in London. Renov, your official reason for going will be to discuss the problems in the Balkans. Those will be with us for a generation. They always have been. The main thing is to establish that nothing has leaked out. Once we know for certain that nothing has leaked, we can decide our next move. I'm very concerned that no approach whatsoever should be made to that young man, surrounded as he may be with priests who may be skilled in extracting information through their system of confessions. The less that young man knows, the better. Are we all agreed?'

Both Maiski and Renov fully agreed. It was going to be an important and interesting task for Renov. Vladimir Renov had enjoyed his last visit immensely. He was sorry that he wouldn't be going down to Slapton again and possibly meeting his future Tsar, but he fully supported the decision to keep the young man in the dark. He would look forward to meeting Mrs Lang – yesterday's bride – again.

As soon as it was reported to him that Mrs Lang was back in London, he drafted his letter. It read:

'Dear Mrs Lang,
    My wife and I were dreadfully sorry to learn of your

215

husband's tragic accident in Spain. Please accept our sincere sympathy. We were sorry not to have been with you at the funeral, but I trust our flowers and sympathy note reached you at your flat in Madrid. It only seems like yesterday that Myra and I were attending your delightful wedding at Slapton College and the lovely reception thereafter at the White Hart. We have often thought and spoken of you both since then. By chance I am coming to London in the very near future, to discuss important Government business with your ministers. It will be an official visit this time, not a private one, but I might well be able to have some time to myself, and I would be very pleased if you would care to be my guest for lunch at our Embassy in London, from which address this letter will be delivered to you by hand. If we cannot meet I will understand, but I hope we may.

    Yours sincerely

    Vladimir Renov'

President Stolypin and First Vice President Maiski had no problem in approving Renov's draft.

'You are quite the letter writer now, Renov. I'll have to think of having you replace my secretary.' This joke had to sustain their humour for the rest of the day. They had pressing matters on their minds. Stolypin was not noted for his humour. He wasn't an 'easy' man, but then his position didn't really lend itself to humour.

The letter was sent in the diplomatic bag to London. Within 48 hours it was being delivered by hand to Charlotte at her mother's home. There was nothing for it, but Charlotte had to take the letter to Sylvia at the House. She waited half an hour before leaving her home with her mother to go shopping, and then she was on her way to the Home Office building. The officers on duty recognized her and she was allowed to park, but she had no pass, as yet, for the House of Commons, so she went via the public entrance and completed the usual form as though she was an ordinary member of the public wanting to see their Member of Parliament.

Sylvia made her excuses to the two Cabinet members sitting either side of her on the Front Bench and made her way to Charlotte.

'Whatever is it, Charlotte? I'm needed back in there. It must be something urgent?'

'Yes it is, but you may not think so. I've just received a letter one hour back from Vladimir Renov in Moscow. I thought you would want to see it immediately rather than tomorrow.' Charlotte produced the letter in its envelope from her handbag.

Sylvia read it. 'Good girl. I'm glad you're going to be my PA. Fancy having a PA who is on close personal terms with the Second Vice President of Russia!

'Listen, Charlotte. He's not to know that you are working for me. So far as the world is concerned, and that includes Vladimir Renov, you will be a personal researcher for a friend of mine, who is a backbencher who isn't standing at the next election. He's never had a researcher before, and he doesn't really need one now, but if he ever did need any help I would let you help him. When you start with me on the first of December, I'll introduce you to him, and you can work with him for a week, just to get to know your way around again. His name is Tim Hughes. He received a "K" for length of service on the back benches. He never was a Minister, but he's a very nice man with interests in the City. You'll like him.'

'Thanks, Sylvia. I'll look forward to meeting him and will make full enquiries about him for practice. How old did you say he is?'

'I didn't. Don't try your Police tactics on me. I can see you haven't forgotten how to ask questions when you want answers. I don't know exactly. I would say about sixty. A lot older than you and I, and at least ten years older than Xavier, so don't get any ideas!'

'Oh, Sylvia. I can see you haven't changed, but I'm not really up to that sort of teasing yet. I will get over things, I

217

must, but it's early days. I'm certainly not thinking of re-marriage – well, not for a very long time.'

The two women got up. Sylvia went back to her seat in the House, bowing to the Speaker on her way, as required by tradition, and Charlotte rejoined her mother in the Home Office car park.

The following morning, George, the Inspector from the Southgate Police Station, arrived at Charlotte's mother's home with a House of Commons Security Pass (temporary) – the real one would carry her photograph. She was described simply as Mrs Charlotte Lang, Researcher to Sir Timothy Hughes MP.

Over dinner with her mother, Charlotte raised her glass of wine and proposed a toast: 'To Sir Timothy Hughes MP and all who sail in her'. After dinner, Charlotte wrote her reply to Renov.

'Dear General Renov,

Thank you very much for your kind letter. I would very much enjoy having lunch with you at your Embassy when next you are in London. Please let me know when. It was very kind of you and your wife sending me flowers in Madrid. I miss Xavier dreadfully, but I have received much comfort and friendship since his tragic death. My mother sends you her best regards. Please give my kind regards to your wife.

Yours sincerely,
Charlotte Lang'

Charlotte carefully addressed the envelope to 'Major-General Vladimir Renov, Care of the Ambassador', marking the envelope 'Private and Personal'. She knew it would be passed through the infra-red machine.

Charlotte, her mother and Carlos had been back from Spain about three weeks when Paul de Sanches announced that he wanted to come to London to meet the family and discuss important matters that needed attention in Madrid and Seville. He would like to see Charlotte and Carlos on his own. This was both necessary and desirable: he would explain all when he came. It wasn't easy on the telephone. That was the way he put it.

Charlotte was at Heathrow to meet Paul, together with her mother. Charlotte thought he would appreciate her mother being present. Since Charlotte was driving, the conversation in the car was really between Alice and Paul. It was both light and general, including enquiries after Marie in Seville and Carlos down at Slapton. They drove to Slapton, as arranged, first, so that Paul could speak to his nephew on his own, and then they would drive back to Southgate in London so that he could talk to Charlotte on her own, if he thought it 'necessary and desirable'.

Paul was looking forward to visiting Slapton during term time. He had never been there before himself, except on the wedding day. Now he would see it in its everyday appearance. Paul was delighted with all he saw, particularly Carlos himself. On their own, Paul came quickly to the purpose of his visit:

'I'm very glad you are keeping in touch with your Aunt Marie and myself by post. We really do enjoy your letters. It seems so long since I read letters written in English. Now, Carlos, I do understand that you are very fond of Charlotte and so are we, and you know that most of your Dad's money will come to you under Spanish law. It will not go to Charlotte unless, of course, you want it that way. I know you are a very generous young man, and you may feel tempted to give all your money to Charlotte. That would be a grave mistake, even if you were capable of doing it. That is why I wanted to speak to you on your own. I know that you think Charlotte is a lovely person. I believe you, but take it from me that many men in this world would also share your thoughts if they thought she had real wealth. If you were to make over any large sum of capital to Charlotte, you would almost certainly lose her. She's very vulnerable just now, missing your father, and she might easily fall prey to some bastard who was after her money. You must act at all times

219

as though you were her protection officer, just as Charlotte acted as protection officer to her friend Sylvia.

'There is another thing. Your Dad's money is in Spain, and it should remain in Spain. I have done what you asked me to do with the flat in Madrid. Everything that Aunt Marie and I thought you might like from the flat has gone to your home in Seville which Maria is keeping in perfect order. She and Manuel particularly asked me to thank you for letting them both continue to live in their flat as their permanent home. They would have had nowhere to go if you had turned them out. I think I know that I can rely on your patriotism to Spain and your love of your family, including Charlotte, to do the right thing. Please say that I am right in my thinking.'

'Uncle Paul, you really needn't have spoken to me as you have done, but thanks for coming over. You really are the best of uncles and trustees. Anything you can do to keep Charlotte as Mrs Lang has my full support. You know that. Strictly between ourselves, I feel that I'm in love with Charlotte and always have been, but I daren't say so at my age or at this time. Dad only died a few weeks ago. Please do all you can to prevent any man taking her out of the family. I feel that Maria and Manuel are part of my family, even if they are not relations; they did so much for Momma I wouldn't dream of putting them out of their home in Seville. I want to make my home in Seville, as you know.

'Incidentally, Charlotte tells me that she's going to start working again, not with the Police, but in the House of Commons, if she hasn't started already. If you feel she does need any more income, you know that you can give her the rent from the flat in Madrid. All I need here is enough pocket money to see me through. I'll need more this year than last, because I'm Captain of Rugger and Head of House. Believe me, Uncle, I'm working as hard as I can for Momma and the family, if that doesn't sound too pompous.'

'Bravo! Good for you, Carlos. You know we're all behind you in Seville. I shouldn't really tell you, but your Aunt and your three young cousins have been saying a rosary for you every night since your father and Miguel were killed. If prayer does have any real power, you will have the best "A" levels, as you call them in England, provided you keep your head down. We are very much looking forward to seeing you in Seville during the Christmas holidays.'

At Alice's home in Southgate, Paul continued his mission, his zeal buttressed by the support he had solicited and received from Carlos.

'Alice, I have enjoyed this meal. I can't think why *Cuisine Anglais* is regarded as such a joke in France. I think it's excellent.' Beyond enjoying his food and wine, Paul knew how to flatter; Alice preened. Paul continued: 'Charlotte, I felt I had to speak to you on your own, but obviously I don't mind your mother hearing what I have to say, if you have no objection.'

This was another clever ploy. 'I've had a good little chat with Carlos this afternoon, as you know. What a lovely and lively lad he is. He's a real credit to his family and, if I may say so, to you. I can tell you that he holds you both in high regard. I'm making all necessary arrangements in Spain. Briefly, Marie and I have stripped the flat in Madrid of all valuables and personal items. They have been taken by road to Seville. I'll be able to get a very good rent for the flat, and I want to tell you, Charlotte, that, if you should need your income to be supplemented, I can let you have that rent or any part of it, since the flat was owned by Sophia and I am trustee of her estate. I know that Carlos would like you to have it if you felt you needed it. I don't yet know the value of Xavier's estate – it may take some time to find out – but it will be substantial. From what I know already, it cannot be less than ten million pounds and will, of course, be many millions in terms of pesetas. If you need any income, please do not hesitate in speaking to me direct in my role as Carlos's trustee. I know he would wish you to do that, and it would save you any embarrassment in asking him whilst he is still a schoolboy.'

Paul de Sanchas had crafted his words with skill. His

English may have been heavily accented, but the message he wished to convey was clear enough. No reference to capital, but interest only, and his reference to Carlos as a schoolboy wasn't lost on Charlotte and her mother.

'Thank you, Paul, for what you've said. I'll confess to you that I was absolutely shattered when Xavier's lawyers in Madrid told me that he had made no provision for me whatsoever by way of a will, but I don't think I will need to ask you for anything. I have been very fond of Xavier's son Carlos since I first knew him when he was a little boy. I should almost feel I was stealing from him if I was to take any money from him out of his mother's trust fund behind his back. I think I can tell you that he himself offered me as much income as I required to save me from going out to work. That boy is a real gem. I just pray that when he grows up he finds the girl he deserves.'

Paul felt mightily relieved. He was going to help build the Lang fortune. He had said 'ten million' to test Charlotte and her mother. A figure of sixty million would have been nearer the mark.

'Tell me, Charlotte, if you don't mind me asking, just what do you plan to do with your life? You know we would love to have you living in Seville.'

'It's good and kind of you to say so, Paul, but that is really quite out of the question at the moment. There would be nothing for me to do in Seville beyond looking after the house, which would be like a furniture shop without Xavier. Here I have my mother, my work and Carlos, whenever I get the chance to see him. He can always come here when he wants, but he's going to be playing rugger most weekends for Slapton, when he's not working, and he's a bit of a workaholic like his father. You see, when I moved out to Spain Mum cleared my room and made it into a boys' room for Carlos and Miguel. Now that I'm back home it's become my room again, and when Carlos comes home for a weekend he has your room, which is all right for one night, but it's hardly home from home when he got used to having his own room. By the way, we hope you don't mind having the box room, but we are a bit cramped, as you can see. The old vicarage furniture only just fitted in. No. I shall stay working as I am for quite a time. The future will just have to look after itself for the moment.'

'Thank you, Charlotte, for being so straightforward and forthcoming, but do remember that the fact that Xavier is no longer with us doesn't mean that we are going to lose touch, and we are really looking forward to seeing you and your mother at Christmas in Seville. Just let us know when you plan to come. I'm sure that Maria and Manuel will be glad to see you.'

The following morning Paul set off back to Madrid and, after he had done his business there, he was off back to Seville and his own home. The following night Alice spoke to Charlotte:

'Charlotte. I think Paul was almost too friendly, didn't you? I hope you don't mind my speaking my mind, but I can't really believe that you are not entitled to any of Xavier's money – his capital, I mean. Paul talked about interest only, and it seems he controls all Carlos's money and now Xavier's as well. He seems a very nice man, but he does have a wife and three daughters. Have you checked properly as to your legal rights?'

'Yes I have, Mum. I do have rights. I could hold the whole of Xavier's estate up by questioning and seeking to find if he did make a will unknown to his Madrid and Seville lawyers, but if I was to take any step in that direction through solicitors of my own it would be sure to get back to Carlos, and I don't want to upset him in any way just now when he's got his "A" levels coming up. I would never forgive myself if I caused him to come a cropper in his exams. What I will do is have a little chat with him when he has taken his exams and he knows the results, and we discuss his own future together. I know I enjoy his complete trust and confidence, and I'm not going to do anything to spoil our relationship, and I don't want you to say anything to him about his father having left me no money. He knows that already, and as you know he said I could have any amount of money from his mother's trust fund to save me ever having to work again.'

'I won't say anything, dear. I know you're very fond of him, but I bet there aren't too many women in this world who would take the view you are taking with all those millions in Spain. I know he's very fond of you. He told me so immediately after your wedding, but then he's still only a schoolboy, but he's no ordinary schoolboy. He seems very much the young-man-about-town to me. See, I shouldn't be talking to you like this as the widow of a vicar, but I am your mother, and I still think it was cruel of Xavier not making a will in your favour. I can't think that Paul hasn't made a will in favour of Marie.'

At the Russian Embassy in London, Major-General Vladimir Renov might have been the Tsar himself, in terms of the respect and attention that was accorded to him. He was after all the Second Vice President of Russia.

All events moved on oiled wheels, not least the very pleasant lunch to which Charlotte was invited.

'Do tell me, Mrs Lang, if you ever feel like taking a further holiday in my country with, say, your mother or a friend including that stepson of yours, what's his name, Carlos, isn't it?'

'That's kind of you, General. Perhaps one day we will. We did so enjoy staying with you and your wife Myra and your little boy, but I'm afraid that will have to wait a bit. I will have to clear up certain family matters in Spain this coming year, and I'm back at work again.'

'Are you now – back in the Police, you mean?'

'No, General. I think I'm getting a bit too old to be a Protection Officer any longer – seriously, it's never easy going back to a situation. No. I've been very lucky. I've managed to secure a position at our House of Commons. I'm working as personal assistant to one of our members called Sir Timothy Hughes. He's a very pleasant man to work for. Of course, you will understand that nothing can be said to be permanent in politics, particularly democratic politics with elections, but I'm finding the work very interesting. See, here is my Pass to the House of Commons.'

Charlotte produced her temporary Pass, which Renov examined with care.

'Thank you very much, Mrs Lang. I find it most refreshing to find someone in London I can speak to who is honest and straightforward, but tell me, if you can, a secret. Are you expecting an election shortly? Is that why you have only a temporary Pass?'

'No, General. I don't know any secrets and I couldn't tell you if I did, but you were quick to spot my Pass was temporary. It's simply that the office which issued the Pass didn't have my photograph. I will be taking a passport sized photo into the office tomorrow, and I will then be issued with a permanent Pass which I can wear.'

This conversation, which had been taped, was dutifully reported back to Moscow by Renov, together with a memorandum to the effect that Sir Timothy Hughes was simply a wealthy back-bencher who had done his 15-year stint to obtain his knighthood. That it was unlikely, on account of his age, that he would ever receive ministerial office and that she, Charlotte, seemed unlikely ever to know any secrets.

Back at the House of Commons Charlotte made full report to Sylvia as to what had passed between Renov and herself, and MI6 was also fully informed. In truth, there was not that much to report beyond the fact that they had enjoyed a pleasant chat over lunch and that Charlotte was working for Sir Timothy Hughes.

Christmas itself would be spent in Southgate. Alice was very pleased. There is something about Christmas in England that is special to most English people. In Scotland, rather more is made of New Year. In Spain, apart from the spiritual significance of Christmas itself, there would be little or no atmosphere, so far as Alice was concerned.

She was very glad to have Charlotte at home. The House of Commons would not be sitting. Sir Timothy Hughes was off to Barbados and would require none of Charlotte's attention, and Sylvia could easily keep in contact from Harcourt or her Ministerial Office in Whitehall. Alice's elder daughter Margaret and her son-in-law Philip could spend Christmas day with her – which they couldn't possibly have done if she'd gone to Spain. Carlos would enjoy himself wherever he was, and Philip would have some male company in Carlos, instead of being with herself, Margaret and Charlotte, as he had been over the years.

Christmas is always likely to prove a difficult period for widows on the first Christmas following their husband's death, and for this reason Charlotte was glad that Carlos had very happily agreed to spend Christmas with her and her mother, and had not insisted on accepting the invitation of his Uncle Paul and Aunt Marie. Charlotte would go to Midnight Mass, whilst her mother went to her old parish church, where her husband had been vicar, accompanied by Margaret and Philip.

Back home, Alice contented herself by saying that she had enjoyed going back to her husband's old parish church and that it was a pity that she, Charlotte, had not come along as well and brought Carlos with her.

'He wouldn't have minded coming. He came to the Garden Party. He doesn't know anybody at that church round the corner.' Alice felt she had made her point.

Charlotte thought it best to make no reply, obvious or otherwise beyond saying that he had enjoyed 'his' Midnight Mass and that she had enjoyed being with him. Margaret and Philip went home, but they would be back for the Christmas lunch, which Alice always arranged for 1 p.m. 'in time for the Queen's speech at 3 o'clock' as she put it. Alice was a great believer in tradition.

The day itself was wet, and the five of them spent the day around the television when they weren't at the dining table filling themselves with turkey and plum pudding.

On Boxing Day Philip and Carlos were off to the Tottenham Hotspur/Chelsea match – a friendly, not a League fixture. Since Philip was a Spurs fan, Carlos for fun said he was a Chelsea man, although, in truth, he would have preferred to watch Rugby Union at Twickenham.

It was Margaret who remarked that Carlos was now taller than Philip – 'So you won't be able to take him in half-price'.

Everybody laughed, particularly when Carlos said, 'I'll pay for the tickets. I'll ask for an adult for myself and a "Senior Citizen" ticket for Philip.'

Philip wasn't an old age pensioner yet, but he was considerably older than Margaret and might easily have been taken for Alice's husband.

A week spent in Seville during the College Christmas vacation passed too quickly for Carlos. His Aunt Marie had cried for joy when he first entered her home. The weather was perfect and Carlos found his Uncle true to his word in terms of hospitality. Aunt Marie and her three daughters were entranced with him.

19

Russia's continuing economic difficulties, made worse by a terrible winter with prolonged periods of snow, ice and sub-zero temperatures, had increased the necessity for an ever-closer understanding and relationship between the financial institutions of Russia itself and its true friends and partners in the West.

In personal terms, this meant a closer relationship between the Orlanskis in Chicago, the Renovs in Moscow and the Sabitas in London. Sylvia's very close relationship with both Mary Orlanski and Charlotte Lang meant that the three women saw much more of each other than would have been the case had Russia not experienced its economic problems.

Sylvia and Mary, who had both become very well-heeled, were extremely sorry for Charlotte in her situation of being left a widow at the early age of 32, and doubly so when they learnt that she had been left penniless beyond any claim she might have, if she cared to pursue it, in a foreign Court.

On her own, Sylvia, herself a Queen's Counsel before becoming Deputy Prime Minister, felt she must try and persuade Charlotte to pursue matters, if need be via diplomatic channels, to obtain a substantial fraction of Xavier's undoubted wealth.

'Charlotte, you can't simply let matters rest with all Xavier's money going to Carlos. You were Xavier's wife for God's sake. He certainly should have made a will and left you properly provided for, if only a life interest. Please let me make enquiries through our Ambassador in Madrid. I know you worry about Carlos's feelings, but he need never know.'

'Thanks Sylvia, but no thanks. I simply daren't do anything until he's taken his exams. You and I both know that information leaks. No British Government since the war has been able to prevent confidential information leaking. If any enquiries were to leak out regarding Xavier, who was prominent and important in Madrid, Carlos would be bound to find out through his Uncle Paul, who knows everybody who is anybody in Madrid as well as Seville. Even you could not guarantee matters not leaking in London, never mind Madrid – and where would I be then? If it makes you and Mary, and Susan too for that matter, feel better, I'll promise to go down to Slapton and speak about my position on the night he has taken his last ''A'' level examination. How's that for you?'

'Very well, Charlotte, but I'll hold you to that promise, and so will Mary and Susan. That boy owes you a lot. His father owed you more. I'm sorry to seem to go on, but I'm only trying to help. I do like Carlos myself, but obviously I'm not as close to him as you are. Do give him my very best wishes. I do hope his ''A'' levels go well, believe me. I also know that in the absence of any close family over here, you're his inspiration. He never stops talking about you at Harcourt when he comes over with my own boys, even when you aren't there.'

On Stolypin's orders, Renov and Maiski were directed to fly to London and pursue Charlotte. Renov invited Sylvia, her husband Carlos and Charlotte to a private dinner at the Russian Embassy. Viktor Maiski was present. During the course of the dinner Renov asked Charlotte, as though casually, if Xavier had ever spoken of any plans he might have had for settling down to live in Russia.

'Good heavens, no. Whatever gave you that idea, General? We enjoyed our holiday in your country, we were particularly pleased to meet your wife and little boy, but he never spoke of living in Russia. I know that Xavier spoke Russian. He had Russian blood in him from generations back, and his

229

two boys spoke some Russian, as I do now, but only for holiday purposes. I couldn't speak to you as I'm doing now in fluent Russian. I could manage in French. I read French at Warwick, but I think you know that already.'

After dinner Renov and Maiski smiled at one another. The would both make report back to Stolypin.

It was June when Carlos sat his 'A' levels. Slapton always obtained very creditable results. Carlos's results were to be no exception.

The examinations over, the Sixth Form were now down to games and, more importantly for those not in the First Cricket Eleven, looking forward to their end-of-term celebrations, including the College Ball.

Charlotte booked in at the White Hart. She wanted to be with Carlos on her own on his last night of the exams. She was not relishing her fulfilling her promise to Sylvia, but it did seem ridiculous having to earn her living as her mother had been obliged when her father had died, leaving little or no money, when Xavier, her husband, had been a millionaire.

She arrived at Slapton at 7 p.m., having driven down from London. She was tired. It had been a very busy week with Sylvia in the House, the Ministry and elsewhere, including Harcourt. She hoped her tiredness didn't show when she changed for dinner. She deliberately had not gone to the College first. She wasn't going to embarrass Carlos by kissing him in front of his pals. In any case, she wanted him to see her at her best. She was downstairs in the hotel lounge when he arrived at 7.30 with two other boys, who were also prefects and who were having dinner with their respective parents. Carlos came straight to her. He seemed a man rather than a boy. He was half a head taller than his two friends. He was obviously delighted to see her. He put his arms around her, held her tight and kissed her on both cheeks. 'Carlos. I'm glad the exams don't seem to have taken all your strength. Come on, sit down and have a sherry. Tonight's on me.'

'Thanks, Charlotte. You're a real brick coming down from London tonight. There's so much for us to talk about. I don't know how I've done. I know I've passed, but it's a question of grades. I hope I've done well, for your sake.'

'It's more important for your sake, darling, I got my "A" levels years ago. It seems a long time since I was at Warwick, but I know you've worked hard. Father Turner told me. Your parents would be proud of you. It's sad they can't be here, but I'm here and I'm proud of you as your stepmum, whatever your results.'

Charlotte decided that she would speak to Carlos about his father's money and her own future after dinner, rather than spoil the meal. One consideration she had was that if it did prove a difficult session there would be a shorter interval between her talk with him and her retiring to bed. She was feeling very tired, and she wasn't going to have a late night if she could help it. The hotel menu was always extensive, and unusually the table d'hote menu contained two fish dishes – this being a Friday night, when there were always a few parents taking their sons from the College.

Charlotte and Carlos settled for the salmon. It was whilst they were eating their desserts that Charlotte sensed that Carlos had gone strangely quiet in both his manner and speech.

'Is there something on your mind, Carlos? You seem to have gone very quiet.'

'Do I, Charlotte? It's these coffee Renoirs. They remind me of that dinner years ago in Chamonix. It was the first time I'd ever taken you out for dinner. I was so glad you made me keep that childish promise. Looking back now, I think it was that night I fell in love with you.'

Charlotte looked at him. What was this boy saying? He was no longer a boy, but an extremely good-looking young man, years ahead of his age. Carlos placed his hand on hers across the table.

'Charlotte. Please look into my eyes. I know you always think of me as a little boy, but I'm not a little boy any longer. Can't you tell I'm madly in love with you? I can't propose to you properly like this across the dinner table. Please promise me that you'll let me propose to you properly when we're on our own, after I've left Slapton.'

Charlotte was completely overcome and taken by surprise. She knew, of course, as any woman in her position would, that Carlos was fond of her. He had liked her since he was a little boy and she had played with him as a WPC and bought him ice creams, but this. She felt the room was beginning to swim, but his eyes never left hers.

'Carlos, darling. You don't know what you're saying.' This was all she felt she could say.

'Yes I do, Charlotte, and I'm waiting for your answer. Don't you think I've been wanting to speak to you for months? I would have spoken to you before, but it didn't seem right when Dad had only been dead for such a very short time – not that much different from the time Momma died and you married Dad. I know you're older than me, but I'm not a child. In Spain, I'm a man. I've already signed a will to benefit you. One day I will make another. I'm growing older quicker than you. I had to explain that to your mother, who I already call Gran.'

'Carlos, what are you saying? Does Gran know you are speaking like this to me tonight?' All manner of thoughts were going through her mind.

'No she doesn't, Charlotte, but I bet if she was sitting here with us she would remember my conversation with her when you were on your honeymoon with Dad. I explained to her that you were roughly twice my age then, but that when I was twenty-one you would not be forty-two!'

Charlotte took in what he was saying, but her mind was spinning. It was to spin faster as Carlos proceeded.

'Charlotte, please look at me. I know you wanted children and so did Dad, but you also know, like me, that he could never have given you a child.'

Charlotte felt her heart was bumping. What did Carlos know that she didn't? Her blank, astonished look told Carlos what he had never understood, her ignorance.

'Don't be cross, Charlotte. I thought Dad must have told you what he'd told Miguel. It was Miguel who told me that after I was born Dad had an operation to prevent himself from making Momma pregnant, and before he married you he had another operation to reverse the first one. It didn't take long for Miguel and me to realize that the doctors had done a first-class job with the first operation and that the second one had failed. I thought you knew.'

'Carlos, I don't know what to say.'

'Don't try, Charlotte. Let's have our coffees here at the table and then we can join the others in the lounge, but please promise me that you will let me propose to you properly in Spain. I would love you to say ''Si''. We could make Gran a proper Gran.'

'I promise I will let you propose to me when we are next in Spain on our own, but please don't ask me to say anything more tonight. I'll never forget tonight as long as I live. God, I wish I could have known your Momma.'

They drank their coffees at the table, and Charlotte went to the powder room to freshen up before joining the parents of the other two boys to make conversation with Carlos. He realized that Charlotte was tired and made some excuse to return to the College on his own, to see that some youngsters had observed 'lights out' in their dormitory. As he made to leave the hotel, Charlotte walked to the entrance with him. She took his right hand in her left hand. She was left-handed.

'Carlos,' she said, 'thank you for everything tonight.' She placed her hands behind his neck, her arms around him. She pulled him towards herself and kissed him on the lips. It was the first time she had ever kissed him on the lips. Carlos was a little taken aback, but thrilled.

'Thank you, Charlotte. Sleep well. Sorry you have to go back tomorrow, but don't forget I'll want most of the dances with you at the College Ball next Saturday.'

Charlotte stood by the door as Carlos walked back to the College drive entrance. Something must have told him that she might still be watching. He turned at the entrance to the driveway and waved.

At the Ministry building Sylvia awaited Charlotte's appearance. She had told her husband what had passed between Charlotte and herself. Susan, who was on duty as usual in her role as Protection Officer, in uniform this morning, knew all about Charlotte's situation. Charlotte came bouncing into Sylvia's office, wearing a smile Sylvia thought she hadn't seen since that terrible day last November, when the news had come through of Xavier and Miguel having been killed. The three women faced one another.

It was Sylvia who led the way. 'Come on, Charlotte. You know what we want to hear. How did you get on with Master Carlos?'

'I got on with "Master Carlos", as you call him, very well indeed. I tell you both now that I find "Master Carlos" the nicest, kindest young man I've ever known. No more questions, please. I'm just glad we didn't start those enquiries in Spain. I appreciated your offer, but I'm glad, more glad than I can say, that I declined. I will hope to be able to tell you both a great deal more in the future. I'll just say this. You and I, Sylvia, will no doubt be at the Slapton Ball this coming weekend. We shall both have a Carlos for a partner. You with your husband, and me with my stepson. I don't want to say the wrong thing, but I bet I'll be the happiest woman in the College and Master Carlos will be the happiest man.'

Charlotte couldn't be drawn, however hard the two of them tried.

The Slapton College Ball is always one of the leading events in the annual social calendar in the south of England. It formed part of what was officially termed 'The Great Weekend' – a mixture of Annual Ball, Sports Day and Prize-Giving.

Other attractions included a golf competition on the College's own golf course and a cricket match between the College First Eleven and a team representing the Old Boys' Club, drawn from former pupils now attending universities. With any number of boys being related either closely or distantly to the aristocracy and leading captains of industry, the national press were always on hand, not least to cover the Ball itself.

The daughters of some families arrived in carloads with their parents, to maintain family links and hopefully create them. There was a joke that had gone the rounds that a foreign prince was in the Sixth Form one year and the press had called the Rector with a request that 'the Prince' give an exclusive. The Rector is said to have replied, 'Which Prince? We have three in the College.'

True or false, no-one could deny the possibility. Naturally, there was a measure of competition for placings at all the major events, particularly the Ball itself. Dame Sylvia Sabita, as the Deputy Prime Minister, and her husband were naturally among those who would be on the top table in the huge marquee that served as the ballroom, illuminated with crystal chandeliers. Had Xavier lived, there could have been no doubt that he and Charlotte would also have been on the top table, but as it was, Charlotte had been placed on Father Turner's table. This was explained quite easily by reason of Carlos Lang being 'Head of House'. Whilst the top table was arguably one of the most distinguished top tables outside London, Father Turner's table contained two Ambassadors from South America, an Old Boy who happened to be a Rear Admiral and a High Court Judge, and their respective spouses.

Other housemasters had their own tables with guests. Those who could not have seats at the housemasters' tables were divided up on an alphabetical basis amongst the staff of the College. This had been the system since 1910, and whilst inevitably there were minor irritations, no-one had come up with a better suggestion.

Sylvia had been down to Lanchester, her constituency, on the Thursday with her husband, together with Susan as protection officer, and Charlotte made the opportunity of staying with her old friend Florence Parmaine – now Lady Bickerstaffe.

Florence was everyone's pet heroine. She was particularly close to Sylvia whom she had known since childhood. At one stage in the past Charlotte had been employed by Scotland Yard to spy on Sylvia's husband, Carlos, and Xavier, long before her marriage to him, at the time when the Police were investigating the murder of the late Sir John Penrose.

It was thanks to Florence that Sylvia had become reconciled to Charlotte, and now they were close friends. Florence had been instrumental in bringing first Mary and then Charlotte and Susan into the Soroptomists. She was now in line for national honours in that organization, if her obligations to her husband would permit.

Although Charlotte was always prepared to back her own judgement, she felt that a completely objective viewpoint, which she knew Florence would give, must be worth having, and she decided to seek her friend's advice. 'Florence, I do want your advice on a very personal matter. Please give me your word that you won't breathe a word of what I'm going to say to anybody – not even John, Sylvia, Mary or Susan. Do I have your word?'

'Of course you do. You've never found me letting you down before. Whatever is it? You're not in any trouble, are you?'

'No, Florence. Not yet. That's why I've come to you for your advice. It's a long story, but I'll come to the point quickly. I think you know that I gave up my job at Scotland Yard to marry Xavier, and he has left me penniless by reason of his not having made a will. I could, of course, make a claim, but any monies I received would effectively come out of the pocket of Carlos, Xavier's youngest son.'

'Yes, dear. I did know that. Sylvia told me, and I gather she's been trying to get you to agree to her making some enquiries, with a view to your making a claim in the Spanish Court through Spanish lawyers. How can I help? I've been out of the law a long time now, well it seems a long time, and in any case my knowledge of Spanish law could be written on the back of a postage stamp – with ample room to spare.'

'Sorry, Florence. It's not your legal advice I require, but your advice as my most trusted friend. I'm glad Sylvia has spoken to you as she has. At least you know a good deal of the background, without my having to go through it all again. How well do you know Xavier's son Carlos, and when did you last see him?'

'That's a funny question, Charlotte. The last time I saw him was about three weeks ago. He was here with Sylvia's two boys. John was showing them his collection of Victorian postage stamps, including his Penny Blacks if that means anything to you. Carlos looked a good deal older than Sylvia's boys. He was very polite, as they were. You must understand I've never had much to do with young boys or men of that age, but I would say he's a very charming young man. He's not in any trouble, is he?'

'No, he's in no trouble yet. Neither am I. The point is, Florence, and this is why I'm speaking to you in confidence, it seems he has fallen madly in love with me and, dare I say it, I have fallen in love with him. Now, before you say I'm mad, I know I'm thirty-two and he's only seventeen, but he seems so grown-up I sometimes feel he's twenty-seven. Last week he was an absolute angel. Effectively he asked me to marry him. I was completely taken aback. Naturally I didn't just say "Yes Carlos, I will marry you", but I felt then and I feel that if I had to make a choice now, I would marry him. Please give me your advice. I won't mind what you say. I'll never quote you.'

'Before I give you any advice, Charlotte, I want you to tell me in detail all that passed between Carlos and you last week. Don't hold anything back. The value of any advice I give to you will depend on how much you can remember and tell me. I'm not being curious. I have to know. It's not like offering sympathy in exchange for full details, if you know what I mean.'

Charlotte looked at Florence, took a deep breath, and started. She told all from first seeing him and inviting him to have a sherry, to her kissing him on the lips. She missed nothing out. She had been a perfect Police witness for years. Xavier's vasectomy and her having no knowledge of it until told last week by Carlos – she missed nothing.

It was Florence's turn to look hard at Charlotte. She, Florence, took a deep breath:

'Charlotte, you've asked the impossible question. Human chemistry is something it's almost impossible to advise upon

237

properly. I can only tell you what I would do. I would study Spanish. I would get Carlos settled in Seville University. I would invite him to propose to me, I would accept his offer and try not to smother him. I would let him give me, say, two children, allowing for your age, and I would hope to live with him happily until old age. Never forget his father was physically old enough to be your father. He was forty-eight and you thirty as I remember it, so forget that aspect immediately. The only thing you'll need to watch is that you don't rush him into marrying you. Let him propose to you out in Seville or wherever in Spain, but you fix the time as soon as you like after he's eighteen and settled in the University, and go out to Seville and make your home there. I'll look forward to coming out to see you if I'm still alive, but one thing I would insist upon – keep this matter completely between yourselves until everything is arranged. I won't say a word to anybody. Thank you for taking me into your confidence. Remember, I'm not giving you advice, I'm just saying what I would do if ever I'd been in your position. How's that for you?'

'Florence, you're an angel. I prayed you'd say something like that, and I'll do just as you suggest. I didn't feel I could discuss this matter with anyone but you.' Charlotte kissed Florence on her forehead.

At the College, preparations had been going on all week. Indeed, they had been going on for months, but now all manner of activities were taking place, from the erection of the huge marquee to the laying out of car parks, the necessary toilets and pavilions for bars adjacent to the playing fields, golf course and rifle range. Side by side with all this activity there was a constant stream of security officers and Police. Father Rector would be glad when it was all over, the boys and their parents dispersed and the Community of the Order could, for a few weeks, resume a pattern of behaviour that the saintly Founder of the Order might just recognize.

Charlotte felt she was walking on cloud nine as Carlos's stepmother. She knew that this was, perhaps, one of her last

238

visits to the College for a long time. Carlos, the little boy she had first known whilst serving Sylvia as WPC was now Head of House, with all the deference given to his rank by the junior boys. She, as his stepmother, was given deference accordingly.

Any number of the parents still offered her sympathy on the loss of her husband, but it was seemingly many months ago, and all her thoughts now were concentrated on Carlos. She took his arm as though they were an engaged couple. He was definitely going to be the man in her life. He was already. She had confessed to Florence that she had not dared to take Carlos up to her room in the hotel. Walking round the College, she felt as near to being 'Royal' as it was possible to feel. She had changed faith for Xavier. There had been times when she had wondered whether she had done the right thing, but she had no doubts now.

Carlos was involved with his Head of House duties on the Saturday morning. He had hoped to play golf, but that had not been possible. He enjoyed Charlotte being with him. He could show off as well as anybody.

In the afternoon he was to play against the Old Boys, who were not much older than himself. He knew some of them, who had been in the First Eleven when he had been lower down the school.

Charlotte joined Susan for lunch. There really was no need for Susan to have been on duty. The whole pavilion was swarming with security, but there was one rather unpleasant incident. A smartly dressed young woman, who described herself as an 'investigative journalist', had gone around asking questions of all boys who would speak to her regarding Carlos and Charlotte. Eventually she spoke to Charlotte herself.

'My name is Lena Jenkins. I'm trying to obtain an exclusive. My friend here has been taking photographs, and some of the boys who know your stepson have been very helpful. Now that you must be one of the richest women in the country, I guess you must be one of the most eligible widows here this afternoon. What would you say are your chances of finding an eligible husband for the second time this afternoon?'

For two pins, Charlotte and Susan would have felt inclined to sort her out physically, but Charlotte controlled her inner anger. 'I would say pretty good, if I was husband-hunting, but I'm not. I hope that'll be a good quote for you? If not, you'd better make an appointment to speak to my press representative in Madrid!'

Lena Jenkins swallowed. She hadn't really expected to receive a reply she could quote verbatim.

She persisted. 'Is it true that you have received any number of marriage proposals including offers from strangers, Mrs Lang?'

'I'm not aware of any offers from strangers. Any offers from strangers will be referred to my press representative. Now, unless you wish me to call the Police, I must ask you to let me start watching the cricket. My stepson is playing.'

Lena attempted a third verbal assault. She held a notepad in one hand and her biro pen in the other. 'I'm sorry, Mrs Lang, but I must have something for my readers.' She got no further.

Susan stood up her full six foot two inches. 'That's it. You were warned. I'm a Police Officer. An Inspector, if you want to report that to your readers. I'm arresting you for conduct likely to cause a breach of the peace.'

Susan placed a firm grip on Lena Jenkin's upper arm, causing her to drop her notebook and her precious notes. 'I'm sure I don't have to tell you, but I'll tell you anyway that you are not obliged to say anything, but anything you do say will be taken down in writing and may be used in evidence.' Susan didn't release her hold, but tightened her grip until two uniformed officers who knew Susan came across.

'Officers, I've arrested this woman for causing a disturbance – conduct likely to cause – please take her to your car. I'll join you presently.'

'Certainly, Inspector,' said the taller of the two men. Lena

Jenkins was led to a police car parked immediately behind the pavilion.

Susan picked up the notebook that had fallen and passed it to Charlotte, saying, 'It'll make a good laugh reading what any of the boys have said. Excuse me, I'll just go and get her released. You watch the cricket. I'll be back shortly.'

Susan joined her uniformed colleagues and the wretched Lena Jenkins. 'Miss Jenkins. I heard all that passed between you and that lady, a recently bereaved widow. I know we all have to earn a living, but all the journalists I know have a code of honour. Now just give these officers your full name, address and telephone number, and I'll let you off this time with a caution, but don't ever let me find you again causing a nuisance of yourself, and think yourself damned lucky that Mrs Lang didn't throw you on the floor and jump on you in self-defence. I happen to know that she holds a Black Belt in karate. You can let her go, officers, when she's given you all the information you require.'

Inspector Susan made her way back to Sylvia.

'You're a bloody lucky woman,' said the younger officer. 'It's a good job for you the Inspector is keen on cricket herself. That Inspector has a very good memory. She wouldn't let you off with a caution next time.'

'Thanks for nothing,' said Lena. 'Where's my notebook?'

'How should we know? We've seen no notebook,' replied the taller officer. Lena Jenkins went back to the pavilion to retrieve her notes, but all she could see was the formidable Woman Police Inspector who'd arrested her. She didn't fancy a further confrontation. She persuaded her photographer friend to go and find her notebook, but he quickly returned, saying he couldn't.

He didn't look that carefully. He felt his afternoon had been wasted. Not entirely. He had obtained one or two quite good shots of Charlotte, but he wouldn't let Lena Jenkins have them. Like her, he was freelance. He would sell his photographs to a better market than Lena Jenkins.

The following night, the local evening paper showed a

number of photographs of the day's events, including a pleasant one of Charlotte chatting to Father Rector.

In Moscow, Renov and Maiski made their verbal report to Stolypin.

'So it comes to this, comrades. Xavier Lang did keep his word to us, and his wife knew nothing of our plans. That's excellent. It opens the doors to two obvious alternatives. We can now pursue the legitimate heir based on heredity, or we just might start to think in terms of Xavier Lang's younger son – the one who was the good skier at Chamonix. What have we got on them both? Can we have a meeting next week, with full reports on them?'

'I think we might, but a fortnight would be better,' replied Renov. 'I know that young Lang sat his examinations recently. He's almost certainly done well. He's remained very close to Xavier Lang's young widow, and I think she feels that he may return to Spain to attend Seville University. She enjoyed her holidays over here, so it shouldn't be too difficult to get the boy to come and spend a holiday with us, and we could size him up together when he comes. Speaking of size, he's a very well-made young man with his father's looks and some Russian for holiday purposes, according to the widow. As for the direct heir, he's seemingly less eligible as time passes. At least we now know who he is. His pictures and news of his whereabouts are in the glossy international press every week of the year. If you could leave the young man and his stepmother to me, perhaps Viktor, with his American connections, could find out all there really is to know about HRH.'

'Thanks, Vladimir, for that suggestion. I'd like to do that, Mr President. It'll mean another trip to the States. What shall I be covering this time? The flooding of the Mississippi and how it matches the flooding of the Volga? That should be enough. It would open the doors to a great deal of money – and much else besides. Yes, I'll do it. I'll call Elmer Orlanski and, perhaps, invite him and his wife over here for a change. You will like her, Mr President. She's American, but before she married Orlanski she was Maltese British. I should say she will be the best-known Maltese we've entertained in the Kremlin.'

Stolypin looked at his two Vice Presidents. 'Go on, you two. I'll look after Mother Russia whilst you're both away. Make certain you do your duty. I'm counting on you both. Lives may depend on it!'

20

As Personal Assistant to Sylvia, Charlotte quickly became one of the best-informed women in British politics. Effectively she shadowed Sylvia, not in the physical sense that Susan did in her role as protection officer, but in all her paperwork and contacts within the Government and Central Office. The fact that she had previously served as one of Sylvia's protection officers herself and had a good languages degree in French meant that she was able to absorb all manner of documentation with an eye to security, whether it emanated from Brussels, Strasbourg, Westminster or Whitehall.

Florence had suggested that she improve her Spanish, which wasn't that bad anyway, having been married to Xavier. She would work to improve her Spanish for Carlos's sake. She couldn't wait to be married to him, but Florence was right. She must not hurry 'the boy'. He wasn't going to be any 'toy boy' – he was going to be the father of her child or children, but all that lay in the future.

An invitation came from Moscow that could not be refused. The invitation was extended to the Prime Minister, but John Senior was very heavily engaged. Sylvia Sabita would have to go in his place. Charlotte would be going as PA, and Susan in her role as protection officer. When these details were relayed to Moscow, via the British Ambassador, Renov used his initiative to have Carlos Lang invited by his wife on a personal basis, with the approval of Stolypin and Maiski.

After leaving Slapton, Carlos had returned to his home in Seville. Maria and her husband Manuel were delighted to have Carlos back home. Whilst the family were away, Maria and Manuel had continued to live in their self-contained flat on the fourth floor of the beautiful house that resembled a museum under wraps. Maria had removed all the cover sheets, and everything was gleaming when Carlos came home.

'Please Carlos, never leave home again for England,' Maria had cried.

'Maria and Manuel,' he replied, 'I just can't continue to live on my own in this house. Keep your flat as it is, but please occupy one of the bedrooms below your flat. Until I make any changes or get married, we might just as well live as one family. You know you'll never have to give up your home upstairs. I've told you that and, as an added precaution, I've made arrangements with the family lawyers.'

Maria and Manuel needed no persuading. It was a matter of comment that lights, not just security lights, could be seen burning in the house on the first, second and third floors, behind the closed shutters at night. Paul de Sanches was as good as his word. He had arranged for Carlos's entry into Seville University, and the Captain of the University Ski Team was very happy to have a Fresher on board with a history of a Gold Medal from the Chamonix School Games. There would be no automatic place for Carlos in the University team, but it was always useful to have good reserves, particularly if the best men and women were in the middle of examinations.

Carlos decided that he would not enter the Martial Arts Club at the University in his first year. This needed considerable practice if he was going to the top, and he had no desire for possible injury until he had established himself in both his work and his marital plans.

Carlos had been back in Seville a month when a letter was delivered to his home from the Russian Consulate in the City. The letter was addressed to him formally as 'Señor Carlos de Sallas Lang'. The envelope was of good quality and bore the Consular Emblem of the Russian Republic. Carlos was fascinated, and he opened the envelope with his father's stiletto-style opener. The letter read:

245

'Dear Señor Lang,

My husband and I do hope that you are now feeling fully settled in Seville. It seems only like yesterday that we were with you at Slapton, and I remember you being a first-class dancing partner. We understand that your stepmother is coming to Moscow in her official capacity as Personal Assistant to the British Deputy Prime Minister in ten days' time. You may be with her unofficially, but if no arrangements have been made for you to join the British Delegation, please regard this letter as a formal invitation from my husband and I to be our personal guests here in the Kremlin. Think what a very pleasant surprise it would be for your stepmother to meet you at Moscow Airport or here in our home.

If you are unable to come we will quite understand, but if you can just let our Consul in Seville, Señor Romov, know by telephoning the number at the top of this page, he will be pleased to make all the necessary arrangements.

The Conference will not last more than three days, so it will not be necessary to bring many clothes. Remember that the temperature in Moscow is very warm at this time of year – almost as warm as Seville!

Sincerely yours

Myra Renov'

This letter was designed to appeal both to a young man's sense of adventure in a country he had only once previously visited with his father and brother, and a personal appeal to 'a truly first-class dancing partner' of recent happy memory.

Carlos was tempted to pick up the telephone and call Señor Romov, but he wasn't his late father's son for nothing. Instead, he called his Uncle Paul. The call to the Russian Consulate was made from the bank. Paul de Sanches would be able to deal with all currency matters, and the Consulate would know that Señor Lang's movements were known to others than Carlos himself.

At Moscow Airport, Myra Renov waited for Carlos to arrive. She was not on her own. She was joined by the Spanish Commercial Attaché, who was a personal friend of Paul de Sanches. Paul was always concerned for security by instinct. He was a very good chess player. It was surprising how often the two things seemed to go together.

After exchange of pleasantries, Carlos was off on his 'adventure', as Myra Renov was to describe it. Myra spoke no Spanish, but like so many educated Russians she had some command of English, and some would have described her as fluent, if slow. She still thought in Russian and translated into English. She never thought in English.

Carlos was to say to her truthfully that her English was a great deal better than his Russian. He had listened to a tape his father had insisted he master for holiday purposes – 'Please show me the way to the Railway Station, etc.', but he could make no real conversation. He was very glad Myra could speak English, even if she did sound somewhat unnatural – it sounded very attractive!

The Renovs' flat was very comfortable, if somewhat old-fashioned. Carlos liked that. His own home in Seville was old-fashioned as the flat had been in Madrid. Even the best rooms at Slapton, outside the classrooms themselves, had appeared 'olde world', as indeed they were. There might be electric shaving points and all the paraphernalia of modern living, but it was set against a solid background of wooden walls that might contain any number of gadgets and marble floors.

Vladimir Renov had given very detailed instructions as to how Carlos was to be entertained. There were to be no drugs or use of alcohol, except as might be offered to any honoured guest. He, Vladimir, had a perfect command of English with little accent. When he spoke to Myra he always spoke in Russian. Carlos had no idea what passed between them. All he knew was that he was enjoying himself with very pleasant people.

Slapton and Seville seemed a long way away.

'Carlos, I hope you don't mind me calling you Carlos,'

started Renov. 'I do have a little surprise for you this morning. I understand that the British Delegation are to arrive at 3 o'clock this afternoon at the airport. Naturally they will be met officially, and I will be one of the welcoming party. There will be the playing of National Anthems and an Inspection of a Guard of Honour. Would you like to join me, or would you prefer to give your stepmother a surprise by meeting her for the first time to-day here in the Kremlin?'

'Thank you very much, General, for giving me the choice. I think I would prefer to give her the surprise of her life by meeting her here.'

'Good. I hoped you might say that. Meetings at airports are always a bit "stiff", as the English say. Anything that isn't stiff tends to be a bit artificial, "*Bonhomie*", as the French say. My surprise for you is that we have half an hour to spare before we set off for the airport, and this will give you the privilege of meeting our President and his Deputy. It won't be a formal affair, you understand, but I'm glad you have a tie and jacket.'

'It's a funny thing you said that, General. My uncle in Seville told me that the Russians and the Spanish are the most formal nations in Europe, and he insisted that I brought my best grey suit – the one you saw me wear at Slapton – will that be best with my OS tie?'

'Your OS tie? What is that, Carlos?'

'I'm sorry. I mean my Old Slaptonian tie – what the English call their "old school tie".'

'Ah yes, excellent. The President will like that. How very English, and worn by a Spaniard. We'll have you dressing like a Russian yet!' Renov smiled to himself at the thought.

Carlos's meeting with the Russian President was hardly to be compared with an audience, but it served Stolypin's purposes perfectly, and General Maiski gave him full marks. In ice-skating terms, if he didn't rate 6s, he was certainly 5.8 or 5.9!

Sylvia's plane taxied slowly and made its way to the official reception area. As usual, there was a smart Guard of Honour and military band. The Russians were a bit annoyed that it was not to be the Prime Minister who was coming himself, but they knew Lady Sabita well enough.

There were formal greetings, shakings of hands and then formalities. The familiar strains of 'God Save the Queen' and the Russian National Anthem sounded out. The general public, particularly the sporting public, had become quite familiar with certain national anthems. Nobody at Moscow Airport was unfamiliar with the two anthems now played, whilst standards were unfurled on the lead cars of the motorcade.

Sylvia had met Renov before, and so had Charlotte professionally, and more recently socially. Neither Sylvia nor Charlotte could honestly say that they felt at home in Moscow, and they were both relieved to be at the British Embassy, together with Susan, who felt very inadequate in a professional sense. How could she act as a Protection Officer in a country where she didn't speak the language, and had not much idea of the plan of the Embassy Building itself or the city outside? For some time, Susan had felt somewhat redundant. She simply liked being with Sylvia and Charlotte again, but her busy doctor husband was concerned every time she went abroad. In the evening there was the inevitable reception for the top delegates attending the Kremlin Conference: the Americans, the British, the French, the Japanese and others.

It was a glorious setting, with the chandeliers of Tsarist days refurbished and dazzling. Sylvia had Susan sitting next to her, but quite unable to render her any protective assistance. This was in fact provided by the KGB. There never were any attacks on foreign dignitaries at the Kremlin. The Russians were only going through the formalities in giving Susan a place on the top table.

General Maiski decided to sit between them, and provided the conversation. He had been annoyed that Susan's place had not been reserved for Charlotte, but that was a rare mistake. Charlotte had found herself relegated to one of the long tables leading off the top table that ran the length of the principal Romanov Palace Stateroom.

249

The dinner passed, speeches were made and at 11.30 p.m. the delegates set off to their respective Embassies. Not all the delegates were included in that generality.

Vladimir Renov had made a point of inviting Sylvia, Susan, Charlotte and the British Ambassador and his wife back to his flat within the Kremlin for a final drink. It was midnight when the electric lift brought the small British party to Renov's flat. Renov himself, Myra who had not been to the dinner, and Carlos lined up as though they were a reception line. Charlotte felt she was in a dream, and scarcely less so were Sylvia and Susan.

Only the British Ambassador and his wife, who had never met Carlos, accepted his presence. They thought Carlos must be a member of Renov's family who they had not previously met. There was a further formal shaking of hands – not so far as Carlos was concerned.

He placed his arms around Charlotte and held her tight.

'Charlotte,' he said.

'Darling,' she replied. 'Where on earth have you come from?'

'I've come from the bedroom, Charlotte. I've been here twenty-four hours. General Renov and his wife Myra kindly invited me to come to Moscow to give you a surprise. They've been very kind. I met the Russian President this morning whilst you were flying high up somewhere over the continent, I suspect. I know you've just come from the banquet. I wish I had been with you, but Myra has been entertaining me very well here in her home, and she's been showing me her Bolshoi collection.'

Renov and Myra made a point of taking in exactly the relationship, as it appeared to them, between Charlotte and Carlos. Uniformed men in period costume almost literally appeared out of the woodwork, pouring drinks.

It was after 2.00 a.m. before the Russian hosts would allow the British to leave.

It had been a very good day for Russia. Returned to the Embassy from the party at Renov's, both Sylvia and Charlotte knew that they were going to have a difficult hour together.

Sylvia knew that Charlotte was very fond of Carlos, but she had to speak:

'Charlotte, we must talk. I didn't say anything until I had you on my own, but we will have to speak both to the Ambassador and our security team tomorrow morning before we go to the Conference. You know what I'm talking about – Carlos being a guest of the Russians. I still can't believe it.'

'Neither can I, Sylvia,' replied Charlotte. 'I was absolutely stunned – gobsmacked – to see him there. I really had no idea, Sylvia. I was just as surprised as you. He told me that he had accepted their invitation, hoping to give me a surprise, and he succeeded. What terrifies me is what is happening to him right now and why they invited him to Moscow in the first place. It can't be that they just like the colour of his eyes. There must be some security element, but I can't for the life of me think what it could be, unless they thought I would betray you in some way to Carlos, who in turn would betray me, but I know I wouldn't and I know he wouldn't.'

'Yes. You know that and I believe you, but that doesn't mean that they don't think they might obtain secrets. They may simply be after his money and a foothold in Spain. There may be any one of a dozen reasons or a combination of reasons. What we have to face is that Carlos is being entertained by the Second Vice President of Russia and his attractive young wife for no obvious reason. Can you imagine the position in reverse, with me entertaining, say, a top young Russian athlete at Harcourt, with his father or stepfather prominent in Russian politics. There would be bound to be questions asked.'

Charlotte was very naturally concerned on the physical side, having heard and read of 'swallows' – young female agents – being invited to have affairs which could be photographed and later used in blackmail. Equally importantly, she could not bear the thought that Carlos was with any woman other than herself. 'He is so young and vulnerable' she thought as she finally fell asleep.

Charlotte needn't have worried, had she known Myra

251

better. Myra was a very competent and accommodating hostess, but she was arguably the last person in Russia to have a 'swallow' across her doorstep for any sexual or political reason. She knew all about 'swallows' being used, but they would never be used under her roof, and she had made that very clear to Vladimir before they were married, and their marriage had been a great success. She had given up her career with the Bolshoi to marry and have a child or children. She had, of course, met many members of the KGB, but those she knew made it their business never to suggest 'swallows' to her. Myra was a woman to be feared. A wrong word or a thoughtless suggestion could have very serious consequences. There was a strongly held belief that certain KGB officers owed their first allegiance to Myra. Certainly nobody, but nobody, would enquire after the welfare of anyone 'taken out' on her orders.

The following morning Carlos was taken on a sightseeing trip by Myra. He did the obvious thing in buying Myra flowers and a bottle of vodka for Vladimir. He had taken his camera, but having read warning notes supplied by his uncle, he was prudent enough to seek Myra's permission before snapping away. He remembered his Uncle Paul saying how amused he had been reading a notice in a Russian hotel bedroom that read: 'As in all countries, no photographs should be taken of bridges, railway stations and other buildings or installations without approval of the Police. Anyone found taking such photographs will risk immediate arrest and imprisonment.'

Staying with General Renov and Myra, with Charlotte also in Moscow, was great, but he had no more desire than anybody else with sense, in wanting to be arrested, never mind being put in prison. Myra seemed to have no hesitation in recommending good viewing points, and seemed an accomplished model when asked. She had worked in the Bolshoi and knew all about being photographed.

On occasions she summoned bystanders to photograph herself and Carlos standing together. Ludmilla could use a camera! Charlotte and Carlos did manage to see more than something of each other, but they were rarely left on their own.

On the third and final night there was to be an international concert to mark the end of the Conference. The Moscow Symphony Orchestra gave a 'musical extravaganza', with music from each of the nations taking part in the conference.

Charlotte and Carlos sat together. Myra had experienced no problem in arranging that detail – her request was an order that nobody would have dreamt of disobeying. Charlotte, when she did get Carlos on her own, out of the hearing of anybody, said:

'Carlos, darling, I've not slept since I first saw you. How are you? Have you slept well? There's so much we need to talk about, and I don't feel we can talk properly here. Please don't come to Moscow again without telling me first.'

'And receiving your permission?' grinned Carlos. 'Don't worry, Charlotte. I've done nothing you wouldn't approve of. You don't imagine I would risk doing anything that might mean my losing you? I don't imagine that you slept with the British Ambassador, so don't you worry about me.'

Charlotte, in her emotional state, didn't know whether to kiss him or slap his face for his boyish impudence. She wisely decided to kiss him on the lips.

'Thank you, darling. I nearly gave you a good slap. Please hold me.'

Carlos put his arms around her, held her tight and kissed her on the lips. Perhaps it was that kiss, the first time he had kissed her on the lips – as distinct from her kissing him – that sealed a wonderful Moscow visit.

Charlotte slept like a log that night. She was as fresh as a daisy the following morning – the morning of her return to London.

Carlos was taken back to the airport by Myra. His plane flew directly to Paris. He changed there into an Iberian Airways flight to Malaga.

Many pages of newsprint around the world followed the Conference, with photographs of all the world's leaders.

Hours had been spent drafting the final Conference Communiqué, but this was par for the course for all international political conferences. More interesting to those involved were the very personal discussions that followed.

In Moscow, Vladimir and Myra compared notes. It was a very interesting and profitable exercise.

'Vladimir, I'm quite certain that the relationship between that young man who you hope to make Tsar, and his stepmother, is very close indeed. I know if you'd had your way completely you might have wanted to test him with a 'swallow'. Thank goodness I was here. You never know how things work out. In ten years' time we will be ten years older, and in twenty years' time we'll be twenty years older, and we'll both want him on our side and, perhaps, even more important, we'll want her on our side!'

'You've done very well for us, Myra. You always do. I could tell that you had him eating out of your hand. Boris and Viktor are very thrilled with the way you handled him, and the cost was relatively trifling. But best of all, the British contingent know nothing, and neither did the young man or his stepmother.'

In London, the whole business of Carlos being entertained was, in fact, receiving the greatest attention. Sylvia had felt honour-bound to speak to the Ambassador in Moscow and to the Prime Minister himself on her return. Security had been alerted to investigate, but what was there to investigate? It might simply have been a genuine act of friendship – a return of hospitality for that afforded to the Russian couple at Slapton, following their attendance at Charlotte's wedding to Xavier.

It was Commander Margaret Stevens at Scotland Yard who came up with a theory. She felt she had to have a woman-to-woman talk with Sylvia that would need to be taped.

'Minister, as you know, I've been put in charge of enquiries. It may all be quite innocent, but for the purpose of my enquiry I have to assume that it's all part of a very clever Russian plot. Let's start at the beginning. We all know that there is a lot of spying going on all the time, and you are at the centre of it, so far as this enquiry is concerned. So much has happened in the world in the last ten years, it's difficult to remember 1985. At Hendon College that year, we had a very bright intake. Three of my girls – I didn't hold my present position then – were specially trained for security work, including protection duties, and it fell to me to allocate them. When those assaults on Ministers started, I allocated three WPCs to you. Various other Ministers were allocated men, but let's stick with you.

'Mary, you know, left us to marry her husband Elmer Orlanski, and he has gone to the top of American banking.

'Charlotte married Xavier Lang. We both know now that he was very senior indeed with Interpol and the Spanish Government, and his brother-in-law is a top Spanish banker. The only one not so successful financially is Susan, but Susan is happily married to her doctor husband, who is a Registrar at Barts.

'What does all this mean to the Russians? It means that they have access through you and your extended family, including my Police girls, to many things. A regular flow of dollars from the States. The same number of pesetas and more from Spain, access to Slapton public school, and most importantly access to you and your husband through Xavier and Carlos. Naturally nobody would ever suspect you of anything, but the only safe thing I can think of is cutting down the size of your family to reduce pressure. I don't like to suggest it, but you must consider terminating Charlotte's employment as your Personal Assistant. You could, no doubt, put her back to work for Sir Timothy Hughes until he stands down, but that's the best I can suggest at the moment.'

'I've heard what you say, Commander, and you may be right. I'll be very sorry to lose Charlotte. She's been a very good friend to me, and you know she may well have saved my life on a number of occasions. I shall never forget how she fought those ruffians in Chamonix. She was magnificent. You'd have been proud of her and your training. I'll consider what you've said, and I'll speak to Charlotte. She's a very understanding girl, but I'm sorry to have to do it.'

255

The following morning, after Sylvia had had time to sleep on matters, and after talking the whole thing through, both with her husband and Prime Minister, she decided with great reluctance to part with Charlotte.

'Charlotte, I need to speak to you on your own. This is going to be more difficult for me than you. If there is any help I can give you I will, but I have to tell you that having regard to Carlos's holiday in Moscow, at the invitation of the Russian Government, and your relationship with him, I must ask you to cease being my PA. It's not really my decision, Charlotte – it's security. I do hope you understand. Security believes the Russians must have some special reason for inviting your stepson to Moscow. I'm very sorry.'

Charlotte had had thoughts of her own whilst in Moscow. She had talked to Sylvia at the Embassy on the night of Renov's party, but this – and so suddenly! A dozen thoughts flooded her mind.

'You're not as sorry as me, Sylvia, but thanks for telling me so frankly. I'm going to miss my work and working for you. You know I've always felt very close to you, even when I had to keep observations on Xavier during those enquiries regarding Sir John Penrose, and to think the same people who had me spy on your family now want you to get rid of me. As somebody once said, "It's a funny old world". When would you like me to go. Today?'

'No, Charlotte. You needn't go today. Let's say Friday. Would you like me to speak to Susan, or would you rather speak to her yourself? What I can do, immediately if you like, is speak to Sir Timothy Hughes.'

'Thanks, Sylvia. I'd be glad if you would. At least that will put me on. I don't think I could stay working in the House of Commons after this. I'll have to consider my own position carefully now. I do appreciate all you've done for me in the past. I know we'll always be friends.'

Sylvia put her arms round Charlotte and kissed her lightly on the cheek. So ended a relationship, but not their friendship. Secretly, Charlotte was devastated. Everything had seemed to be going so swimmingly. Now she was losing her

256

job, and Sir Timothy Hughes was, at best, a put-on. It would mean looking for another job, and if it was Security that had pulled the plug, and she didn't doubt it, there would be no way back into the Police. She didn't doubt she could find some other job, but her whole career was gone. Gone that is, except for Carlos, but that would be a whole new way of life and, perhaps, a long way off. Suppose Carlos was to change his mind and attitude towards her?

She went quite cold at the thought – and how was she going to explain to him that she'd been sacked because of his relationship to her? The whole thing seemed like a nightmare, but she wasn't sleeping. She was as wide awake as anyone in London. She would speak to Florence again. She wouldn't tell her own mother immediately.

Sylvia did speak to Sir Timothy Hughes, who happily agreed to have Charlotte's paid help for a month.

At the weekend Charlotte went to stay with Florence. She poured out her heart and all the relevant facts. Florence listened carefully, as she always did. On their own, Florence held Charlotte's hand.

'Charlotte, do it now. Pick up that phone and call Carlos in Seville. Tell him you want to see him as soon as possible. Do what he's asked. Invite him to propose to you as soon as you see him, and make sure you accept. I'm not advising you, I'm telling you that's what I'd do!'

Charlotte squeezed Florence's hand. Even in this moment of excitement she could not fail to notice how frail and thin Florence looked, but she had that gleam in her eye that never deserted her. She didn't need to look for Carlos's number in Seville. It was engrained on her mind as her own Police number. She pressed the required digits. Seconds later, a vaguely familiar Spanish voice answered. It was Manuel. A few seconds later, it was Carlos on the phone.

'Carlos, darling. It's me. I'm speaking from Lady Bicker-staffe's in Lanchester. I can't speak for long now, but I do want to see you. I really need to see you as soon as possible. When can I come?'

'Do you have wings, Charlotte?'

'How do you mean, do I have wings?'

'If you have wings, you could fly to me now. If you haven't, catch the first plane out of Heathrow or Gatwick tomorrow. Let me know which flight you're on, and I'll meet you at Malaga or Seville. Just come as you are. No need to pack, just overnight things. Call me back when you've made arrangements. I'll tell Maria to get your bedroom fixed up, and give my regards to Lady Bickerstaffe and her husband.'

21

'Well done, Charlotte. I heard every word he said. Don't let him down. Come on, you've work to do. First get a booking and then call that man, what's his name, Sir Timothy something, and tell him you've been called to Spain and that you'll be with him a week on Monday. That'll give you quite long enough to get things fixed up between Carlos and yourself. After all, you're not marrying him next week. You're just going to get yourself engaged. One thing before you do. Make me a promise.'

'Anything you like, Florence. What is it?'

'Please let me be your Matron of Honour. It would be nice to be a Matron of Honour once in my life. I don't expect a second chance.'

'Florence, you're on. That's the least I can do for you after all you've done for me, but let me get myself engaged for certain first. Once I've said "Yes" to Carlos, you can start ordering your dress or suit. I haven't given a thought as to what I might wear. I still have the dress I wore for Xavier, but I think it would be tempting providence to wear it again, and it wouldn't really be fair on Carlos?'

'No, it certainly wouldn't, Charlotte. You must make a completely fresh start with Carlos. He's not your "little boy" any longer. He's going to be your husband and the father of your children. I hope you have two. It's not too much fun being an only child. I never had a brother or a sister. I've had good friends, very good friends in the Soroptomists, including Sylvia, Mary and yourself and Susan, of course, but that's not quite the same thing.'

They continued chatting for a further ten minutes, by which time they were joined by Sir John.

'Charlotte has been called to Spain, John. I've told her she can make the arrangements from here.'

'Certainly, Charlotte. You carry on,' said Sir John airily. He knew nothing of what had passed between Florence and Charlotte. So far as he was concerned Florence, who was still careful with her money, had given her approval, and that was sufficient for him.

A quarter of an hour later, and the booking was made on a cancelled morning British Airways flight to Malaga from Heathrow. That would be a Monday morning flight out, with a return flight on the following Friday. Being a scheduled flight, it would be more expensive than a charter flight, but that couldn't be helped.

She phoned Carlos with the details. It only remained to call Sir Timothy Hughes and a courtesy call to Sylvia. There would be no problems beyond the necessary collection of a small amount of cash in pesetas from the Exchange Bureau at the airport. She didn't require much. She had maintained a very small account in Seville for emergencies. Charlotte knew it would be very hot in Seville and that she would only require a few light clothes accordingly. She still would say nothing to her mother about losing her job with Sylvia. She didn't want her mother to think she was throwing herself at Carlos – even if she was.

'Perhaps, Sylvia has done me a good turn,' she thought to herself. 'Carlos and I would already be engaged if he hadn't made me promise to allow him to propose to me formally,' she told herself.

The flight to Malaga was on time – one of the big advantages of travelling 'scheduled'. The familiar voice of the Captain indicated that they were starting their descent quite shortly after they had passed Madrid on the right-hand side far below.

Within a very short time, long as it seemed to Charlotte, the plane was dropping gently over the hills to the immediate north of Malaga. She could see the reservoirs, short of water she thought, the roads, the neatly laid-out vineyards, and now they were down, with the engines giving their familiar reverse thrust to slow themselves down on the runway.

Carlos was waiting and waving. Within minutes of passing through Spanish customs, having passed through Passport Control already, she was in his arms. He kissed her on the lips now as though he had always kissed her thus, but with a fervour that she immediately recognized with both pleasure and relief. He was still the same Carlos who had last kissed her in Moscow. He looked the picture of health.

'Come on, Charlotte. Don't let's waste time. I'll take your case. I said don't bring much. Maria has got your room ready, and I've booked dinner at the Alphonse tonight, so you don't have to start cooking the first thing you arrive.'

Carlos was wearing his boyish grin again which she loved so much. He drove along the, still new, road that linked Malaga to Seville. Conversation was happy and easy between them, until Carlos referred to the Moscow Conference.

'The photos have come out very well, Charlotte. I've sent a set to Myra and her husband. They really were very kind to me, but what is all this I hear about you stopping working for Sylvia?' Charlotte was completely taken aback.

'What do you mean, Carlos? What have you heard?'

'You old fraud,' chuckled Carlos. 'I do believe you weren't going to tell me, were you?'

'I was, Carlos, but not until we got to Seville. Tell me, who told you?' Charlotte was using her Police training in fencing off a direct question.

'Uncle Paul, of course. Who else? It seems that Sylvia's Carlos telephoned Uncle to say that I had to be sure to be very kind to you whilst you were here this week, and I gathered that you might have had to give up working for Sylvia because of me. I'm sorry if I've caused you to lose your job. I can't think why, unless she thinks that you and I are going to sell secrets to the Russians, but if Sylvia's action has brought you to me now, I say "Good old Sylvia".'

'Carlos. You're always kind to me. Please pull off the road

261

when it's convenient.' Carlos said nothing, but pulled off the road as Charlotte asked. He applied his handbrake and looked to his right, deep into her eyes.

'What is it, Charlotte? Come on, out with it.' Carlos could see her eyes were full.

'Please put your arm round me, Carlos. I need you so badly. I feel so ashamed at not having told you about my having to leave Sylvia myself. You're so open with me. You tell me everything. I feel I only tell you what I want you to know. Please forgive me.'

Carlos, who had placed his right arm around her shoulders, pulled her towards himself and kissed her on the left eye, which he smudged in the process.

'Come on, Charlotte. I know you didn't want to upset me by saying that I'd caused you to lose your job. I do wish you had told me. I don't need Uncle Paul to tell me to be kind to you, but he meant well. Don't you say a word about this to either him or Sylvia's Carlos. We are together, and that's the important thing. Listen to me talking to you like this. You know you can always count on me, just as I counted on you when I was a little boy and you were my "Superwoman".'

Charlotte pulled herself together sufficiently to enable Carlos to remove his right arm and enable him to release the handbrake and continue driving to Seville. Carlos felt he had to try and say something.

'Come on, old girl. Get your mirror out. I've smudged your left eye. Tell me if you want me to stop again. See. Use my handkerchief.'

'Thanks, darling. You're a tonic.'

Carlos drove at speed towards Seville, slowing down only at the 'Welcome to Seville' sign in four languages. He felt at home.

In minutes he was. He sounded his car horn, and Maria and Manuel appeared at the front door.

'Welcome back home, Señora Lang,' said Maria in her broken English that Carlos had taught her to speak with some difficulty. Charlotte, who knew that Maria spoke no English at all beyond 'Yes, No. Please and Thank you', was

262

impressed. She kissed Maria on both cheeks and repeated the same greeting to Manuel, who had tried to appear very British by extending his hand as though to shake hands. He seemed surprised and confused, as many men do in such situations, but he was pleased.

Manuel took Charlotte's one bag and disappeared with it upstairs. Although afternoon tea is essentially an English creation, thought to have been started by the Duchess of Bedford in the seventeenth century, Maria had, in accordance with Carlos's instructions, prepared a very English afternoon tea, replete with sandwiches and cakes and tea served from a large silver teapot, that usually resided in a display case of silver in the magnificent hall of the house.

'I guessed you'd have had something on the plane, Charlotte, so I just asked Maria to put up a traditional English-style afternoon tea. She seems to have done us very well. Don't feel you have to eat it all. Don't forget we're going out to the Alphonse this evening. We'll be eating at nine, so you can work that out. I thought you might want a shower and a good lie-down after your journey. Don't worry yourself about me. I've to go to the bank, and there are one or two other things I need to do in town. Now that you're back for a few days, I suggest that you and I start talking to each other in Spanish. I know you can, and it will make Maria and Manuel feel much better and much closer to you.'

'Thank you, Carlos. You think of everything. I will.'

Carlos hadn't had any lunch himself, and he helped demolish Maria's afternoon tea with a vengeance. Maria was delighted to hear Charlotte speaking in Spanish which she could follow, even if she did sound 'posh', speaking in her perfect Castilian as though learnt from a textbook. She didn't know that Charlotte always understood what she said in her very local accent, but she made a very good attempt to speak slowly and with gestures.

Charlotte went upstairs to 'her' room that Maria had made ready. She looked in at Carlos's room and recognized any number of silver framed photos of Sophia, which had obviously come from Madrid. She said nothing, but she noticed.

263

There were now two enlarged photos of Carlos and herself – enlargements she had not seen before and which he had obviously had printed. These were in attractive wooden frames. She looked into Carlos's room again after showering, and could not fail to notice that there was now only the one large sepia-coloured photograph of Sophia that she had last seen in the flat in Madrid. There was no photograph of Xavier in the house.

'What a lovely man Carlos is,' she thought. The word 'boy' never entered her mind. This was Carlos's home now. It was no longer Xavier's home. Although she was older than Carlos, this counted for nothing. She was almost wishing he would be as masterful as Xavier had been, and ideally more so, and yet he was so gentle.

She suddenly felt very feminine in a way she hadn't felt since before she'd joined the Police years ago. She had no problem dozing off. The House of Commons seemed far away, further away than Moscow. This was going to be her home just as soon as it could be arranged, but she would want to be married first before she ordered any new curtains or whatever. Perhaps she wouldn't. Carlos had obviously removed photographs for her sake, but she wouldn't make too many alterations to start with. That would only upset Carlos and the faithful Maria, who was still obviously devoted to the memory of Sophia.

Carlos must have been out for three hours. He had spent a whole hour and a half with his uncle and the family lawyers, going through what seemed like a mountain of papers, which Paul had taken him through with his usual meticulous care. Carlos was careful by training, but Paul de Sanches was thorough to the point of being a pain in the proverbial. There was no question of 'please sign here and here, Carlos'. Fortunately, Carlos liked his uncle and aunt and their chil- dren, his cousins, but not in any romantic way. He hoped he would like their husbands when they married, as they surely would. There hadn't been an unmarried member of the de Sanches family over the age of 30 in the last 100 years, male or female.

Back home, Carlos changed after showering. He decided to dress smartly to the extent that he would wear a very lightweight suit and his old School tie.

The Alphonse XIII Hotel in Seville was one of the smartest hotels in Spain. Downstairs now, Charlotte looked at her best. She was wearing an off-the-shoulder dress which complemented her lightly tanned skin. She not merely wanted to look well herself, she wanted Carlos to be proud of her. She couldn't make herself his age, but age didn't come into it – 'The heart has its reasons' she told herself. In any case, she wasn't that old. She could easily have passed as 25.

'Charlotte. You look perfectly lovely in that dress. Let's have a sherry together before we go to the Alphonse, and whilst we have it you can sit down and tell me exactly what it is that you really needed to speak to me about when you were at Lady Bickerstaffe's.' Charlotte looked at him adoringly.

'Thank you, darling. Please close that door and lock it. It's very private. I don't even want Maria and Manuel walking in.' Carlos was somewhat surprised by her request, but he had no hesitation in doing what she asked. 'There you are, Charlotte. Now out with it. You needn't have worried about Maria and Manuel. All you had to do was speak in English.'

'Darling, just pour that sherry and come and sit next to me,' she replied. Carlos poured out two generous sherries into white wine-size glasses. He brought them across from the wine cabinet to where Charlotte was sitting on the comfortable settee. 'There you are, Charlotte. Get that down you and fire away.'

'Thank you, darling. Just sit down, please. When we were at the White Hart at Slapton, before you came out here, I made you a promise. I promised you that the first time I came out to Spain I would allow you to propose to me properly. Please, darling, make your proposal now.'

Carlos was taken by surprise, but like so many men he had prepared his lines – so far as any man can.

'Charlotte, darling. Who's proposing to who? Please, for God's sake say "Yes". You know I've always loved you.

Nobody could love you more than me, and nobody ever has. Do please agree to become my wife, yesterday if possible, and if not, just as soon as we can, and have as many of my children as you want.'

Carlos's proposal did not sound prepared the way he made it. Charlotte was transfixed. Xavier's had not sounded one half so romantic, as best she could remember. She didn't like to make comparisons, but perhaps it was inevitable. Within a second, Carlos had raised himself from his half-sitting, half-kneeling position. He was holding her and kissing her. She felt she was in heaven as their lips met.

'Yes, Carlos. A thousand times yes. Thank you for proposing so beautifully. Please kiss me again. I want to hold you so tight. You must never ever let me go.'

Carlos held her as tight as he could and kissed her again. 'There's no chance of my letting you go, Charlotte. You know that. Just you make sure you never leave me except to go into hospital to have our babies.'

'Darling, I can't wait to make you a Daddy, but not just now. I'm all dressed up for dinner.'

'We'll try and become Daddy and Mummy, I hope, on our wedding night, Charlotte, not before. I'm Spanish, remember. You know you can trust me. Come on, let's go and have that good dinner at the Alphonse. We really have something to celebrate, with Cava before the main course.'

Over dinner, conversation flowed quickly between them. The head waiter, who knew Carlos both as the son of Xavier, an honoured customer over the years, and the nephew of Paul de Sanches, was at his most attentive. He and the General Manager of the hotel always gave their select clientele the feeling that it was they who, as individuals, kept the palatial hotel going – the sure hallmark of quality service.

'The first decision is when and where we are going to get married? It's your choice, Charlotte. You're the bride. I suppose it must be London or Seville.'

'London would be very much easier, darling, but Seville has its attractions. To start with, we're here, but it's asking a lot of mother, my sister and her husband and John and

Florence to fly out. It's not just the expense. John and Florence aren't getting any younger.'

'You're saying it's London. That's all right by me. Do you mean Southgate or somewhere up west, like Brompton?'

'No, I mean Southgate, darling. Please let it be Southgate or better still, Wood Green, where I was received into your church.'

'Very well, Wood Green it is, but after the wedding we come straight back here to live – that is, after our honeymoon in, say, the Cotswolds or the Lake District.'

'I agree, Carlos, and thank you, darling. The next question is, when?'

'As soon as possible, Charlotte. I'll be eighteen next month. I'll leave it to you to fix a date. Just let me know. I'll make arrangements here in Seville, including the reading-out of the banns and all that. By the way, how are you fixed for money? Let me give you a cheque tomorrow. I don't want you working up till our wedding day for Sir Timothy Hughes or anybody else.'

'It's very good of you, Carlos, offering to give me money. I don't have a lot of money, it's true, but I do have sufficient. I'd like to save Mum the expense of a second wedding. Two weddings for the same daughter in twelve months! That's one of my reasons for wanting the wedding in London.'

'Charlotte, you know that my home is yours now. Even your bedroom will be our bedroom when we come back from our honeymoon. There's another thing, Charlotte. I know it's nothing to do with our wedding, but how well did you really know my father?'

Charlotte thought she might be going to blush, but she didn't.

'How do you mean, darling – how well did I know your father?'

'I don't mean physically, Charlotte. I mean did my father ever speak to you of your living with him in Russia together on a permanent or semi-permanent basis.'

Charlotte suddenly felt quite uneasy. This was the odd question that General Renov had put to her at Slapton,

267

Moscow and London. How well had she known Xavier? He hadn't told her of his vasectomy. He had let her undergo medical examinations. He had made no will. He had certainly never mentioned living in Russia, and here she was being asked a perfectly straightforward, if odd, question by Xavier's son, who she intended to marry just as soon as she could make the arrangements at the Catholic Church in Wood Green.

'No, Carlos, he didn't. Why do you ask? Did he ever say anything to you?'

'No, Charlotte, not in so many words, but you did know, didn't you, that my father was one-quarter Russian, and that makes me one-eighth Russian. General Renov and his wife Myra were very kind to me in Moscow, and I certainly want them to be invited to our wedding! Come on. Don't let this steak go cold. I always enjoy French mustard with steak, don't you?'

'Yes I do, darling.'

Charlotte's mind was everywhere: Wood Green, Moscow, the House of Commons, Harcourt and Sylvia's Ministry Office.

'I'm sorry, darling. I was just thinking. There really is so much to think about and plan. I do agree this steak is delicious, and so is the Reserve Rioja.'

'Charlotte, can I leave it to you to let everyone know in England? I'll naturally let everyone know here who needs to know, including a "Forthcoming Marriage Notice" in the Seville press.'

'I'm sorry, darling. I do hope you don't mind, but I'd rather not put a notice in the press. I will, of course, let those coming to the wedding know, but I'd like to tell them myself first. There may be one or two who may be both surprised and upset at my marrying you so soon after your father was killed. I'm fairly certain to be accused of cradle-snatching, if you know what I mean?'

'Yes, I do know what you mean, Charlotte, but surely not those who you think Gran will invite to the wedding. So far as the rest are concerned, I would say "Stuff them", and that isn't an expression I learnt from Father Turner, but I can speak strong words in English as well as Spanish. It's only envy or jealousy, but if you like, I won't say a word to anyone, not even Maria and Manuel, until you return to London on Friday.'

'That's very good of you, darling. I didn't like to ask, but I think it'll be best for both of us in the long run. Just you let me have a list of those you want inviting, and I'll see to it that Mum invites them. We will have to keep numbers down, I'm afraid. Mum won't let you make any financial contribution to the wedding. Please don't think she doesn't like you. She's very fond of you. She loves you calling her Gran, but I'll have all my work cut out persuading her that I haven't thrown myself at you and made you marry me.'

'What about your friends the Sabitas, the Bickerstaffes, the Orlanskis and Susan?'

'I think they'll be very nice, but that's why I want to tell them myself rather than have them find out from reading *The Times* or the *Telegraph*. I know the Bickerstaffes will be delighted, but you see I'm very young still to them. The others – well, they may think I'm a bit too old for you.'

'Well, I don't think you're too old for me, Charlotte. You would have been ten years ago, when you were twenty-four and I was eight, but our ages have caught up and will continue to grow closer, you wait and see.'

'Thank you, darling, and you're quite right. I've loved you since you were a little boy at Slapton. I loved being with you when you won at Chamonix and you first took me out for dinner, and ever since. You're the most precious thing in my life. Nothing and nobody will ever stop me loving you, and I promise I'll never try and stop you doing something you want to do. Please kiss me, Carlos.'

Carlos got up from the table and kissed her. Charlotte was very full, but she kept control of herself. She too had prepared her lines, and Carlos kept topping up her glass with Rioja when the wine waiter didn't. Carlos felt today was the happiest day in his life.

It was a happy couple who made their way home from

the hotel. The General Manager thoughtfully and tactfully provided a chauffeur from his staff.

Manuel and Maria were still up and about when Charlotte and Carlos returned from the Alphonse. Carlos paused before entering the house as Manuel opened the magnificent studded oak door.

'Charlotte, is it tonight or on our return from London that I carry you across the threshold?'

'Shush, darling. Not a word. Thank God you're speaking in English. You promised not to say anything.'

'Sorry, Charlotte. I forgot. Come in. Just think, when we come back from London married, we shall be sharing a bedroom. I wonder how many in our position would wait until then?'

22

Returned from Seville, Charlotte felt as happy and as confident as any Spanish Princess. Carlos had proposed to her as though he was a character out of a top-class novel.

He had bought her a lovely cross-over diamond ring on the day following their engagement, and he had given her a cheque for one million pesetas – the equivalent of fifty thousand pounds. He had insisted that she place the money on deposit, to attract interest, at his uncle's bank.

'Family money mustn't leave Spain, Charlotte, unless it's essential and I mean essential,' Carlos had said.

Charlotte liked Paul de Sanches, Sophia's surviving brother. He thought at this stage that the capital sum of one million pesetas represented the settlement of any claim that Charlotte might have had and made against Xavier's estate. He thoroughly approved. He thought Carlos had done very well.

Back in Palmers Road, New Southgate, Charlotte wondered what her mother's reaction would be. She didn't have long to find out.

'Mum, I have some big news for you. I'm going to get married again next month. I'm going to marry Carlos.'

'You can't be serious, Charlotte. Carlos who?'

'Xavier's son, Carlos. Who else, Mum?'

'Charlotte, you can't. He's only a boy. He's my grandson. You are joking?'

'No, Mum, I'm not. Carlos isn't really your grandson. He's your step-grandson, and that's quite different. He isn't a blood relative of either of us. You could marry him if he

271

asked you, but he proposed to me and I've accepted his proposal. He proposed beautifully. Please say we have your blessing and approval.'

'Charlotte, you know I'm very fond of Carlos, but he's only a boy. He's only eighteen, isn't he, and you are over thirty. When he's sixty you'll be over seventy. You simply can't marry him. You'd better get on that phone immediately and tell him that you've had second thoughts. Let him down gently. You owe him that, but for heaven's sake do it and do it now. Whatever would your father have said, and what do you think Margaret and her husband will think and say? It's not just the age difference, Charlotte. It's the fact that Xavier was Carlos's father, and he hasn't even been dead twelve months.'

'Mum, I've listened to all you've said, and I thought you might start like this. I'm not your daughter for nothing. Don't you think I've thought on these lines myself for hours, but please listen to me. I'm marrying Carlos, whether you and Margaret like it or not. Frankly, I couldn't give a fig what Margaret or her husband think. I love Carlos and he loves me, and that's all there is to it. This last week has been the happiest week in my life, and if you think I'm going to give up Carlos to please anyone, it's you who must be joking. Now, please listen to me again. We both want you to arrange the wedding – at Wood Green this time, on a mini-budget. I have the money, Mum. Please Mum, I do need your help and love. I don't want to have to make all the arrangements myself. You will do it, Mum, won't you?'

'Yes, love, I will if you insist.' Charlotte moved round the table, put her arms around her mother and hugged her.

'Thanks, Mum. I knew I could rely on you. Now before I do anything else, let me ring Florence in Lanchester. I know she'll be delighted. You can listen to the conversation.' Charlotte knew Florence's number without looking in her diary.

'Florence, it's me, Charlotte. I'm back from Spain with Mum. I've just told her that Carlos and I are engaged to be married. What do you have to say to that?'

'Congratulations, Charlotte! I'm so glad you're going to

272

remain Mrs Lang. What a clever girl you are, and what a lucky young man Carlos is. I want you to keep your promise. I will order my Matron of Honour suit just as soon as you let me know what you'll be wearing. Do give my love to your mother. Tell her that I'm delighted.'

'Thank you, Florence. I felt sure you would be pleased. Mum is stood right next to me so she can hear what you are saying. Please give our love to John. I can't give you any details yet, beyond saying that the wedding will be here in London this time, not Slapton.'

Next Charlotte phoned Susan, who sounded equally supportive. Susan had appreciated Charlotte's support when she had married her doctor husband from Barts Hospital in London. David had been, and still was, a Registrar at St Bartholomews Hospital, and he had come from Barbados. Charlotte had been one of her Bridesmaids – the second and Chief Bridesmaid had been David's sister. Having heard the reaction of both Florence and Susan, Charlotte's mother was breathing quite normally again.

How would Margaret, her elder daughter, react? Margaret was out, and so was Sylvia.

Charlotte put a call through to Seville. She had promised Carlos that she would phone to let him know that she had returned safely and to let him know her mother's reaction.

'Carlos, darling. It's Charlotte here. I'm speaking from Mum's. I've told Mum that you and I want her to arrange the wedding, and she says she will. Just hold on, she wants to speak to you herself.'

Mrs Johnson didn't know that she really did want to speak to Carlos, but Charlotte had forced her hand. She could hardly refuse.

'Hello, Carlos. This is Gran speaking. Charlotte has just told me that you are to become my son-in-law, so I won't be your Gran anymore.'

'Yes you will, Gran. Wait till we have children. You'll be the proudest Gran in London. I'll always continue to call you Gran. Thanks so much for agreeing to arrange our wedding. Sorry I can't do much to help from over here, but

I look forward to your next visit to our home here in Seville.'

Carlos was very diplomatic. He quite deliberately used the phrase 'our home'. Mrs Johnson felt a tear was developing in her left eye. She passed the instrument back to Charlotte. 'There you are, darling. Now I mustn't run this call up. I'll call you again, but better still you call me, say, eight o'clock to-night. I'll make a point of being in. Before I go, Florence and Susan are very pleased for us. Perhaps, I will put notices in *The Times* nad the *Telegraph* just as soon as I've booked the Church, and leave it to me to collect brochures on the hotels in the Cotswolds and the Lakes. I'll send them to you. That's your choice. Love you.'

Charlotte replaced the phone and kissed her mother on the cheek.

It was during the afternoon following Charlotte's return to London that Carlos made an interesting discovery. Like many men of his rank, not to say wealth, Xavier had had one of the rooms in his home in Seville converted into a private office, that was furnished to the highest standard both in its general furnishings and its state-of-the-art electrical equipment.

Nobody had ever entered the study during Xavier's lifetime, and Carlos had made an early decision that he would follow his father's example and practice. He had allowed Maria into the room, but only in his presence. Maria had wondered whether she really should, but she had agreed only on the basis that Carlos would stay in the room with her whilst she cleaned. It was when Carlos was going through the second drawer down on the left-hand side of his father's desk that he came across a small tape he had not noticed before. Although no expert in electrics, it only took Carlos seconds to have the tape playing. Carlos listened fascinated. He had only learnt 'holiday Russian' at his father's command, and he could not follow the conversation, but suddenly as it seemed to him, he recognized his father's voice. Anyone who has lost anyone close knows the feeling of a loved one's voice again. Carlos determined to listen to the

274

tape. He thought he recognized a second voice, but he could not be sure. He was, however, in no doubt but that it was his father's voice. He would recognize that voice for the rest of his life, and his father had not been dead twelve months. There was only one thing Carlos could think of. He must have it translated, but by whom? Uncle Paul would know the answer. He would have known the answer himself once he'd started at the University, but that was all of two or three months away. Like so many young men, and young women for that matter, he wanted the translation now, if not yesterday.

Carlos assumed it was a play-reading or something of that nature, and so he described it to his uncle, who put him in touch with an elderly Russian lady whose parents had escaped from Stalin's Russia in the long-ago.

Lady Florence Bickerstaffe was genuinely quite excited at the prospect of acting as Matron of Honour at 'young Charlotte's' wedding.

'What am I going to wear, John?' she had asked her husband.

'Clothes, my dear, I expect,' Sir John had replied unhelpfully. He was in the middle of a paper he was preparing for the Shire Bank, of which he was now a director, having been appointed by Elmer Orlanski of the Chicago Temperance Bank, which held a controlling equity share in the Bank in Tib Lane.

'Seriously, dear. I've no idea. You'll have to ask Charlotte what she's wearing and, dependent on her answer, you'll know exactly what you want to wear and what you're going to wear. Is it to be another white wedding, or is it to be suited? Please find out whether I'm expected in my old morning suit. I think I've had it thirty years now, but men's fashions don't change that much, except there's more grey about than black.'

Florence decided to phone Sylvia. She would know, or would she? Did she even know there was going to be a wedding? She would surely be one of the guests? Florence asked herself these questions as she called Sylvia at Harcourt. Sylvia was on a speaking tour of the North, but after some gentle persuasion, as Lady Bickerstaffe, she was given a Harrogate telephone number.

'Deputy Prime Minister, this is Lady Bickerstaffe speaking.'

'You don't have to tell me, Florence. How did you get this number? Don't let me guess. Tell me when we are not on the phone. There's nothing wrong is there, for you to be phoning me up here?'

'No, Sylvia, it's the best of news, but surely you've heard?'

'No, Florence, what is it? Are you expecting or something?'

'No, of course not, silly, but yes I am. I'm expecting to be Matron of Honour at Charlotte's wedding next month.'

'Charlotte's wedding? Charlotte who?'

'Your Charlotte, of course, Xavier's widow. Obviously you haven't heard. Charlotte is going to marry Carlos – Savier's son. I'll bet Charlotte has tried to speak to you and hasn't been able to get through to you. I'm delighted myself. In fact I may have played Cupid, but more of that when we speak. I really rang to see what we're all wearing. I'll have to call Charlotte again and find out what she's wearing. I only know that the wedding is to be at Wood Green this time, and it will be a smaller wedding this time, for obvious reasons.'

'Florence, you've taken my breath away. Perhaps I'll let her call me, just in case Carlos and I are not invited.'

'Oh, you're sure to be. I'm sure Charlotte has forgiven you for giving her the push, even if she's nothing to forgive. I'll speak to you again before the wedding. Bye for now. Oh, John sends his love.'

There were continuing problems in Moscow. There are always problems political and economic in all countries, but 'at this moment in time', as the politicians are so fond of saying, Moscow was having greater problems than usual.

276

What was really needed was a benevolent dictator and a new currency – rare species, particularly in a democracy!

There was absolute delight in Myra's heart and mind when the formal invitation arrived from Mrs Johnson – Charlotte's mother – enclosed with a personal letter from Carlos written as from London. The invitation itself was in wedding style in pale lavender, as the last invitation had been, and was formally addressed to Major-General Vladimir Renov and Madame Myra Renov. It contained a formal RSVP, but it was the letter that held the fascination. It read:

'Dear Vladimir and Myra,

Please forgive my familiarity in addressing you by name rather than by rank. I remember very clearly your very kind hospitality. As you can see from the enclosed formal invitation, I am to take the place of my late father in becoming the husband of his widow, Charlotte, who has always been my best friend in this world since I lost my mother, father and brother. I do hope you can both come to my wedding. If you can't come, both Charlotte and I will fully understand, but do come if you can.

Yours very sincerely
Carlos de Sallas Lang'

Myra immediately decided that she was coming. Vladimir said that most unfortunately he simply could not be away from Moscow. It was essential that the President, Maiski and himself be in complete charge. To leave Moscow and Russia now would be almost treasonable and an open invitation to very real problems.

'You go to London, Myra. You know what we've discussed and what we want. This may afford a wonderful opportunity.'

When eventually Sylvia did manage to get hold of Charlotte, she, Sylvia, was full of it: 'But don't you think you're taking a terrific risk, Charlotte? You'll have to be extremely careful you don't smother him. Never forget it was you who really took his mother's place years ago when he was a small boy

277

at Slapton. Don't get me wrong. I know you will do your best for him and he for you, but you are sixteen years older than him. It won't be easy.'

'Perhaps not, Sylvia, but I coped pretty well, I think, with Xavier, and he was eighteen years older than me. Carlos and I have spoken to each other very freely on the subject of our ages. When I'm sixty he'll be forty-four. If Xavier had lived when I'm sixty, he would have been seventy-eight. If it was simply a question of ages, which would you have preferred?'

'Putting it like that, I suppose you're better off with Carlos than Xavier, but I'm sorry I said anything now. You know that we all wish you every happiness. If you'd still been working full-time at my office, you might not have been able to marry Carlos. Perhaps one day you'll forgive me for having to drop you?'

'You were forgiven a long time ago, Sylvia. Both Carlos and I look forward to entertaining you both in our home in Seville later in the year, or next year at the latest. As to the wedding itself, it's only going to be small. You and Carlos are being invited, of course, and Mary and Elmer if they can come, and Carlos has insisted on those Russians, Vladimir and Myra Renov, being invited. I don't really see why, but as you say I mustn't try and mother him. Apparently they were genuinely very kind to him when he stayed as their guest whilst we were attending that Conference together.'

Myra's command of the English language was still somewhat limited, but she never failed to make herself understood. She left it to Vladimir, however, to write her letter of acceptance, which she signed.

Carlos prepared himself with his arguments.

'Uncle Paul, I've got really important news for you and Aunt Marie. I'm going to get married next month. I'm going back to London to marry Charlotte, but don't worry, we're coming back to Seville to live. I want you to be my Best Man. Please say "Yes".'

'Sit down, Carlos. What are you telling me? You are joking,

aren't you? Do say you're joking. It isn't the First of April, is it?'

Carlos sat down. 'No, Uncle. I'm not joking. I'm marrying Charlotte in London next month. I'm in love with Charlotte, and she's in love with me. Do tell Aunt Marie that I want her to come to the wedding with you and the girls. I know you think I'm too young and stupid, but I'm not. Try and look at it this way. Charlotte will become Spanish properly. Our children will be Spanish, and Momma's money and property will stay in Spain.'

It was an incredible performance, worthy of a professional actor ten years his senior. Paul sat back in his comfortable leather chair. He looked hard at Carlos, facing him for a full half-minute.

'Carlos, you're impossible. You're your father over again, but you're better. Your Momma would have been proud of you.'

'You're wrong, Uncle. Momma is proud of me. Everything that I do, from skiing down, I do for Momma and the family. I want Charlotte to remain a member of the family properly, together with you, Aunt Marie and the girls. Please say you will be my Best Man.'

'Carlos, you have a Best Man. Come on home with me. We'll break this news to your Aunt Marie together. Don't expect her to be as easy as me. You and I share the same blood bond, but Aunt Marie is very fond of you.'

To Paul's surprise and relief, his wife was delighted with the news. It is always difficult for any man to know exactly how another man's mind might work in any given situation, and 'quite impossible for a man to know how a woman's mind works'. Had she been given a completely free choice, Marie might have wished that one of her daughters, all three attractive and bright, might have married Carlos, but as cousins that might have been risky – and in any case, which one? They all liked Carlos, which wasn't surprising. Equally important, Marie really liked Charlotte.

Following Xavier's death, she had felt that Carlos was very vulnerable as an attractive wealthy young man. Marie might not have been a de Sanches by birth, but she knew how many pesetas made ten as well as any woman in Spain. Moreover, years of marriage to Paul had taught her the ways of the world of finance – and much else besides. She had not felt able to give Carlos the protection she would have liked, what with Carlos being away at school in England, with her stuck in Seville, without appearing to push her daughters at him. Charlotte would certainly protect him. The family would remain constant, and Sophia's lovely home, which she liked so much, would remain in the family for the benefit of them all.

'You lovely, lovely boy,' Marie cried. 'What a clever young man you are. Of course, you must marry Charlotte and have lots of children. I know three girls who will be disappointed, but they couldn't all three have married you. You would have been an absolute idiot if you'd let Charlotte slip through your fingers.'

Queen Alexandra could hardly have spoken more movingly. Carlos was delighted at Marie's response to his news. Paul had led him to think that Aunt Marie might not be easy. The three girls extended their congratulations in rather more subdued tones, but all were pleased at the prospect of a visit to London to attend the wedding. None of them had set foot on British soil before. They all spoke English, albeit with Spanish accents. Carlos had been their hero. No doubt he always would be, and although each of them was younger, it had more than crossed their individual minds that they would love to have had him as their husband. The three girls did like Charlotte, however, and they were, in their own way, as relieved as their mother that Carlos was not 'marrying out'.

All six of them ate a hearty dinner together at the de Sanches home, a converted farm set among vineyards. At the conclusion of the meal, Paul toasted 'To Carlos and Charlotte'. It was a happy Carlos who was driven back to Seville that night.

Events moved quickly following Charlotte's return from Seville to London. Arrangements went ahead for her wed-

280

ding to Carlos at Wood Green. It was not going to be a grand occasion as it had been at Slapton, but it would be nice. There would be 18 guests only including Mary and Elmer from Chicago, Sylvia and her husband Carlos, Sir John Bickerstaffe and his wife Florence, and Susan and her husband.

Florence would be Matron of Honour and Uncle Paul would be Carlos's Best Man. He would have his wife Marie and his three daughters with him. Myra Renov would be there with her bodyguard Ludmilla.

Charlotte looked radiant as bride wearing a cream outfit with a Cossak style hat and Florence was in her element. Fortunately the weather was kind for October, but this mattered less than it had done at Slapton since the guests only had to travel a very short distance from the Church to the Falcon's Head Hotel where the wedding breakfast was held.

Like most weddings, a small crowd on a Saturday morning in London became a large crowd when it got around, as these things do, that the wife of the Second Russian Vice President was attending together with the Deputy Prime Minister. MI6 and MI5 co-operated with the Metropolitan Police and officers of the KGB. They could co-operate when required.

The Nuptial Mass took its usual form. Confetti was thrown notwithstanding pleas from the altar, but Security prevented too close contact.

The meal itself was good. Once again the wines were best Spanish with Mary and Elmer feeling a shade isolated sipping lime and lemonade!

Sir John Bickerstaffe proposed 'The Bride and Groom' as he had done at Slapton. Carlos replied on behalf of 'My wife and I' in a most amusing manner and it was left to Uncle Paul to respond to the toast to 'The Matron of Honour'. He spoke in fluent, but accented English, taking the opportunity of adding his personal thanks on behalf of all the guests, including his wife and his three daughters, to Mrs Johnson for her 'most generous hospitality'.

It was what happened within the next few minutes that

would live with Charlotte and Carlos for years to come. They rose to leave the room on their own for the first time as man and wife. They took up a position in an adjoining room to shake hands with everybody again whilst after-lunch drinks were served.

Charlotte spoke to Myra slowly, but distinctly. 'It really is most kind of you to come all the way from Moscow to be with us today. My husband and I are most appreciative.'

'Mrs Lang. You are very kind. I do claim a special favour of you. Please do not think me too demanding. May I please have your husband Carlos for no more than ten minutes completely on my own. I know it must seem a very strange request on your wedding day, but you must know that I do not make the request lightly or for any – how do you say it? – improper purpose. I really need to have Carlos completely on his own for ten minutes, perhaps whilst you are changing into travelling clothes. Will you please permit Carlos to come with me? We shall not leave the hotel, and Ludmilla will stay with you to protect you, or she can come with me to protect Carlos and me if you prefer?'

The request, so quaintly put, seemed preposterous, and yet from the earnest way in which she spoke Charlotte could not envisage any harm in her agreeing. She looked at Carlos, who was standing next to her in his morning suit.

'What do you say, darling?'

'Certainly, Myra, but only ten minutes, please. This is our wedding day. We don't want our guests thinking that I'm running away from my wife already!' He too spoke slowly for Myra's benefit, but she laughed and so did Charlotte.

'That would never have occurred to me, Carlos. Remember, I would have to answer to my husband, as you will have to answer to your wife in future. Please come with me upstairs. I will not keep you from your bride for long, I promise.'

'You lead the way, Myra. We shan't be long, Charlotte.'

Myra led the way to room 14, which she had had reserved ostensibly as a place to which she might retire if the British food had caused her to feel ill. Carlos followed her, followed in turn by Ludmilla. Having arrived outside the room, there was a short conversation in Russian between Myra and Ludmilla.

Carlos didn't understand a word that passed between them, but it was obvious that Myra was giving instructions to Ludmilla to stay outside the room and not to let anyone come in or stand at the door listening. Ludmilla, after satisfying herself that there was nobody in the room except Myra and Carlos, took up position outside the door in accordance with her instructions.

'Please sit down, Carlos, and you listen very carefully to me, yes.'

Carlos sat down and wondered what was going to happen next. Myra took from her handbag what was clearly a compact miniature tape recorder.

'Carlos, you listen carefully, yes?' Myra pressed a button, and the conversation that he had heard played in his home in Seville started to play, his father's voice and the second voice he thought he had recognized. It was the same tape!

'Myra, I know this tape.' Myra looked at him in astonishment. 'Carlos, how do you know this tape? You cannot know this tape.'

'Myra, please believe me as I trust you. I do know this tape. It meant nothing to me, so I had it translated. That is my father's voice. I thought it must be a stage play reading or something. I tell you I have a copy,' Carlos thought quickly, 'in my bank in Madrid.'

Myra looked at Carlos in a way he had never seen before.

'Carlos, you know what this means? You are now standing in your father's shoes, yes? You are my "Spanish Eagle". I want you to be my future Tsar, and I want your bride to be Tsarina. We only have a few moments left together on our own, Carlos. You have a duty to God and to Russia. Russia and Spain are friends now, and you can, and will, make the friendship closer and better. Please say that we may meet again in Moscow with your bride. Our time is up. I promised ten minutes, and I always keep my word.'

'Thank you, Myra. You have given me a lot to think about.

I promise I will speak to Charlotte, and if we can come to Moscow again we will, but as to my becoming your Tsar and Charlotte your Tsarina, that must, for the moment, be just between ourselves and God, of course. Come with me and we will rejoin the others.'

Charlotte had not left to change yet. She knew she only had a limited time with Mary and Elmer, who had flown over specially from Chicago. Mary had taken the opportunity of staying with Elmer at her parents' home in Shoreditch, and Elmer had done some useful work in Tib Lane, but Charlotte felt certain that she would see more of the other guests before she saw Mary and Elmer again.

After a further half hour, during which many photographs were taken, Carlos and Charlotte retired together to the room Charlotte had reserved for changing. She hadn't removed her hat before she started:

'Carlos, what on earth was all that about? Whatever did she want with you on our wedding day, for God's sake?'

'Calm down, Charlotte. There's nothing for you to worry about as between you and me, but there may be a hell of a lot for you and me to think about when we get home. We must be very careful about what we say, and certainly you must promise me that you'll say nothing to anybody, not anybody – and that includes Sylvia and all the others here – but it seems that Myra wants me to be Tsar of Russia and you Tsarina.'

'You're joking, Carlos. You're pulling my leg.'

'I'm not, Charlotte, believe me. That's why she wanted me on my own. She could hardly have made such a statement like that at the dinner table, could she? You do know that her husband Vladimir is the Second Vice President of Russia?'

Charlotte didn't know what to think. 'Carlos, I wasn't cross. I'm just bewildered. Come on, we best get changed quickly. You can help me fasten up. I can't wait to get to Grasmere. They've a heliport in the grounds of the hotel. We'll be there in a very few hours. Come on, let's change.'

She took her hat off, readjusting her hair.

'First of all, Charlotte, you give me a proper kiss and tell

284

me that you do trust me with Myra or any other attractive female.'

Downstairs again, changed for going away, Charlotte and Carlos looked as well as any bride and groom, even if Carlos had not fully succeeded in removing all Charlotte's 'stay-firm' lipstick from his own lips, following his request for her trust. They made their tour of guests for the last time. Charlotte made a point of speaking at greater length to Myra than she might otherwise have:

'I am so glad you did not run off with Carlos, Myra. It is very kind of you to invite us to see you in Moscow some time in the future. We are so very sorry that your husband could not be with you. I will try and learn some more Russian before we come to see you. I hope I have not spoken too quickly just now, but we do have a plane to catch, and thank you very much for your very kind gift of vodka decanters. I can promise you that I will try to acquire a taste for vodka before we come to Moscow.'

'You are very kind to me, Mrs Lang. I hope we become very good friends. Your husband, Carlos, will tell you all that I said upstairs. You will have full protection when you come to Moscow. I can promise you that, but I cannot say more than that now. Please look after yourself and Carlos. You have the best wishes of my husband and myself.'

It was a somewhat artificial conversation, but that was not surprising given what had been said earlier between Carlos and Myra, and allowing for Myra speaking very correctly, if slowly, in her attractive Russian accent.

Eventually they were away in a London taxi to Heathrow. Two hours later they were in Manchester, and an hour later they were at the Wordsworth Hotel, Grasmere. It had been a wonderful wedding day, with unexpected Russian overtones.

Britain, Spain and Russia had moved closer, but none of the other hotel guests could have known.

23

At Moscow Airport, Myra Renov and her bodyguard Ludmilla were met by Vladimir Renov and a group of very senior Russian Army officers.

Within the hour Myra and Vladimir were in the presence of President Stolypin and General Maiski.

'Tell us all, Myra. How did it go? We've been very busy with our own enquiries whilst you've been away.'

'It's gone very well, Mr President, with possibly one serious breach of security, but I'll come to that presently. First, I attended the wedding, and they are well and truly wed. An agent from our Embassy obtained a certified copy for our records. I have it here. The wedding itself was a pleasant occasion. There were twenty present. Bride and groom and eighteen guests, including the British Deputy Prime Minister and her husband. I didn't attempt to speak to them beyond being polite. After the meal I managed to speak to Carlos Lang completely on his own in a private room. Ludmilla stood outside to prevent our being overheard. I played him the tape and, to my amazement, it seems he'd heard it before – and that's where there must have been some lack of security. Presumably that tape you gave to Xavier Lang was not self-destruct or, if it was, he took a copy on some machine of his own when he played it to himself in Spain. That's not my department. I'm only guessing, but it's something you should look into. I had a good five minutes with him, as I say, on my own, and if our plans do go ahead I think he will be perfect for us and for Russia. I believe he trusts me completely, and his wife Charlotte is very nice.

286

'I wouldn't really expect them to come to Moscow without invitation, but I think they would come together if I was to invite them. I believe they will keep their own counsel. I didn't think it sensible to make threats.'

'You've done very well for us again, Myra,' said Stolypin. 'Now let's give you our news. We've made further investigations. It seems that Xavier Lang was not completely honest with us. "Economic with the truth", I believe the British call it. It seems that Xavier's great-grandmother was indeed a Romanov. So far as we're concerned, Xavier Lang was a Romanov, which means that Carlos Lang is a Romanov and his children will be Romanovs. I don't think we need to consider further any claims made by other would-be pretenders.'

Maiski added: 'Once the announcement is made, all manner of claimants will be only too glad to swear allegiance and give up their claims to titles in exchange for roubles – if we have any to spare. A few medals and decorations in exchange for pledges of loyalty to our Tsar, together with our promise to take out any who fail to honour their pledges at home or abroad. That should be a very fair exchange!'

Stolypin, Renov and Myra smiled. 'Now the next thing is timing,' continued Stolypin. 'We will, of course, have to have them over here when the announcement is made. Let's keep things as they are. Nothing in writing. We'll have to have them over here when the announcement is made, together with anyone who might be got at by the Western media, Charlotte's mother, for example, but perhaps they don't all have to come. It would be sufficient if we were to provide embassy cover. We'll also need to have a ready-made dacha home for them, but that's no problem. It's just a question of keeping the whole thing secret. The one thing we must avoid at all costs is having the Western media speculating and damaging us in any way. Fortunately, young Carlos Lang appears a very sensible young man with plenty of money, so he'll not be inclined to indulge in chequebook journalism.'

'No, he won't do that. I'm certain that's not his style,'

added Myra. 'Although I say it myself, I would put a lot of roubles on him.'

A very different conversation was taking place at the Wordsworth Hotel.

'That conversation, Carlos, you had with Myra Renov. I really ought to report it to somebody.'

'No you mustn't, Charlotte. I only told you what I did because I trust you completely. I would be very sorry indeed if you were to talk to anybody, and I repeat, anybody. If the whole thing isn't a charade, Myra Renov will have put her life on the line speaking to me as she has done, and I'm not going to be the one to pull the plug on her, and neither are you. It's quite obvious to me now that my father told you nothing of his plans and hopes for the future. He told you nothing about his physical condition, and he left you no money. Can't you begin to understand how I feel having my own father treat you very badly? How do you think I feel now towards his memory when I virtually worship the ground you stand on, and he treated you just as a plaything?'

Charlotte looked at Carlos, whose eyes were flashing. 'Darling, I won't say anything to anybody. Please don't upset yourself about your father. You're my husband now. You always will be. Please just hold me tight, as tight as you like. We've all our lives together. Never look back in anger. There's no profit in it. Anything you say to me stays with me unless you want me to repeat it. You know that. Trust me, darling, like I trust you.'

Carlos took Charlotte in his arms and held her tight.

'Thanks, Charlotte. Whether we remain Mr and Mrs Lang or Imperial Majesties lies in the future. For now we're simply Carlos and Charlotte. We're going to enjoy our honeymoon. The world will still be revolving tomorrow morning.'

There was another interesting conversation taking place at Harcourt.

The wedding of Charlotte and Carlos had brought Mary and Elmer Orlanski to London from Chicago, and Sylvia had been pleased to invite Florence and John Bickerstaffe to join them for dinner and an overnight stay. Relations between Sylvia and Florence went back a long way. Sylvia had known Florence through her father when she, Sylvia, had been Head Girl at St Monica's in Yorkshire, then when she had been at St Hilda's at Oxford, and then as a barrister at Lanchester before she had entered Parliament.

Her relationship with Mary did not go back so far, but Mary had been her closest confidante as her first Protection Officer, and it was Mary and Florence between them who had saved her political career when she had married Carlos Sabita. It was to Florence and Mary that Sylvia felt she must once again turn for help.

Sylvia felt that Britain was singularly ill-informed as to what was going on in Russia, beyond what every nation knew. Who was really wielding power, and who would be wielding power in 20 years' time? She felt they were well equipped to help her, since Mary was now married to Elmer Orlanski, the eminent banker from Chicago, an appointed International Banker and Chairman of the Chicago Temperance Bank, which was outstripping the Bank of England in aiding the Russian economy.

Florence was now married to Sir John Bickerstaffe, himself a part-time banker in Tib Lane. Sir John had, after all, been her first Permanent Secretary at the Ministry of Information. Between them, the six who sat around the dining table at Harcourt that Saturday evening were some of the best-informed in the Western world. Sylvia's husband was argu-ably less well-informed than the others, but he was an international businessman in his own right, with many inter-ests. He spoke four languages and regularly visited Brussels, Paris and Madrid.

'I don't want to spoil a lovely day with political and econ-omic conversation,' started Sylvia, 'but you must all have been surprised that young Carlos, our bridegroom, should have invited Myra Renov to his wedding? It was Charlotte who told me that he had insisted that the Renovs be invited. Did any of you get a chance to speak to her? I didn't myself beyond pleasantries, but I did notice that she took Carlos

289

out of the room with that large female minder. I wonder what she was up to?'

This opening led to a full discussion.

Mary was first. 'I don't know, Sylvia, but they were only away for ten minutes or less. I timed them, habit I suppose. I can't imagine she got up to much. Carlos looked no worse for his tête-a-tête with her, and had there been any nonsense I'm quite sure Ludmilla would certainly have been able to give any assistance that might have been required. What a woman! I think I'd have found her a very formidable opponent.'

Florence advanced the conversation: 'I think it was a wonderful wedding and a perfect end to what had seemed so sad. I must say, I think Carlos is a superb replacement for Charlotte. I don't know what the relationship was between Xavier and the Renovs, but clearly they think a lot of young Carlos. Myra Renov was almost purring with delight, getting Carlos to herself. I understand that the Renovs entertained Carlos in Moscow when you, Sylvia, were in Moscow yourself, attending that Conference. Charlotte and Susan were with you, as I remember you telling me yourself.'

'Yes they did,' replied Sylvia, 'and as I remember it, Charlotte was very worried at that time. She had no idea he was going to be there. I do miss Charlotte sometimes. I always feel I let her down when she was spying on us, on instructions from Scotland Yard, to find out if Xavier had any possible connection with the murder of Sir John Penrose. Effectively I had her posted away, and then I dropped her again as my Personal Assistant following Xavier being killed at that accident. She must be the loveliest girl to continue to treat me as a close friend!'

'Yes. She is a lovely girl, Sylvia,' added Florence. 'I do hope she finds happiness with Carlos, after all she's gone through. There's a big difference in their ages, but I'm sure she'll handle herself very ably. She could so easily smother him.'

'I don't think you need to have any fears in that direction.' It was Sir John Bickerstaffe who surprisingly contributed to the conversation now. 'I've only known young Carlos Lang for a very short time, not like you for years, Sylvia, but I think I'm still a fair judge of character. I'd say young Carlos is quite capable of being very masterful in his own way. No doubt Charlotte will run his life for him, in the domestic sense, but when it comes to big decisions, I think Carlos will be found to have a lot of his father in him. I remember Charlotte herself telling me that she hoped Carlos would be masterful. I forget the exact words she used, but it was to the effect that she knew that Carlos would be no "toy boy", that she was very glad about that, and that the thing she liked most about Carlos was his dominant character. For all her abilities, I suspect that she may enjoy being dominated by Carlos, at least in some ways. I think the more dominant Carlos is the happier Charlotte will be!'

'I've not said anything yet,' commenced Elmer, 'but I guess we haven't heard the last of Carlos and Charlotte. I don't know much about the Renovs, but Mary and I have come to know Renov's friend General Maiski. Maiski has been in our home as our guest. He's a very good guest, charming and an excellent pianist. I believe he also plays a good game of cards and chess. He's been a very good friend to the Bank in Moscow and, now I come to think of it, he fairly pumped Mary and I for all we knew about Xavier, his boys and Charlotte. We told him all we knew, but that wasn't much. He seemed to know more than us.'

The conversation drifted on into the night, with Sylvia's husband refilling the brandy glasses.

The honeymoon had proved extremely happy and successful in every way. Even the weather had been perfect. Perfect weather could never be guaranteed in the Lake District, but 'Fortune favours the Brave'.

Returned to Seville via London and Paris, Charlotte surveyed her prospects. In some ways, it seemed all she had to do was take up where she'd left off. She had been married to Xavier, but now she was going to make a new life with Carlos. There was another big difference. When married to

291

Xavier, she had spent most of her time in Spain living in Madrid. Now the flat in Madrid had been let at a good rental. Life with Carlos would be more provincial.

It was still Sophia's home. During her marriage to Xavier, nothing had been changed. Xavier had laid it on the line that nothing was to be changed which might upset the boys and she had gone along with that, but now Xavier and Miguel were both dead and lay buried with Sophia in Madrid. 'If I don't make a move now, I'll be living in Sophia's shadow for the rest of my life.' These were her thoughts. She must communicate them to Carlos without upsetting him. He was still very close to his mother, much closer than he was to his father, although his mother had died first and long ago in real terms.

'Carlos, darling, there is something I feel I must talk to you about. I love this house and I would never think of moving, but I do want it to be our home. At the moment I feel that we're living in your parents' home. I don't want to make any real alterations, but if we could have the rooms redecorated in the nineties style rather than the sixties style it would be so much more our home, don't you think?'

'Yes, I suppose you're right, Charlotte. It must be our home. I'll leave it to you. Have all the redecorating you want doing, but leave all the furniture as it is, and then we'll see whether any of that needs changing when the redecorations are carried out.'

'Thank you, darling. You are good. It will cost quite a lot, with two new bathrooms and a new kitchen, but if we have it done well it will last well into the next century. We will have to move the furniture about a bit and, of course, the pictures will have to come down. We'll have to make a note of where they've all come from, but we may put them back slightly differently. We don't want too much light spoiling any of them.'

Charlotte said this last sentence to give herself the opportunity of replacing only those which she liked. How anyone could like those pictures of bullfights was beyond her.

'I know you don't like them all, Charlotte. You can't

deceive me. I'll take all those you don't like into my study. Then I'll get them valued. If they're any good, I'll either keep them for investment or sell them here in Seville or Madrid.'

'Good for you, darling. If you do get good prices, it will pay for the alterations and decorations. Now, before we go to bed, play that tape for me which you said Myra played for you.'

'No, Charlotte. If you don't mind, I'll play it for you tomorrow morning after breakfast. I know you think I'm naughty, but I don't want you going to sleep with my father's voice in your head, even if he was speaking in Russian. I can be selfish sometimes. I want you completely to myself – particularly at night. I'll play it for you first thing tomorrow after breakfast, I promise. Say you agree!'

'All right, I agree,' Charlotte said with some reluctance. She was annoyed at not getting her own way immediately, but secretly she was glad she had his complete attention and devotion. He manifestly wanted her rather than hearing his father's voice, and she also noticed Carlos was always now referring to his father as 'my father' and no longer as 'Dad'.

Carlos had moved his large framed photograph of his mother from his former bedroom to his study, together with a silver framed photograph of Miguel. There were no photographs of Xavier to be seen anywhere. One or two that had been about had clearly been removed from sight.

The following morning, Carlos kept his word. Maria had set up the breakfast with coffee and rolls at 8.30 a.m. The two interior designers arrived with their brochures, wall-papers and paint charts.

'Señora Lang. You set us a very difficult problem. The kitchen and the two bathrooms are the easy part. See. We've brought these brochures. They show the best designs for kitchens and bathrooms in Spain. It's the rest of the house that worries us. Do you wish the house to look English or remain Spanish?'

'Remain Spanish, of course,' replied Charlotte without any prompting by Carlos, who smiled his thanks.

'Good, Señora. Then there'll be no need to make any

alterations. We shall simply need the best modern materials to make good all the decorations and lighten the whole house to show off your furnishings and paintings to the best advantage. We'll start at the top and work our way down. No doubt you'll want an estimate of our professional fees, labour, materials and taxes? We should have that within two weeks, allowing for information coming to hand from Madrid, and if you agree we will start three weeks from today.'

The two men started their survey. They returned after Siesta to complete their review. In the meantime, Carlos played his tape for Charlotte. He provided her with a copy of Señora Vishinski's translation. Charlotte listened as carefully as she could. Although she was not fluent in Russian, she recognized Xavier's voice immediately.

Charlotte and Carlos listened to the tape three times and then studied the translations together.

'You see what I mean, Charlotte, about my father not telling you about his plans?'

'Yes, Carlos. I find it very upsetting. The question is what are we going to do about it, if anything?'

'I say we do nothing, Charlotte. Certainly we mustn't go public either to the press or security. Dad' – it was the first time he had used that word for a long time – 'may simply have been acting. Let's see if any approach is made to us. In the meantime, promise me it's just between ourselves.'

'I promise, Carlos,' she replied. They always seemed to be promising things to each other. Who would be the first to break a promise, and what would be the consequence?

24

Whilst Carlos and Charlotte were enjoying their private lives and the early days of their married life in Seville, the world was not standing still.

In Moscow, political and economic life was in a whirl. President Stolypin decided the time had come. He summoned Maiski and Renov. The months of detailed planning were over and about to bear fruit.

'Comrades, I believe we must now put "Operation Spanish Eagle" into effect. We simply cannot allow the present drift to continue. I've worked out a detailed plan that simply requires fleshing out and personal directing. The roles of the Army, the KGB and the media are vital. We need a prelude, and that can start today or tomorrow, Renov, just as soon as you can organize it. You know what we've discussed. Spontaneous demonstrations here at the Kremlin and on Red Square. Portraits of Nicholas II and plenty of placards with the words in Russian and English, which will appear well on the American and British television. Not too well-printed and painted. They must appear spontaneous, as though printed by volunteers. You, Renov, will arrange full TV and radio and press coverage across the Federation. Slogans like "Bring back the Tsar" and "Death to the Tsar's enemies" will do for a start. Do make sure that reliable KGB men and women lead the demonstrations, with detachments of Interior Police to marshal the demonstrators and take out any opposition.

'Maiski, the Police and the Army are your department. There will be promotions for the most ruthless. We shall

295

succeed within a week. There will be no political prisoners. People are either for us or against us. Once the world sees us winning, as we will, there's certain to be a bandwagon effect.

'In the meantime, Renov, please have your wife invite young Carlos Lang and his wife to Moscow for a holiday as soon as possible. I'll need to speak to Señor Carlos Lang myself, and your wife, Renov, is the one to get them both over here. Carlos Lang must be made to realise his duty to God and Holy Mother Russia and his obligations to his wife, their unborn children and his family.'

Myra wrote to Carlos and Charlotte the following day. Her husband had worked late into the night with Stolypin and Maiski. Plans were being dovetailed.

By 3 a.m. Interior troops were taking up positions. Tanks from the 24th Guards Brigade controlled all bridges, Moscow Airport and the main city television station.

Myra's letter, drafted by Vladimir, read:

'Dear Charlotte and Carlos,

Now that you are settled in your home, we would like you to spend a short holiday here in Moscow. Please come before you, Carlos, start at the University and before you, Charlotte, find it unwise to travel too far! I do hope that you do not think I write too personally, but I know how quickly babies come if you both want. I was the same age as Charlotte when I married Vladimir. You will never regret having a family. Please let us know when you could come. I promise you a happy time with us.

Yours sincerely
Myra Renov'

Charlotte, mindful of the tape and having seen the international news on Spanish TV, thought it prudent not to rush a reply. When she did, she wrote:

296

'Dear Myra,

It is very kind of you to write to us with the offer of a holiday in Moscow. We are in the middle of alterations here in Seville. If it was possible for us to visit you both sometime next year we should be delighted.

Yours sincerely

Charlotte Lang'

Myra showed Charlotte's letter to Vladimir.

'That won't do at all, Myra. We need to have them here next week, not next year! You'll have to speak to them on the telephone. No time like the present. Make sure you speak slowly. You'll know what to say. Just get them both here as soon as you can.'

Vladimir pressed the required digits.

'Good morning, Señor Lang. This is Myra Renov speaking from Moscow. Please thank your dear wife for her letter. I do know how difficult it can be with builders and decorators in the house. Look. Please do not wait until next year. Do explain to your wife that Russia is a democracy now. Vladimir may not be re-elected next year. Please speak to your wife and say you will come next week or the week after. You will be away from all the dust which always goes with building work and decorating. Feel free to speak to our Consulate in Seville tomorrow, when you have made up your minds which day suits you both best, and I will ask Vladimir to make all the necessary travel arrangements. I was absolutely delighted to be with you both on your wedding day. Vladimir was so very sorry he could not be with you. Do give your wife my best regards. When I put this telephone down I will speak to our Consulate in Seville.'

Carlos did not need to repeat any part of Myra's message. Charlotte had been listening on the bedroom extension without interrupting.

'Well, Charlotte, what do you say?'

'I don't really know, darling. I would rather be here to keep an eye on things, but it's very tempting. Having a lot of the work done while we're away would save a lot of dust,

297

as Myra says. We can't, of course, go this week. There's far too much to do, but next Tuesday, say. Yes, let's say next Tuesday. We'll do that. We may never get a second chance. To be entertained by the top Russians is something many people in the West would give their right hands for – well, not literally – but come on, let's go. We'll have to have everything sorted out here in terms of storage security, but we can arrange that. I suggest we take a few photographs of the house as it is now and then we'll see the difference when we get back, although I think I heard the interior decorators say they always did that and presented their customers with a "Before and After" album.'

The flight from Madrid to Moscow via Paris was arranged by Renov. More exactly, it was Renov who arranged for their flight on a scheduled service. Charlotte took the precaution of taking two evening dresses, and Carlos packed his dinner suit. If they were to be entertained by the Second Vice President of Russia, albeit for the time being, they would not let him and Myra down, or themselves.

At Moscow Airport, both Charlotte and Carlos were surprised to find themselves being separated from their fellow passengers and escorted to what was obviously a VIP lounge.

Myra Renov emerged from a large doorway escorted by Ludmilla, who had escorted Myra at their wedding, together with three rather obvious security men.

Myra went straight to Charlotte and kissed her on both cheeks. She then turned to Carlos and kissed him in the same way. Myra seemed very excited. At the Renov's Kremlin flat, Charlotte immediately detected a high state of security. It appeared far more evident than when she had last been in the flat, on duty herself as Sylvia's Protection Officer. Now she was a guest of honour together with Carlos, and their bedroom was perfectly laid out, with flowers and copies of the London *Times* and the Madrid *Expresso* on a side table. Nothing had been omitted. It wasn't just fresh towels and sheets.

The whole room would have matched any palace bedroom in any part of the world. The twin beds were tactfully placed side by side and together.

Dinner was to be taken in a private dining room that led off the main hall of the flat, itself a beautiful room with a 25-foot-high ceiling.

'I do like your dress, Charlotte,' started Myra as Charlotte and Carlos walked into the hall from their bedroom. 'We do have a surprise for you both, Vladimir and me. We are not dining alone, we do have three other guests. We are very honoured to have as our guests this evening, President Stolypin and his wife Olga, and General Viktor Maiski. If we behave very well, we might persuade Viktor to play the piano for us. He plays very well. You will find he makes the most perfect dinner guest, and he does not speak very slowly like me.'

Carlos and Charlotte smiled their surprised look at Myra and then, as opportunity arose, looked at each other with questions in their eyes. They didn't have long to wait. They had no sooner seen Vladimir pour out their first vodkas than President Stolypin himself and his wife Olga were announced. Stolypin bowed rather stiffly towards Charlotte, taking her hand in his and kissing it. Olga shook hands and kissed her on both cheeks in a much more informal, not to say friendly, fashion. Stolypin shook hands rather stiffly with Carlos, but again Olga seemed ready to receive Carlos's kisses on both cheeks.

It was Vladimir Renov who led the conversation. 'Mr President. My wife and I feel very honoured to have you and your wife as our guests this evening and to meet our friends from Seville. I had the honour to be invited to attend their wedding in London. You may remember my telling you last month. Unfortunately, I was prevented from going because of my duties with the Chinese trade delegation, but Myra has told me that it was a splendid affair. Señora Lang, as you might imagine, looked the radiant bride she was.'

Charlotte wondered whether her blushing was obvious. Both she and Carlos felt they were on stage. The conversation, in perfect English, seemed stilted and prepared.

'Myra told me all about it, Señora.' It was Olga who was speaking now. She seemed and sounded much more natural.

'Now I want to hear all about your home in Seville. I've never been to Spain myself, but I hope to do so one day. No doubt you will be able to give me any number of tips from the woman's perspective. I believe you lived in Madrid last year, but I think Seville is more like Paris on a small scale, yes?'

'Yes it is, but it's not that small. Expo 92 was held in Seville, and it was quite a large city before then. Hopefully it will never be the size of Paris or Madrid. I like it just as it is, as did our King's daughter on her wedding day! If the opportunity arose, I would be very pleased to show you around.'

The conversation continued in a more relaxed mood, not least since Vladimir was a generous host with his decanter. They had just finished their second drink when they were joined by Maiski, who oozed charm from every pore from the moment he arrived. Within seconds it seemed Maiski was talking of his last visit to Chicago, his meetings with the Orlanskis and how he hoped he might visit Malta one day, where Mary Orlanski's family came from. After further conversation, a uniformed waiter announced that dinner was served.

To Charlotte's surprise, not to say amazement, Stolypin took her arm and led her to the dining room like in some old-fashioned film. Myra had placed name cards, and Charlotte felt certain they had been placed with diplomatic care since she was not placed facing Carlos. It would be difficult for her to communicate with him by her eyes. Again, surprisingly Charlotte thought, Vladimir pronounced Grace in Russian. Two uniformed attendants commenced serving the meal with wine from the south.

The first course was a generous portion of caviar with salad. At the conclusion of the first course, Vladimir proposed the first toast of the evening to 'Our guests, Mr President, Madame Stolypin and our friends from Spain.' Vladimir and Myra stood, raised their glasses and downed their remaining wine. Resuming their seats, they started conversing again as the second course arrived, a generous fish course with French wine – a quality Muscadet. When this had been consumed, it was Maiski who rose to propose a toast to 'Russia and Spain'. Maiski didn't just say 'Russia and Spain', but made a little speech.

'Mr President and friends. We do not often have the pleasure of entertaining friends, particularly young friends from Spain. It gives me great pleasure to propose a toast to Spain and to our own country. In particular I drink to the long life of the King of Spain and all the people of that great country and, of course, our own great country.'

Stolypin, his wife Olga, Maiski and the Renovs rose and toasted 'Russia and Spain'. Carlos felt he had to say something. Charlotte was too far away to offer guidance. He rose, rather unsteadily, Charlotte thought.

'General Maiski. May I thank you for your very kind words, and whilst on my feet thank you, General Renov, for your very kind hospitality to my wife and myself.' Carlos felt he had said enough and sat down. His Russian hosts clapped their hands. Charlotte felt relieved. The second course was cleared and the third course arrived.

The table was cleared by the staff, who were clearly acting on Myra's instructions, given by her pressing a concealed button. It was a credit to the chefs who had prepared it. 'Steak a la Moscow', according to the printed menu. A rich red wine was poured from large cut-glass decanters. It was impossible to know the origin of the wine, but presumably it came from the sunny South. It tasted like a quality Bulgarian wine, but nobody enquired.

It was halfway through this course that President Stolypin rose from his chair.

'Comrades and friends. There are occasions when I have been called upon to speak for an hour at a time. This evening is not one of those occasions. We all know that once upon a time Russia had its own throne, now sadly vacated. That throne was occupied for many years, with distinction, by members of the Romanov dynasty. I feel honoured to share this dining table with the present head of the Romanov dynasty.

'We have conducted enquiries in depth, Señor Lang, and it now appears to us that your late father was not completely honest with us when we had that discussion with him, of which I believe you hold a copy, and various other discussions we had with him over a period of time. It now seems to us that your late father was, if not in direct line of succession, sufficiently clear for Russia to have acclaimed him Tsar if that had been possible. Following your father's tragic accident, it follows that you stand in the shoes of your late father and elder brother. It only remains for me to propose the toast of the evening: "The Romanov dynasty".'

Everybody rose, including Charlotte, who rose at a glance from Myra, and drained their glasses. There was a pregnant pause in the conversation when they all sat down, but the Russians clapped, including Stolypin himself. Carlos felt he should rise again, but he did not know what his hosts would expect him to say, and he had already drunk far more than usual at this stage of the dinner.

The uniformed attendants had already refilled his glass from time to time. Maiski came to his aid by striking up a conversation in relation to the Russian Season in terms of the forthcoming Bolshoi productions. This was the cue to Myra to carry the conversation forward, which she did with graphic descriptions of behind-the-stage scenes and musical gossip, which she always seemed to pick up. She went frequently to the concerts and rehearsals of every description. There was seemingly no end to her fund of knowledge concerning the Bolshoi, its past, present and future. Since she was ostensibly the hostess for the evening, not even Stolypin sought to restrain her. At the conclusion of the main course a variety of cheeses was produced with yet further wine, with vodka on hand for any who preferred it.

Charlotte had warned Carlos about the amount of wine that would be offered, but even she was feeling merry and light-headed. Further toasts were proposed. Charlotte and Carlos between them could hardly recall all that had been toasted, but the Army came into it somewhere.

Eventually the meal came to an end and Maiski took himself to the piano, where he gave a pleasant if short recital – Rachmaninov. Everybody applauded. On the stroke of midnight Stolypin made his excuses and, together with the amiable Olga, departed into the night with Maiski and a phalanx of security people, both men and women who had been entertained by Ludmilla. The Russian guests departed, Myra started on Charlotte:

'We really have enjoyed you being here tonight, Charlotte. May I call you Charlotte now that the others have gone? You made such a good impression on the President and, perhaps more importantly, on his wife Olga. She really is a tremendous person. So full of fun and so clever. They say she was responsible for siting the SS-20 missiles years ago, and they have lovely children. I do not know where she gets the energy from. I pray you do become Tsarina. You must promise me that you will work on your husband to become Tsar when the time comes!'

Charlotte was stunned. She knew that she had been drinking, but now she was alone with this earnest Russian, who clearly was at the very heart of the Government and who was trying to get her into 'working on Carlos', as she had put it, to become Tsar, but when and how? The whole thing seemed like a dream. She frantically pulled herself together to make reply. She did remember to speak slowly for Myra's benefit:

'Myra, you have fairly taken my breath away. You have given us a glorious first night. No first night at the Bolshoi could have been better, but I have drunk far more wine than I should, Please let us talk tomorrow, and then I will speak to Carlos.' What other reply could she make?

'Thank you, Charlotte. That will do very well. I know we are going to be good friends, you and me. It's the men who make the decisions, but it is we women who must make them make them. President Stolypin himself would not be President without Olga. I think it will be you who makes Carlos into the Tsar, if that's what you want, and you must. Too many good men and women have given their lives for freedom for selfishness to prevent the restoration. I'm counting on you, Charlotte. There are others who would be Tsar if they could, in line of succession I mean, but Vladimir has been through them very thoroughly. He wants Carlos, and so do I. I wanted your first husband, but then he was killed. Our men fought with their bare hands' to try and get him and Miguel out of that car in Spain. See, I've said too much. I've been drinking, too. Those Russian businessmen on holiday were not businessmen, they were Vladimir's men on special duty. They fought with their bare hands' – Myra was repeating herself, a sure sign that she was tired – 'to save him and his son. Thank God you married Carlos. I can say no more now, the men are coming back from wherever they have been, but please remember what I have said. I shall pray for you tonight. Yes. Russian women can still pray, after seventy years.'

Charlotte's mind was spinning. Even her first-class Police training at Hendon Police College could be no real training for this situation. The best she could do was look pleasant and keep a cool head and say as little as possible.

When Carlos and Vladimir did come back from wherever they'd been – she couldn't care less at the time – she made her excuses to retire 'after such a long day travelling and such a glorious evening', as she put it. By the time Carlos came into the bedroom, Charlotte was fast asleep. He was desperately tired himself. He didn't try and waken her. He did kiss her before turning the light out. He was asleep himself within three minutes.

Myra wasn't sleeping. She made full report to Vladimir on her conversation with Charlotte. Vladimir was now as excited as his wife.

'Did you say you wanted to conceive our second child tonight?' he asked before turning his bedside lights out.

The following morning, Charlotte waited her opportunity before speaking to Carlos in relation to her last-minute conversation with Myra of the night before.

'Darling, we're in a desperate situation. It seems that the Russians really did want your father to be proclaimed Tsar

304

at some future date, and now they want you to stand in his place, with me as Tsarina. It all sounds like something out of a fairy story, but it isn't. Supposing you said "No", you don't imagine they would just say OK, do you? It seems they have invested very heavily, and Myra said to me last night that too many good men and women had died in their cause. The trouble is that we know so little, and if we were to tell anybody of our predicament God knows what position we might find ourselves in!'

'You're quite right, Charlotte. General Renov was on to me as well as Myra being on to you. If I'd agreed last night, I really do think we might have been proclaimed this morning. I didn't say "No", in fact I implied "Yes", but I made it clear that I would not make any decision without your agreement, and in any case I couldn't agree to anything immediately because arrangements would have to be made for your mother, sister and brother-in-law and my own family in Spain.'

'Thanks for that. Just imagine a proclamation followed by hordes of journalists and photographers in Palmers Road, New Southgate, and my sister's place. Life could never be the same for them. I'm glad you told Renov it wasn't on this week. We'll have to have a good long think about our future and, for the moment, certainly this week, we must not be got at individually. Myra wants me to work on you to persuade you to say "Yes".'

Carlos nodded his agreement.

Charlotte continued, 'Good. Let's present a united stand then on what you've said. We'll agree to think about their proposition, but we will have to make arrangements in both London and Seville, and we simply cannot make the arrangements from here. I suggest we tell them both this morning together.'

'Thanks, Charlotte. I'm glad I married you. I do love you. You know that. Give me a kiss.' They embraced warmly. Charlotte's mind was in overdrive. No-one could receive training for this situation.

Over breakfast, Carlos took the initiative. 'General Renov,

305

or may I continue to call you Vladimir, as I did after all that wine and vodka last night? Charlotte and I have been talking to each other this morning, as I promised you last night. We are both very flattered and honoured at what has been suggested, but we must have "time and space", as they say in England. I know from what you said last night that you would like to make some announcement to your friends this morning, but you don't seem to realize what problems any public announcement would cause in London and Seville. We must be able to alert our families to what may be announced, so that proper arrangements can be made for them. You have no idea what pressures they will come under.'

'I hear what you say, Carlos. Believe me, we have given a great deal of thought to your two families, and every facility will be afforded to them by our Embassy in London and our Consulate in Seville. We know your TV and press media will be after your families for interviews and "exclusives", but they can easily receive full protection through our contacts in England and Spain in "safe houses" until the immediate news period is passed and suitable articles can be drafted out for them. How does that suit?'

'It suits very well, Vladimir,' started Charlotte, 'but we must fly back, tomorrow if need be, to inform our families and make other arrangements, including our alterations and decorations in Seville, the storage of furniture and many other things. It simply cannot all be done from this building over the telephone, quite apart from the possibility of the telephone or radio waves being intercepted by any number of people and organizations.'

'You are going to be a perfect Tsarina for us, Charlotte. I'm very glad you appreciate the security aspect. If I can rely on you both to come back to Moscow in a fortnight's time, having made all your "arrangements" as you call them, without a word of what we intend going to anybody outside your families, I think I could arrange to have you back in London tomorrow morning with full back-up from our Embassy for any reasonable requests you might make.'

'You can rely on us, Vladimir,' replied Carlos. 'It just may be desirable for us to bring Charlotte's mother and sister back here to Moscow, for a short time at any rate. Our arrangements in Seville are more at a business level, but we needn't trouble you with our business affairs. When we do come back, I assume you will have separate accommodation for us – a flat like this, perhaps – what the British call "a grace-and-favour residence".'

'Yes. We would certainly do that, and Myra will be pleased to show you today the place where I fancy you would like to be, and you will be receiving the fullest protection as from today, depend on it. I'm sorry I can't be with you for the rest of the day, but Myra will be and I will be with you for the concert this evening and the supper afterwards back here.'

Both Charlotte and Carlos were conscious that they had nothing in writing. It was all verbal. No doubt this was for security reasons. The Russians were not going to make themselves hostages to fortune in providing evidence that could be used for any purpose.

At the moment they simply had the word of Renov and his wife. It was all they were going to receive. Myra was her usual charming self. She continued to speak slowly in English, but occasionally Charlotte attempted to use her Russian, to Myra's slight amusement.

The flat they were to occupy within the Kremlin was indeed a grace-and-favour residence of some splendour. It had been used on previous occasions as a guest residence for very top guests of the old Soviet Government, and more recently by the Republic of the Russian Federation.

Before Renov left, Charlotte pumped him as best she could as to exactly what she and Carlos would be expected to do with their time. 'You do ask the most searching and sensible questions, Charlotte. I suspect Carlos will carry out all those functions that, say, the King of Spain carries out, and you will carry out those that the Queen of Spain carries out. The exact work programme will be a matter for detailed planning, but I imagine that you will both want to start, once you're settled in here, with two or three extensive tours of the Republic – but by then we shall be the Russian Empire once again. Then there will be your entertaining foreign royalty and others, and your visits abroad, including Brussels and Strasbourg. You are going to have very busy lives, and best of all, you will hopefully have children of your own.'

'You certainly make it all sound very exciting and demanding, Vladimir,' was all Charlotte and Carlos could say. A telephone call was made to Charlotte's mother in Southgate.

Twenty-four hours later, Carlos and Charlotte were at her home in Palmers Road. Unknown to them, they were spotted at Heathrow and followed by Russian security agents, who reported to Moscow their safe arrival. Alice was delighted to have them back home. She had not expected them, but the telephone call had given her time to air the bed in the guest bedroom and get in extra food. They would only be staying for two days, but that was heaven for her. After dinner, Charlotte spoke for both of them. They had planned together that Charlotte should do the talking.

'Mum, we haven't just broken our journey back to Seville to come and see you. We do have some tremendous news for you, but you must keep it completely to yourself. No, I'm not expecting yet, as far as I know. It's this. Carlos and I have been asked to take on very responsible jobs in Moscow, and it will mean our going to live there, probably on a permanent basis, with visits to London and Seville. We can't tell you – not even you – any more at the moment. Something, anything, may come up to prevent it happening, but if it does come off we want you to be in Moscow with us in ten days' time. What do you say to that?'

'Charlotte, I don't even know what you're talking about. What can I say?'

'You could say "Yes, Gran." ' It was Carlos speaking now. 'Just say "Yes", and we'll fix it up for you, Margaret and John to come with us to Moscow. You won't have to stay with us long if you don't want, but I know you will never forgive yourself if you don't come. Don't press Charlotte for any more details. Just say you will come, and bring Margaret and John with you. We have given our word to say nothing. You will come with Margaret and John, won't you? It will cost the three of you nothing. I will see to that, and hopefully the Russians will be paying anyway.'

Alice Johnson looked at her daughter and son-in-law. She was very fond of them both, and after looking at them both for a whole minute in silence, said:

'All right, but there isn't a mother in London who wouldn't need and want to know a lot more. I'll get Margaret to agree, and hopefully John as well, but I'm sure they'll want to know more than you have told me. Come to think of it, you've told me nothing except that you want the three of us in Moscow when your new job is announced. That's about the size of it, isn't it?'

'Yes Gran, but we won't let any of the three of you down, and I think I can safely say that you'll be grateful for our keeping you in the dark for security reasons. Remember, it isn't that long ago that Charlotte was under strict security control, looking after her friend Sylvia.'

'Carlos, I've said I'll come. You'll have to leave it to me to persuade Margaret and John to come as well. You just fix up the tickets and the hotel in Moscow.'

'No problem, Gran. I'll fix them up tomorrow morning. You'll be flying British Airways. There will be five of us. You, Margaret and John, and Charlotte and me. You won't need to take too many clothes. Just take say two changes, just in case you had an accident with soup being poured over you in a restaurant.' Carlos winked at Charlotte, both at his own humour and to say 'well done'.

The remainder of the conversation continued quite normally. The conversation with Margaret and John was more difficult, but with Charlotte's mother already coming, it didn't take Charlotte more than half an hour to persuade them to come along.

The arrangements were quickly made, and by using code General Renov was informed by the Russian Embassy that Mrs Alice Johnson, her daughter Margaret and son-in-law would be coming 'to resume the holiday arrangements which had been made for Mr and Mrs Carlos Lang'.

In Seville, matters were much simpler. Uncle Paul was briefed sufficiently by Carlos, with Charlotte in attendance, and Maria and Manuel, at the family home, thought there was nothing whatsoever unusual in Carlos and Charlotte going to live in Moscow and St Petersburg, provided they weren't going to live in England, and they would be sure to come and live in Seville at least once a year and, yes, they would be happy to have a holiday in Russia at some future date. Neither of them had ever flown in an aeroplane, but if Carlos had wanted it they would travel on donkeys to please him, but it would be rather too far on donkeys!

The Russian Consulate informed the Renovs of 'very satisfactory arrangements for Señor Lang and his wife to resume their holiday, which they had been obliged to cut short on account of Señora's illness in London'.

The code was preserved intact, with no possibility of interception. British Airways made Moscow the first stop.

25

Experienced officials of MI6, the British Security Service dealing with external affairs, checked the list of passengers flying from Heathrow to Moscow on the scheduled flight.

Carlos and Charlotte, Charlotte's mother, sister and her husband were checked against their luggage 'Excelsior Hotel, Moscow'.

At Moscow Airport, a large black Zil limousine displaying a 'Hotel Excelsior' sign awaited them. The Excelsior was one of the four best hotels in Moscow. Rooms had been booked through the Intourist office in Piccadilly.

MI6 were fully aware of the political and economic problems facing Russia. It was thought an elementary precaution to check who was visiting the Russian capital.

The Langs were well known. Carlos Lang was the son of Xavier Lang who, though now dead, was still something of a hero figure, following his information and flair that had saved the Palace of Westminster two years ago. It was well known that his widow Charlotte had remarried his son, Carlos. MI6 also knew that Charlotte had first served as Protection Officer to Sylvia, still Deputy Prime Minister, and had very recently worked as her Personal Assistant.

Why should she be travelling to Moscow with her husband, her sister and brother-in-law? Perhaps it was just a family holiday? Carlos Lang was, after all, a very wealthy young man, but it wasn't obvious why they should be holidaying in a capital that seemed wracked with problems. The Foreign Office was not actively encouraging travel to Russia, but was stopping short of advising against.

MI6 reported their findings to the Thameside Headquarters in London via the British Embassy in Moscow.

The Excelsior was checked, and 'Yes, Mr and Mrs Lang, Mrs Johnson and Mr and Mrs Harrison were booked in. They had separate rooms, a double for the Langs, a double for the Harrisons and a single for Mrs Johnson with a surcharge paid in advance.' No further comment was made or required. Their luggage taken to their rooms, the happy quintet commenced taking dinner in the huge dining room. They liked what they saw and enjoyed their meal.

Whilst the diners were dining in Moscow, Sir John Bickerstaffe and Florence were arriving at Harcourt. After changing for dinner, Florence came downstairs and passed an enveloped marked 'Personal and Confidential' to Sylvia. It only took Sylvia a second to open the envelope. The letter was the most amazing that Sylvia had ever read:

'Dear Sylvia,

I feel I must write this letter to you in haste. Forgive my not trying to speak to you by phone, but you must know that I could not be certain that our telephone conversation might not be tapped and taped. I have asked Florence to deliver this letter to you. Please pray for Carlos and me. As you read this letter, Carlos and I will be in Moscow, as guests of the Renovs. It is possible that we settle here at the highest level of Russian society, but please believe me, if we do become Russians, I will always regard you as one of my closest friends, and there will be no question of my betraying any British secrets known to you and me. Please give my best love to Carlos. You know you have my undying friendship and gratitude.

Charlotte'

Sylvia passed the letter to her husband who in turn, at Sylvia's suggestion, passed it to Florence and Sir John.

'What on earth has happened?' started Florence. 'This

312

can't be true. Let me read it again.' Florence re-read the letter and passed it back to Sylvia.

'I must call MI6 immediately and see if they have any information,' began Sylvia. 'I'll have to advise them of my having received this letter, but we'll have to be careful. I don't really mean us. I mean the Embassy staff in Moscow. I'd love to be able to speak directly to Charlotte before she takes any rash action, but I simply can't fly out myself, and in any case anything she and Carlos want to do or say they may already have done or said.'

'First things first, Sylvia,' said Sir John quickly. 'Get Susan to call MI6 and take it from there. The PM will have to know immediately. This is the very last thing I expected.'

Sylvia thought for a moment, and pressed the required digits.

Within three minutes she was speaking directly to the Prime Minister on the red line. 'Prime Minister, I feel I must speak to you as a matter of urgency. You will, of course, remember Charlotte, who worked for me most recently as my Personal Assistant?'

'Yes. What of it, Sylvia?'

'I have a letter from her delivered to me within the last few minutes. It's in my hand as I speak. It seems that she and her new husband are in Moscow, and she writes of the possibility of becoming Russian, with all that that might mean in terms of security. I felt I just had to let you know immediately. I'm going to call MI6, if you agree, to let them know and see if they know anything. She's been a real treasure to me over the years. I don't like to think of her doing anything wrong, but I feel we must know what is happening.'

'You're quite right, and thanks for letting me know. Go ahead. Call MI6. See if they know anything, and tell them to keep both of us fully informed.'

'Thank you, Prime Minister. Leave it to me. I'll come back to you myself as soon as I have any information.'

Within seconds Sylvia was speaking to Thameside Head-quarters.

'Yes, Minister. Mr and Mrs Lang flew out of Heathrow this

morning, together with a Mr and Mrs Harrison and a Mrs Alice Johnson, and they all arrived safely and they are staying at the Hotel Excelsior. We have checked at the hotel, and they are booked in there. We don't know more than that, but the booking was apparently made via the Intourist office in Piccadilly here in London. We haven't made any further enquiries. They only took a small amount of luggage. It was all labelled to the hotel. We could get you the number of the hotel if you would like to try and call them yourself, or we could try and call them from here, but, of course, they might not be in the hotel itself when we call.'

'Thank you. Get me the number and I will try and call,' replied Sylvia. It was several minutes later when Sylvia received the Moscow number from MI6, but that was the easy part. There was a delay on all calls to Moscow, and Sylvia spoke no Russian. She rang back to MI6 and asked them to make contact either by phone or through the British Embassy in Moscow.

'Tell them I want Charlotte Lang to speak to me urgently, very urgently. She knows my number here.' MI6 could make no satisfactory contact either by telephone or through the Embassy. Embassy officials did call at the hotel. They met a blank wall. The Head Porter, flanked by two rather obvious KGB officers, was terribly polite but uninformative. Yes. Mr and Mrs Lang, her mother Mrs Johnson and two friends or relatives of hers were booked in, but they had gone out for the evening. He had no idea when they would be coming in, but if they cared to leave a message he would be pleased to see that it was delivered to Mrs Lang's room.

'Russia is a free country now, gentlemen. We don't attempt to track and follow our guests' journeys around the city.' This was relayed back to London. A message had been left. There was nothing more the Embassy could do, unless they were required to maintain observations, but what were they supposed to do beyond conveying the Minister's message? There were a number of concerts in the city. It would be like looking for the proverbial needle in the haystack to search the city. The probable answer was that they were being entertained by their friends, the Renovs. If that was the position, London would just have to await Charlotte's call. There was no way the Embassy staff could be discovered keeping the Kremlin itself under observation without possible fearful consequences.

In truth, Charlotte never received the message that Sylvia had sent the Embassy, and when MI6 did eventually get through on the telephone to the hotel, there was the polite but bland answer that the Embassy men had received.

Myra Renov and her constant shadow Ludmilla had seen their five guests arrive at the hotel and had been kept fully informed of their progress. Myra decided to make her move when they were halfway through their dinner.

'Charlotte. How very nice to see you again in Moscow, this time with your family, as I remember them at your wedding.' There was kissing and shaking of hands. 'Now, do not let us spoil your dinner. When it comes time for coffee, you must all come back with Ludmilla and me back to our flat.'

Myra was speaking as usual very slowly in her attractive accented English, but she spoke in Moscow with an air of authority. She wasn't so much asking them, but telling them that they were coming to have coffee in her flat. Twenty minutes later they were all at the Renovs' flat, where coffee was served and glasses were laid out for after-dinner drinks.

'Now please let me tell you what we have arranged. Vladimir will be here shortly, and he will be able to confirm all details. Firstly, you will not be going back to the hotel. You will all be staying here tonight. I have given instructions for all your belongings to be brought here from the hotel, and they will probably arrive quite shortly. Tomorrow is going to be a very busy day for all of us, and a very thrilling day. Do you all know what I am talking about?'

'I've no idea, Myra,' said Alice truthfully. 'Charlotte simply told me that she wanted me to come with her for some important reason concerning Carlos's future work. She has refused to say more.'

'Same with us, Myra. Charlotte can be very secretive when

315

she wants. It feels very funny not knowing why we are here beyond being on holiday.'

Myra looked at her captive audience of five. 'Good, very good. I am glad you kept your promise, Charlotte. Now we will have to wait for Vladimir to see if it is going to happen. In the meantime, let us have another glass of coffee.'

Everyone present exchanged glances whilst Ludmilla poured more coffees.

Quite suddenly, as it seemed, Vladimir was with them. He greeted Myra as though they hadn't seen each other for a week. In fact, he had been with her and the Stolypins during the day.

'Carlos, I have the honour to inform you that tomorrow morning at ten o'clock Moscow time, a Proclamation will be issued. You will be proclaimed Tsar of Russia and all the Russians. You, Charlotte, will be proclaimed Tsarina. By that time you will be in your own flat here in the Kremlin, with Ludmilla as your protection officer. We have a team of twenty picked men and women as your personal protection unit.'

Although Carlos and Charlotte had expected something like this, the others simply held their breath. They could not take in what was being said. As if by instinct, Carlos shook hands formally with Vladimir and then kissed Charlotte, Myra, his mother-in-law and sister-in-law. There was more kissing and shaking of hands.

The whole atmosphere was so unreal, but now here was General Stolypin, together with his wife Olga and General Maiski.

General Stolypin made a short prepared statement: 'Tonight is one of the great nights of my life, but tomorrow will be a great day for all Russia and the Russian people. Russia will have its Tsar and Tsarina. Let us drink to victory. I propose a toast "To the Romanov Family and its Restoration".' All present raised their glasses.

Carlos felt he had to say something. He had prepared himself so far as he could, but again there could be no real

316

preparation for such momentous and unbelievable events unknown to the world outside.

'Mr President and friends. I hardly know what to say, beyond saying that my wife and I feel very honoured and yet humbled by your news and toast. We pledge ourselves to all of you here present that we will do our very best for Russia and all its peoples.' Carlos said these few words in Russian, to the delight of his hosts. 'At the risk of asking the obvious, what happens next, Mr President?'

'You are very quick, Carlos. Very soon I will cease calling you Carlos. You must now assume the name of Nicholas to become Nicholas III, and there is much work for you to do tonight. You will come with me to have your message to the Empire and the world filmed for release tomorrow morning. You will, of course proclaim a National Public Holiday. Even as we are talking, any number of Army and Interior Police units are taking up strategic positions just in case there was to be any trouble.'

Charlotte lost colour visibly at these last remarks, but Olga quickly comforted her with the words: 'Please do not worry yourself. There will be no problems. The only real problem will be for the Police to marshall all the crowds who will be waving to you on Red Square tomorrow. It is going to be a great day of rejoicing. It will be interesting to see which Royals acknowledge you first. By the way, do not worry about press "exclusives" as you call them. We have prepared all manner of texts, and the Western press will not be allowed within one hundred metres for at least three months, so there is nothing to worry about. No doubt you will be wanting to speak to your friends who attended your wedding. If you could let me have their numbers, there will be no problem. Now, before we do anything else why do not you all, except Carlos, come with me to your new home in Moscow? I do hope you like it. All previous occupants have loved it, and you will have time to meet your staff and security officers – Ludmilla will introduce you to her team. Do not trouble about your luggage. All that will follow us. Once tomorrow is over you will be able to plan your future. It is going to be a very exciting few days, and I imagine a very exciting few years ahead for all of us.'

'You go along, Charlotte. I'll be all right,' said Carlos. 'I'll come to you just as soon as I can after filming or whatever else has to be done.' The little company broke up. Carlos went with Stolypin and Maiski, Charlotte and her family with Renovs.

Carlos was observing by the second even the route he was being taken. He was asked to give his measurements, and these were checked. Within half an hour he was wearing a Russian Army Officer's uniform. A short speech had been prepared for him, and this he read three times before filming commenced. The speech would be heard and seen throughout Russia and extracts, no doubt, throughout the world. The speech was very short, and there were underlinings in red and yellow where emphasis was required. The speech read:

'One hour ago I had the honour to be proclaimed Tsar of Russia and all the Russian people. My beloved wife Charlotte has been proclaimed Tsarina. We pledge ourselves to the service of Russia and all loyal citizens of the Empire. Our policy will be to develop a window of opportunity for our nation and peace-loving nations throughout the world. We believe in friendship with all democratic countries, but until world peace can be fully guaranteed we will seek to preserve our glorious armed forces in a state of full effectiveness with all the power at our command. We live in difficult times. With God's help and the industry of all loyal Russians, Russia will prevail.'

There was nothing remarkable about the speech itself. Carlos could have read a speech written for him lasting for hours with no greater effect. His short speech repeated on the hour, every hour, for the next 24 hours, would penetrate everywhere. For an hour after the filming. Carlos spent time meeting any number of people he had never met before and being given a quantity of reading in Russian and English.

Charlotte and her mother, sister and brother-in-law spent their time in equally exhausting conditions. Ludmilla, it seemed, did speak some English, which was a help. Their new home was a magnificent suite of rooms, which the word 'flat' could not begin to describe. There were three principal reception rooms, ten bedrooms, each with en-suite facilities, and substantial domestic offices. The dining room could seat 40 without difficulty, and the kitchen looked like something out of a Hollywood production. There was a resident staff of 12, in addition to security staff quarters.

Within two hours, the time Carlos was away with Stolypin and Maiski, Charlotte began to feel at home, so far as anyone could in her situation. It was a very tired Carlos who returned to his new home with his mentors.

'We are going to leave you now so that you can have a good long sleep after all your travel and excitement. Remember, we rise early in Moscow. I suggest you set your alarms for five o'clock.' With these words Myra crossed the room towards Charlotte and kissed her on both cheeks.

The Stolypins, Maiski and the Renovs departed.

Carlos and family were on their own at last – not completely alone. Ludmilla and a security staff of four would not be going anywhere. They would be on duty all night – certainly until 6 a.m., when a fresh team of KGB security officers, two men and two women, would arrive to take over.

In bed, at last, Carlos turned to Charlotte.

'Darling, I do love you. I don't know what I'd do without you. I just pray we're doing the right thing for ourselves, our children when they come, and for Russia. I can't even begin to think what anyone outside our life may be thinking.'

'Don't talk, darling. Just hold me. You know you'll always have me and my support. I'm very tired tonight, darling, but I can't let you go to sleep without telling you something I believe is happening.'

'What is it, Charlotte? Do tell me.'

'I think, darling, you are already a Daddy tonight. I will test again, but when I tested in London, I was positive!'

Carlos's tiredness was gone in a flash. Beyond kissing Charlotte, he was up immediately and opening a bottle of

319

Champagne and pouring out two glasses. They toasted each other and sipped freely.

She was right. She had conceived on her honeymoon. Russia would have a Tsarevitch within nine months.

By 9 a.m., large crowds were gathering on Red Square. There had been practice 'spontaneous' crowds for days, but this time it was for real. Word had been sent out to any number of factories and offices, and some 40,000 troops were on special duty.

At 9.30 a.m., all the bells of Moscow's churches started pealing, and the nation was advised by television and radio that the President would speak at 10 a.m.

A number of foreign embassies besieged the Kremlin for advance information as to what was to be announced. Complete security was maintained, on Maiski's specific instructions. Nobody who valued his or her life would consider breaking the imposed silence. Maiski had never been known to take prisoners.

All world satellite listening posts were alerted, including the British listening post at Cheltenham and the United Nations Center in New York. On the stroke of 10 a.m., Moscow time, the main news of the day commenced. The familiar red, blue and white lined flag of Russia was depicted, flying from its familiar flagpole on the Kremlin.

Slowly the flag appeared to be lowered, to the astonishment of viewers, and the features of President Stolypin appeared. He started speaking slowly and deliberately:

'Comrades, I am speaking to you this morning from my home here in the Kremlin' – in fact it was pre-recorded.

'Today is one of the greatest days in Russia's great and glorious history. One hour ago His Imperial Majesty Tsar Nicholas III of Russia was proclaimed Tsar, and his wife proclaimed Tsarina. I shall remain your President, and Parliament will remain answerable to democracy as in the past. However, today Russia has a Tsar, and I salute him as your President. Even as I am speaking to you, the flag of the Imperial family – the flag of the Imperial Eagle – is being unfurled over the Kremlin and in all cities of the

320

Empire. I ask you all who hear me now or who come to hear what I have said today to join me in saying or singing "Long Live the Tsar".'

The President's features faded, and the Eagle standard was seen by viewers being hoisted for the first time over the Kremlin since 1917. Television now showed a Royal Salute of 200 guns from the Kremlin Wall, and a large military band on Red Square started playing the Russian National Anthem.

Then the well-known newscaster appeared, dressed on this occasion in army uniform. 'Comrades, it is now my privilege to invite His Imperial Majesty, Tsar Nicholas, to address the city and the world.'

The picture of the newscaster faded, and the unmistakable features of Carlos de Sallas Lang, now Tsar of Russia, appeared dressed in his smart new blue Army uniform.

Carlos started his prepared speech. He spoke the text in perfect Russian: 'One hour ago I had the honour . . .'

Charlotte and her family watched the TV set along with 60 selected and carefully vetted guests. Immediately it was over, the scene went back to the Imperial Flag, now flying freely over the Kremlin. Now it was the newscaster again:

'Comrades, the Tsar has announced that tomorrow will be a National Holiday and a National Day of Prayer. Russia is rejoicing at the Restoration of the Tsar, and messages of congratulations are already being received in the Kremlin. In five minutes' time the Tsar and Tsarina will appear before a large and happy throng within the Kremlin, and hopefully will shortly thereafter appear on Red Square itself.'

The 'large and happy throng' was well organized. The Imperial Anthem, 'God Save the Tsar', unheard for years, was now heard, led by a selected choir. Cheering broke out as Carlos, wearing his blue uniform, with Charlotte at his side, appeared at a balcony window. The scenes on Red Square itself were without precedent. It seemed now that all Moscow was coming on to the Square. Church bells were still pealing, guns still discharged their blank salvos. It was like the '1812 Overture', but for real. Large genuine crowds, including thousands of soldiers and others in uniform, poured on to the Square.

Cheltenham had, of course, been monitoring Moscow for hours. The BBC and other television corporations, in co-operation with the Russian State Television Service, were sending reports and commentary all over the world.

The British Cabinet sat in the Cabinet Room at No. 10 Downing Street and the American President and his Cabinet sat in the Oval Office of the White House.

Sylvia could hardly believe her eyes. She just had to burst out: 'Prime Minister, I know the Tsar and his wife, and so do you. They were married here in London. I was at the wedding. The Tsar's father was Xavier Lang, who was my husband's best man. You were at the wedding with your wife at Lanchester. The Tsarina is as British as any of us. She was my Protection Officer from Scotland Yard, and the Tsar himself is a close personal friend of my son John. Do tell me, someone, that I'm not dreaming!'

The whole room, from the Prime Minister down, stared at Sylvia, but nobody spoke. Eventually – that is, after a few seconds that seemed like an eternity – the Prime Minister did speak:

'Are you quite certain, Sylvia?'

Sylvia nodded in her excitement. 'Yes I am, Prime Minister. As certain that I know that you are John Senior and Prime Minister. Remember that letter I spoke about and showed to you? The Tsar is Spanish. He was at my son's school, Slapton, and you will remember meeting the Tsar's father here at No. 10. I'm referring to Xavier Lang. The Tsar is Xavier's son.'

Sylvia could say no more. She was quite overcome, as well she might be. She sat motionless. At this moment the telephone on the great table rang. The Cabinet Secretary answered:

'Sorry to interrupt, Sir Roger. May we have your immediate instructions? Are we to recognize the newly proclaimed Tsar of Russia, or should we check first with Moscow, Washington and Brussels – I mean our Embassy in Moscow?'

'I can't just say "yes" or "no", Carruthers. I'm in Cabinet. I'll have to come back to you immediately a decision is made here. Have you any news yet as to whether anyone else has recognized?'

'We cannot be certain, Sir Roger, but we understand that the French and Spanish Ambassadors in Moscow are at the Kremlin now, and they won't just have gone for coffee. We'll let you know immediately we have any information, but I can tell you that our Embassy reports that the whole exercise has obviously been very well planned – yes, hold on – yes, France and Spain have recognized and sent their congratulations. It's coming through from Cheltenham as I speak.'

'Thank you, Carruthers. I'll come back to you just as soon as possible.'

'You heard that, Prime Minister? France and Spain have announced their recognition of the Tsar and sent their congratulations. The Foreign Office await your orders. Do we recognize immediately, or do we wait until we have spoken to Washington and Brussels? Paris and Madrid have not been on to us. They may have had prior information.'

All eyes turned to the Foreign Secretary. 'Prime Minister, it's a very difficult decision. Of course, I would like us to give instant recognition, but you know how fluid things are in Russia, and the last seventy years can't simply be forgotten. Supposing the Tsar was to fall as happened in 1917, where would we be then? So much is at stake, with so many British now working in Russia. I must plead for time. Within the hour, we can have spoken to everybody we need to consult and give full instructions to our Ambassador in Moscow and prepare the text of your congratulations and those of the Queen.'

Sylvia looked at John Senior. 'I've heard what the Foreign Secretary has said, Prime Minister,' she snapped, 'and I suppose in his position I would have said the same, but you and I are not in his position. I say grant immediate recognition and leave it to our Ambassador to make his own contribution. Please believe me, gentlemen, I know the Tsar and the Tsarina as well as I know my own family. By all means let us delay an hour or more if we must, but we don't want to be the last with our congratulations. The Tsar and Tsarina could be the best friends we, as a nation, have outside these islands, but if I know the Tsar, who I know as Carlos not Nicholas, thinks that we've slighted his beloved Charlotte we shall pay a very heavy price indeed. At best he will order a "Buy British Last" campaign, and France will be ahead of us for ever and a day. I've said all I'm saying, but I want my words minuting, Prime Minister, for reading in thirty years' time, when the present Cabinet papers are published.'

Silence fell over the Cabinet.

'May I speak, Prime Minister?' It was the Home Secretary who spoke. 'Dame Sabita has said some very important things. I think all of us around this table accept that she's correct in what she says, namely that the Tsarina of Russia was her Personal Assistant until recently. It follows quite possibly then that the whole of MI6 could be at risk so far as Russia is concerned. I'm not worried about Inspector Charlotte Johnson of yesterday becoming Tsarina of Russia, but I'm very concerned for our Intelligence personnel in Moscow and elsewhere in Russia!'

'Home Secretary, as Prime Minister that's my responsibility. I don't want to get side-lined into a debate on security. Certainly that aspect requires urgent consideration. In fact, certain enquiries are already under way ever since my deputy alerted me to the fact that her former Personal Assistant, Mrs Lang as she then was – the former Inspector Johnson for those of you who don't know – had gone to Russia with her husband and family, but clearly none of us knew that she was going to be proclaimed Tsarina. The question before this meeting now is, do we acknowledge and send our congratulations and advise the Queen to do the same? Time is not on our side. It seems to me that we either tell the Foreign Office to send our congratulations immediately, or we delay an hour to sound out our allies?'

'No, Prime Minister. You decide for us, and we'll back you whichever way you choose,' said the Chancellor of the Exchequer. 'We'll soon find ourselves spending hours perusing minutes. I move you decide, Prime Minister. I'll back you for certain. Nobody will be against you.'

The Prime Minister looked around the table. Various heads nodded. John Senior decided. 'Call the Foreign Office, Sir Roger. Tell them to acknowledge and send our congratulations. Tell them to let me have a draft for Her Majesty that I can take to the Palace this afternoon after I've dealt with Prime Minister's Question Time in the House.'

'Yes, Prime Minister.' Sir Roger called Carruthers back. Britain's congratulations were on their way via the British Ambassador in Moscow within half an hour. Congratulations were already on their way from many nations, including the United States and Japan.

In Chicago, Mary Orlanski simply could not take it in that her friend and colleague of Metropolitan Police days was now Tsarina of Russia. Secretly she had feared for Charlotte marrying Carlos, particularly after the death of Xavier, but her fears for her friend had nothing to do with her exalted position today. Just how does a private citizen, however wealthy, communicate with any Head of State, particularly a newly proclaimed Tsarina or Queen? The only obvious way, Mary thought, was a faxed letter to be sent via the Temperance Bank's Moscow Office. There was no time to lose in Mary's mind.

Within an hour of the announcement, Mary had drafted her letter that would be typed up on a word processor and faxed to Moscow:

'Dear Charlotte,

Elmer and I have just been watching you and Carlos on Chicago Television. Please accept our loving prayers and congratulations. You never said anything at your wedding. You and Carlos must be the very best poker players in the world, or the very best actors. We are both very thrilled for you. Do please look after yourself and give our love to Carlos. I can't wait to see you. Make a State Visit to America as soon as you like, and if you can't come please arrange, if you can, for Elmer and

me to come and visit you. We would stop over in London and see my parents, and perhaps Sylvia and Florence en route.
    Affectionately yours
        Mary'

The letter was faxed to Moscow with a covering letter of instructions. The fax was delivered to Charlotte together with a number of other letters and messages. Greetings came in shoals.

What was concerning Stolypin, Maiski and Renov was not greetings from abroad, welcome as they were, but greetings from within. To aid matters, Renov had sent out 3,000 Tsarist greetings to those 3,000 he and others at KGB Headquarters thought most important.

The merrymaking was going very well in Moscow and St Petersburg, but Russia does not consist of two cities only. There would inevitably be some opposition, and it would be the duty of the KGB to find out and sort out. Promotions would go to the most ruthless in weeding out 'enemies of the state', and 'Peoples' Courts' would give summary justice. 'There is no political problem that cannot be resolved by the machine gun.'

This awesome saying was repeated again and again. Within a week, there was no overt opposition. No doubt many citizens might have their reservations, but long experience had taught that it was sensible to keep one's opinion to oneself.

In Moscow, Imperial signs were to be seen throughout the city. Cities throughout the Empire, as it was now described, quickly followed. Sylvia could hardly wait to speak to her husband, but before she did so she had to sort out her own position vis-à-vis security. The point raised by the Home Secretary had to be cleared up.

'I have every confidence, Prime Minister, that the Tsarina, who I know as Charlotte, would never do anything to betray the Official Secrets Act. Furthermore, she never worked for MI6 except when she met up with certain Security people, when Major Renov, as he then was, was seeking to trace

326

certain senior deceased Imperial Russian Officers from the First World War and their descendants. She certainly never met any of our MI6 officers in Moscow except when accompanying me. Naturally I'll advise you and security of any contact I have with her in the future, but I don't think I could do more than that. If you really feel that I personally represent any threat to our national security, or my husband for that matter, then I would seek to resign from my present position. I don't say that lightly, and although I say it myself I don't think my resignation – which would certainly be regarded as forced – would advance our interests.'

'You're right, Sylvia, and I don't want or seek your resignation,' replied the Prime Minister quickly. 'What I would like you to do is maintain and if possible further develop your friendship with Tsarina Charlotte, as long as you keep both me and Security fully informed. You will not tell her anything without Cabinet approval, but you might easily glean information that could be very helpful in developing good Anglo-Russian relations. Don't you agree, Foreign Secretary?'

'Yes I do, Prime Minister, and we'll have to take the Leader of the Opposition into our confidence on a Privy Council basis, and other party leaders. No more than a handful need know outside the Cabinet.'

'Are we all agreed?' Cabinet members nodded their heads, and nobody spoke against. The Cabinet proceeded to other matters.

Even whilst the Cabinet meeting proceeded, Britain's congratulations were being extended to the Russian Government through the British Ambassador in Moscow. The Russian Government was acknowledging the messages and timing them as they were received on a minute-by-minute basis. This information would be stored for posterity, but was immediately made available to President Stolypin.

Before returning home to Harcourt, Sylvia dashed off a note to Charlotte. She had the same photographed – half a dozen copies.

'Dear Charlotte,
    Congratulations! It will take me some time to get used to addressing you as Your Imperial Majesty! Carlos and I were very thrilled to learn of your proclamation this morning on our TV sets. You know you could have trusted me. We do pray that all goes well for you both, and I can't wait to talk to you properly and privately. Do give our love to Carlos and let me hear from you just as soon as possible.
    Affectionately yours
    Sylvia'

In Moscow, events were moving forward in many directions. It was quickly apparent that there was no real objection to the turn of events; and salary increases, in real terms, and an increased volume of Western aid and Eastern aid from Japan was reflected in the growing Russian economic confidence.

President Stolypin, Maiski and Renov were not simply motivated by political considerations internally, but externally. Russia's increasing role within NATO and the European Union was to be pressed further. Russia wanted its elected representatives in Strasbourg and Brussels just as much as any other country. Russia would want at least the same voting rights as Germany.

The nations of Western Europe were very mindful of Russia's vast mineral resources – still largely untapped. Already Russia was providing much-needed gas and other energy sources.

The roles of Carlos and Charlotte in pressing Russia's claims and aspirations were obvious enough and would involve them in much travel and entertaining, but first they must travel extensively within the Empire. A detailed plan was worked out. Postage stamps bearing Carlos's likeness in Army uniform were printed and circulated. Charlotte's condition was explained, and she would be carefully checked and not allowed to overdo anything. Invitations literally flooded in, and were dealt with officially by the Tsar's office, drawn from the ranks of the Foreign Service, and the KGB who were charged with security. The Tourist Office was also represented.

One 'innocent' result of the Intourist influence was the presence of a substantial detachment of the Army dressed in Imperial costume, who paraded daily within the Kremlin together with a matching military band. The Changing the Guard was modelled on the same ceremony as takes place outside Buckingham Palace in London and outside the Royal Palace in Copenhagen.

Charlotte was pleased to receive Sylvia's letter and she wanted to have an early opportunity of speaking to her on her own, but how could she? There was no way she could leave Carlos and Moscow to travel to London or anywhere else without formal invitation and the approval of the Russian Government.

It was Mary in Chicago who had the bright idea of coming to Moscow on her own as a private holiday maker. She decided, however, to tell Sylvia of her plans and succeeded in persuading Sylvia to join her. It was not as simple as that. Arrangements had to be made with diplomatic care.

'I think Prime Minister,' Sylvia had said, 'It would be useful, if you could spare me for a few days, to let me join Mary Orlanski on her trip to Moscow. I would take my Protection Officer with me and I might just learn something from the top.'

'Yes, you might Sylvia, but you must be extremely careful. This must be a strictly private visit. There will be no Guards of Honour or Ambassadorial security as there was on your last visit.'

At Moscow Airport Charlotte waited with Ludmilla and other security officers for the American Airways jet that had flown from Chicago via Heathrow. No one was allowed to leave the plane until Sylvia, Mary and Susan had alighted first by invitation. A large black Zil car took them to the VIP lounge where Charlotte greeted them all with kisses. All three guests were mindful of the uniformed security guards, both men and women.

'Don't bother with your luggage Sylvia. Security will look after that,' said Charlotte airily, 'It will be collected by Ludmilla's officers after the remaining passengers have disembarked. Come with me. You must all be tired. We'll go straight to my home. A good shower and change and we'll all feel better before dinner.'

The four women climbed into a large gleaming Mercedes car – an immediate gift from the German Government to the new Russian Royals. In a very few minutes, or so it seemed, the four of them arrived at the Kremlin, preceded and followed by a uniformed motor-cycle escort. Upstairs in the lift Carlos was waiting to greet them surrounded by three senior army officers. The officers saluted and departed.

'Do tell us Carlos,' started Sylvia, 'do we still call you Carlos or is it Nicholas now, or Your Majesty?'

'You can still call me Carlos, Sylvia. You don't want me to start addressing you as Deputy Prime Minister do you? Charlotte lays down the House Rules here. We can be as stiff and formal as anybody when we need to be, which is much of the time, but on our own or with friends we are just as you knew us a very short time ago.'

Mary started: 'Charlotte. You really must tell us when do you propose making your first State Visits to London and Washington?'

'Now that's a difficult one Mary. Obviously, I can't answer right now,' replied Charlotte, looking at Carlos as she spoke. 'Firstly we would need to be invited. Secondly, we would have to see when we could come, and thirdly, Carlos's government would have to give the green light. Again, I imagine it will be just the same with your Queen. It seems funny me saying "your Queen", but you know what I mean. In theory I could simply book a ticket and come, but that is not going to happen. Effectively, Carlos and I are cogs, albeit important cogs, in a huge machine. The machine is very well oiled and runs smoothly.'

It was Sylvia's turn to intervene and make her contribution. By this time they had all moved into the dining room. The table was set for eight.

330

'Do tell us, Carlos, if you feel free, when did you first know you were going to become Tsar? I can still hardly believe it. Elmer is absolutely thrilled for you both and the bank and what it may hold for Russo/American relations, but the whole thing seems like a fairy story.'

'I'll tell you all I properly can, Mary, but it's quite impossible to summarize all that has happened over the last one hundred years over dinner. I've no doubt that new books will be written about it. The strict answer to your question is the night before the Proclamation, but Charlotte and I came to Moscow knowing that there was the possibility of a Proclamation being made. One day I might write a Family Memoir for the Russian people, but that's a long time off. The Bolshevik Revolution of 1917 didn't just happen overnight, although sometimes it's convenient for casual historians to put a date on it for examination purposes. The day of my being proclaimed will, no doubt, be a date students here in Moscow and throughout the world will have to learn, but in real terms the Restoration began years ago. The architect and hero is General Stolypin, our National President, who has at all times had the support of his wife and family, General Maiski, who you've known in America, and General Renov and his wife Myra. Those five people are the heroes of Russian history in terms of the Restoration, outstandingly President Stolypin and all who stood behind him in the Army.'

'Come on, Carlos. You're not giving a lecture to the Duma. This is home and a dinner party. I know you think highly of General Stolypin, and so do I, but let's eat our dinner first and you can tell us the remainder of the story afterwards.'

It was Charlotte who stopped Carlos. Carlos wasn't minded to continue. He enjoyed eating and drinking as much as anybody, but more importantly he adored Charlotte and he relied on her very heavily. She knew how to encourage as well as any wife, but she also knew how to control his youthful drive and maintain her control of any dinner party she was hosting – or any other activity!

Everyone around the table got the message, and the

dinner table conversation became instantly more social and humorous and less political. The superb dinner and its liquid content went down very well, and Susan added greatly to the amusement of the diners with her gift for mimicry of any number of people who they all knew. Mary spoke of her children, her parents and Malta, and Charlotte's family spoke of their homes in London and their thoughts of returning or selling up and coming to live in Moscow. After dinner, Sylvia was anxious to have Carlos carry on where he'd left off at Charlotte's command.

'Carlos, you were telling us all before dinner all about your being proclaimed Tsar. I know Charlotte stopped you, and I think I would have stopped my Carlos talking hotels and restaurants at home, but please do tell us more about General Stolypin. How did he manage to find you and put you on the throne?'

'As I was saying before dinner, it's a long story. You know, Sylvia, in Britain the Victoria Cross is awarded "For Valour". I translate that word as meaning inspirational bravery – the sort of bravery that is so exceptional that it's calculated to inspire otherwise timid men to be brave themselves. That's General Stolypin's principal attribute. He has other attributes, of course, but that's his chief one. I don't know all the details, perhaps nobody does, but the story of the Restoration began in the 1920s. I don't know how much you know about life here in Russia under the Bolshevik Regime during the period 1919 to 1924, never mind all the years since then.

'Did you know, for example, of the millions who literally starved to death here in Russia, quite apart from all those killed in the Civil War between the Reds, the Whites and the Greens? You can't imagine that nobody was hurt. I don't just mean deaths and injuries. That's obvious. What I mean is that the whole nation suffered in a way Britain has never suffered. At the very time when millions were starving in February 1920, your David Lloyd George was telling your Parliament at Westminster that "the corn bins of Russia are bulging with grain" at the same time as he was receiving reports of "complete economic collapse" from his own

332

Foreign Secretary. I suppose you would call that economy with the truth. I would call it lying, and so did the Stolypins.

'Then in World War Two Stalin was able to appear as "the Goodie", but thankfully the Stolypins were able to hold on and recruit. It's a hell of a story, but you don't imagine there aren't thousands of old scores to be repaid with interest. My job is to help make a completely fresh start, from Chechnya in the south to the North Pole, and from St Petersburg to Vladivostok in the east. With Charlotte's support, I'll do it. You have your chance, Sylvia, tomorrow morning to help me and Anglo/Russian relations into the bargain. Now that we have our new chervonet currency, what Russia wants is membership of the European Union, with the same voting rights as Germany.

'Then Britain, Spain and Russia will form the pyramid from the extremities of Europe. If the extremes can hold together, the centre of Europe will hold together. If the whole of Europe is based on the centre, say, Germany, there is the danger that Britain, Russia and Spain will be isolated. Surely you can see that?'

'Carlos, you absolutely amaze me. How on earth have you put all this together in a matter of days, weeks at the most?' asked a bewildered Sylvia.

'Sylvia, I was blessed with good parents. Sadly I was an orphan when I was seventeen, but my character was formed by then, and now I have Charlotte. Without Charlotte I would be nowhere. You once said, Charlotte may have saved your life at Chamonix. She saves my life every day and, as a bonus, she's giving us both a baby this year.'

'I'm not often lost for words, Carlos, but you absolutely amaze me,' said Sylvia truthfully.

'Sylvia, I won't talk any more politics tonight, or I'll find myself upsetting Charlotte. She mustn't be upset. These next few weeks are critical, I believe, but I will tell you this. I look forward to learning of your support tomorrow of Russia's application to join the European Union, with no nonsense about voting rights and voting blocks. If you can support us, I'm fairly confident we might be able to support Britain's continuing to hold a permanent seat on the Security Council at the United Nations. You'll understand that any such decision lies with the Russian Government, not with me, but you have a saying that was invented in Spain, "one good turn deserves another".

'One day, Europe will be one united trading block. Didn't some comedian once suggest that the Swiss should run finance, Germany the business, the French the foreign policy and the Russians the defence? That still leaves room for the British, the Italians and the Spanish. I'm sure there's room for us all.'

At this point, Carlos was summoned by one of the uniformed attendants to the telephone.

Sylvia, Mary and Susan found themselves on their own with Charlotte, the others having retired for the night. Perhaps this was the moment the four of them had been waiting for.

'Do tell us, Charlotte. What is Carlos really like as a husband, and how does it feel to be Tsarina of Russia?'

It was Mary who asked the two questions they all wanted to ask. 'I'll tell you, but only on your promise not to breathe a word.' The three women nodded eagerly. 'He's absolutely marvellous. Of course, I have to take control. Sometimes I feel absolutely dreadful. He's so kind, open and generous, and I find I have to keep rationing him in so many ways, but God, he really has made my life.'

Four days later Sylvia, Mary and Susan together with the Foreign Secretary returned to London. Mary flew on to New York and Chicago.

At 10 o'clock on Monday morning Sylvia made her personal report to the Prime Minister having already dictated a formal Memoranda and *aide mémoire* for the Foreign Office before leaving the British Embassy in Moscow.

'Prime Minister, before you read my report I thought you would like me to let you know immediately that we really have no fears for ourselves or the country so far as Charlotte, I mean the Tsarina, is concerned. She was very friendly and forthright. Naturally I put it to her, when we were on our own, that she should have let us know what was happening or likely to happen before she flew from London to Moscow.

'She didn't exactly turn on me, but she made it quite clear that she had said nothing on my advice. She was referring to advice I had given to her about her owing her first loyalty to Spain just before her first marriage to Xavier. It all came back to me when she reminded me that I had used the phrase "you will always be a daughter of the Sceptered Isle."

'She now naturally feels that what I said in relation to Spain applies equally to Russia. I have absolutely no doubt that she is very much in love with her young Tsar and if we are sensible, Anglo/Russian relations will improve dramatically, if not quite so quickly, as Russo/Spanish relations. Do remember that the Tsar, who I suppose I will always call Carlos rather than Nicholas, is Spanish with some Russian in him, but no English, apart from his education at Slapton and his marriage to Charlotte.

'From what he said to me, and believe me he isn't just a boy of 18, he regards himself, not as the ruler of Russia, but as an important cog in a vast machine, and that he is not at his most useful when bestowing medals or whatever, but in flying "kites".

'The "kite" he flew for me concerns drug addiction. The way he put it was both sincere and a shade ruthless. He said that, as a young man, he was very concerned about the spreading drug scene throughout Europe. He reminded me that as a "House Captain" at Slapton he had the duty to report to his housemaster any signs of any drugs entering the College. From this simple statement of fact he went on to suggest that our Royal Navy should work jointly with the Russian Imperial Navy in preventing drugs entering Europe by sea, the Russians assisting us with their Atlantic Submarine Fleet that forms part of the new Imperial Navy. It wasn't just this suggestion, but his polite cross-examination of myself.'

'His cross-examination of you Sylvia?'

'Yes, Prime Minister. The way he put it to me was that the

335

Russians might question our determination to really smash the drug trade. Now how did he put it? He asked what revenue we as a government made out of taxation in relation to tobacco and alcohol and whether we were thinking of legalizing cannabis or any other drugs to improve our tax revenue on cannabis sales? You see what I mean. He's not just another teenager; my advice is that we treat him at all times as though he was our age and equally well informed.'

'Thank you very much Sylvia. You've done very well. I say, wouldn't it be good if we could have him as a future back-bencher on our side? Perhaps not. He just might take over from you and me. All I will say at this stage is "God Save the Tsar".'